SPECIAL MESSAGE TO READERS

Mary de Laszlo trained as a fashion journalist in the mid sixties, working for *Queen* magazine in London and *Jardin des Modes* in Paris. In recent years she has had various stories published in women's magazines, both in the UK and Paris, and broadcast on BBC Radio 4's 'Morning Story.'

The mother of three children, she is also a director of her husband's travel company. She lives in West London.

THE WOMAN WHO LOVED TOO MUCH

Ever since they were little girls, Grace's cousin India has got what she wanted. Yet pretty, privileged India has always been secretly jealous of Grace. So when Grace falls in love with charismatic Jonathan Sheridan, India knows she must have him — the fact that Jonathan marries Grace only sharpens India's desire to wrest him from her. Grace knows how much India wants her husband and she is so anxious to keep him that she fails to see the weakness in their relationship that one day will jeopardise all she has worked so hard to preserve, all she loves so much . . .

Books by Mary de Laszlo
Published by The House of Ulverscroft:

BREAKING THE RULES

MARY DE LASZLO

THE WOMAN WHO LOVED TOO MUCH

Complete and Unabridged

ULVERSCROFT
Leicester

First published in Great Britain in 1997 by
Headline Book Publishing
London

First Large Print Edition
published 1998
by arrangement with
Headline Book Publishing
a division of Hodder Headline Plc
London

Cover artist: John Hancock

British Library CIP Data

De Laszlo, Mary
   The woman who loved too much.
   —Large print ed.—
   Ulverscroft large print series: general fiction
   1. Domestic fiction
   2. Large type books
   I. Title
   823.9'14 [F]

   ISBN 0–7089–4012–9

Published by
F. A. Thorpe (Publishing) Ltd.
Anstey, Leicestershire

Set by Words & Graphics Ltd.
Anstey, Leicestershire
Printed and bound in Great Britain by
T. J. International Ltd., Padstow, Cornwall

This book is printed on acid-free paper

1410188 2

With love to my mother and
in loving memory of my father.

Very many thanks to the friends I plagued endlessly about legal and business procedures. Natalie and Peter Blenk, Ian Henderson, Phoebe and John Olcay, Jenny Redhead and Jeffrey Rucker. My thanks as always to my agent, Judith Murdoch, and my editor, Anne Williams.

Part One

1

1984

'Ninety-nine . . . one hundred . . . coming!'
Grace heard India call. She felt sick with
apprehension. They'd find her at once, she
knew they would. She could already see
India's pert, pretty face twist with derision.

'Grace, it's such an obvious place, *surely*
you can think of somewhere better to hide.
It's so boring playing with you,' India would
say loudly enough for the others to hear,
instead of keeping quiet and slipping into
the place with her, as the game Sardines
required, until there was only one person left
who had not squeezed into the hiding place,
and so had lost the game. The others, who
all thought India was wonderful and wanted
to stay on the right side of her, would giggle
at her remarks and agree with her.

Grace shrank back into the large disused
fireplace behind its tall Victorian screen, in
this room that was only used as a sort of
overflow sitting room if there were lots of
young people staying in the house.

She felt the cold stone of the fireplace hard

against her back, smelt the stale, sour smell of long-dead wood fires.

Grace hated all these games her cousins so adored. She felt awkward and out of place. They were so confident, so full of easy laughter; they never seemed to mind making fools of themselves, not that they ever did. However stupid the game they carried it off with a youthful elegance and charm that she could never achieve.

No doubt it helped that their parents, her uncle and aunt, were so sophisticated. Aunt Flavia was renowned for her generous and imaginative entertaining. Prime Ministers and Presidents, even Royalty had been known to come to her parties. All the most interesting and fashionable people came, rather (it must be admitted) to the consternation of her uncle, who was happiest with his dogs and horses; but the children were quite used to playing Racing Demon with a Cabinet Minister or sitting next to a famous writer or artist for dinner.

Grace had left the door to the room slightly ajar and she heard the chattering, muffled laughter and running feet as some of the group of young people ran past the room and up the back stairs. She heard Caspar, India's brother, say, 'I bet she's in the airing cupboard in the old nursery yet again.'

4

India giggled and said, 'She must be able to think of somewhere different. With all the masses of rooms to choose from, surely she can find somewhere else.'

Grace felt as if she was going to faint but the running feet went on up the stairs and dispersed across the landing. People were meant to hunt in pairs — that was another nightmare, finding someone to pair up with — but this time it seemed to Grace they had stayed in a pack. She let out her breath slowly, feeling calmer. Then fear prickled up her spine as she heard the heavy creak of the door being pushed open further. She crept to the very back of the fireplace, then stood up, the top half of her in the wide, black, sooty chimney.

Someone came into the room. Their step was firm. Grace did not dare to breathe. She heard them move about the room, heard the swish of the heavy silk curtains as they looked behind them. She heard them come up to the Victorian screen which was stiff and browning with its collage of glued-on pictures and move it gently aside, then step into the fireplace. Like a small child she scrunched her eyes shut as if by not seeing them they would not see her. Someone touched her. She almost screamed.

5

'I've found you.' It was Jonathan Sheridan, whose mother and stepfather were staying in the house this weekend.

'I'm never any good at this game,' she said apologetically, opening her eyes. She was relieved it was him and not India or Caspar, but his good looks and charm made her feel even more gauche and self-conscious than ever.

He sat down on the floor of the fireplace, his long legs out-stretched until they almost touched the other side. 'I hate these games, I'd much rather ride, or play tennis,' he said. 'Does one ever have a chance to do that here? I mean, they've got stables full of horses and a tennis court.'

Grace sat down beside him, feeling a little frisson of excitement at being so close to him. He was eighteen, almost two years older than she was, and he was surely in love with India who teased and joked with him in the most natural way.

'Sometimes they do ride or play tennis, it depends on their mood,' she said, thinking that she probably hated riding and playing tennis with them even more than playing these games.

'Serve underarm, Grace, if you can't get it in otherwise,' India had said crushingly last time they'd played tennis. As for the horses: the old ponies she was given either refused to move, conserving all their energy for tearing at the grass, and however hard she pulled the reins she could not get their heads up, or they were too fresh and bolted on the turn for home.

'Those stables are something, aren't they? And those racehorses. Do you think I'd ever be allowed to ride out with the lads in the morning?'

'I don't know . . . if you're an experienced rider Uncle William might let you. Why don't you ask him?' She looked at Jonathan surreptitiously. It was dark in the fireplace, with just a little light from the window squeezing past the screen, but she knew his lean, well-honed face, with its wide, laughing mouth, his blond hair flopping over his eyes, his almost arrogant poise.

Jonathan gave a slight laugh. It was the first time he had stayed at Elmley Park. 'Well, I don't know. I wouldn't like to upset him. I mean, he looks quite fierce, doesn't he?'

'I suppose he does.' Grace could feel the warmth of him as they sat side by side. She kept her body tightly curled into itself so she wouldn't touch him, though she longed to. Longed for him to slip an arm affectionately round her shoulder, to show a relaxed camaraderie with her as he did with India.

'Don't you know?' He sounded surprised and before she could answer, stammer some excuse, he went on: 'It must be wonderful for you coming here so often, having such . . . ' He hesitated. She suspected he was going to say 'rich', but thought that might sound rather gauche, so he said instead, ' . . . such exciting relations, with this huge, wonderful house and grounds. Racehorses and everything.'

'Yes,' she said, lying because she dared not confide in him and confess that she hated coming here with Aunt Flavia giving her all India's cast-offs and sighing about the fate of Grace's mother, her only sister.

'How *is* your mother?' she'd said despairingly when Grace had arrived to stay this time. 'Is your father making *any* money from his pictures?'

'She's fine, sends her love,' Grace answered, feeling sick, anticipating some devastating remark. She'd rather die than admit to the endless crippling money worries of her parents. She adored her father and it was hardly his fault that no one liked his pictures enough to pay the prices he deserved for them.

'Really, when I think of all the boyfriends

8

she had, *why* she had to go and marry the most penniless . . . ' Flavia said, tossing her beautiful head and smiling complacently at her grey-haired husband. He was twelve years her senior, but a baronet with a stately home and a fortune. Then, seeing Grace's expression, she smiled kindly and said: 'Not that I don't *adore* your father, but if only he'd give up this painting idea and get a proper job. He could always paint at the weekends after all.'

Grace flared up at her remarks. 'Daddy's paintings are marvellous, so intricate and detailed, they are worth far, far more than he's paid for them. And he works so hard, sometimes late into the night. So much harder than some people in other professions,' she'd cried, furious with her aunt, with her uncle who seemed hardly to work at all.

She'd almost burst into tears of frustration at the unfairness of it, but Aunt Flavia had patted her shoulder and said in her special voice she used for those she deemed 'unfortunate':

'My dear Grace, please don't take such offence. I simply *adore* his work.' She put on her sublime expression. 'We've bought some after all, and would have more, only they don't hang so well with the Raeburns and the Turners, dear. Perhaps he should do some smaller ones, flowers, bowls of fruit, pretty scenery, subjects that fit in anywhere.'

Grace turned away, knowing that to explain her father's work to her aunt was as pointless as explaining the work of the Impressionists to a chimpanzee.

To make amends Flavia had gone through India's cupboards and drawers like a whirlwind and insisted that she had grown out of almost everything and given Grace three extra suitcases of clothes. Grace knew that it was natural with families like India's to hand down their good-quality, barely worn clothes, despite the fact that some people might take offence at it; but most of them were far too smart for her home and school life, and she wouldn't dare wear them here for fear of India's pitying eyes upon her, knowing she didn't look nearly as good in her clothes as India did.

Grace had often begged her parents not to keep sending her to Elmley Park, but her mother had explained that she had to work and so couldn't always give her enough time, and really it was so good for her to be able to stay at such a beautiful house, to experience a more lavish lifestyle, to meet such influential people. Grace also guessed that her absence saved her parents precious money and the clothes heaped upon her helped eke out their finances further, so she gritted her teeth and went on visiting.

'I'd love to own racehorses like your uncle,' Jonathan said, stirring beside her in the fireplace. 'It's so exciting seeing them racing, especially if you know the owners of the horses. I had a bet last week, for the first time, and I won.' He turned to her and in the gloom she could see the excitement in his eyes.

'It is fun,' she said, then, feeling she ought to say more, said, 'do you often go racing?'

'No . . . it's so expensive, isn't it? But if Robert and Mother are going and I'm around, I try and tag along. Robert pays then, he is awfully generous like that.'

'Where's your real father?' she asked, suddenly daring.

He shrugged. 'I don't know.'

'Oh.' She gave a little gasp, afraid that something terrible had happened to him and she had upset him with her prying. 'I'm sorry . . . I didn't mean . . . ' She felt hot and awkward, and wished she could get up and run away.

He laughed, putting his hand on her arm. 'Don't be sorry, I'm not. He's what my grandmother called a 'bounder'. He gambled, drank, oh, thoroughly lived it up, but thought a family commitment too much.

I haven't heard from him in ages. But Robert has been a marvellous stepfather, all things considered.'

'I'm glad,' she said weakly, feeling the touch of his hand glow through and through her. He moved his hand away, and immediately she felt cold and abandoned.

'What about your parents, do they have a huge estate too?'

'Oh, no.' She couldn't help laughing. 'My father is an artist, he makes next to nothing. My mother runs a bookshop. We live in a tiny house in Kew, with a studio built into the garden. It's almost bigger than the house.' She didn't know why she was telling him this, she'd wanted to impress him, hadn't she? Though she knew that in front of India she would impress no one.

'It sounds so romantic.' He smiled, hugging his knees to his chest. 'Did your mother elope with him, the penniless artist whom her father disapproved of?'

'Her sister disapproved of, more like.' The words slipped out before she could stop them.

'I see.' He seemed amused. They giggled together like two children with a secret joke. He lowered his voice. 'She is rather terrifying, isn't she? I mean I always feel she's thinking how bad my table manners are, or expecting me to wipe my nose on the curtains or something.'

Grace let out a peal of laughter.

'Hush.' He put his fingers over her mouth, bending close to her, until she felt her blood would boil though her veins. 'They'll find us, and the game will be over and we'll have to play something else.'

His fingers felt so soft on her mouth, and when he took them away she could taste the salt from them on her lips. She felt it was the most intimate moment of her life, and she could not help herself leaning towards him until she could smell the scent of him.

'So she disapproved of your father?' he said, seemingly not minding her proximity.

'Yes, but you know . . . ' She felt so close to him, closer than she'd ever felt to anyone, apart from her parents. 'I think sometimes she's jealous. They're so in love, you see. Even though they've been married for ever, they still love each other like . . . well, you know, young people who have just fallen in love. And Aunt Flavia and Uncle William . . . well, I'm sure they *do* love each other . . . ' she said doubtfully, knowing that she thought her aunt saw her husband as just a provider of a title and an income.

'I don't think they love each other at all,' Jonathan said. 'I think they think love between themselves is rather indecent. They've done their bit producing an heir, they needn't do it again.' He laughed once more.

She felt ridiculously happy, almost light-headed, being here with him in this sooty, chilly fireplace, joking and gossiping together.

'Love can be a bore though,' he said suddenly. 'I mean, I find it quite difficult seeing my mother being so fond of my sisters, them taking up so much of her time. Of course I understand that she wanted more children when she married Robert, but she does make such a fuss of them. They're so spoilt.'

'Sometimes I feel left out too,' Grace admitted, feeling a rush of understanding for him. 'My parents mean so much to each other I often feel as if they don't need me in their lives. I feel as if they didn't really want to have me . . . not that they don't love me, and are very kind to me, but they didn't have any more children. You'd have thought, wouldn't you, that if they liked children they'd have had at least one more after me.'

'They may not have been able to afford it,' Jonathan said. 'I mean if you say they are badly off.'

'They said they only wanted me,' Grace

14

said, feeling a sudden rush of homesickness as she remembered her father hugging her and laughing, telling her what a silly she was, and how one precious jewel was enough. 'I used to ask for a brother. I'd have loved a brother.' She thought of Caspar, arrogant and dismissive and very spoilt, but he and India were so close, they didn't have to speak. Just one look and each knew what the other was thinking. She envied that.

'I think you're lucky. Our whole house centres on my sisters. I can't have my friends round in the evenings, or play my music too loud in case I wake them up. Their toys, hideous dolls in nylon dresses, are everywhere — ' He stopped suddenly. They both heard the door open, quick steps cross the room and part of the screen was whisked back.

'Found you,' India said, her black eyes glittering with malice at the sight of them both sitting together side by side. 'Really, Grace, you do choose the most grubby places. I absolutely refuse to get in there. Jonathan, I don't know how *you* could. It's not compulsory to join the other person if they've chosen an impossible place, you know?'

Grace felt the full force of her disgust, and waited for Jonathan to agree with India.

15

She felt isolated and sick with despair. Just for a moment she'd felt wonderful, sitting here secretly with Jonathan, alone. They'd got on so well. He'd made her forget her awkwardness and her shyness. She hardened her face, bracing herself for his betrayal.

But he laughed. 'Oh, India,' he said, 'that's not playing the game properly. I think this is a perfect place. We've had a great time, waiting here to be found, haven't we, Grace?' He turned to smile at her, and all at once she felt as if she would burst with happiness and float up the chimney and out into the sky.

In her joy she did not see the venom in India's eyes, the sneering cruelty in her mouth, but before India could form any words to wound her, the others crowded in, saying: 'Found you, so that's where you were.'

Jonathan got up and went over to join Caspar. The two were at school together, in their last year, though not in the same house. India threw them a look of contempt and flounced out of the room, announcing that she was bored of playing games. The four other young people, Ned and Charles Porter, and Emma and Charlotte Harbord who lived locally, followed her. Ned, who'd been in love with India all his life, ran to catch up with her, offering suggestions to

16

alleviate her boredom.

In a moment Grace was once again left alone in the fireplace, but she stayed there happily for a while, savouring the time spent with Jonathan.

That evening they were all having drinks together in the huge drawing room before dinner, when Uncle William caught her eye and boomed: 'Grace, my dear, India wants a new horse for hunting, she has grown too tall for Moonlight. I thought you might like him, he'll do you another year I think.'

His words provoked a tiny silence among the smartly dressed people in the grand gold and blue room. Grace was dumbfounded, struggling for something to say to this quite unexpected gift. India, sleek and sophisticated in red silk, leapt into the centre of the room, eyes sparking like an angry cat.

'You can't give away Moonlight, Daddy! I've had him for ever. You can't give him away.'

'No, really, Uncle William, I've nowhere to keep him. It's so sweet of you to think of it, but . . . ' Seeing her uncle's expression harden, his eyes freeze with severity, Grace tailed off, not knowing how to get out of this appalling situation, feeling everyone's eyes homing in on her.

'As you like, but I don't have room for two

17

horses at the moment. If you want a new one, India, then Moonlight must go. I thought it would be nice for you to know he was going to a kind home. If he was with Grace you could visit him whenever you wanted to.' He finished his whisky, went over to the drinks tray, picked up the cutglass decanter of sherry, and went slowly round the room refilling glasses.

'But we have plenty of room, and Grace doesn't like riding much, and as she said, she doesn't have anywhere to keep him,' India said defiantly.

'There's a good stables not far from her that I know of, and naturally I'll see that Grace's parents will have no extra expenses,' he said dryly, still circulating with the sherry decanter. 'But if you want to keep Moonlight and not have a new horse, India, that's fine by me. I'll buy that filly I saw last week. If she won't win me any races, she'll do as a brood mare.'

'But, Daddy, you never said we couldn't keep Moonlight when you agreed to get me a new horse,' India cried in anguish.

'I won't have him, India does so love him,' Grace blurted out to no one in particular.

Jonathan, who had been standing by the window with Caspar and Ned, came over to her. 'What a wonderful present, you can ride every day,' he said quietly to her with a smile. Grace saw him give India a rather contemptuous look, but she felt too wretched to feel any joy in it.

There was a slightly awkward atmosphere in the room as the other guests quaffed their drinks, not quite knowing what to say. Some were looking distinctly bored. Then Flavia, with a big smile, skipped over to her husband. 'You're such a darling, I'm sure when India sees her new horse she'll get over Moonlight. Now tell us about your day's shooting, how are the birds this year?' Skilfully she got off the subject of Moonlight, weaving in amusing anecdotes about mutual friends' shooting parties, drawing out experiences from the guests, until everyone except India and Grace had forgotten the baronet's offer.

For the rest of the evening Grace felt wretched. Dinner seemed interminable, and though she'd been hungry before, now she could hardly eat. India kept shooting little darts of hatred from her dark eyes, as if Grace had personally forced India's father to give her Moonlight. Grace sat next to Charles and Caspar, and when they found that she made no effort to entertain them, they ignored her, laughing loudly with the Harbord girls.

Grace sat there in the panelled dining

room with its vast and magical chandeliers, the miles of pale green washed silk curtains falling like lustrous waterfalls from the tall windows, desperately wishing she was at home in their tiny, snug sitting room, with her parents, and perhaps some friends, talking animatedly about the art world, or about books or the theatre. Their clothes would be shabby, the wine and food inexpensive, but the atmosphere would be one of cheerful, undemanding affection.

2

'But, Mummy, why should I share a dance with Grace? Her friends will all be so dull, and I have so many people to invite and Daddy can't ask more than two hundred and fifty.' India's voice had an unattractive whine to it, her beautiful face bunched with anger. 'I can't share one with her, I really can't.'

'But, my darling, she won't have many friends, and besides they will be quite lost in the crowd of your own,' Flavia said sweetly, pouring herself some more tea from the bone-china pot on the table in front of her. She stole a glance at her husband at the other end of the breakfast table to gauge his reaction.

'But, Mummy . . . ' India began again.

Her father slowly lifted his eyes from the racing page in *The Times*, lowered the paper and regarded her sternly. 'That poor child has nothing, and you, my dear, have too much. The least you can do is let her share your dance. You are both eighteen this year, and her parents can't afford to give her a party.'

'That's not my problem!' India cried. It really was too bad. Her parents had always preferred Grace to her. Having her here whenever they could, giving her all India's clothes, saying she'd grown out of them even when she hadn't — clothes she'd loved and wanted to wear again. But the worst thing was when they'd given Grace Moonlight to make way for her new horse. India had never forgiven her father for that, never forgiven Grace for accepting him, and now Grace was going to ruin her dance by *sharing* it with her. Goodness know what her friends, *if* she had any, would be like.

'It should be your problem, she is your first cousin after all,' her father said coldly, his flushed face hardening as he looked at her, his bushy eyebrows adding emphasis to his displeasure.

'I'm sure she didn't mean it like that, my dear,' Flavia hurriedly broke in. The last thing she wanted was for India to upset her father so much that he would cancel the dance altogether. 'She just means that, well, that dear Grace is not so sophisticated as she is and that she . . . and her friends might feel left out.'

William Gratton sighed loudly. India quailed inside, though she refused to show it. She knew that sigh signalled intense tedium

22

with a subject. He'd been known to pull out of whatever idea he'd been discussing, and refuse to discuss it ever again. He'd done it over Moonlight, after that disastrous weekend when Jonathan Sheridan had come to stay, and for the first and indeed the only time in her life, India had felt really attracted to a young man, met someone she'd wanted to belong to. She was used to men falling in love with her, they had ever since she was fourteen, but she could never be bothered with them. Not like that wimp Ned Porter who'd change the weather for her if he could.

Jonathan had something undefinable that tantalized her. It was difficult to pinpoint exactly what it was — Caspar had so many attractive friends he'd brought back from school, and now university — but there was a sort of aura about Jonathan, an animal magnetism, an energy, that all the others, despite their posing and boasting, didn't possess. She'd felt very jealous when she'd found him hiding with Grace in the fireplace that day. But thank goodness it was only Grace and not one of the Harbord girls. Someone as good-looking and charming as Jonathan would never fancy Grace.

But she felt she'd lost ground with him when her father, after she'd worked on him for ages, and made him agree to buy her a new horse, had come out with that bombshell about giving Moonlight to Grace. She knew she should have hidden her feelings until she was alone with her father, but she hadn't been able to stop herself sounding like a spoilt, selfish child. She'd not noticed until too late Jonathan's expression change from amazement at her father's generosity to disbelief at her reaction to his gift to Grace.

Later when Jonathan had said his goodbyes he had barely bothered to look her way and had made a far warmer farewell to Grace. If Grace hadn't received this with such gauche awkwardness, she'd have been quite jealous. She'd seen him a few times since then and found as her body stirred into full womanhood that she wanted him even more. But her pride and fear of his rejection — for he and Caspar often joked together about their successes with the girls — kept her aloof from him, determined that he would come to her so she could keep the upper hand in any relationship they might have.

She got up to help herself to more coffee from the silver pot on the sideboard. She took some bacon from one of the square silver dishes lined up beside it. She knew that if she wasn't careful there would be no dance, and that would be a disaster as she'd already boasted about it to her friends and asked so many people to it.

'Mummy's right,' she said to her father. 'I think it's misplaced kindness, like sending boys from working-class families to Eton. It's not their fault they don't fit in. She won't have anything to wear, and it'll be cruel for her to have to wear one of my cast-offs.' She didn't add that they never suited Grace: she was so tall and dark and Grace slight and blond. The brilliant colours India wore usually wiped Grace out, with her pale complexion.

'It will not be at all like sending working-class boys to Eton, India,' her father said with irritation. 'Grace has spent a great deal of her childhood with us, she fits in beautifully. But you're right about a dress . . . ' He stared thoughtfully at his plate of congealing kedgeree. 'Thank you for pointing it out, India, I hadn't thought of it.' He gave her a quick smile. Then, looking over at Flavia who was holding her breath in readiness for him to say he'd thought better of having a dance and would far rather spend his money on a new racehorse; 'Arrange for her to have one made, my dear, at the same place you go to for India. Let her choose whatever she wants.'

'Of course. How kind and generous you

are, my dear.' Flavia, in her relief at him not cancelling the dance, got up and scuttled down the long room to bestow a kiss on his forehead. He swatted at her as if she was a tiresome wasp.

'This kedgeree is cold, get me some more,' he said grumpily, picking up the newspaper again and retreating behind it.

India was about to protest, but seeing her mother's severe gaze on her, kept her peace. One more complaint and her father might well dig in his toes and refuse to give a dance altogether. But it was so hateful them preferring Grace to her. Always, ever since they'd been babies, she'd been encouraged to share with Grace, let her have a turn first because she didn't have the advantages India had. It was so unfair, especially as Grace was such a timid little thing and seemed more afraid than grateful at all she was given.

She picked over the bacon on her plate, then settled down with her coffee and lit a cigarette. There was another thing, which she hated to admit, but she was jealous of Grace's parents and, of her easy family life. Her house was horrid, all small and poky, quite unlike this eighteenth-century mansion with its Robert Adam interior, its wonderful pictures and priceless furniture, its rolling lawns and glorious trees. But there was

26

a feeling of such happiness there: Grace's parents were so in love with each other, so proud of their daughter, that the warmth of their feelings engulfed everyone else.

India knew too that Grace did not like leaving that haven for this grand house, for India's parents who now barely tolerated each other. There had always been rumours of her father and his stable girls, but recently he'd shown uncommon interest in the wife of a trainer who lived on the other side of Newmarket. Her mother was no better, she often left her father alone here for weeks at a time while she stayed in their house in London. When India questioned her, she said airily that she was just seeing old friends; her father hated London, he would be quite miserable there. India knew some of their acquaintances were betting on who would leave whom first. Recently she'd heard one so-called friend of theirs remarking: 'He'd kick her out tomorrow, but we all know Flavia so adores her title and position that she'll do her damnedest to hang on to them.'

This remark had terrified her. She'd tried to discuss it with Caspar, but he was too occupied with his own love affairs to take much notice of her concerns. Yet what would happen if they did split up? Might her father

27

marry this trainer's wife and bring her here to ruin Elmley Park for India?

For the first time in her life India started to feel insecure, terrified that this vital backdrop to her life, this house that she loved so much, would be taken from her by her father's new woman and that she would no longer be welcome here.

Recently she'd also realized, or perhaps finally admitted to herself, that her mother did not love her father. Perhaps she never had. Now she was more mature, India saw that her mother's lack of love for him hurt and bewildered him, and persuaded him to seek company elsewhere. Flavia had chosen William Gratton for his possessions, his title and estate, which she used to their full advantage. Why shouldn't another woman do the same?

Grace was the only person she'd ever met who was not the slightest bit envious of or impressed by her lifestyle. It was as if she knew that she was the lucky one because she came from a home of love and stability, which in the end, India suspected, was far more precious than Elmley Park and all its glory.

★ ★ ★

'I wish we didn't have to go downstairs and could just watch from behind somewhere,' Grace said to her parents as she waited for them to finish getting ready for the ball.

'Nonsense, my darling. Everyone must see you. I've never seen you look so lovely.' Her father, giving a last twirl to his bow tie, turned to look at her. Love and admiration shone from his face. 'Suddenly you're no longer a little girl but a beautiful woman,' he said a little wistfully. 'It makes me feel old, but also very proud.' He came forward and kissed her.

'Oh, Daddy, I haven't been a little girl for ages,' she laughed affectionately.

'I know, I've been trying not to notice. But tonight you'll outshine them all.'

'Not with India there,' Grace said without envy. 'No one can ever touch her.'

'She is lovely.' Her mother bustled in from the adjoining bathroom, taking off her dressing gown and going over to her dress which lay on the bed. They were all staying at Elmley Park for the dance and they were due to be downstairs in ten minutes for a drink before dinner.

William Gratton was a stickler for punctuality. He often stood waiting with his gold watch open in his hand counting the seconds that ticked past the allotted time

29

he had set, more like a general planning a military exercise than a host expecting guests.

Olivia Penfold stepped into her dress and Grace zipped her up.

'You look wonderful, Mummy,' she said, thinking how good her mother still looked and how the eau de nil chiffon dress with its beaded top suited her, giving her a glamour she wasn't used to. Olivia had found the dress in a second-hand shop in central London and had been thrilled with it.

'I only hope it didn't belong to one of the guests,' she'd laughed when she'd proudly shown it to them. 'That would be terribly embarrassing.'

'You look wonderful too.' Olivia patted Grace's hand. 'Be happy, darling,' she said suddenly, as if, Grace thought later, she wanted her to choose the right person to love as she had, not choose someone for their position or money as her sister, Flavia, had.

There were twelve guests apart from them staying in the house and most of them were downstairs in the drawing room on time. India looked wonderful in cerise silk, the colour bringing out the dark lights in her hair and eyes, giving a rosy glow to her skin. But as she walked in, feeling rather shy on her father's arm, Grace was suddenly aware of people's eyes on her, and their glances were more admiring than any she had ever known before. Even Caspar with his dramatic good looks, immaculate in his dinner jacket and a jade-green silk cummerbund, stopped talking to the pretty girl with him and said: 'My! Grace the ugly duckling is now truly a swan.' His voice was kind and his smile warm, making a little burst of pleasure break in her.

Flavia bore down on her. 'You look lovely, my dear. Isn't her dress just the right colour for her, that lavender blue, the colour of her eyes, and so pretty with her fair hair, don't you think?' She smiled at the other people in the room, holding Grace's hand as if showing off her own creation. Awkward, Grace kept her eyes down, frantically following the patterns of the Persian rug under her feet.

'My dear Flavia, you have such good taste in clothes, in everything.' Her father stepped forward to rescue her. 'You look sublime yourself, that apricot gold is perfection on you.' He smiled and she blushed, simpering like a much younger woman.

'Oh, Leo, you're such a flatterer,' she said with a coyness that made her appear ridiculous.

Ned Porter, still hopelessly in love with India but always kind to Grace, came up at

31

once to talk to her, to compliment her on her dress, to put her at her ease. A glass of champagne was thrust into her hand and in a moment the whole room had regrouped and was talking together again and Grace, to her great relief, was forgotten.

For the rest of her life Grace remembered and judged other dances by this one. She kept forgetting that it was her dance too, and that she was sharing it with India. India was excessively nice to her when they were surrounded by guests, which was a new departure from her usual behaviour towards her.

'This is my cousin, Grace Penfold,' she'd say to yet another love-sick young man who hung round her, desperate for even the smallest morsel of attention. 'You *simply must* dance with her. Isn't she pretty, and don't you just love her dress?' She would smile her dazzling smile that made the young men gasp like drowning fish and agree with her and before she knew it, Grace was off with one of them to dance, knowing in her heart that however polite and kind they were, it was India they wanted to be with and it was only to please India that they danced with her.

Dancing was held in the long gallery, the room resplendent with wonderful pictures and gold-coloured silk walls. From the high ceiling hung a row of crystal chandeliers shimmering like diamonds shot with gold reflected from the walls.

Grace's friends, all from Kew or the small, private convent school she'd been educated at, clustered round her excitedly, quite bowled over by the splendour of the setting. But all the time she was looking through the well-dressed, chattering crowd for Henry Buchan, her boyfriend she supposed she should call him now. She'd known Henry for ages, but a few months ago he had suddenly kissed her, and both of them, rather amazed by the pleasure it gave them, had kissed again. Their relationship had sped out of the safe, cosy confines of friendship and she supposed that they were now in love.

Suddenly she caught sight of him. Her heart gave a little lurch as she saw him looking rather apprehensively around him. He looked good in a dinner jacket with his wide shoulders and slim hips, his brown hair uncharacteristically tidy. She skipped up to him, pleased he had come, pleased to be with someone so dear and so familiar.

'So this is where you escape to,' he greeted her. She saw to her dismay that there was resentment in his voice and in his eyes.

'Oh, Henry.' She tugged at his arm. 'Yes,

33

it's no big deal . . . I'm not part of it.'

'Yes, you are,' he said, 'and remember this is your dance too.'

'I do keep forgetting, but you know it's not really my life. I can hardly help it if my aunt married my uncle who owns all of this. It is so beautiful, but I know there are more important things to life.' She tried to smile, to will him to laugh, make a joke, be himself again. But instead he looked sullenly round at the other guests so obviously enjoying themselves, at the phalanx of champagne bottles lined up on damask-clothed tables with a line of liveried footmen ever waiting to fill up the proffered glasses.

'You always said you hated coming here and I thought . . . well, I didn't think it would be like this.'

'What did you think it would be like then?' she said a little impatiently.

'A big house of course, but this . . . ' He swept out his arm. 'Is that a Rembrandt? And that furniture. Just that French commode is worth more than a year of my father's salary.'

'Oh, come on,' she said, pulling him on to the dance floor, feeling rather irritated by his reaction. Having got used to all this splendour as just another backdrop in her life, she felt annoyed with Henry, that he was somehow disapproving of it, and had turned it into something to hold against her.

'Look,' she said, hoping to cheer him up, 'that's my cousin India. Isn't she beautiful?'

India was standing on the edge of the dance floor with four young men clustered round her. One held her hand trying to pull her on to the floor, she was laughing as she resisted. Another leant over her shoulder.

'She is beautiful, but not my type.'

'I should hope not!' She tried to laugh, to pull him closer to her. She felt disappointed in him. She had so looked forward to having him here, dancing with him in this sumptuous room, feeling relaxed and happy with him, knowing she would feel dreadfully shy and gauche with India's sophisticated men, and now he was spoiling it.

In a while they stopped for a drink and gradually he relaxed and became the old Henry she was used to.

'Tell me about your house party?' Grace asked him eagerly. Henry and her other friends had been put up at various houses in the district. 'I'd quite forgotten you'd been put up with that trainer and his wife. You know rumour has it that she's Uncle William's girlfriend?'

'Yes, I remember you told me. They're very nice, her husband only appeared just

35

before dinner, but she is an attractive woman,' Henry said. He looked round the room, 'Look, there she is, standing by the curtains.'

Grace turned to look. She saw a tall, red-headed woman dressed in a dress of green shot silk. She had a thoroughbred look about her, and though not strictly beautiful was very handsome. She was talking to an elderly man whom Grace recognized as a former Cabinet Minster, but her gaze seemed to be skittering round the room as if she was looking for someone else. As Grace watched her gaze stopped, her face lit up and a little smile played on her mouth. Grace saw her uncle, dancing with her mother, catch that gaze and hold it a moment, his face suddenly alive, as she had never seen it before, then being forced to lose the redhead's look as he turned away in the dance. Looking back at the woman, Grace saw her face had taken on a warm glow as if she knew that she was not forgotten.

'She's very nice,' Henry went on, 'a bit brusque at first, but I think that was a sort of shyness. Well, she couldn't have been as shy as me.' He laughed awkwardly. 'It's all a bit above me, I don't mind admitting, Grace. I shall be glad to get you back to Kew.'

She felt a dash of sympathy for him. 'But

they're not grand, are they?' she said. 'Not like this?'

'No, their house is quite ordinary, large, rather a mess actually, but her husband, Peter, can be rather offhand. I don't think he wanted to come tonight.'

'Poor man, I don't suppose he did if the stories about his wife and Uncle William are true.'

'There must always be stories about men like your uncle,' Henry said. 'They can't all be true.'

'No, though I think this one is. But my mother says Aunt Flavia won't let him go so I expect it will all work out.'

'One rule for them,' Henry said sarcastically, 'another for the rest of us.'

They danced again and close in his arms Grace felt content. This beautiful house and the splendour of the dance was like a dream, not their real life at all, but she was glad she had shared this evening with Henry; she hoped it would be a happy memory for them to store away and think of again when they were together.

Suddenly, however, her warm feelings for him were swept away by something stronger. There walking on to the dance floor with a girl was Jonathan Sheridan. She hadn't seen him since that weekend two years ago, and had only thought of him occasionally. He looked so confident, so alive with an energy she found mesmerizing. He was no better looking than most of the other young men but he seemed to stand apart from them. He held the girl by her hand and whirled her round on the dance floor, catching her in his arms and holding her to him, his fair head against hers.

Grace felt a stab of envy. Suddenly she longed to be the girl in his arms, have him hold her so close. He turned and their eyes met. For a second he didn't recognize her, then he smiled, released the girl in his arms a little and said: 'Why, if it isn't Grace. Last time I saw you we were in a fireplace together.'

'What were you doing in a fireplace, Jonathan?' The girl looked petulant.

Henry stopped dancing and stood awkwardly by her side. Smiling rather frantically Grace introduced them.

'This is Melanie Douglas,' Jonathan said easily, his arm still round the girl. 'So this is your dance too, Grace? It's only good manners for me to dance with my hostess.' He smiled at Henry and handed him Melanie. 'We'll just go round once or twice, you two don't mind, do you?'

Neither dared say if they did mind and

before she knew it Grace felt Jonathan's arms encircle her as he swept off her round the floor. The music now changed from the more old-fashioned tunes her uncle had demanded to something with more of a beat. He held her hand, spun her to him and away while they gyrated to the rhythm.

They only danced for a few minutes and the music made it impossible to talk but it was enough for Grace to know with a sad certainty that she'd never felt so alive before, and that no other man, including Henry, could match him.

When the music finished, India suddenly appeared beside them. She ignored them all but Jonathan.

'My dance, I believe, Jonathan,' she said, laughing, taking his arm and pulling him away into the crowd, leaving Grace feeling rather flat and the shimmering splendour of the room suddenly dimmed.

3

'Grace — how are you?'

Grace, who had just finished choosing a cashmere jersey for her boss's mother, turned and saw India. 'India, it's been ages. How are you?' They kissed rather awkwardly. Grace thought how pale India looked, but unlike other people to whom illness and tiredness gave a rather bleak, pinched look, she just looked more fragile, her features finer, but still beautiful.

'It has been ages,' India said. 'What are you doing in Harrods, buying expensive cashmere?' She glanced over at the counter with its pale blue twinset on a plastic model, an expensive silk scarf and various gold chains elegantly furled round its neckline.

'It's for my boss's mother's birthday. I work just across the road and every year he makes me come here to buy her birthday and Christmas presents. I think it's awfully lazy of him. He spends enough time at his club but can't find the time to shop for his mother. But if *I* don't do it,' she sighed, 'the poor old thing would probably get nothing.'

'Maybe she's a wicked old thing who's

40

ruined his life and he only sends her presents out of duty,' India snapped back vehemently, her face going quite pink. 'Parents' selfishness can muck up their children's lives dreadfully, you know.'

'Of course they can,' Grace said hurriedly, surprised at India's vehemence. There was a change in her, she thought, surreptitiously examining her.

India was dressed in an expensive dark green suit with a cream silk blouse; her glossy dark hair had been newly done; her make-up was subtle and flattering, but there was a look of desperation in her eyes.

'It's good to see you, Grace. You look wonderful,' India said. 'I like your hair longer.'

'Thanks.' Grace was amazed at her compliments, the almost childlike desire to please that was quite alien to India's character. It was true that Grace hadn't really seen her for at least a year, apart from in the gossip columns or unexpectedly, like today. Then India would give her a curt wave, or a hasty kiss depending on her mood, say she couldn't stop, she was in such a rush, and dash off with the air of someone never out of the social whirl for a moment.

'Have you time for a coffee and a chat, we haven't seen each other for so long, or

41

have you got to get back to work?' India said with a hint of eagerness in her voice, again quite uncharacteristic.

'I must get home. We've damp coming into the drawing room and I've got to be there to let in the builder. Mummy's at work and Daddy's in Wiltshire painting a picture of someone's country house.' Then to cover her surprise at the obvious disappointment in India's expression she rushed on: 'My boss is good at giving me time off. He said to buy his mother's present then go.'

'Could I come too? I . . . I haven't been to your house for ages,' India said hesitantly.

'Of course.' Grace hastily examined a display of handbags to hide her surprise. What had happened to India to change her so? She hadn't heard through the family grapevine that anything dreadful had happened. 'It's quite a trek though.'

'I don't mind. Do you go by bus?'

'No, tube.' She glanced at her watch. 'If you're sure, only I ought to set off now to be there on time. We've got to get an estimate, you see,' she added rather defiantly, sure that India's parents would never need an estimate, but would just get in the best people for the work and hang the expense.

'How long have you been in your job?' India asked Grace when they had settled themselves on the train.

'Almost two years now. I keep thinking I'll get something better, but so far I haven't, not that I've tried very hard. What have you been doing? I heard you'd been abroad.'

'Yes, that was after our dance. I went abroad for a year, on and off.' She smiled a little sourly. 'Doing art courses, languages, you know, the classic filling-in-time thing one's parents think is a good idea.'

'I'd have loved to have done something like that. I mean, art and languages are useful for all your life, they enrich you, broaden your horizons. Secretarial college only gets you a job, not that that's not important, essential as far as I'm concerned, but so narrow and boring.' Grace could not help a sliver of envy creeping into her. She had left school at eighteen after A levels, as had India. Then she had gone on this secretarial course, while India had lived it up in exotic and exciting foreign countries, when she wasn't embarking on an endless round of parties and other social events. Grace had had to work almost straight from school and after a few temping jobs she'd got this one, working in a firm of architects, while India was still free to enjoy life, no doubt financed by a huge allowance from her father.

India just smiled, then, biting her lips as if

to stop the words escaping, lost the battle and burst out: 'Caspar was off with his regiment somewhere. I was sent abroad to be out of the way.'

'Were you? I thought you just went to be polished, as it were.' Grace tried not to sound scornful.

'No, not really. Oh, Grace, you must have heard the rumours, you know . . . ' She looked round the carriage as if there might be someone she knew who was listening in to their conversation.

Grace frowned. Her mother had told her, not that she didn't know already, that both Aunt Flavia and Uncle William had flings with other people. Then there'd been that red-headed woman she'd seen exchange smouldering glances with Uncle William at her dance, but, as her mother had remarked, if they were both at it, no doubt it suited them and they'd carry on that way.

Grace didn't know how to answer India's question. She didn't know how much India knew, or how much she wanted to know about her parents' alleged affairs. She just nodded sympathetically and waited to hear more.

'Mummy's moved out of Elmley,' India said in a low voice. 'Oh, no one, not even your mother, knows it's official. Mummy's in the house in London, Daddy's down at Elmley. It's been like that for the past year, and so far it's been kept out of the gossip columns.'

'How dreadful.' Grace was shocked. She felt rather shaky inside as if a great institution and well-known landmark had suddenly crumbled and collapsed.

She remembered her father's words: the rich live their lives differently to the rest of us poor mortals. They have enough houses to live happily apart from each other with whomever they wish and still feel disposed enough towards each other to appear together whenever duty calls.

'It wasn't too bad at first,' India went on. 'Mummy came down to Elmley if she had to entertain, be there as Daddy's wife, the great hostess, you know. I was often around, and all the staff are there, and Daddy of course, so it didn't seem much different, but . . .' Her face clouded over. To Grace's horror it almost looked as if she might cry. At the same moment she realized they had reached their stop and, taking India's arm, she whisked her off the train, avid for her to continue.

India pulled herself together, hunted in her pocket and her bag for her ticket, finally found it and handed it in. As they walked up the road to Grace's house, Grace said: 'What's happened now to make it different?'

'I'll tell you when we're inside,' India said, sticking her hands in her pockets and striding up the road.

In five minutes they were home. Grace snapped on the lights and drew the curtains against the oncoming dusk. 'Tea, coffee?'

'I'd love some coffee.' India followed Grace down the passage to the kitchen/dining room. It was done up in old pine. Some of the cupboards were original and her father had spent ages searching for other old pieces to blend in with them. There were jars of herbs and dried flowers dotted about. One wall held a bookcase stuffed with cookery books and a message board cluttered with cards and scraps of paper. There was a small recess by the window with a cane sofa tucked into it. On its bright striped cushions lay Horatius the cat, who opened one eye disdainfully before closing it again and continuing his sleep. In the middle of the room was a square pine table that was used for eating and preparing food; a large blue and yellow pottery bowl stood in the middle of it evoking the sunshine colours of a Mediterranean clime. The room had a comfortable, homely feeling of happy chaos.

'Do you want to sit here, or next door?' Grace said hurriedly, knowing that the drawing room was smarter, though probably no tidier.

'Here's fine,' India said, sitting down on the sofa next to Horatius.

'Move, you lazy boy,' Grace said, seeing India eyeing the cat doubtfully. She scooped him up and put him on a chair. He shook himself crossly and took himself off.

Grace made the coffee and opened a tin of biscuits, putting them both in reach of India. Then she sat down opposite her and said as gently as she could, forcing herself to curb her impatience, 'So what's happened?'

India took a sip of coffee and lit a cigarette. She leant back and regarded Grace with her fine dark eyes. 'Anthea has moved into Elmley with Daddy.'

'Anthea?'

'You know, Grace,' she said impatiently, 'Peter Millard's wife.'

'The trainer? I know, that red-haired woman. Moved in?' Grace sat up now.

'Yes. Before they just met wherever. Mummy still ran Elmley even though she wasn't there very often, but now' — her mouth drew in as if she had swallowed lemon juice — 'Anthea has taken over, and I haven't been back since. I can't bear to see what horrible things she's done to it.' Her voice was frantic now, her face agonized. 'I love Elmley, you know I do, more than anything. It's the one place I feel I really belong to. I know it was silly, naïve of me to imagine it would always be there for ever and ever without changing, but I did. Even when Caspar inherits, I felt I'd still be able to go there. It would stay the same, with all the pictures and furniture that I love, always in their places, but now . . .'

'But what will she do? She can't pull it down,' Grace said quickly. 'Your father loves it too, and no one more than he knows his duty to it. I've heard him say more than once that he considers it a privilege to live there, be custodian of that wonderful house and its treasures for his lifetime, and how he must guard it well.' Grace began to feel sick herself. India's unhappiness was infectious, and although she hadn't been back to Elmley for at least two years, and certainly didn't want to live there herself, she did love the house, and enjoyed its sumptuous beauty. Who could fail to? It was her relations, except for Uncle William, who had made her feel uncomfortable.

'Just her being there will change it, the atmosphere, I mean. But you know how Daddy hasn't really any taste, I mean he doesn't need it, with everything there already, but she might change it, paint it terrible colours, sell things . . . '

She seemed so distressed that Grace knew there was more to it than just the presence of someone else in the house. 'Oh, India, I'm so sorry. But you have your mews house in London, and your mother's house, and you could go down and see it for yourself? Surely your father wants to see you?' she pointed out, as if India were saying that she was homeless and had nowhere to go.

'I can't go back,' India said. 'Don't you understand, Grace?'

For a moment there was a hint of the old, supercilious India, saying, 'How boring you are, Grace, can't you think of a better place to hide?'

'If I go back and see and feel the changes I'll lose the memories I had of it for ever. I'll never get them back. If I feel the one stable place in my life has gone, I'll never get over it,' she said dramatically.

'I see that,' Grace said, and thought she did understand. Although she did wonder if India, so used to Elmley being the perfect backdrop for her beauty and her way of life, was also being goaded by selfishness.

'Besides' — India looked defiant in her hurt — 'with her there, I may not be

49

welcome. Mistresses don't want their lovers' children around, do they? They might show them up for what they're really after. So I want you to do me a favour. You're the only one that can do it as you know Elmley as well as I do.'

'But Caspar . . . '

'He's in Northern Ireland with his regiment, so you must do it.' Her voice was firm now, bossy, telling her to serve underarm and stop holding up the game. 'You must go down to Elmley and see exactly what she's done. I want to know everything, do you understand, absolutely everything she's changed.'

'But, India, I — ' She was interrupted by a ring at the doorbell. 'Damn, that must be the builder. I'll go and let him in or he'll go away.' She got up and ran to the front door quickly as if India would disappear while she was thus occupied.

'I understand you've got some damp?' The builder, a sturdy, robust-faced man, greeted her cheerfully. He came in, wiped his feet and began to look around.

'Yes, it's in here,' Grace said, longing to get back to India, yet knowing she had to ask all the questions her mother had listed, and be sure he gave an estimate for redecorating as well.

He took for ever, tapping and banging and

looking glum. 'It needs replastering. Have to dig all this wet stuff out,' he said at last with an almost gleeful look in his eye, 'then put in some dampproof plaster, replaster it all.' At last he went promising to send an estimate by the end of the week. Grace went back to India.

'So,' India greeted her, 'I want you to go down as soon as possible for the weekend.'

'But, India, I can't just turn up there uninvited!' She gave an incredulous laugh.

'Yes you can, you know Daddy is fond of you. You just appear and say you were in the district and wanted to see him. He's bound to ask you to stay the night, or anyway for a meal. But if you ask in advance *she* will put you off. It's the only way, Grace, you must do it.'

'I feel . . . ' Grace didn't like say it was the last thing she wanted to do: go down there alone, uninvited, and snoop round? But she'd never seen India so upset before. It must be hellish for her, her father moving in someone else like that, someone who might not want his grown-up children around. Thank God her parents were so besotted with each other she'd never had to worry about that problem. She looked round the warm and familiar room filled with so many things that held happy memories. This was hardly Elmley, but she'd hate it if another woman moved in here and started putting her mark on it.

'You must go, Grace, you're the only one who can. I'll get your train ticket, unless you have a car. I can hardly lend you mine. But you've got to go.' Her voice held a mixture of pleading and authority.

Grace felt again her childhood fears of inadequacy, of failure to belong to that gilded group, seep back into her. But she steeled herself. She was twenty-three now, no longer a child, and she couldn't just go back to Elmley without an invitation.

'You must come too, India,' she said. 'If we go together it will be much easier. Once you've done it — '

'No,' India interrupted her firmly. 'I want you to go, Grace. You've got to do it for me, you just don't know how unhappy I am.' Her dark eyes looked soulfully into Grace's, her soft mouth trembled and although part of Grace told herself that India was surely putting on this act, she knew her cousin did feel devastated at her parents' break-up and her fear of someone else ruining Elmley was genuine, even though it might be rather exaggerated.

'All right,' she said sighing with affected heartiness. 'But it will have to be at a weekend and I can't go this one. I'm sailing with Henry.'

'Who's Henry, can't you put him off? Or can't he go with you?' India looked petulant.

'No, I can't. I promised to sail in this race with him ages ago, Henry's depending on me,' Grace said firmly. Henry made plans for them most of the time. She just went along with them, out of habit.

'Well then, I suppose it will have to be the weekend after,' India said with impatience.

'It will,' Grace said. 'I don't have a car, so I'll have to take the train. Then what? I can't just take a taxi without ringing your father first, can I?'

India thought a moment. 'Take a taxi to the Rutland Arms, ring him from there. Say you're passing and could you drop in.'

'And what if he's not there?'

'He will be, he's always there. Though do it about five, after shooting. Then he'll ask you to stay. It'll be too late for him to expect you to go somewhere else for the night,' she said briskly, as if there were no more to be said on the subject,

'All right,' Grace said, admitting to herself that she was curious to see the new set-up at Elmley.

India looked more relaxed. 'Who is Henry?'

she asked. 'The man in your life?'

'Yes, I suppose he is. He came to our dance, remember? Henry Buchan.'

'I don't remember. You've been going out with him all this time? Will you get married?'

'I . . . I don't know,' Grace said. Apart from the time that Henry had spent at Edinburgh University they had been together. It was an easy, contented relationship, but it didn't have the passion her parents still had. But then she often supposed that many relationships worked in a more low-key way than theirs. 'Have you anyone special, India?'

India smiled a little secretly. 'Not really. Most British public-school men are pretty predictable, don't you think? There was a friend of Caspar's I thought had a bit more to him though . . . not that I've seen him for ages. Now that Caspar's away . . . and of course things being how they are, we don't have those huge house parties any more.'

Grace was about to ask her who the friend was, whether he was someone she knew, when they heard the front door open and Grace's mother, Olivia, came in.

'India, how lovely to see you,' she said with surprise, putting down her shopping on the table and coming forward to kiss her. 'I haven't seen you for such a long time. How are you and your parents?'

Grace tensed, knowing how upset her mother would be when she heard that Aunt Flavia had been usurped by the trainer's wife and banished from Elmley, but India, returning her embrace and smiling broadly, said: 'Everyone's fine, thank you, sends their love.'

'Good, I must ring your mother. I'm hopeless at keeping in touch, we only seem to contact each other at Christmas and birthdays. I don't know where the time goes.' She smiled again, taking off her coat and hanging it up in the small passage.

'She's in London at the moment,' India said, having thrown a warning look at Grace. 'I'll tell her I saw you. I met Grace in Harrods, buying cashmere for her boss's mother.' She ran on, and watching her Grace knew that no one would guess at her inner turmoil.

She wondered why Aunt Flavia hadn't told her own sister about the situation, or why India was pretending that everything was all right. But then as she half listened to India prattling on as if her life was wonderful, she realized it was pride that made them keep their failures secret. Flavia had always despised her sister for marrying a penniless man and expecting to live off love alone, while she had gone for the big catch. Now that her marriage had floundered and another woman had secured her prize, it would not be easy for her to admit to it.

'Do stay for supper and the night too,' her mother said, when India paused in her discourse.

'Oh, thanks but I can't. I'm having dinner with Freddie Fitz-Hunter, and I must get going. Can you ring for a mini-cab, please, Grace?' She threw her a dazzling smile, that Grace knew was a thank you for saying nothing about the collapse of her parents' marriage.

Grace felt ridiculously pleased as if she'd at last been allowed to join that hallowed gang.

'Isn't Freddie Fitz-Hunter the heir to the Duke of — ' Olivia started only to be quickly interrupted by India.

'Yes, he's waiting in trepidation for it to happen any day now. The poor old boy is not at all well,' India said as if she was tired of talking about the subject. 'I'll ring you next week, Grace, about that weekend.' She gave her a deep look, then said to Olivia, 'Just a weekend party I want her to come to.'

'How lovely,' Olivia said, beginning to unpack her shopping: a few groceries, some vegetables and pasta for supper. 'At Elmley?'

'Yes,' India said, then added in her best-mannered voice. 'How is Uncle Leo?'

'He's well, thank you, India.' Eagerly Olivia went on to tell her about the picture of the country house he was painting and how he had got quite a few similar commissions lately.

Grace, watching her, felt a pang of affectionate sympathy for her, knowing her mother was trying to convey to her sister, through India, that some people did appreciate his talents, and he was not a loser. She wished she could tell her that her sister's superior marriage had failed and that all the money and status in the world was nothing if you were rejected and on your own. But she knew she would say nothing, but be instead an accessory to Flavia and India's courageous attempt to pretend to the world that all was well.

4

'It seems that poor old Great-uncle Arthur is going to snuff it at any minute and I really don't much feel like being a duke,' Freddie Fitz-Hunter said to India as they sat over dinner. 'I suppose you wouldn't marry me, help me out?' He lifted his glass of wine and emptied it, throwing her a half-despairing, half-sardonic glance.

India gave a little laugh. 'Oh, Freddie, you know it wouldn't work.' She didn't love him, he didn't much like sex and she didn't want to be a duchess.

'Thought you wouldn't,' he said easily, clicking his fingers for the waiter to bring them another bottle of wine. Impatiently he pushed back the lock of brown hair that kept flopping over his eyes, stretched his long legs out and leant back in his chair. 'I'll have to settle for one of those horsy, doggy girls that adore being stuck in the depths of the country in pouring rain for months on end.'

India laughed, though a little sadly as she thought of the fate of Elmley. 'I do love the country, rain and all, I just wouldn't make a good duchess. Anyway, I don't want to get married just yet, or ever perhaps. You know, Freddie' — she leant forward on her elbows, cupping her face in her hands — 'I saw my cousin Grace today. Her parents are so in love it's unreal. When my aunt talks of her husband her whole face lights up as if she's a teenager in love for the first time. That's what marriage should be.'

Freddie gave her a crooked smile. 'That is extremely rare, my dear. You know my parents weren't that happy, and yours not at all. Too much is expected from marriage these days, and it's all change your partners at the first sign of trouble or boredom.'

'So why do you want to marry then?' she said. 'Just to have an heir?'

'Not just that, companionship too, and you and I, we'd have a giggle being Duke and Duchess. We get on fine in an uncomplicated, contented way. Besides, you're used to the life, wouldn't make a hash of opening the church fête.' He smiled his charming, boyish smile, and she couldn't help but smile back. Encouraged, he went on, 'It would solve your problem of not having Elmley to go to whenever you wanted to. You'd be mistress of your own pile.'

'But, Freddie, it's miles away in Scotland and I'd miss all my friends . . . '

'You're right, I feel the same. Pity our family seat had to go to some rich Arab to pay off death duties.' He sighed. 'My uncle should have sold Scotland instead.'

'I know, those wretched death duties have ruined so many families, broken up priceless art collections, let lovely houses go.' India knew her father had entailed Elmley to Caspar. There were four more years before it legally became his. She sometimes wished it was sooner then perhaps Caspar would move in and the trainer's wife and all her changes would be sent packing.

'So will you live in Scotland and run the estate when your great-uncle dies?' India said to take her mind off the pain thinking of Elmley gave her. It was there when she woke each morning, and it disturbed her in the darkness of the night: a sick, hollow pain that would not go away. Why couldn't her parents continue as they always had? Living together, yet leading separate lives? It wasn't as if they wanted to settle down and start families with new people. Anthea was too old to have more children, wasn't she?

Freddie shrugged. 'I don't know yet. I'll have to spend some time up there, see to the estate. There's a lot of fishing and shooting which will be fun. That's the only good thing about it I can think of. I can have huge house

60

parties with all my friends.'

'I suppose it's too late for your uncle to have a child?' she said, fighting to put thoughts of Elmley and possible new stepbrothers and -sisters from her mind. At least her brother was the heir to it all and couldn't be usurped by a new brother, unless he got killed in Northern Ireland, or in a car crash — he drove far too fast. The thought terrified her.

'Oh God, yes. He's seventy-eight and I don't think he likes women much. He's always preferred his dogs and horses. You can trust animals, I remember him saying when I was a child, they never let you down. Sad, really.' He gave her a quick smile as if he felt the same way, but didn't want to admit to it.

'Some men father children right into their eighties,' she said cheerfully, recognizing his sorrow and trying to lighten it. 'There have been cases of men hiring women to give them heirs.'

'If I could hire one to give him a son I would,' Freddie said with feeling, 'but I'm afraid he's past fathering one. He expects me to be his heir now. Of course he always thought my father would get the title, no one thought he'd die so early.' His mouth clenched. India put her hand over his as it moved restlessly over the tablecloth.

'That was hell, but at least he died doing his favourite sport.'

'I know, but the sickening thing is it was a freak fall. Just a low fence; he'd jumped far higher many times. I thought he'd die hunting, but when he was about ninety, not fifty-four. He had so much vitality.'

'I know he did.' She remembered his father on the hunting field and in other walks of life. He'd had enormous energy, but unfortunately most of it had been passed on to his three daughters and by the time Freddie had come along there was not much left for him. Any one of his sisters would have made a far better duke.

When they got close to her mews house off Cadogan Square, Freddie said: 'Can I spent the night, just have a cuddle? I don't feel like going home.'

'All right,' she agreed, knowing there would be nothing more. She recognized his loneliness and knew she felt it too — a sort of helplessness at not being able to make life go the way one wanted it to go. He would have to be a duke many years before he'd thought he'd have to. She was losing Elmley in a way she hadn't considered.

There was nowhere to park in the mews and India had turned her garage into a dining room, so they had to park in Lennox Gardens. As they waited to cross the road to go into the mews, a dark Maserati slid past, slowing down to let them cross. Glancing inside at the driver she saw in the glow of the streetlamp that it was Jonathan Sheridan. She felt her heart leap, her blood quicken; she would have spoken to him, but by his side, her hand on his knee, was a woman. Her pride came to her rescue and she crossed the road, holding on to Freddie's arm. But her body and mind were in tumult. Why did Jonathan attract her so? She'd had lovers, enjoyed being with them, but never once had she felt that all-consuming attraction for any one of them. She hadn't seen Jonathan for over a year, though he'd often come down to shoot with Caspar before he'd been sent to Northern Ireland. He had always been perfectly friendly to her, but nothing more. She, who was used to men falling in love with her, couldn't understand why he hadn't fallen for her. But it was a new challenge and she certainly wasn't going to throw herself at him.

The other men she knew seemed to be cast in the same mould. They were charming, amusing, sometimes childish, but all conforming to the same behaviour and holding the same views. But Jonathan seemed not to care if he was part of the public schoolboy herd or not. He stood alone and seemed content. He had an elusive quality about him, untamed, unowned by anyone, a master of himself, and this intrigued her.

'Why so quiet?' Freddie said, snapping on lights in the hall and going into the drawing room to do the same. 'Are you tired? I am, exhausted. Can I have a whisky? Pour you one?' He was over at the drinks tray before she could answer him.

'I am tired,' she said, taking off her coat. At once he was by her side helping her off with it. He laid it on the chair.

'We won't be late, shall I bring the whisky to bed?'

'If you want, I won't have anything.' She went upstairs into her pale peach and green bedroom and sat down at her dressing table, staring at her reflection in the mirror. Who was the girl with Jonathan? She hadn't seen her face. She felt jealousy worm into her, imagining them going home somewhere together, Jonathan taking the girl to bed, making love to her. She gave her head a little shake as if to dispel the pictures of them entwined together. How she yearned to be that girl.

She wondered how, without losing her pride, she could contact him. She supposed he was in the phone book. She didn't want to ask Caspar for his address. She could hear him say with an enormous roar, 'What unsavoury reason do you have for wanting it, India? Don't tell me you fancy him.'

Freddie came upstairs and carefully put his whisky glass down on the bedside table. He went into the bathroom and in a few moments came out again dressed only in his boxer shorts, his clothes over his arm. These he arranged carefully on a chair. He got into bed.

'Hurry up, India,' he said good-naturedly but without passion.

India slowly undressed, put on her night-dress and took off her make-up. All the time she wondered what it would be like if it was Jonathan here with her. Would he tear her clothes from her, take her with a vigour and an impatience that would disarm her pride for ever, and make her abandon her life to him?

She got into bed beside Freddie. He put off the light and snuggled close to her.

'Will you still care for me when I'm a duke?' he said in the darkness.

'Of course, and I'll visit you often,' she said, feeling the pain of losing Elmley creeping into her again. She wished Grace would go there this weekend to find out what that woman had done to it.

They lay close together like children, comforted by the warmth of each other, each crying out silently into the night at the helplessness they felt at the sudden changes to their once predictable lives.

5

Grace gazed round the little church of St Stephen Walbrook with delight. It had worked marvellously, she thought, the pure white dome above with the exquisite moulded flowers and the plain altar designed by Henry Moore. There was an almost mystic feeling of space, light and peace and it was in this frame of mind that she went out into the street.

It was a beautiful autumn day, the changing leaves shining bronze and gold in the sharp sunlight. She was glad she'd come into the City early on her way to the train to Newmarket and Elmley. She'd always wanted to see some of the little churches crammed into the corners of the City of London and, feeling that her parents wanted to be alone, her father having returned from his painting trip late last night, she had decided to take advantage of needing to be in this part of London, and look at them.

Still in a reverie after seeing the church, she wasn't altogether looking where she was going and she crashed into someone who was rushing out of a doorway.

'Oh, I'm sorry.' She felt she was falling

and clutched at the person only to feel their arms steadying her.

'Oops.' The man looked contrite but a little annoyed, then as he stared at her a flash of recognition came into his eyes.

'It was my fault,' she said, looking at him, feeling her heart lurch. She blushed. 'Oh, Jonathan, it's you. It's Grace Penfold.'

'Of course, the fireplace at Elmley. Fancy seeing you again like this. I didn't hurt you, did I?'

'No. I wasn't paying much attention to where I was going. I've just been to see St Stephen's and I was wandering along in rather a dream. It's so peaceful, it sort of doped me, I'm afraid.' She laughed, then realizing that they were still holding on to each other, took away her hands from his arms.

'The churches here are superb. When I have time I often pop into one. Sometimes they have concerts at lunchtime, you know, very uplifting in the middle of the day.' He was looking at her intently, his grey-blue eyes taking in each feature of her face, his long mouth curved with a smile.

Grace felt as if a light was switched on inside her and was glowing out through her eyes and skin. She had an overwhelming compulsion to put her hands back on his arms, but she forced herself to hold back, scolding herself for her extraordinary desire.

'What are you doing here on a Saturday? Do you work in the City?' Jonathan asked her.

'No.' She paused, then, needing to share her anxiety about her errand, said, 'Actually I'm going down to Elmley. I'm on my way to the station.'

'Staying the weekend?' He eyed the bag over her shoulder.

'I . . . I don't know.' How awkward this was. She'd been feeling apprehensive about the whole thing all week. She couldn't confide in her parents, not until her aunt had told her mother about her marriage breaking up. And what would Uncle William think of her turning up so suddenly out of the blue like this? Why, if she knew she was going to be in the area, hadn't she telephoned him before? She was bound to make a complete mess of it all and India would be furious with her.

'Don't know?' He looked surprised. 'You mean you're going down on spec?'

She sighed, bit her lip then blurted out: 'Sort of. You see, oh dear . . . I don't know how to put it.' She didn't like to break India's confidence, or indeed reveal the state of her uncle and aunt's marriage.

She was sure Jonathan was trustworthy but the more people that knew about it, the more likely it was to get into the gossip columns.

Seeing her discomfiture Jonathan smiled reassuringly and touched her arm briefly. 'Don't tell me if you'd rather not. I know how mysterious families are. Have you a moment for some lunch before you go?'

She glanced at her watch. It was ten to twelve and she'd thought about taking a train in the early afternoon. 'That would be lovely,' she said shyly, feeling suddenly relieved that she had someone to take her mind off her worries for a while.

As he took her arm and began to walk her up the street she felt bubbles of euphoria running through her. She'd never felt like this with Henry, she thought suddenly, guiltily. It must be the shining, golden day, the beauty of the tiny churches, a contrast to her apprehension about going to Elmley.

They went into a small restaurant. It was dark and intimate, with wooden panelling and red velvet. He led her to a table and after they'd sat down said, 'So what have you been doing with yourself all these years? Not married, I see' — he glanced at her ring finger — 'or engaged?'

Now she blushed, squirming a little awkwardly. What could she say? She wasn't officially engaged to Henry, he'd never actually asked her to marry him, but he'd sometimes made remarks like 'When I've finished my accountancy exams we'll be in a position to marry', or 'I'd like to live in the country when we're married, near somewhere like Bath, what do you think?' She had just agreed with him, assuming that one day they would be married and live in quiet contentment somewhere. She did love him; he was honest and kind; they had a lot in common. More exciting men, she often told herself, never actually having got involved with one, would be more trouble than they were worth. You would never quite know what they were up to when you weren't with them.

'I see you must be,' he laughed. 'Is it a secret?'

'I'm not really engaged, but I have a boyfriend. We're very close,' she said.

'I've just broken up with my girlfriend. She was so demanding, wanting to know what I was doing every minute of the day and night.' He threw her a smile. 'I can't bear to be put in a cage like someone's pet. Just because you're in love with someone it doesn't mean you have to own them, does it?'

'No, of course not. But sometimes . . . if people feel insecure about someone, they're afraid of letting them out of their sight,' Grace said, knowing girlfriends who had that problem. She was so relieved that she never had any cause to worry about Henry.

'Insecurity is too difficult to live with,' Jonathan said. 'I can't bear to be with someone who keeps prying into every corner of my life, as if they can't trust me, or criticizes the way I spend my money. I do work damn hard for it after all. I've been working this morning.' Then, as the waiter appeared, he asked her what she wanted to eat and drink.

After she had chosen beef and oyster pie and a glass of red wine she sat back and regarded him. His features had hardened into those of a man now, all the softness of extreme youth gone. But his attraction and his vitality were still there. She liked the way his thick hair waved back from his face, his mobile mouth ready with sudden laughter. What, she thought with a glow of warmth, would it be like to kiss it? No doubt, she thought wistfully, he had an electronic organizer full of girlfriends, he was someone who would never be alone for long.

'I suppose I couldn't come down to Elmley with you?' he said suddenly. 'I mean as your visit seems so vague, would it make any difference if I came too? I could drive you down, my car's parked close by.'

'Oh, I don't know . . .' She was momentarily taken aback by his suggestion. Why on earth would he want to come with her?

As if he guessed her thoughts he said: 'I'd love to see the place again. Now that Caspar's in Northern Ireland I haven't been down for ages. I quite like his father, though I found his mother terrifying.' He shrugged, a nonchalant smile on his lips. 'Just a thought. I'll quite understand if you'd rather go alone.'

Now that he'd suggested it she desperately wanted him to come. She would feel so much better if he was with her, but she'd have to confide in him and was that fair to India? But he may know more about the break-up of her relations' marriage than she did, after all he was a great friend of Caspar's. She said tentatively, 'India asked me to go . . . She hasn't been for some time. She wants to see if there are any changes.'

'Changes?' The waiter came with a basket of bread and a bottle of wine, which he poured into their glasses.

When he had gone Grace said, 'Her parents . . . their marriage . . .'

'It was never strong. Remember we discussed it, among other things, in that chimney?' He took a sip of wine. 'I understand they both sleep around, but if they both do it . . . ' He shrugged. 'Good luck to them.'

'It's just that Uncle William's . . . ' she struggled — how should she describe the trainer's wife? ' . . . girlfriend,' she muttered at last, 'has moved in. Promise you won't say anything, but my aunt now lives in London and India wants to know what changes this woman has made to Elmley. She so loves the place, you know, and now that Caspar isn't there to report back to her, or even to keep an eye on things, she asked me to go down and see it isn't painted in lurid stripes or something equally awful.'

'How dreadful. These so-called open marriages nearly always end in tears, don't they? But I'm surprised India hasn't barged down there and made quite sure there are no lurid stripes herself. She's hardly timid,' he laughed.

'I know, but I was surprised' — again she felt a nudge of disloyalty — 'that when I saw her last week, for the first time in ages, I must admit, she had changed. I think the possibility of losing Elmley, the Elmley she knew, depended on if you like, has cracked her self-confidence. When she knew she had it all, when we were staying that time, she

74

felt she was . . . superior, I suppose, could lord it over us all.'

'Maybe you're right, but it still surprises me. She was so in control of herself, so beautiful, with every man under her spell.' He smiled as if he rather despised them. 'The praying mantis type I call girls like that — gobbling up the male when they've had enough of them.'

'I thought you liked her,' Grace said, suppressing a little thrill of delight at his description of her.

'I do, in a way. She's so beautiful, and the sister of one of my best friends, but I don't want to become another of her victims. Remember that poor Ned Porter, dashing round like a puppy trying to please her? She destroyed him, I hear. He's taken to the bottle.'

'I don't think that's quite fair, I heard he just went a bit wild, drunken parties, girls and such.' Grace liked Ned, and she hadn't taken much notice of the gossip. After all Caspar had been through some wild times alongside Ned and no one had accused him of doing it because a girl had broken his heart.

Jonathan shrugged, then said, 'About Elmley, I could be a help, I know the place quite well, not as well as you, of course, but I might notice different things to you.'

'I'm not sure how to play it,' Grace said, feeling suddenly enormously pleased that he was coming with her. 'India said to get down about teatime, after shooting, and ring and say I was passing. She said Uncle William was bound to ask me to stay the night.'

Jonathan smiled. 'We'll manage it perfectly. Much better if there's two of us and in a car. After all, you don't often drop in after a train journey, do you?'

★ ★ ★

The journey down to Suffolk did not take long in Jonathan's Maserati. He drove well and Grace enjoyed watching his firm and capable hands on the wheel. He must be quite rich, she thought, to have such a car. She said nonchalantly, 'What's your job?'

'I work in Meadows and Laing; you know, the investment firm. It's a good job, good money. I have to admit to a weakness for a luxurious life. My parents are comfortably off, but I want more and I'm prepared to work for it. Somewhere like Elmley' — he laughed, catching her eye, — 'would suit me fine.'

'It's too big for me,' she said, matching

76

his laugh. 'It's superb, but . . . '

'And the stables. There's one of those racehorses, Dark Emperor, that I want to look at. It's bred to be a winner,' he ran on before she could explain why she wouldn't want the responsibility of owning such a place.

'So you're still interested in racing?'

'Yes. I like a bet from time to time. Adds to the excitement of life.' They had arrived in Newmarket; he slowed down and said, 'We're not far now. What's the plan?'

'I must telephone Uncle William. It's almost dark, he must be back from shooting now.'

'We'll stop at the Rutland Arms, ring from there.' He drove on a few more yards until he reached the hotel.

Feeling suddenly rather nervous Grace went in, located the telephone and dialled the number. It was answered by Frobisher, the butler.

'It's Grace, Frobisher, how are you?' She could picture his long, grey face breaking into a smile. He'd always been kind to her.

'Very well, thank you, Miss Grace, and how are you keeping?'

She told him then asked if her uncle was there. In a moment she heard his booming voice on the line.

'My dear Grace, what a nice surprise. I haven't heard from you for so long.'

Feeling guilty at the subterfuge, she blurted that she and Jonathan were passing and could they drop in?

'But of course, my dear, come to tea. Better still, stay for dinner, or even the night. What do you say?'

'But there's two of us,' she said ridiculously, knowing there were at least ten spare bedrooms, a house of staff and a larder full of food.

'We've enough room for twenty. Do come, I'd be pleased to see you. Your family well?'

'Yes, thank you.' She did not ask about his.

Twenty minutes later they drove up the long elm-lined drive to Elmley. They were shown straight into the drawing room. Grace looked round curiously. Everything seemed the same, but Jonathan whispered, 'Did you see those awful box trees cut like jockey caps as we arrived?'

'No, it was too dark.'

'Look in the morning.'

'I will.'

Uncle William and the trainer's wife, as Grace still thought of her, were sitting by the huge fireplace in which almost a forest of logs was blazing. Uncle William got up at once and strode over to her.

A tiny dog resembling a rat leapt at them, barking furiously. The woman called fiercely, 'Shut up, Moo, come here.' With another series of furious barks ending in a yelp the dog slunk back to her. Uncle William took no notice of it whatsoever. Grace wondered where his two golden Labradors were.

'My dear Grace, how good to see you.' He gave her an awkward kiss and said in his bluff way. 'My, how you have blossomed, my dear, you are so pretty, just like your mother.' He turned to Jonathan and shook him by the hand.

'Jonathan, how nice. I'm sorry you didn't come in time to shoot. Next time?'

'Thank you, I'd like that,' Jonathan said. 'Have you heard how that old devil Caspar is?'

'Not lately, but he's all right. Nothing he likes more than a bit of action, though it's a damned difficult situation out there.'

Grace looked round the room. Apart from a basket with a cushion covered in patterned Liberty cotton for the rat-like dog, everything seemed to be exactly the same. The smell of the house was the same too, a subtle mixture of wood smoke, old stone and beeswax.

Uncle William, now looking rather red,

coughed, then said in the voice of a general giving orders, 'May I introduce Anthea Millard?'

'How do you do?' Jonathan said easily and went forward and took her hand.

Feeling rather disloyal to India and indeed her aunt, Grace did the same.

Anthea was in her early fifties, tall and rangy, her red hair tucked behind her ears. She wore dark trousers and a blue jersey. She smiled and said in a perfectly friendly way, 'How nice that you could come. I'm sure you're hungry, do tuck in.'

'Yes, tuck in,' Uncle William said, gesturing towards the tea trolley, which held scones and jam, a chocolate cake and a plate of homemade shortbread.

Uncle William and Jonathan immediately began talking about shooting and then racing and Grace was left to talk to Anthea. She'd arrived determined to dislike her, egged on by India's assurance that she 'would ruin the place', and be no more than icily polite to her, but when Anthea gave her a friendly smile and asked her pleasantly what she was doing with her life, she answered her readily enough.

'How nice to work in Knightsbridge, so near the best shops and the V. & A.,' Anthea said. 'I lived in London when I was a child,

80

but now I'm afraid I much prefer living in the country.'

'I love London,' Grace said, 'but when one comes down here, especially on a wonderful day like today, I wonder why I don't want to give it all up and live in the country too.'

'You must come down here whenever you want to,' Anthea said cheerfully. 'I understand you spent much of your childhood here. You must look on it almost like home.'

Grace thanked her but could not help wondering if this woman were just sucking up to her, or did she really mean it? Would Uncle William marry her, and what had happened to her husband, the unfortunate trainer?

'I'm going to have my bath,' Uncle William announced suddenly. 'You two can sleep in the cream and green rooms, you know the ones at the end of the passage. Help yourself to anything you want from Caspar and India's rooms. See you back down here at a quarter to eight.' He took out his watch to check the time, and snapped it shut again.

Grace could not help smiling, remembering he was a stickler for punctuality.

She used the time before dinner to look surreptitiously round the rest of the house. Nothing had changed that she could see.

81

She popped down to the kitchen, wanting to see Mrs Bates, the cook, who'd been there most of Grace's childhood, but also wanting to glean some gossip.

'My, what a fine young lady you've grown into,' Mrs Bates said beaming. Her hair was quite grey now, but her face still round and shining. 'Why haven't you brought India with you?'

'She's . . . ' Grace hesitated, she didn't want to start any gossip herself. 'She'll be down soon, she's just so busy.'

'I expect she is, all parties and young men, no doubt. I often see her picture in the papers. I see you've brought that nice friend of Caspar's. He your young man?' She dimpled, her dark eyes teasing her.

Grace blushed, stammered, 'Oh, I . . . '

She winked. 'Don't be shy, my dear. You make a good pair. I said to Frobisher after I'd seen you arrive. Those two look good together.'

'It's not like that,' she began, wishing desperately to get on to another subject, afraid Mrs Bates would embarrass her by saying the same thing to Jonathan.

'Love is everywhere,' Mrs Bates continued, putting a couple of brace of pheasant, their breasts covered with streaky bacon, into the oven. 'Look at Sir William,' she giggled.

'That was a turn-up for the books, wasn't it?'

'Things have changed,' Grace said, knowing if she waited long enough she'd hear everything.

'I'll say, not that I didn't like your aunt.' Mrs Bates bustled into the larder and came out with a bowl of jellied stock. 'She didn't love him, though, just kept him sweet so she could have what she wanted. But' — she clicked her tongue — 'poor old man, he was so often alone here, night after night while she was gadding off somewhere. Frobisher and I would serve him dinner in that huge dining room, him sitting there with just the dogs for company. It wasn't right. You can't blame him for looking elsewhere.'

'Does she live here?' Grace asked.

'Oh yes, dear, like man and wife.' She winked again. 'You should see their bedroom. That's the only room she's done up so far, all pink and flouncy. You wouldn't credit it, she doesn't look the feminine sort, does she? Goodness knows what the rest of the house will turn out like. She's nice though, good tempered.'

'Is she going to change more things?'

'Don't ask me, dear.' Mrs Bates cut some bread very thinly and put it in the oven to make melba toast to go with the soup.

Frobisher came in followed by Connie, the girl who helped in the kitchen, with a bowl of peeled potatoes in cold water. The talk ceased at once. Grace remembered Frobisher was not keen on gossip, especially in front of young girls like Connie, who, as he'd once put it, didn't have the respect that the older staff had, always gossiping to their boyfriends who might well turn their stories into cash if a newspaper reporter got hold of them.

Grace went back upstairs and wondered where Jonathan was. She would have liked to have talked things over with him, but after what Mrs Bates had said about them she felt shy of knocking on his bedroom door. If any of the staff saw her it would add fuel to Mrs Bates's fanciful opinion of them. Instead she went into India's room to find something to wear for dinner.

The room was just as she'd always remembered it, blue and cream, the fabric copied from an old French design, though it was quite faded now. There was still the stain of nail varnish on the carpet that she remembered India spilling as she rushed to get ready for a lunch party when they were younger, half hidden by the frill round the dressing table. She felt rather sad for India as she stood here. She who had everything, beauty, money, who

84

had felt that coming from such a house gave her a superiority over other people, was somewhere deep inside herself still a child who yearned for her home to be the same as it had always been, a sumptuous bolthole to protect her from the realities of life.

Her parents may never have been happy together, but there'd always been a house full of caring staff to look after her, giving her stability and a much-loved home. How strange, she thought, remembering Jonathan's surprise at India, of all people, not dashing down here herself to see what was going on. India had a weakness after all: she could not bear to think of Elmley being taken from her.

She went over to the vast mahogany wardrobe and opened the door. So many clothes still hung there as if any moment India would be back to wear them. Grace wondered if she needed them in London, but she hadn't asked her to bring anything back for her. She settled on a simple black ribbed silk dress and after a bath hurried downstairs, not wanting to be late.

Uncle William was standing by the fireplace in the drawing room. He was dressed in an old bottle-green smoking jacket, a glass of whisky in his hand. There was no sign of either Jonathan or Anthea.

'Grace, my dear, let me pour you a drink. Sherry? Gin and tonic?'

'Sherry, thank you,' she said, feeling suddenly shy alone with him like this. Hastily she tried to think of something neutral to say but was forestalled.

'Have you seen India lately?'

'Y . . . Yes. I was in Harrods and I saw her and . . . '

He didn't look at her, but took a gulp of his whisky, and said, his eyes staring thoughtfully into the fire, 'I expect, Grace, that you are shocked to see my, um' — he coughed — 'my new living arrangements.'

'I . . . ' Grace didn't know what to say.

'Your aunt was a good woman in many ways,' he went on as if he were discussing the merits of one of his brood mares, 'but she never loved me.' He looked embarrassed as if he was confessing to a weakness in himself. 'Lots of people are impressed by titles, possessions, but in the end we are all the same. Flesh, blood and emotions. Anthea knows that.' He looked at Grace defiantly as if expecting her to disapprove.

Grace felt very awkward, as if he was suddenly going to spout forth the facts of life to her. She didn't think she could bear it. To field off any more intimate details she blurted out, 'India is afraid the house will be changed.'

His bluff, weather-beaten face broke into a smile. 'It has changed, my dear,' he said simply, 'it is full of love.'

His words were so incongruous: there he stood, a picture of typical English landed gentry, tall, old now, with white hair and a flushed face; a man who preferred shooting and racing to anything else in life; a man who found it easier to communicate with his dogs and his horses than a woman, admitting he was in love. She felt suddenly rather pleased for him, and went over and kissed him.

'I'm glad for you, Uncle William,' she said spontaneously, then, remembering India's unhappiness, immediately felt guilty.

Grace was spared any more discomfiture by Jonathan's arrival. He had on Caspar's dark blue velvet smoking jacket and she felt again a thrill of pleasure as she looked at him. The cut and elegance of the clothes emphasized his natural grace and good looks. He smiled at her and said, 'That suits you so well, Grace. What a fine pair we make in our borrowed finery.'

'Indeed you do,' Uncle William said, offering drinks, then he looked at his watch.

At eight exactly Frobisher appeared to say dinner was served and Anthea walked in, dressed in a long beige and black kaftan. She was smiling. She held out her hands to Sir William.

'Here I am, Billy boy,' she coquettishly, 'you can put away that watch and breathe easy.'

He beamed like a happy schoolboy at her. 'My dear, you look magnificent.' He took her arm and walked her in to dinner. Jonathan winked at Grace and slipped her arm though his.

'Billy boy,' he whispered, 'how India will cringe at that.'

As the evening progressed Grace felt the glow of her uncle's obvious happiness, combined with good wine and food, infuse her. She found herself often smiling at Jonathan, liking the fact that he was there across the table from her. He was witty and convivial, telling her jokes, winking at her when her uncle and Anthea made some remark that they both knew would kill India. It was as if they were bound together in some sort of secret.

After dinner the men stayed in the dining room with their port, while she and Anthea sat drinking coffee in the drawing room.

'Are you shocked at your uncle and me?'

Anthea broke the companionable silence.

'N . . . no, of course not,' Grace said hurriedly. She'd never admit to being shocked, knew it was mean of her to imagine that old people should do without illicit love.

'I know the children are horrified . . . well, now that I've actually moved in. But you know, we didn't see why we should go on with this hole-in-the-corner affair, as if what we felt for each other was something to be ashamed of. It wasn't fair on my husband either, and, contrary to what you all might think, I do love William, very much.' Her voice was brisk, as if she were describing a rather dull domestic arrangement instead of a love affair.

'I do see how difficult it must have been,' Grace said, but Anthea went on as if she hadn't spoken.

'If he hadn't got all this' — she gestured round the room, taking in the Turners, the Constables, the priceless furniture — 'a title and all, no one would think much about it. I don't care for all this, you know, it's rather like living in a museum. When Caspar gets back from Northern Ireland, I'd like him to take it over, and go and live with William in some little house somewhere else.' She smiled ruefully, stroking the rat-like dog that lay curled in her lap. 'But I doubt anyone will believe me.'

'I'm sure they will,' Grace said, liking her suddenly and wondering what she was going to tell India.

She smiled again, shrugging. 'Children are always difficult to please. I know they hate me, and are afraid of what I might do to their father, this estate, but they are both old enough to accept that he deserves to be loved.'

'They will in time . . . ' Grace said, wondering if she ought to say how afraid India was of her changing Elmley.

'Ah, time. That is the one thing we never have enough of.'

Grace pondered this for a moment, wondering if she was insinuating that Uncle William was running out of time. Then Anthea said, 'I like Jonathan, you suit each other.'

'Oh, no, you're mistaken. He's a friend of Caspar's, we just met on the way here.' Then, afraid Anthea would guess that India had forced her to come down here to check her out, she went on: 'I have a boyfriend, Henry. He lives near me in Kew.'

'Oh, I see. I'm sorry, I've misunderstood, you seemed so very close.'

Grace felt mortified and guilty about

Henry. For the rest of their stay there she remained remote from Jonathan. After lunch on Sunday they drove back to London. As they sped up the motorway he said, 'So, what do you think? Apart from those terrible box tree jockey caps, it hasn't changed, and what's more they are in love. You have to allow them that.'

'I agree. I felt much closer to Uncle William than I ever did as a child. I think he's mellowed, having Anthea.' She looked out at the countryside, the golden leaves glittering in a shaft of bright sunlight against a grey-blue stormy sky.

'So do I. Elmley is a far more relaxing place without Flavia.' He paused, glanced at her. 'But you,' he said, 'you seem to have gone all quiet, is something wrong?'

'No.' She gave him a quick smile. 'Except that India will be unhappy.'

'That'll be a new sensation for her. I thought you were cross with me. We seemed to get on so well, and then . . . ' he turned to her. 'Have I done or said something to offend you?'

'No,' she said too quickly.

'There is something, won't you tell me?' His voice was warm and persuasive.

She said defiantly, 'Only that Mrs Bates and Anthea got the wrong end of the stick about us. It's so annoying when I've got Henry.'

'Is that all, Grace? You shouldn't take any notice of gossip.' He laughed, put his foot down and roared on up the motorway.

6

'So tell me everything,' India said with controlled impatience. She sat on the edge of her chair in her mews house, her dark eyes boring into Grace's face as if she were interrogating her.

Grace curled up on the sofa and smiled to hide her unease. She took a nervous gulp of wine. She felt intimidated by India, just as she had as a child, inwardly bracing herself against her crushing remarks.

'Well, go on, Grace, tell me however bad it is. I'd rather know the worst. Has she pulled down all those Adam columns or painted them like candy sticks? Tell me,' she urged bossily.

'She's done nothing like that,' Grace said quickly to ward off India's attack. She'd agonized for hours over how much to tell India about her weekend. India had rung her on the Sunday night and, realizing that Grace couldn't talk in front of her parents, had demanded that she come round here on the Monday after work, stay the night, and tell her everything.

There was nothing much to say about

93

Anthea, except that she loved her father, and had not destroyed Elmley Park. It was taking Jonathan with her that worried her. Would India be angry that she'd told him her secret fears? Could she get away without mentioning that he was there at all?

'Well, what has she done then? Do get on and tell me,' India ordered, drumming her fingers on the arm of her chair.

'She's just put two box trees cut — or should I say topiaried — into jockey caps on the front steps in huge, rather pretty actually, stone urn things.'

'How naff! I don't believe it, jockey caps!' India wrinkled her nose in horror. 'God, I'll go down there and put weedkiller on them at once,' she said in the tone of voice that suggested she'd like to put weedkiller on Anthea. 'What else has the woman done?'

'Nothing . . . but the bedroom,' Grace admitted nervously, as if she herself were responsible for the pink flounces.

'The bedroom, whatever's she done to that?'

'Well, I didn't actually see it, but Mrs Bates told me it was all,' — she swallowed — 'pink flounces.'

'Like a brothel, no doubt, pink nylon or what?' India's voice was like a whiplash.

'I told you I didn't see it, India. I couldn't

really go into their bedroom, could I?' she reasoned timidly, bracing herself for a further attack.

'What else?'

Grace tried to think of something else. She tried not to remember that she had liked Anthea, been pleased that she had made Uncle William happy. She felt so confused, feeling sorry for India, but also feeling that her father did deserve a bit of love at this time of his life.

'She had a dog, a bit like a rat, called Baa . . . no, Moo. It had a basket with a Liberty lawn cushion — one of their prettiest lawns,' she added quickly in case India was going to sneer at it. She couldn't help smiling, it sounded so ridiculous.

'Good God! Where were Hades and Petra? Why didn't they eat this rat?' India was beside herself now.

'They didn't take any notice of it,' Grace said. Then she added quickly as if each word would cause an explosion. 'She doesn't want to change Elmley, really she doesn't, India. She loves your father, and he was so happy with her.'

'Rubbish! Surely, Grace, you're not so naïve as to fall for that old story. She's no one, married to a once-successful trainer who hasn't turned out any good horses recently and is going through a difficult time. She was quite content to see my father elsewhere while Peter was doing well, but the minute things began to go wrong, she saw her chance and moved in.' She lifted her hands dismissively. 'It's not difficult, Grace, to seduce a man if you put your mind to it.' Her tone suggested she was instructing someone with very little intelligence. 'Especially an old man. The only comfort is he didn't go for one of those money-grubbing bimbos. Mummy's to blame too, of course, always going off with some 'friend', though they're getting thin on the ground now that she's getting older,' she said waspishly. 'But if you do leave your husband lying about, especially a titled, rich one, you can only blame yourself if some go-getter grabs him.'

'I don't think it was quite like that,' Grace said bravely, remembering the glow in her uncle's eyes. She wondered if she should tell India that Anthea wanted Caspar to take over Elmley, so they could move out to a more cosy house together, but she decided against it, imagining more histrionics from India who might accuse Anthea of plotting to take some of the priceless furniture and pictures with her; or selling them to buy this cosy house. She looked round the perfect, expensively decorated room, and wished she could go home now, not stay for further hours of interrogation.

'So who else was there?' India shot at her.

Grace swallowed. She didn't want to mention Jonathan. She wanted to forget him altogether, but her dreams had let her down. While she slept he was there with her in her mind, laughing, kissing her, but always spinning away when she reached out to him. He had driven her home and stopped for a while, charming her parents with his easy manner. Then his eyes had caught sight of the piano in the drawing room and he had asked if he could play it, he so rarely had the chance these days.

'Of course,' her father, who played wonderfully himself, said.

Jonathan had sat down and for a moment the whole house had vibrated with Chopin. She had felt as if the music was seeping into her body and her mind, taking control of it. When he came to the end, the silence in the house was almost more potent. He laughed, sprang up from the stool and, cheerfully dismissing their praise, said his goodbyes. He'd blown her a kiss and had gone, leaving her feeling bereft.

'So who else was there? Really, Grace, what's got into you? You look quite daft.

Don't tell me she's sacked all the staff?'

'No. I saw Mrs Bates and Frobisher; they hope to see you soon. Mrs Bates has been keeping up with you through the gossip columns. I saw Connie, and I assume the dailies are still there, but they don't usually come in at the weekend unless there's a house party, do they?' She rattled on, vainly trying to chase Jonathan from her mind as if by doing so India would not find out about him being there.

'So there was just you, Daddy, that woman and the rat-dog?' India said, staring at her with her X-ray eyes.

Grace felt she'd faint. She'd always been hopeless when faced with India. She despised herself for being so weak, but if she didn't tell her about Jonathan, she was bound to find out from someone else and make the whole thing out to be far worse than it was.

'Oh . . . ' Grace forced herself to sound offhand, 'that friend . . . you know . . . ' She drained her wine glass. 'Could I have some more wine please, India? It's so good.'

India, holding the bottle over the carpet so that it wouldn't drip on the table, poured Grace, then herself, some more wine. 'What friend? Do you mean Clive Ashworth? He's always there, I believe, now that his wife is dead.'

'No, Jonathan.' Grace found it an almost sensual pleasure to say his name. She was being such a fool, she told herself firmly. She had Henry, she mustn't do anything, think anything, to jeopardize that. Jonathan wouldn't care for her. He might play with her, just for a moment while he was between girlfriends, but he wouldn't love her or want to care for her for ever, like Henry did.

'Jonathan?' India raised her finely arched eyebrows, drilling her with her eyes. 'Which Jonathan?'

'Sheridan, you know, Caspar's friend.' She hoped she sounded non-committal.

'Whatever was *he* doing there?' India demanded fiercely. 'Caspar wasn't back for the weekend, was he?'

'No. I ... well, I was in the City. I thought I'd see some of those lovely churches, I'm not often there and — '

'Stop rabbiting on, Grace. Whatever are churches to do with Jonathan?'

'Nothing, except I met him in the City when I was looking at them and he suggested that he drive me down to Elmley.'

India's eyes glittered dangerously; her mouth went sour; her breath came fast. 'Drive *you* down,' she said in a voice that implied that he must have been mad to drive Grace anywhere. 'Did you make him drive you? Tell him everything.'

'No,' Grace lied. 'He asked me what I was doing in the City and I just told him I was going to Elmley to see Uncle William and he said he loved the place too. He hadn't been there for some time as Caspar was away and he suggested that he drive me there.' She went on spilling out words as if they would stall India's derision. 'I didn't see any harm in him coming with me, he being Caspar's friend and all. It looked more plausible too, dropping in in a car, instead of a train.' She looked away from India, wondering why she looked almost . . . jealous. But why should she be jealous? She who had every man at her feet, yapping like dogs on the end of leads held firmly by her. Besides, the gossip columnists had decided she was going to marry Freddie Fitz-Hunter, who was certainly very good looking and about to come into a dukedom. With him in her grasp why would she care about Jonathan?

'I didn't know he wanted to go down so much. He could have asked me to invite him,' India said coldly.

'Your father asked him back again to shoot.'

'When?'

'They didn't fix a date. He just said, you

know how people do . . . come again to shoot.'

'I see.' India gave her a hard look as if she longed to say more but was damned if she was going to demean herself.

Grace bleated, 'You ought to go down there, India, see for yourself. It's really not so bad.'

'Not yet. God knows what other horrors she'll come up with,' India said coldly. She got up and left the room to go to the kitchen. 'Ready for supper? I got Mrs Glen to prepare something. Smoked chicken salad and an apple pie, I think. That OK?'

'Lovely,' Grace said and followed her into the denim-blue-painted kitchen.

'We'll eat in here. I've all my papers for my Christmas Fair arranged on the dining-room table. Remind me to give you an invitation,' India said, lighting a candle on the already laid kitchen table.

'Thanks. What's it for this time?' Grace asked, relieved to be on safer ground.

'Children with cancer.' India went on to grumble about the inefficiency of the stall-holders. Mostly they were people like themselves who painted waste-paper baskets, or children's names on various objects, or sold hearty accessories like green wellington bags for country lovers and their dogs. This

101

subject stirred up India's bad temper again and Grace tried to steer her on to another tack, but in her anxiety her mind went blank.

She said without thinking, 'How is your mother?'

India put the salad on the table, pieces of smoked chicken heavily garnished with coloured lettuce leaves, baby tomatoes and olives. 'Not too well, if you really want to know.' Then, seeing Grace's expression, added, 'Oh, she's not ill like . . . ' She gestured with her hands as if to pick the words from the air. ' . . . cancer or flu or something. It's just she's sort of defeated. It's all very well having lots of lovers when you're young and pretty, but life being how it is, women who've had too many lovers and are losing their looks are discarded, while men in the same situation are still in demand.'

'I'm sorry.' Grace didn't know what else to say.

'Don't be,' India said callously. 'She should have stayed with Daddy. He wouldn't have discarded her if she hadn't behaved as she did.'

'Mrs Bates said Uncle William was left alone, except for the dogs, night after night,' Grace felt guilty that she was telling tales, but she did feel more sympathy for her uncle. 'She said it wasn't right.'

'Trust old Batey to moralize, she's always adored Daddy.'

'Oh, India,' Grace had to laugh at this remark, imagining shiny-faced Mrs Bates's chances with Uncle William.

'You know how some misguided women do. Men must be put first in everything, be waited on hand and foot, a woman's life being solely to serve the male.' She laughed. 'Thank God we're not brought up like that any more.'

The doorbell rang stridently, making Grace jump.

'Oh, God,' India said impatiently, 'just as we're about to eat. Who on earth can that be?'

'Shall I go?' Grace was nearest the door.

'If it's religious maniacs tell them I'm an atheist, or if it's someone selling something, I've got it already,' India said curtly.

Grace opened the front door. Freddie Fitz-Hunter stood, or rather lolled there against the side of the door. His face was chalk-white, his eyes frightened like a small boy's. He looked at her in bewilderment. He'd only met her once or twice. Grace suspected that he didn't remember her name, or even know who she was.

'India?' He looked past her into the tiny hall.

'Who is it?' India called.

Relief passed over his face. He came into the house, tossing Grace a rueful smile. 'Oh, India,' he said thankfully, 'it's me. I've been called to hover round the death bed. Uncle Arthur might not last the night. I wondered if you'd come with me.'

'But, Freddie, I can't. It's miles away. He's in Scotland, isn't he?' India came forward and stood beside him in the hall.

'I'm no good at death, I hoped you'd come,' he said pitifully.

'But, Freddie, it's not a party, and your sisters will be there, won't they?'

'Yes, they're ready to leave now. I just thought you'd come, spot of moral support, you know.' His voice was now resigned as if he had expected her refusal. He let out a laugh that smote Grace's heart.

'I might be a duke in the morning. Hell, isn't it?' His mouth was smiling but his eyes were fearful.

'You'll be a very good one, Freddie,' India said briskly. 'Look, have a drink before you go, you're not driving all that way, are you?'

'No, we're taking the night train. I've got to go, the girls are outside. I just thought you'd come with me.' He gave her a sad, rather brave smile.

He looked like an old man with a boy's face, Grace thought, feeling the fear and the insecurity seeping from him. She wanted to tell India to go with him, she'd be fine here, but before she could there was a call from outside.

'Freddie, do hurry up, we'll miss the train.'

'Coming, Harriet.'

Freddie threw one last beseeching look at India, who gave him a hug, kissed him on the cheek and said firmly, 'Courage, Freddie. I'll ring you tomorrow.' She bustled him out of the house and Grace heard her talking with Harriet.

'Poor Freddie, he's such a baby,' India said when she returned. 'Hell for him being the much-wanted boy after three sisters. They all bossed and spoilt him, then his father died prematurely a few months ago. He always thought he wouldn't inherit until he was at least fifty.'

'You could have gone with him, I'd have been all right here,' Grace said, thinking from what she'd read in the papers that India was just about engaged to him, and should indeed be with him at this time.

'It's nothing to do with me, Grace. Why

should I be mixed up with someone else's family drama? Mine's bad enough. He's got his mother, three sisters and hundreds of other relations all milling round. He doesn't need me as well,' she said crossly, savagely cutting up the loaf of French bread.

'I thought, well, the papers keep pairing you off,' Grace said with an attempt at a laugh.

'The papers know nothing, as always,' India said dismissively. 'I'm very fond of Freddie, but I don't want to marry him. I've never met anyone I even remotely want to marry . . . ' Then her voice tailed off, her eyes taking on a glazed, wistful look.

Grace, watching her, guessed that she was thinking of one person that she would marry if she could. Seeing her expression she wondered who it was, and if perhaps he was married already, and out of her reach.

7

'I thought we'd go skiing at Livignio this year? I believe it's a very good resort, and not too ruinous,' Henry Buchan said to Grace as they drove back to London one Sunday evening after an afternoon's sailing.

'Mmm, I've heard it's a nice place,' Grace said non-committally, staring out of the window at the string of car lights reflected in the dark road, glistening with rain. She felt cold, cold from sailing on this sharp November day and cold inside because she knew she no longer loved Henry.

It had come on her slowly after that weekend a month ago when she'd gone down to Elmley with Jonathan. It wasn't, she told herself firmly, that she had transferred her love from Henry to Jonathan, but that she realized that she felt far more alive just being with Jonathan. That she felt more drawn to him, both physically and mentally, than she ever had to anyone else. She felt she had betrayed Henry, yet she also felt these intense feelings were beyond her control.

She wondered what to do. To struggle on with Henry as they always had, in their safe, predictable way, until at last they married and probably had a child or two. Or to hurt him, finish their relationship for no other reason than the immature hankering after an out-of-reach man, and take what life gave her.

Jonathan hadn't even rung her since that weekend so it wasn't as if he had any interest in her. Even during the weekend he'd done no more than kiss her cheek in a brotherly way. It was just that, since seeing him, her body had begun to feel somehow dead with Henry, and her mind stupefied as she walked ever behind him in life, her feet as it were in his footsteps. If only he had done something that she could throw at him, eyed up other women, drunk too much, spent too much, something she could point at and say, 'Our relationship just won't work, your faults may not be serious now, but they will become so and will ruin everything between us.' But there was nothing to complain of. He was good and kind and would plod contentedly through life, happy to have her and a family by him until the end. Such men were gold dust, she knew, but she felt she couldn't go on with it, that she'd shrivel up and die before her time. Yet how could she tell him this without hurting him irrevocably?

'You seem very silent, anything wrong?'

he said, giving her a quick glance. His face was yellow from the streetlights. It was a nice face, a face she had loved, kissed in the passion of lovemaking, but now it irritated her, and she was cross with herself for feeling so, when he had done nothing to provoke it.

'I just feel . . . ' She stopped. What could she say? Trapped? Trapped by what? Him, the predictability of life with him? She wanted to escape, but where to? Not some other country to explore unseen terrain and cultures. She wanted to throw away her safe life with Henry just for a gamble. A gamble that Jonathan might throw her the occasional glance. It was utter madness and she knew it.

'Did you catch cold? It was pretty nippy today,' he said, quite oblivious to the possibility of any deeper reason.

'A bit, but . . . Henry, don't you ever feel our life is too predictable? That we should do something else before we settle down?' she said frantically, wishing he would somehow guess what she was trying to say and instantly understand. Perhaps if they had a rest from each other, she would realize what a fool she was being and everything would be as it was before.

'Like what?' He gave her an affectionate

smile. 'You mean go and find ourselves in India or something?'

'N . . . no. I just feel perhaps we're being unfair on each other. Seeing each other all the time, never doing anything with anyone else.' Her words tailed off; she just couldn't bring herself to say: I've had enough. I'm bored of you. I just want to be alone for a while, to wonder why another man whom I hardly know and who does not care for me has filled my mind and my senses more completely than you ever have. I'll never have him, but since being with him, I feel my life with you would only be half lived.

'I do do things with other people. That regatta with Michael and David. Then I have the golf lot and we play tennis with Jenny and Stephen.'

'I know but . . .'

'And you have your girlfriends and those smart cousins of yours. You had that weekend with them last month.' He frowned, studying the road ahead. 'There's nothing wrong . . . about us, is there?' he said suddenly, his voice slightly hurt.

'Oh, no,' she said too quickly, so afraid of wounding him. Then she was angry with herself, knowing that these things could never be done without pain. She felt ashamed of herself for her cowardice and resolved to forget Jonathan, get on with Henry and be thankful she had him.

'What then?' he said. 'What are you getting at?'

'I just felt that neither of us has ever had another boy-or girlfriend.'

'But I don't want anyone else!' he cried out. 'We were lucky, we found each other at once. Most people experiment with other people because they don't find the right person the first time. We were lucky, or don't you think we were? Grace, have you met someone else?'

They had arrived outside her house now. He stopped the car and turned off the engine.

'Answer me,' he said in a very quiet, controlled voice.

She looked out at the familiar street. She'd lived here all her life and knew every stone of it. She wished one of the houses would answer for her.

'There is someone, isn't there?' he said bitterly. 'Was he with your smart relations at Elmley? Ever since you went there that weekend you've been different. At first I thought it was because you were unhappy about your aunt and uncle's marriage break-up, but there's more to it, isn't there? Who else was there?'

111

'He doesn't care for me.' She heard herself saying, then knew with a sickening, sinking feeling that she had started wrong and had admitted that there was someone else.

'But you care for him?' Henry's voice was anguished. 'I know it's one of those rich, smart young hoorays, isn't it? All braying about the place, guns at the ready.'

'No . . . no, you don't understand.' She felt his pain and turned to him in despair, feeling the goodness of their relationship shattering like glass in front of her, never to be repaired. She put her hand on his arm. 'It's not like that,' she said anxiously. 'I don't love anyone else.'

'But you don't love me. *I'm* not good enough for you, I suppose.' He shook off her hand as if it revolted him.

'Henry, it's nothing like that. You're too good for *me*. Why must you always think my uncle's possessions and his way of life are so important to me? They're not, I don't want to live like that.' She willed him to understand, knowing that he had always had a chip on his shoulder about Elmley and that part of her life, and was now making out it was the enemy that had destroyed them.

'No? Well, you don't want to live in a miserable little flat in Kew with me either, do you? Which is all I can offer at the moment.'

'It's not that . . . I don't care where I live, you must believe that. I do love Elmley, I can't help it, it's so beautiful. But it's not my world and I know from seeing what's happened to my aunt and uncle that it doesn't bring happiness. I just feel . . . '

'That I am not good enough for you.'

'No, you mustn't think that. Oh, Henry, why can't you try and understand? I'm afraid, afraid and confused at my feelings. I want to talk to you about them,' she said desperately, thinking that if she told him about Jonathan, how her feelings for him were unrequited and quite irrational, no worse surely than a crush on an actor or a pop singer, he would understand. Might even laugh her out of them, make her see that life with him was right after all.

'Talk to a counsellor, then,' he said shortly. 'I can't cope with it. I can't change who I am, or ever earn enough to keep you how you expect to be kept. You should never have gone back to Elmley, Grace. The place and the people have made you dissatisfied with me, and the sort of life I can give you.'

'No, Henry, it's not at all like that,' she tried again, the tears running down her face.

'I think it is.' He sighed heavily. 'I'd like you to get out of the car now. I suppose the only good thing is we found out before it was too late.'

'I want you to understand,' she sniffed, feeling her heart torn by his misery.

'I do,' he said, 'and there's nothing I can do about it. I hope you'll be happy with that sort of person. Wasting their lives at other people's expense. I never thought you'd turn out like that, Grace.'

'I haven't. Let me just tell you about it, I'm confused too. We should, after all this time together, be able to talk honestly to each other.'

'Just go,' he said and turned away so he would not see her leaving.

8

The idea of not spending Christmas at Elmley filled India with a deep misery. She had never spent it anywhere else and every year the old ritual of decking the place in garlands of evergreens, of decorating the huge tree that stood in the hall and another slightly smaller one in the drawing room, enchanted her. It filled her with a sense of security, of excited joy of memories called up from childhood. The house was always full and cheerful with people and although she and Caspar often grumbled that the Christmas arrangements never changed, they would in fact have hated it if they had. But this year she didn't know what would happen.

Her mother, much subdued since her banishment from Elmley, but still holding on to a vestige of her fighting spirit, announced that she would be opening her house for everyone who was alone on Christmas Day. Knowing this meant other sad and discarded friends and relatives, India was not too keen to be included.

She hid her pain under her pride, trying hard to ignore the festive shops and the sparkling lights. She thought she might go skiing, but then she felt guilty about leaving her mother alone to organize her party, even though Caspar would be home on leave. Then her father, whom she hadn't heard from for some time — she certainly wasn't going to call him in case she got hold of 'the trainer's wife', as she thought of her — rang her one morning.

'My dear, we shall be away with Anthea's family for Christmas' — he coughed awkwardly, as if rather ashamed of himself — 'but why don't you and Caspar come here for New Year? Make up a party. You know — Grace, the young man she brought one weekend, Freddie, that girl of Caspar's, or whoever he's with at the moment.' He laughed jovially. 'We could have quite a party, like the old days, invite over some of the locals. What do you say?'

India was about to refuse. The last thing she wanted to do was to go down to Elmley at Christmastime with all the changes that the trainer's wife would have made by now. They'd be hard enough to stomach any time, but at Christmas it would be torture. She dreaded to think what her decorations would be like. A whole hedge topiaried like Father Christmas complete with sledge and reindeers, no less.

116

Then she thought of Jonathan. Ever since Grace had told her that he'd gone down to Elmley with her she'd been trying to think of a way to see him again. It was not in her nature to ring him directly and make some excuse to see him. Men always rang her. She had never grovelled after anyone in her life, and she certainly wasn't going to start now with the one man she really found attractive. But if there was a party to ask him to and he came down to Elmley for the New Year holiday there would be plenty of opportunity to ensnare him.

'Yes, Daddy, that would be fun. How many shall I ask?' She didn't want to say, 'How many can Anthea cope with?' She also wondered suddenly how Anthea would cope. Her mother was wonderful at parties, but what would Anthea's be like? Perhaps she'd better organize it all herself.

'I . . . I don't know, I'd ask . . . Umph, well, what do you think, darling? Ten in the house apart from us?'

India knew he didn't have a clue about entertaining. It wasn't something he'd ever had to think about, her mother had always sorted everything out. She wondered if Anthea had put him up to this invitation as a sort of seasonal olive branch, but then she dismissed the thought. If only she could get Jonathan down, it would be worth it, no matter whose idea it was.

It took her a bit of time to get Jonathan's telephone number. He was not listed in the telephone book. She rang Caspar, in Northern Ireland, who was vague about it, saying he thought he'd moved. She was forced to ask Grace, in a sort of roundabout way when she asked her to join the house party, she didn't know it either.

'I know where he works.' Grace's voice had suddenly perked up. India thought she'd sounded rather down when she'd first invited her, had not seemed particularly keen to come to Elmley at all. Not that India minded, but she wanted to be sure that the other girls in the party were 'safe' and unlikely to make a play for Jonathan. Grace would be perfect, but if she couldn't or wouldn't come she'd have to find someone else. 'Meadows and Laing. You might get him there.'

'Thanks, I'll try. So you don't think you can come?'

'Well . . . ' Grace paused then said in a rush, 'I'd love to come, India. I was asked to another party, but I can get out of it. It sounds fun, thank you.'

'I'm glad I've cheered you up. You don't

118

sound your usual self at all,' India said briskly.

Grace gave an apologetic laugh. 'Oh, I'm just feeling a little down. I've broken up with Henry and . . . '

'I'm sorry, did he go off with someone else?' India assumed that he must have. Poor Grace, she was much prettier than she used to be but she was hardly, well, sexy. No doubt he'd got bored and moved on.

'No, it was me who broke it off.'

'*You* went off with someone else?' India sounded incredulous.

'No, not really . . . I just felt a bit stifled,' Grace said lamely.

'I see, well, I'll see you at New Year. Come down on the Friday for lunch if you can get off work. Most people I know are not working that Friday . . . or tea if you'd rather, let me know,' India said, bored of Grace's love problems and impatient now that she had Jonathan's number to ring him.

When she heard his voice India felt weak inside, a feeling she was quite unused to.

'Caspar will be back and I thought I'd get together a party of his friends,' she began, her voice sounding rather offhand in her vain attempt to sound nonchalant.

'New Year . . . Well, I was going skiing

but things' — he gave an easy laugh — 'have changed. Yes, I would like to come, thank you.'

'Come on the twenty-ninth, stay over the weekend. Caspar will be pleased to see you. There'll be some shooting, of course.'

'Thank you, India,' he said again, 'I'd like that.'

She put the phone down and sat still in her chair. Just the timbre in his voice had made her feel exhilarated, as if every muscle in her body was tingling and alive. Of all the men she had known, he was the one she most wanted. She was so bored with all the men who fawned over her. She wondered wryly if the romantics were right when they said there was one man for every woman? She laughed at herself; that was surely nonsense. It was Jonathan's elusiveness that interested her. She would do her very best, in the most subtle way, of course, to capture him that weekend.

She looked through her list of guests. Freddie, sadly, couldn't come. There was Sophie, Caspar's girlfriend, who was quite besotted with him and wouldn't bother with Jonathan. Melissa and Claudia were rather plain and preferred a day's shooting with the boys than seducing them. Elizabeth was newly married and Pippa so in love with Alexander, who was also invited, she would not notice any other man, and Grace. She had nothing to fear from Grace. She smiled to herself. The party was perfect: the beautiful women were already paired up; the plain, jolly ones would know they didn't stand much of a chance in the romantic stakes with such an attractive man as Jonathan, and would be content with the company of the other men she'd invited, the 'old faithfuls' who fitted in perfectly, being great friends with them already; and Grace was just Grace. She didn't count the local girls who were coming, they wouldn't be in the house long enough to do any damage.

She smiled, hugging herself in her chair; the scene was set and Jonathan would surely fall straight into her lap.

She went down to Elmley on the Wednesday. As she neared the gates she felt sick, just as she had when she used to go back to boarding school. She took a deep breath. Caspar being already here would make it easier, but she dreaded seeing the changes, dreaded seeing Anthea's attempt at Christmas decorations, dreaded seeing Anthea.

But when she went inside the house, it was almost exactly the same as it had always been. The tree was in the hall, the stairs and the walls decorated with evergreen garlands but this time tied with dark red ribbon with oranges, fir cones and holly berries nestling in the dark shiny leaves; and hanging from the centre of the hall was a large ball of bay leaves studded with whole lemons, their scent mingling with the smell of burning apple wood in the open fire. There was no sign of topiaried Father Christmases, or jockey caps for that matter.

'Hi, Sis.' Caspar came forward and kissed her. He was dressed in his riding clothes. 'The old man's in his study. Anthea's in the drawing room. Do you want to come riding with me?'

'No.' India shot him a look of contempt: surely he too wasn't seduced by that woman?

He interrupted the look and smiled and said in a low voice, 'She's fine, she won't bite. The old man's so happy, much happier than he was with Mother, you can't begrudge him that.'

'I don't . . . It's just . . . ' She sighed, letting the atmosphere of Elmley seep into her again. It felt like home, and yet it didn't because she knew things were not as they used to be, and she felt as if Anthea was like an alien waiting there to spoil everything for her. But Caspar, being a man, wouldn't understand that. As long as the house was still standing with all its beauty and treasures intact, and there was a good meal on the table and a good wine cellar, why complicate things by emotions?

Frobisher appeared and when they had greeted each other, India said, 'The decorations are lovely, did you do them yourself?' He had helped her mother every year so it was hardly surprising that he had done them himself this year.

'No, Mrs Millard helped me. She asked me how it used to be and added a few of her own touches.' He gestured to the ribbons and fruit and the ball of bay leaves and lemons. 'I think it's very festive, don't you?'

It took a moment for India to realize that Mrs Millard was the trainer's wife. She had obviously captured Frobisher's heart too. She said coldly, 'Yes. I'm in my own bedroom, I suppose?'

'Yes, of course. I'll see your cases get taken up there.'

'Thank you. I'll go and see my father now.' She swept along to his study feeling sick and furious. The trainer's wife had obviously won over everyone and had secured her place here. However much her mother hoped for a reconciliation she would never get one now.

'My dear India.' Her father got up from his huge desk and embraced her. 'Let me look at you, it's so long since I last saw

123

you.' He stood back and looked her over. 'You look pale, it's that London air. A few days down here will soon put you right. How are you?' He gestured to a chair and she sat down looking round the book-lined room. When they were children they had not been allowed in here to disturb him, but now it was familiar: sporting prints hanging between the bookcases, the furniture solid and gleaming with the rich glow of much polishing.

'I'm fine, and you, Daddy?' She had to admit he looked years younger, even his grey hair seemed more vigorous.

He blushed like an awkward youth. 'My dear, I'm very happy. I know it's difficult . . . ' He coughed, looked away, then said in a brusque tone as if to play down any sentimentality, 'You're old enough to know, India, that your mother and I were never really . . . ' He paused. ' . . . compatible. But I was lucky enough, privileged enough, to meet Anthea.' As he said her name his eyes shone with pleasure. India felt a pang of jealousy.

'I know, Daddy,' India said, anxious not to prolong this awkward conversation. 'I know Mummy behaved very badly, I don't blame you, it's just,' — she shrugged — 'difficult to cope with the changes.'

124

'But there aren't any, my dear. The same staff are here to look after us, the house is the same, and Anthea, well, you'll like her,' he said in his simple way, looking quite surprised that she found the changes difficult to cope with.

India guessed this. She knew he didn't want to face any messy emotional upheavals. She, like Caspar, must accept things as they were now. Whatever she might feel about Anthea she had to hide it. She knew her father would not stand for any disrespect or dislike towards her, nor would he be prepared to listen to any long outpourings of hers over hating Elmley without her mother, hating the feeling that someone else had taken it from her. After all, if her mother had behaved herself things would still be as they were.

'Let's go and see her,' her father said, looking quite animated. India followed him slowly.

'Here is India, darling, safe and sound,' he announced, striding into the drawing room. A small dog sprang from the chair and yapped menacingly. India shuddered; Grace was right, it was just like a rat. Hades and Petra arrogantly ignored it.

Anthea was sitting by the fire reading the *Field*. She looked up, smiled and held out her hand. 'How nice to see you, India,' she

125

said, then called for the dog, who jumped on her knee, shivering violently and, giving India a contemptuous sniff, curled up and went to sleep.

India took her proffered hand and smiled mechanically, sensing that her father was watching her as if she was a child again expected to perform properly in public. Anthea could put on an act of being nice and friendly as much as she wished. She wouldn't be fooled by it. She seemed to have got her father just where she wanted him but India was determined to be vigilant, to fight stealthily to keep Elmley safe.

9

Breaking up with Henry had left Grace feeling wretched. She knew she had hurt him deeply and this added to her pain. She also thought that she was a fool, giving up a kind man just because another, whom she barely knew, made her feel intoxicated with life, with desire, with sheer joy at being near him.

Her parents had been out when she'd returned that evening. But late in the night when she crept downstairs to make herself some hot chocolate — more because she couldn't bear another moment of lying in misery isolated in the dark, than because she wanted it — she saw the studio lights were on. Her father often worked at night, finding the stillness and strangely the darkness an incentive to his creativity.

He was standing by a huge canvas of the Natural History Museum. Through the leaves of a tree she could catch glimpses of the arched windows, the towers, the honey-coloured stone. People of various races mingled on the pavement, all in national costumes, bright against the pearly light of late autumn. If she looked closely there were animals, tigers, elephants, bears hiding in the garden in front. She loved the magic of his work, the way you had to look deep into it to see all the details he hid there. Yet it did not sell well. Once she'd heard an art critic remark that it was neither one thing nor the other. He could almost be a children's book illustrator, yet again they would not translate well on to a mere page.

He turned round and smiled. 'Hello, darling, can't you sleep?'

'No. Do you want some chocolate or coffee?'

'No, thanks. I'm nearly through, what do you think?' He stood back, wiping his brush on a rag.

'It's wonderful.' She meant it, but somehow the misery in her came through her voice and he looked anxiously at her.

'Is something wrong, darling?' She felt like a child again and threw herself into his arms and wept.

At last through her sobs she told him everything, about her and Henry, even about her uncle and aunt's separation. He stayed quiet, just stroking her hair, until she had finished. They were sitting, her on his knee, in the huge, battered chair that stood in the corner of his studio. Outside the blackness of the night made her feel closer to him, and relieved that she had confided in him.

'Poor Henry,' he said at last. 'But even if he had listened to you and realized that you have these feelings for a man you say you hardly know, it would still hurt him. Being rejected is one of the worst pains to bear.'

'So what can I do?' she sniffed. 'Shall I write to him and try and explain?'

'I'd let it go for a while.'

'Do you think I'm being a fool over Jonathan?' she asked him, searching his face for his answer.

He smiled and kissed her. 'Who is to know, my darling? None of us knows what life is going to throw at us, or how we, or our relationships will stand up to it. Henry, for reasons we don't know, has always found it difficult to accept your rich relations.' He laughed, and she had to smile, for she knew that he had always found them rather a joke.

'They're your relations too,' she said.

'Only by marriage.' He smiled wickedly, then looked serious. 'But poor Flavia, she managed to hook herself a baronet, then let him go. She'll never forgive herself. No wonder she never told us, her pride must be in tatters.'

'I suppose it is. Daddy, am I mad to think

I prefer Jonathan, who must have dozens of girlfriends, and anyway hasn't even contacted me since that weekend?'

Her father gently eased her off his knees to sit squashed beside him in the chair, complaining that his legs were no longer young enough to support her for long. He leant back and regarded her gravely.

'That one time he came here and played the piano I saw how you looked at him. It can't just have been the music' — he grinned — 'after all you've been plagued with my playing all your life, but I said later to your mother, it was strange how you looked more in love with him than ever you had with Henry.'

'Did you? Did it show?' she asked, mortified in case Jonathan had seen.

'Not to anyone who doesn't know you. Wait and see, you're very young yet. It's silly to settle down with the first man you meet. I like Henry, you couldn't ask for a nicer man, but if you can find someone who lights up the world for you, as your mother has done for me, then go for it.' He smiled tenderly as he mentioned her mother. 'You know we've been through some pretty tough times. No money, evicted once because I couldn't pay the rent, a very painful miscarriage.'

'Miscarriage? When? I didn't know.' She was aghast.

'You were about two,' He paused. She saw the sadness in his eyes. She hugged him tightly to her, hardly able to bear it.

'Your mother nearly died,' he said tonelessly. 'I hate to think of it. It was a terrible time.'

She felt the full shock of his revelation and struggled to find some words to ease his obvious distress, but he shook off his pain and said cheerfully, 'But through it all we never stopped loving each other. I know we're lucky, and I don't mean to sound sentimental, but believe me, darling, if you can find that, nothing else in life can touch it.'

She lay her head on his shoulder and wept again. She wept because she knew how rare such a love was and suspected she would never find it.

She had yearned for Jonathan to ring her, but he had not. Despite the kindness and concern of her parents, she had felt so alone and unloved; so many of her friends were also Henry's and seeing them was difficult, as they too could not understand why she had left him. Many times she nearly rang Henry, wanting him back, just to be loved again. But she knew in the depth of her heart that that would be unfair, because if by some miracle Jonathan did call her, she would dump Henry again and go with him.

So when India asked her to Elmley for New Year, she'd instantly refused, feeling in no mood to be interrogated and bullied by her. But when she mentioned Jonathan it was as if a warm sun had pushed away the dark fog in her. She felt exhilaration course back through her, intoxicating her with life.

A week later Jonathan rang her. 'Do you want a lift to Elmley? Or will you be wanting to wander through the City churches again on your way to the train?'

'Oh, Jonathan . . . I . . . ' She could hardly breathe when she heard his voice. She forced herself to remain calm. 'I'd love a lift . . . Shall I meet you somewhere, save you coming all the way out here?'

'No, I'm not working that day, I'll collect you. India said teatime, didn't she?'

'Sometime like that. I'm not working either, my boss has been generous this Christmas.' She wasn't going to say she'd been asked to Elmley for lunch if it meant missing a lift with him.

'What time's teatime, about four?'

'I should think so. But I'm miles out of your way,' she added, feeling quite weak with excitement. A weekend with him and the whole drive down, she couldn't believe it.

He arrived in a Golf. She'd been watching for him from the window. But when she saw the car arrive with him at the wheel, she dashed over to the sofa, sat down and picked up the newspaper as if he could see her inside the house and would know how impatient she was to see him.

'Hi.' He kissed her easily on her cheek. 'All ready?'

'Yes. My parents are both out, I must shut the door from the inside and put on the alarm. If anyone breaks in, the insurance will make a fuss about paying if I forget,' she said breathlessly, wishing she was more in control like India would be. She wondered if he'd come into the hall or if she'd have to shut the door in his face.

He followed her into the narrow hall. She felt quite faint having him so close to her. 'I'll carry your case,' he said, not seeming to notice her agitation. 'Got everything?'

He waited while she put on the alarm and then together they went out.

'New car?' she said to break the tension she felt in herself.

'Yes.' He settled her in. 'I had to get rid of the Maserati, more's the pity.' He grinned. 'You know how it is. Here today, gone tomorrow. But I'll get it back, or perhaps

I'll buy a Ferrari, or a Porsche next time.'

She didn't know what he meant, or feel confident enough to ask. Had he lost his job? Or been paid less, or experienced financial difficulties?

'So India's got over her aversion to going down to Elmley,' he said. 'I thought she would. She's not one to sit back and let people take things from her, is she?'

'No, but to be fair she does so love the place, and was very hurt by her parents' break-up,' Grace said, wondering why he wasn't at India's feet like all the other men.

This feeling was strengthened soon after they arrived. India was looking wonderful. Dressed in a plover's-egg-coloured jersey and beige trousers she came out as soon as she heard them arrive. For a split second Grace thought her eyes narrowed as she saw that she was in the car with Jonathan, but maybe it was a trick of the fading light, for in a moment India was hugging her and saying; 'Grace, how good to see you.' She then offered her cheek to Jonathan and said in her imperious way, 'What's happened to the sports car? Caspar said you had a Maserati.'

Jonathan at once looked defensive. 'Oh, I had to get rid of it. I'm between cars at the moment,' he said airily, with an elegant gesture of his hand. But even in the dim light, Grace could see he was uncomfortable. She had a sudden feeling of sympathy for him, having so often herself suffered from India's scorn.

Anthea — she insisted that everyone called her by her first name — was pleased to see them. As she chatted about this and that, Grace couldn't help noticing her eyes kept sliding off towards India, as if she was convinced she was being watched, afraid of being judged and found wanting.

Caspar, still arrogant and obviously delighted with himself, was none the less pleased to see her. 'You look wonderful, Grace. Jolly brave of you to come down with that old rogue Jonathan, hope he behaved himself, kept his hands on the wheel.' He winked at Jonathan. 'Brought your gun, old man? Out at first light tomorrow.'

'I have. So how's playing soldiers going?' The two men wandered out of the room together and although the room was full of people she knew, Grace immediately felt rather lost.

'Always talking about guns and things like small boys,' Sophie, Caspar's girlfriend said affectionately.

Anthea smiled and replied, but Grace, watching the others in the room, some eating tea, others just reading the paper or leafing through the glossy magazines laid out on a table by the window, saw India's eyes follow Jonathan as he left the room with Caspar. Her eyes had a sort of wistful yet determined look that Grace found disturbing.

Uncle William appeared, pink and windswept, and was greeted by everyone who sprang out of their corners to their feet, discarding their papers and magazines as if they had only been passing the time until he had come.

'My dear Grace.' He kissed her heartily. 'How nice to see you. Your parents well?'

Before she could answer he was off round the room greeting the others, his two dogs following him like faithful courtiers. The rat-dog shivered in Anthea's arms, having exhausted itself yapping at each new arrival.

Grace did not see Jonathan alone for most of the weekend. If they weren't shooting they were walking, or playing wild games of Gin Rummy or Racing Demon. The other people in the house party were friendly and fun and the hours swept past. Falling into bed exhausted each night Grace admitted that she was enjoying herself.

But sometimes in a small lull between the frenzied activities she noticed India with Jonathan. She seemed to be engaging him

136

in deep conversation, laughing a lot into his eyes, flirting with him. Grace felt the familiar pang of resignation and envy. India could have her pick of any man she chose and it was naïve to suppose that Jonathan would prefer her when there was India. But she also observed — wondering if it wasn't perhaps wishful thinking on her part — that Jonathan, though polite and friendly enough, did not seen exactly enamoured of India.

On New Year's Eve they had a long and delicious dinner. Grace sat at the opposite end of the table to Jonathan; India sat next to him. She looked wonderful that evening in a rich purple silk dress and Grace knew she could not match her. She felt sad, but she told herself firmly that she'd always known her feelings for Jonathan would never be reciprocated. He liked her, and she must be content with that. After all, friendship was probably a more durable relationship than love. She knew she must seem to enjoy the evening, for a lot of effort had been put into it, and she did her best to sparkle with the people at her end of the table.

After dinner they played games until midnight, then with popping champagne corks they toasted the New Year and each other and kissed all round. Uncle William and Anthea then went up to bed. Grace had noticed everyone but India had kissed Anthea at midnight. They all sat round feeling rather drunk and disappointed now that the object of the evening was passed.

Jonathan, who had helped pour out the champagne, was slumped in a chair a little apart from everyone else. India had been pulled into the group of other young men who were all asking her to tell her wishes and hopes for the year ahead.

Laughing, her eyes often straying over towards Jonathan's direction, though she could not see him as the others were in the way, she told them: 'I'm going to travel a lot this year.' This was greeted by whistles and 'where to?' and 'take me too'.

'Get a job.' This was greeted by loud guffaws.

Grace, also a little apart from the laughing group, suddenly glanced up and saw Jonathan looking at her. The game had now progressed: Caspar was loudly proclaiming his desire for promotion this year and Ned Porter, who was still supposed to be in love with India, was rather intoxicatedly saying he wanted an exciting love affair.

Jonathan slipped from his chair and motioned to Grace to do the same. In the general commotion of the moment no one noticed them slip away.

'It's so noisy, thank God for some peace and fresh air. All that cigar smoke,' Jonathan said, taking her arm. 'I hate New Year actually, so false and rather flat after it all.'

'I feel the same,' she said as they walked slowly across the immense hall and down a passage. 'The dinner was fun, but it's that long waiting for midnight to strike that I dislike.'

'Me too.' They'd reached the door of the room where they had hidden all those years before while playing Sardines. He opened the door. 'Remember that game? I don't think we have to sit in the fireplace this time though, do you?' He smiled at her and she felt the warmth of his breath on her cheek.

'I'd rather not in this dress,' she said.

'It's beautiful. *You're* beautiful,' he said softly, and once they were safely inside the room he took her in his arms and kissed her on her mouth, holding her close to him.

She felt her whole body respond to that kiss and yet half of her held back as if he were making a mistake. At last when she could breathe, she said: 'Surely it's India you want to be kissing, not me?'

'Whatever makes you think that?' He linked his hands round her waist. 'She'd eat me. Poor little Grace, always in her shadow, but don't you realize you're a beautiful,

139

sensual woman in your own right?' He kissed her again, this time more urgently and though she wanted to respond, wanted him to make love to her, she was afraid to here. Feelings of insecurity, apprehension of her inexperience flooded her. He must have made love to so many women; he would surely find her a disappointment. What if they were discovered like when they were playing Sardines?

She struggled in his arms and when he released her, looking a little irritated, she said urgently. 'Oh, Jonathan, not here, I couldn't bear to be found out.' She just stopped herself saying, India will be furious with me being with you instead of her.

'OK, where shall we go? There must be somewhere in this vast house where we won't be disturbed.'

'The attics.' The words slipped out before she could stop them. She blushed, wondering if he'd think her too forward, when in truth she felt shy and nervous.

'Come on then.' His voice was breathless. Keeping his arm round her, he very quietly opened the door.

India was standing outside the drawing room at the other side of the hall. Their passage was in darkness and it was probable that she couldn't see them, but they both stood transfixed, peeping out through the chink in the door watching her. She was obviously listening, wondering which way to go. She seemed about to cross the hall towards them when Ned Porter and Caspar came out of the drawing room.

'Where are you going, India, darling, surely not to bed?' Ned said to her.

Caspar said, 'You can't be tired yet, India. That's not like you at all. We're going to play Charades, we can't do that without you.' They lumbered off to the downstairs cloakroom and then some of the girls came out and asked India what she was doing.

'I'm looking for Grace,' she said.

'She's probably gone to bed, let's go and wake her,' one girl said and, laughing, they all ran up the grand staircase.

'Quick,' Jonathan said urging her on. They nipped up the back staircase in the dark.

'If we go on up we'll get to the attics, we should be safe there,' she whispered, terrified lest they meet India, yet also brave and excited at Jonathan being so close to her. She knew India was looking for Jonathan and wouldn't be able to believe that she was with him.

They reached the attics and in a daze she led him through the series of interconnecting rooms. In the past they had been servants'

141

quarters, but Uncle William had made more modern accommodation downstairs, leaving this whole floor of the house as a storage area. They dared not put on a light but made do with the pale gleam from the moon shining through the dusty windows. Dark shapes of unused furniture and pictures loomed up beside them. It was very cold and Grace could feel the dust stirred up by their feet in her throat.

When they had almost crossed the entire house she pulled him into a small room that she remembered Caspar hiding in as a child. She remembered also how India had hated it as it held various display cases of stuffed animals and birds. It was their staring eyes she couldn't bear, saying they made her feel guilty as if she had been responsible for stuffing their dead bodies and enclosing them behind glass.

'It's so dusty here . . . Goodness, look at these,' Jonathan said, going over to a vast glass dome holding the remains of some owls, their claws forever clasped round a branch.

Grace told herself he would make love to her perhaps just because it was New Year, not because he loved her. But she thought: Even if this is the only time and he never looks at me again, it will be worth it.

'Is there somewhere more comfortable than

the floor we could lie on?' He took her in his arms again and kissed her, running his hands down her back.

Desire for him merged with her shyness and apprehension. When he paused a moment in his passionate kisses, she said; 'I . . . I don't know, let's look.'

Arms round each other, they went into another room where Grace had remembered seeing some rolled carpets. After searching in the moonlight, between kisses and laughter, they found some heavy velvet curtains wrapped in a plastic cover.

'Luxury,' he said, pulling them out of their covering. 'Let's take them back to that room with the animals where there's room on the floor.'

Together they dragged the curtains into the room. Grace slipped out of his arms and went and closed the door. He pulled her back to him laughing. 'No one will find us here, we'll be safe until morning.' He kissed her hungrily, unzipping her dress and tossing it to one side.

The moonlight glinted off the glass cases and Grace was momentarily startled in her passion by the gimlet eyes of the watching weasels, rabbits, stoats and owls. They reminded her of India. She pulled Jonathan closer to her, as if India was in one of the glass cabinets and would suddenly break from it and snatch him from her.

* * *

It was the cold that woke them. Even wrapped in the old velvet curtains they could feel it seeping through to their bones. It was pitch dark. Jonathan said, 'We ought to go back to our beds before everyone's up. Caspar wants an early start to the shoot.'

'I can't find my clothes.' Grace felt stiff. She stayed close to him, savouring the feeling of his warm, firm body beside her, hearing his heart beat against her ear. She thought sleepily, sadly: This might be the last time we lie together.

'Do you think we dare put on a light, if there is one?' he said.

'I think we'll have to, but must we go now?' She kissed the hollow in his neck, winding her legs and arms round him as if she couldn't bear to be parted from him.

'In a moment we must. There'd be such a flap if we were caught. Everyone knows that Sophie and Caspar sleep together, but they always wake up in their own beds.' He laughed. 'Such is propriety, my dear.' Then he made love to her again, still laughing.

They nipped on the light for a second.

It was half past five. Quickly, shivering almost uncontrollably in the cold, they dressed, tidied away the curtains and tiptoed downstairs to their rooms, still holding each other's hands. At her door he kissed her. 'Will I see you at the shoot?'

'I suppose so,' she whispered back, hating the moment when he released her and she had to go into her room alone.

Despite her ferment of love for him, for the raging emotions of love, desire, fear of losing him and sadness that nothing would come of the affair, she slept and when she woke she saw to her horror that it was eleven o'clock. She had missed breakfast and the start of the shoot.

When she was dressed in her warmest clothes, she went downstairs and begged a plate of porridge off Mrs Bates. The house was almost silent as everyone else had gone shooting. She heard Anthea's rat-dog barking from her room and wondered if she had gone out with them.

'I'll take you with the lunch in the shooting brake,' Frobisher told her. 'They're lunching over by the far farm.'

When they arrived, the shooting party was just straggling into the farmyard. Grace looked keenly about for Jonathan. She saw India, dressed in her shooting tweeds, her gun broken over her arm, walking briskly beside her father. She did not look in the direction of the shooting brake, but Grace instinctively knew that she knew she was there and that every fibre of her was spitting out fury and hatred at her.

Frobisher laid out the lunch and Grace was greeted by the rest of the party, except for India who pointedly ignored her. Grace, wondering why she was so angry, was working up the courage to go and ask her when Jonathan and Charles Porter joined the party and for a moment there was no one else in the world for her but him.

'Sleep well?' he said, and his words sounded to her like a love song.

Lunch was a cheerful affair, everyone talking to everyone else, stamping their feet against the cold, taking huge bites from Mrs Bates's meat pasties. Grace joined in, but all the time beneath the bantering, she was aware of India's hostility.

The day had started bright but was now beginning to draw in. The sky was grey and the wind was cold. When lunch was over the guns and beaters made their way to the copse at the end of the field for the last drive. Grace walked beside Claudia who had embarked on a boisterous story about skiing off piste after being dropped by a plane. Grace didn't feel

146

like beating today and preferred to stay with the guns. Jonathan, with a quick wave, went off with Caspar and she did not like to push herself in with them.

They reached the outskirts of the copse and fanned out. Grace could hear the cry of the beaters working the copse and sending the birds up. As they came over the guns the shots rang out and she could hear the flap of the wings, the leaden thud as their bodies hit the ground. Then all was quiet and the dogs were sent in to retrieve.

It was nearly dusk now and the party began to disperse, most of them going back through the copse to the road and the drive home. Caspar and Jonathan and a couple more men had decided to go down to the lake and try for some wild ducks before going home.

Jonathan caught Grace's eye as he passed her and the warmth of his glance touched her like a fire. She wandered after the others, a little behind, basking in warm thoughts of him and of their night together.

She heard the crack of a twig behind her and turning round saw India, her gun broken over her arm, her face set hard.

'So where were you last night, Grace? You weren't in your room or Jonathan's. I checked. I know you were with him.'

'What if I was?' Grace said with as much

147

bravado as she could muster.

'Did you sleep with him?' Again India's eyes bored into her.

Grace felt herself blushing, but she stood her ground. 'What if I did? We're both free.' Her voice sounded so much weaker than her words.

'You are a slut, Grace,' India hissed, 'such a slut.' And before Grace could protest, she came up and slapped her hard on the cheek, nearly knocking her over.

'Ow, India, don't!' Grace cried, clamping her hand over her stinging face, the tears jumping into her eyes.

But India walked past her, tall and erect as if she didn't care if she had killed her, leaving Grace to struggle through the boggy ground in the encroaching darkness, her head reeling, her cheek on fire.

10

'Perhaps we should give a party,' Flavia said to India as they sat together over a scrap lunch in her house. India, feeling rather guilty that she hadn't seen her mother for a while, had popped in on her way back from the hairdressers.

Her father had suggested that Flavia make their London house, in one of the streets near Harrods, her permanent home. He disliked London and if he had to come up he could always use his club.

'What sort of party, Mummy?' India said wearily. She was exhausted with anger and jealousy over Grace's behaviour with Jonathan. No doubt she had thrown herself at him and he, like most men, who were hardly better than small boys being offered sweets when sex was on offer, had happily helped himself. But what made her really angry was the fact that he seemed to like her, and when she saw them driving off together back to London after tea, she had felt so livid and jealous she had crashed round the gun room — her father had always insisted that both his children clean their own guns — knocking

149

things over until Caspar had sworn at her and told her to leave. At that moment she would have quite happily shot them both and Caspar as well.

'You seem to be down in the dumps, darling, although your hair looks so nice. It suits you shorter,' Flavia remarked airily, patting her own now too-blonde hair. 'It's a wretched time of the year, I know. We should be in the Caribbean. I nearly went with Polly and Hamish last month, but . . . well, without a man, I thought I'd feel rather a gooseberry.'

'I don't know why we women all have to depend on a man before we can enjoy ourselves,' India said irritably. She threw her mother a contemptuous look. She wondered how to remark on her rather startling appearance. It had given her quite a shock, but she'd said nothing as Flavia had seemed rather agitated at her unexpected arrival, which was quite unlike her. Usually she almost fell into her arms, greeting her with a delight bordering on gratitude. Her hair was rather bright and brassy and she had on more make-up than India'd ever seen her wear before. Her skirt was far too short but India continued their conversation while she thought of a tactful way of remarking on Flavia's alarming new look. 'I'd have gone if I'd been you, although Polly and Hamish are quite the dullest people. I think I shall go away.'

'Where to, darling?'

'I don't know. I've had enough of England, of Anthea taking over Elmley.' She felt her anger curling in her, screwing tighter and tighter. If Anthea hadn't gone to live at Elmley, she wouldn't have had to send Grace down to look for changes and she wouldn't have met up with Jonathan again and had a whole weekend to spend with him. She spat out suddenly: 'I wish you'd never left Daddy. Surely you could have been more discreet, or spent more time with him, not left him for this woman to grab?' Then, thinking again how ridiculous her once-smart mother looked, her clothes more suited to a teenager than a middle-aged woman: 'Why is your skirt so short, Mummy?'

Flavia went pink, her eyes a little watery at the sudden shock of India's accusation. Self-consciously but with defiance she pulled her skirt down a fraction over her still shapely legs. 'That's all over now,' she said. 'I may have been foolish, but I'm afraid to say your father is very dull.'

'Then you shouldn't have married him,' India said, snatching up her plate and putting it roughly in the dishwasher.

'There is something bothering you, darling, isn't there? I mean more than our broken marriage . . . and my skirt,' Flavia said briskly. She did not like to be reminded of her foolishness, of throwing away her smart lifestyle for the sake of a few lightweight affairs.

India said nothing, but snapped on the kettle to make herself some coffee.

'That's why I think a party would be fun. Let's ask all our old friends. It'd cheer us up at this dreary time of the year. What do you say?' she said coaxingly as if India were still a small child to be cajoled into good behaviour with the promise of a treat.

India thought at once of asking Jonathan. She would not ask Grace. She would pretend that they were strapped for numbers, so they weren't asking family, or already had more than enough girls, but before she could agree, Flavia said, 'You and Grace could have a party . . . have it here and I'll ask a few of my friends, and Grace's parents. A cocktail party's the easiest and we could have a salad or something cold if anyone wanted to stay on for supper.' Her eyes shone as mentally she began thinking of guests and menus.

'Not Grace,' India burst out, 'why should she be in on it? We don't have the same friends, or even move in the same circles.'

'But of course we must have Grace. If I ask Olivia and Leo, I can hardly miss her out,' Flavia said with gusto. 'And we'll have dear Freddie — I wonder how he's getting on as a duke? — and I suppose his sisters, and the Porters, and I'll ask — '

'Mummy, do stop.' India almost stamped her foot. 'Count me out of this . . .'

'But why, dear? It'll be such fun. You used to love parties, and just because we are no longer at Elmley, I don't see why we can't entertain. If we move the furniture we can have about thirty people in this room.'

'I just don't feel like it. Anyway, I think I'm going skiing. I just must get away.' Her voice was frantic.

'Why won't you tell me what's happened?' Flavia said, looking at her shrewdly. 'Am I wrong if I think it's to do with a man? It's not Freddie, is it?'

''Course it's not Freddie! Freddie's such a baby, he doesn't need a woman, he needs a nanny.'

'Oh, darling, that's not very fair. You used to be very fond of him. *I'm* very fond of him. I was very fond of his father, and if you'd marry him . . .'

'You married for a title and look where it got you,' India said darkly. 'I do like Freddie, but I certainly don't want to marry him.'

'Who is it then?' Flavia said impatiently. She'd nursed hopes of having her daughter as a duchess, going to stay at their estate in Scotland.

'Oh, no one you'd know,' India said, trying to stamp out the image of Jonathan shepherding Grace out to his car, his arm protectively around her, her cheek still flushed from the slap she'd given her. Grace's eyes had been defiant as she'd gone with him. If it had been just a one-night stand India could have coped with it, but it looked like something more and for that she would never forgive Grace. Never forgive her for taking from her the only man she'd ever really wanted. *Grace* of all people. She'd have understood if Jonathan had gone for Sophie, or even one of the Harbord girls, but not Grace. What wiles had she used to get him?

'Tell me anyway, you know it helps to share a trouble, and I won't breathe a word,' Flavia said.

India shrugged, making out it was not important. 'Oh, you know, Mummy, that old chestnut of loving someone who doesn't love me.' She gave a brave little laugh.

'Does he know you love him?'

'No.'

'You know what British men are like in

the romantic stakes, darling. Don't know what's under their noses unless it's a dog or a horse — look at your father.' Then she remembered that William had somehow, in between horses and dogs, noticed the trainer's wife, and she coughed hurriedly. 'You know we have to make the running, discreetly of course. Now if we had a party . . . a dinner party, that's more intimate, and asked him, then he would have to ask you back, and . . . ' Flavia opened her hands as if she was revealing the solution to India's problem.

'It might not work that way . . . He might not come.'

'We'll give him two dates. If he says no, you say, well, I'm having another party on the twentieth, or whatever. We could have eight. I'd make myself scarce of course, or you could have it in your house, though it is so small. What do you say?'

India paused. It was an idea. Maybe by now Jonathan was sick of Grace. After all it was almost a month since New Year. Then she had another idea: what if she asked him to join a chalet party to ski? He had a good job, she knew, so he could probably afford to come, if he wasn't going already. But Grace, always strapped for cash, would probably not be able to afford it. Also she'd probably never been skiing, so could be safely left behind on the nursery slopes even if she did come.

The idea took root and began to grow, but Flavia, thinking her idea of a dinner party was taking shape and that India was going over a possible guest list in her mind, chirped on cheerfully, 'Now, darling, who shall you ask? This man, and Freddie, and why not Grace?'

'For the last time, Mummy, I shall *not* be asking Grace to anything. Is that quite, quite clear?'

'But she is your cousin, and — '

'So what? You thrust her on to me when we were children, giving her all my clothes before I'd worn the half of them, and Daddy gave her Moonlight, even though she hardly ever rode him and a child at the stables took him on, and now she . . . ' She bit her tongue before she blurted out, 'She's taken the only man I've ever wanted.'

'What has she done, India?' Flavia asked her, wide-eyed at her tirade.

'I just don't want her in my life and there's an end to it,' India said sharply. 'Now I think I might ring round and try and get a skiing party together. We could have everyone to dinner first, to make the plans.' She smiled brightly at her mother and went to fetch her Filofax from her bag.

Flavia glanced surreptitiously at her watch, and said, 'Well, darling, why don't you do that at home? I've a few calls to make myself, things to do, you know.' She smiled a little too brightly.

'Oh, OK,' India was surprised. She hadn't seen her mother for about three weeks and usually she hated it when she left. She never said anything, but she always looked a little sad, offered another drink or started on another piece of news to try and drag out her visit a little longer. But today, what with her new teenage look and her impatience for her to leave she was sure something was up. She opened her mouth to ask, but Flavia forestalled her firmly.

'It was lovely seeing you, darling. I'll ring you tomorrow and see how your plans for the dinner party are going. Shall we try for the middle of next week? Or the week after?' She got up from her chair and walked purposefully in the direction of the front door as if leading India out.

'I'll ring you,' India said, collecting up her things, pushing down a small stab of hurt that her mother wanted to get rid of her. She had been like this when she was a child, so often too busy for her, pushing her off to the nursery or to the garden. It was only since her father had chucked her out that she'd been so grateful for her daughter's company.

India allowed herself to be kissed and ushered out. She walked slowly down into Walton Street, deciding to go to Harvey Nichols to buy some make-up and look at their jerseys on her way home.

Just before she turned into Walton Street she nearly ran into a young man. He was impeccably dressed in a dark coat, his hair coiffeured into a thick wedge speckled with blond highlights. He smiled, apologized, a gleam of attraction for her flashing momentarily in his eyes, then he walked on.

Something made her turn and watch him. He walked down the road she had just left, stopped at her mother's house and, taking a key from his pocket, opened the front door and let himself in.

11

'Feeling better, love?' Jonathan came out of the sea and lay down on the sunbed on the sand beside Grace.

'Yes, thanks.' She smiled at him from her chair under the shade of a large tree. She'd been very sick these past couple of days, poisoned, she thought, by something she'd eaten on the plane. She was furious at starting this glorious week in Morocco with Jonathan being sick every five minutes or so. It was so unromantic, apart from making her feel wretched.

Jonathan had been kind about it, though she had done her very best to hide the worst of it from him. 'Rotten luck,' he'd sympathized. 'Shall I get a doctor?'

'No,' she'd said, preferring to use the remedies her mother had insisted she take with her. 'I'll keep out of the sun and drink lots of bottled water. I'll soon be fine.'

She smiled at him now, taking pleasure from the sight of his taut, lithe body lying gracefully beside her, his skin just beginning to tan. Often during these last few months she'd felt she was dreaming, could not believe the sheer joy she felt at being with him.

After New Year at Elmley he had driven her back to London, and suggested that they stay at his flat for the night. He couldn't fail to notice the red mark covering her whole cheek after India had slapped her; she'd winced with pain when he'd touched it, but when he'd asked her about it, she'd said she'd walked into a tree in the dusk on the way home from shooting. She did not want to talk about India. She guessed India was so angry with her because she had scored a conquest. India may not want every man in their circle to make love to her, but she certainly didn't want anyone else to have them, unless she herself had discarded them first.

She had not seen India since then, nor did she care to. She had time for no one but Jonathan. Her life had become a whirl of being with him, waiting for him, loving him. They got on so well together, but she was wary, giving him the time he seemed to crave to go racing on his own, without her ever grumbling or remarking on it.

'There's a race meeting on Saturday I want to go to,' he'd say nonchalantly. 'I'll see you in the evening, OK?'

She never asked to come with him, and

he never suggested it. Grace was used to men wanting to have interests apart from the women in their lives, and she didn't resent it. She'd seen her father totally absorbed in his painting, totally excluding the rest of them. Besides, she'd never forgotten the time Jonathan'd told her that he wouldn't put up with anyone who caged him like a pet or pried into his life, making him feel that they didn't trust him. She resolved that however difficult it was to curb her curiosity, she would keep to that.

Then he'd told her, laughing in his charming way, that India had asked him if he'd like to go skiing with her and a group of friends to Val d'Isère. She was giving a dinner party to discuss it, she hoped Caspar would manage to wangle some leave and come with them too.

'Wouldn't you like to go with them?' Grace teased, hiding the sudden fear that he would accept and that India would seduce him, or worse still he would beg her to come too and India would show her up by skiing wonderfully and whisking Jonathan away from her far away on some high mountain range.

'No, I'm too broke at the moment,' he'd said but, four months later, here they were in this most expensive hotel with its beautiful cultured garden growing right down to the edge of the beach.

'I'm taking you away,' he'd said grandly, 'for a week of exotic and erotic luxury. Oh, don't worry' — he'd seen the flash of anxiety in her expression — 'it's my treat.'

'But Jonathan . . . ' she'd begun, remembering how broke he'd been these last months. She'd copied out some of her mother's recipes and cooked supper for him in his flat to save him having to take her out. He always insisted on paying when they went out even when she offered to contribute.

'Don't worry, things are fine now. You've been a darling never grumbling or asking for anything these past weeks, cooking those delicious dinners for me. Now I can spoil you again.'

'If you're sure . . . Have you had a rise or a bonus?' She laughed, holding him close.

'A bonus . . . yes, that's it, a bonus,' he grinned and kissed her. Despite his assurances Grace felt a pang of disquiet in the back of her mind, but it was easily swamped by the excitement of the magic week ahead.

The week spun past. Grace pushed her ill health away and even though she was sick a few more times she managed to enjoy herself.

'If only we could be here for ever,' she

162

said on their last afternoon as they lay together, sated, content after lovemaking. 'I so understand why some people throw up their lives of routine and dreary weather and just come and live in the sun, don't you?'

He gently pushed a tendril of hair from her face. 'I think I'd get bored,' he said, then, seeing her crestfallen look, laughed and added, 'oh, not of you, or of making love to you, but I need a buzz to life, and wonderful though it is being here, part of me longs to get back to the action.'

'I know what you mean,' she said, 'one's mind is hardly taxed at all here.' Although she hadn't wanted to admit it, and he certainly hadn't shown any boredom with her company, she had felt him becoming restless. He couldn't lie on the beach for long, was always jumping up and rushing off to sail or to ride. She'd gone too and enjoyed it, but she sensed it was his mind that yearned to be stimulated, not his body. Once or twice he'd gone to telephone, saying he couldn't make the call from the room, but there was a kind of office place he'd rather use. He'd laughed when he explained.

'It's just withdrawal symptoms from the office, I need to sit behind a desk and make my calls. Do you think I'm mad?'

'Probably,' she said. She hardly gave this

behaviour a thought. She believed him, having heard that there were special rooms fitted out in the City for men who had lost their jobs and needed the security of an office to sit in. She never thought he was ringing another woman. Although he took a healthy interest in other women, she had never once since he had first made love to her had any cause to doubt his fidelity.

'Anyway, back home we'll still be together,' he said, 'it's not as if we won't be seeing each other again, is it?'

'No,' she said happily and kissed him so passionately that he had to make love to her again.

★ ★ ★

It was six weeks later that Grace found out she was pregnant. She could not believe it.

'Apart from the first time, we've always used contraceptives,' she said to the young woman doctor she consulted. 'Once I knew this relationship was going to continue I went back on the Pill. I haven't missed it once.'

After questioning her on her brand of pill, the doctor said, 'Have you vomited recently, for a few days perhaps?'

'Yes, I got food poisoning . . . I was very sick . . . I . . . ' Then the realization hit her.

'Oh, my God, you mean I could have sicked the Pill up, and it wouldn't work?'

'Yes, especially if you were sick for a few days.'

'I was.' She sat there stunned, hardly listening to the doctor's quiet voice.

'Are you in a stable relationship? How will the father of the child take it?' She heard the doctor ask.

'Father?' She looked at her stupidly, 'Oh, father.' Jonathan was to be a father, and she a mother. Suddenly they were no longer just Jonathan and Grace, two free people in love with each other, there was a third person, created by them both, who had to be considered.

The following day was Saturday and they had planned to go and look round some antique shops for some dining-room chairs Jonathan wanted. It was a hot, clear day and Jonathan was in a buoyant mood. Grace did her best to emulate him, but when they were in about the tenth shop looking at some Empire-style chairs, her mind glazed over. It was a full two minutes before she realized that he was talking to her.

'Grace, Gracie.' He flicked his fingers in front of her eyes. 'I said, which do you prefer, these, which are quite expensive, or those straight-backed ones in the first shop?

165

I think these are more elegant, don't you?'

'Oh, yes . . . ' she said, having quite forgotten what the other chairs looked like. She forced herself to look at them. 'These are very nice.'

He studied her carefully then, taking her arm and telling the shop assistant he'd be back, he led her outside and down the road. 'There's something wrong, isn't there, Grace? Usually you love antique hunting and we come back with all sorts of odds and ends, pretty plates, little boxes and so forth. We've seen lots today, but you haven't shown the slightest interest in any of them. It's not like you.'

He seemed almost like a small boy, cross because his playmate didn't want to play any more. Grace, fraught from her discovery of her pregnancy, having confided in no one but the young doctor, burst into tears.

'My love, what is it? Are you ill?' He took her in his arms and there on the street outside the antique shops she told him, blurting it out all in a muddle when she had promised herself she'd wait for a good moment to break the news to him carefully.

'It was when I was so sick in Morocco, I sicked up the Pill and I never thought about it. We should have used something else as

166

well,' she sobbed, terrified he would think she had somehow tricked him into this.

He said nothing. His face went white and he stood rock solid, holding her in the street. At last he stirred, took his handkerchief from his pocket, handed it to her and said, 'We can't stay here, let's go back to the car.'

Standing away from the warm bulk of him Grace felt shattered. Was this the end of their affair? Now that the play time had got serious, was it too much for him? Would he leave her? He wouldn't be the first man to behave so. She longed to cling to him, to cry out: Don't leave me, please don't leave me. I'll do anything to keep you, anything. But some pride in her kicked back, and she blew her nose fiercely and walked tall beside him back to the car.

Neither said anything as they walked, but he held on to her arm and when they reached the car he opened the door for her and helped her in.

By now Grace felt cold, cold right through her, dreading what he would say. Dreading the end of their perfect affair.

He turned to her, his face still white, still shocked. He took her hand and gave her a little smile. 'We'd better get married then,' he said.

'Married?' It was the last thing she expected

him to say, 'But . . .'

'Unless you don't want to?'

'Oh yes, I do, of course I do! But I don't want to force you into it . . . I don't know what to think about the baby . . . I only knew for sure yesterday . . . and I still can't take it in.'

He shrugged and gave her a wan smile. 'A roll of the dice. It's happened, and we'll make the best of it. We get on well, we're fond of each other, we suit each other . . . let's give it a whirl. Do your parents know?'

'Not yet.' She wished she felt pleased, relieved at the way he'd taken it, but she didn't, she felt numb. She wished he'd said he loved her, couldn't live without her, that the baby was proof of their love and he would welcome it. But then she thought he was never one for passionate endearments. He showed how much he loved her in bed and they were happy together, well suited as he said, what more could she realistically ask?

Then the picture of her parents and their intense love for each other came unbidden into her mind.

'What are you thinking of?' Jonathan said gently.

'My parents. How much they love each

other to the exclusion of everyone and everything else.'

'But they love you, that's obvious when you see them with you.'

'I know.' She gave him a brave laugh. 'I'm just selfish, greedy for more. Or maybe I'm jealous. It's pretty rare these days for two people still to be so much in love with each other after almost thirty years of marriage.'

'I'll say, but us . . . Are you trying to say we don't love each other enough to get married?' He looked at her candidly and for a moment she thought he was giving her a way out of his marriage proposal, or maybe even regretting it altogether, but he went on: 'I do love you, Grace, very much, and I think we have as much chance as the next person to be happy, but I also . . . ' He paused and she saw him struggle with emotion a moment. She put her hand over his as it fiddled restlessly on the steering wheel.

'I love you and we will be happy,' she said. 'It's just a bad way to start.'

'You know my father abandoned me when I was a baby,' he said with difficulty, as if he hadn't heard her. 'I couldn't do that to a child of mine, it makes you feel' — he gave a bitter laugh — 'as if you're not quite good enough. I mean if your own father doesn't want you . . . '

'Oh, darling.' She put her arm round his neck and laid her head on his shoulder. 'Don't torture yourself like that. Men ... *some* men can't identify with a baby. They find it much easier to be a father to an older child.' She yearned to find excuses for his father's actions to comfort him.

They sat together a moment, hunched rather uncomfortably over the gearstick, then he straightened, kissed her and said, 'That's enough of my misery. We'll make the best of it.' He counted on his fingers. 'It'll be born about February then?'

'I suppose so.'

'Well,' he said, starting the car, 'there it is. I suggest we go back to your house, tell your parents, then I'll tell mine. We'll get married as soon as we can. We can live in my flat after all.'

'But it's only got one bedroom,' she said, thinking of the smart study he'd just made out of the second bedroom.

'We'll manage,' he said grimly. 'We'll manage.'

★ ★ ★

Once all the parents had been told — Grace's mother showed more concern for her health than any moral disquiet — the plans for the wedding went ahead swiftly.

Only their parents knew of the coming baby, but when Sir William got to hear of the impending marriage he at once offered Elmley Park for the reception.

'I am so delighted, my dear, and such a nice young man, friend of Caspar's,' he boomed down the telephone. Then preceding her name with an awkward cough as he always did, he added, 'Anthea and I would love you to use Elmley, you know how beautiful it is in the summer.'

'Oh, Uncle William, that's so kind, but I don't want to put you to any trouble.' She thought of India and wondered how she would react to this news.

'Talk it over with your young man, my dear, and let me know. Any date you want — oh, except for the last weekend in August when we have the Church fête, but any other time.'

'How wonderful of him. Elmley.' Jonathan looked happier than he had for days. 'I hope you accepted, Grace. We can get married in the church in the village; it will be perfect.'

'But what about India?' she blurted out.

'What about India? Surely she can't object to her cousin having her reception at Elmley? We won't be changing anything, painting bluebirds on the pillars or anything.' He took

171

her hands in his. 'Oh, it will be lovely. Now let's get the date organized and go for it.'

The date was set for three weeks hence. It was not to be a big wedding; the staff at Elmley offered to do the catering and the flowers were to be produced from the vast gardens. A friend was found to make the dress and Jonathan's sisters, who were twelve and ten, were to be the bridesmaids.

'Do you think your father will come?' Grace asked Jonathan tentatively, not wanting to unleash the pain of his abandonment again but feeling she ought to ask.

'I doubt it,' Jonathan said curtly, 'but since our engagement appeared in *The Times* and *Telegraph* I've had various letters from the most unlikely people — masters from school, people I used to work for — so he may get in touch.'

Caspar sent Grace a jokey letter of congratulations, humorously warning her off Jonathan. He was to be the best man. But she heard not a word from India. She then found out through the family grapevine that she was with friends on a yacht cruising round the Greek Islands. She was due back in England the day before the wedding.

★ ★ ★

172

Grace and her parents stayed at Elmley the night before the wedding. Sir William and Caspar tried repeatedly to get hold of India at her London house. Friends and her mother had been detailed to let her know so she could get down to Elmley in time for the ceremony.

Grace prayed she would not come, prayed that her plane would be late, delayed until the day after the wedding.

After a good dinner they all went to bed early. Grace kissed her parents goodnight and her father held her a moment in his arms.

'I wish you every happiness, my darling,' he said.

'Oh, Daddy.' She hugged him tight, feeling a moment's panic. Tomorrow she would marry Jonathan and she still couldn't believe it, believe that she was going to spend the rest of her life with the man she loved more than anything in the world. She just hoped he loved her enough, that she would make him happy.

She tried not to think that his suggestion to get married was just made on impulse or from a desire not to abandon his child in the way he'd been abandoned. She worried that, caught up in the whirl of preparations in the three short weeks before the day, she had not given him sufficient time to reconsider or duck out of it.

Since the day she'd told him about the baby there had been no time to talk about it, really discuss whether they were doing the right thing in marrying so quickly, though she knew he wasn't the sort of person to ponder and analyse every move in life.

In the middle of the night Grace was woken by the rush of her bedroom door being opened violently, then closed. The light was snapped on and there stood India. She was shaking with anger, her dark eyes boring into Grace.

'So you tricked him,' she spat. 'I bet you anything that you're pregnant, you slut.'

'India . . . ! It wasn't like that at all.' Grace sprang up in bed, terrified she was going to attack her, tear at her face with those sharp red nails.

'You had to have everything of mine, didn't you,' India hissed, coming so close to her that Grace could feel her breath and feel little flecks of spittle on her cheek. 'You threw yourself at this man, didn't you, like a cheap tart, and now you've tricked him into marriage. Well, it won't work, he'll soon get bored of you once that baby's squalling and puking about the place. He'll soon leave you.'

Each word was like a blow to Grace, made worse because they echoed her secret fears.

'Why do you care so much who I marry?' she asked. 'You can have your pick of any man.'

India leant over her, her mouth contorted with fury. Grace felt the fear shoot up into her, threaten to strangle her; she could hardly breathe. She tried to move away, get out of the bed and escape from her, but India's words pinned her down.

'I want him, he's the only man I've ever truly wanted, and I shall have him. Whatever I have to do, I shall have him.' Her smile was venomous. 'It was just my luck to be away when you grabbed him and I only heard about it a couple of hours ago. But marriage doesn't mean you own him. I'll get him, see if I won't.' And she whirled out of the room.

Grace did not sleep again that night. She tossed and turned, tortured by India's words, by her snarling face. She was convinced that she would find some way to stop the marriage, to ruin their day.

She decided she'd tell her mother but when she came to it, it sounded so foolish: India's said mean things to me because she wants Jonathan. It would be like a child telling tales, so she said nothing. She braced herself, reassuring herself that India couldn't do anything about it at this late stage. She was spoilt and being spiteful because Grace had married before her. She didn't love Jonathan. How could she? She didn't really know him. Grace doubted she loved anyone but herself. She would probably now be ashamed of her outburst and show it by being sulky and superior when she saw her.

It was a beautiful, sunny day and Grace did her best to join in the excited anticipation that spun through the house.

'I heard those wedding bells that weekend you both came down. Such a good-looking man,' Mrs Bates said triumphantly to Grace when she went down to the kitchen to admire the cake.

'Elmley really comes into its own with a party,' Anthea said from the dining-room window, watching the men put out small tables and chairs on the terrace, 'and it looks like it will stay fine all day so everyone can be in the garden which is so lovely at this time of year.'

'It's terribly good of you and William to have it here,' Leo said, 'my studio only holds a dozen people and a hotel isn't half so nice.'

'Only too glad,' William boomed, 'pity it isn't one of mine. It's high time Caspar got down to producing an heir, and India, well' — he winked at Grace who felt sick at the mention of her cousin's name — 'she can't find anyone good enough it seems.'

Grace excused herself from the breakfast table, thinking: She *has* found someone good enough, only he's mine, but for how long? She felt the shiver of tears in her throat and firmly went upstairs to start getting ready. As she passed India's door, her whole body screaming with tension, it opened and India came out. At the same moment Olivia came up behind them.

'Good morning, India,' she said warmly. 'I'm so glad you got back in time for this special day. It wouldn't be the same without you.'

'I'm not staying,' India said coldly. 'I've much more important things to do.' She swept past them imperious as a queen. Only Leo and Caspar coming up the stairs to join them stopped Grace unburdening to her mother India's jealous tantrum in the night.

Grace arrived with her father at the church, her dress simple but elegant, made from heavy pale cream silk to tone in with her wonderful old lace veil, the one her mother had worn for her own wedding. The bridesmaids were also in cream with large, pale blue sashes, and matching blue flowers in their hair.

'All set, darling?' Leo said. 'You look wonderful. A little pale, though, are you all right?'

'I'm fine,' she said, determined to put India out of her mind.

As she stood at the entrance to the church, her bridesmaids and the dressmaker running round arranging her dress and veil, she heard a noise and in her agitation she almost jumped out of her skin. An old man with a few days' growth on his chin, dressed in a crumpled suit, came out from behind a gravestone. He stared intently at her. He looked vaguely familiar.

Her father, seeing him and feeling her start, said quietly, 'Don't worry, darling, it's only some poor old tramp. Give him a smile, it will make his day.'

It was just like her father to say something like that, she thought and she turned and smiled at the man. He nodded to her and she turned away, wondering why she felt so sure that she'd seen him before.

'Have you seen India?' Jonathan said to her during a lull in greeting their guests. He looked so good, she thought in his silver-grey morning suit, no wonder India wanted him.

'Only for a moment. She has something

178

else to do,' she said quickly, not wanting to spoil the day by telling him of India's jealousy. He seemed more relaxed now they were out of the church. He had, they both had, been very tense during the marriage vows, as if fully realizing for the first time the magnitude of what they had taken on. Later she would tell him of India's threat in the night, needing his reassurance that India could do nothing to part them.

Caspar came up to them. 'So you've beaten me to it,' he playfully punched Jonathan in the shoulder, 'but you've started my old man up again suggesting that I settle down.' He glanced over towards his father and Anthea. 'It's funny India not staying. She says she's something more important on,' he grinned. 'Perhaps she's jealous.'

'She's probably got some new boyfriend she'd rather be with,' Jonathan joked.

Caspar laughed, Jonathan joined him. Grace forced herself to smile. She felt a great sense of relief that India wasn't there.

Seconds later, some of her school friends came up to talk to her, shooting flirtatious and envious looks at Jonathan. Finally Grace began to enjoy being the centre of affectionate attention, standing in the beautiful garden at Elmley with the huge house a perfect backdrop. The bridesmaids were running across the lawn with the two Labradors, each dog with large blue bow to match the bridesmaids' sashes tied by Anthea in their collars. Anthea's rat-dog had been left in her room as she was fearful of it being trodden underfoot by the guests.

Jonathan caught her gaze. 'Time to cut the cake,' he said.

In the sea of faces listening to the speeches Grace was certain she saw India. Here and there among the guests her face would appear, her dark eyes homing in on Grace. She looked away, forcing herself not to look at those compelling eyes. When the cake was cut and the speeches and toasts finished, she looked again, but she couldn't see her.

'I thought I saw India,' she said to Jonathan.

'Maybe her important date finished early,' he said, slipping his arm round her waist.

She did not see India again until she was changed and ready to leave. She had a few girl friends with her, standing at the top of the stairs chattering and giggling. Grace had her bouquet in her hand and some of her friends were about to run down to the hall hoping to catch it. India came up the stairs slowly. She wore a plain silk dress but no hat. The girls stood aside to let her pass, still chattering, leaving Grace standing there, watching her coming up.

Grace steeled herself for the confrontation, but then Jonathan appeared on the landing, pushing past the group of girls, laughing and calling out to Grace to wait for him. At the same moment India reached the top of the stairs. She went up to him, put her hand firmly at the back of his head and kissed him full on the lips.

The girls giggled nervously, Grace froze, but Jonathan pulled himself away from her and said rather shakily, 'What a send off, India.' He took Grace's hand and ran with her down the stairs. Grace forced herself to smile at the cheerful crowd of well wishers that packed the hall to watch her leave. She could not help feeling that Jonathan was running away from India, not running out into their married life together. Numbly she wondered if he had enjoyed that sudden kiss.

They left the reception in a flurry of rose petals and confetti, on their way to a hotel near the airport where they were booked to stay before flying off to a villa, lent to them by some friends in the South of France.

'That's it,' he said, holding her hand in the back of the car, 'we've done it.' He did not mention India and she did not like to, afraid to see desire for her in his eyes.

'We've done it,' she repeated, thinking suddenly of the coming child that she carried and how in a few months their lives would be changed even more. She laid her head on his shoulder and prayed that they would be happy.

When they reached the hotel, they fell exhaustedly into bed and he made love to her, making jokes about it now being legal. He fell asleep almost at once but she lay awake, unable to stop thinking of India.

She heard a footfall in the passage outside and lay frozen with fear, certain it was India coming again to shout at her, to turn Jonathan against her. She could not help thinking that their hasty marriage might be more vulnerable, easier for India to wreck than one arrived at after more time and consideration.

Vainly she tried to soothe herself, tell herself that despite her threats, India couldn't do anything. Besides, Jonathan was not so malleable that he would simply go to her. If he had shown any interest in her, he had had plenty of opportunities over the years to show it. Anyway, hadn't he nicknamed India 'the praying mantis'?

It was just a bluff, another of India's tantrums at not being the centre of attention. She was safe, she told herself, putting her hand out to touch Jonathan. They were married and they would make a success of it.

Then she felt a sharp pain in her stomach, echoing the dull pain she'd felt in her back all the afternoon. Something wet and sticky was running down her legs and when she snapped on the light, she saw that she was bleeding heavily.

12

'But, Mummy, it's so degrading,' India said waspishly, not caring that she had obviously hurt Flavia deeply. 'This ... this Jeremy person is young enough to be your son, you'll be the laughing stock of London.'

'Age is nothing,' Flavia said defiantly, 'it's the person that counts, not their age ... or race or religion for that matter. We just get on so well.' Her voice held a hint of desperation; her face, caked with too much make-up, sagged. For a second she looked older than she was.

India stabbed at her salad; they were lunching in Harvey Nichols. India had insisted that her mother come here with her, on her own. Jeremy was always coming into her house, letting himself in with his key and smirking smugly at her.

'And how's the lovely India today?' he'd say, his eyes unashamedly undressing her.

'I feel quite sick all of a sudden,' she'd retort and she would leave at once, saying heavily to her mother, 'Ring me if you need me.'

She did not want to ask Flavia round to

her house as she used to, in case she brought Jeremy with her. She certainly didn't want him in her house, suspecting that once he had been there, he would keep on coming.

'Can't you see he's using you, Mummy?' India said firmly, pouring her out some more white wine. 'Are you giving him anything?' She couldn't bring herself to say money, knowing that it sounded too much as if he was a paid companion, but also not wanting to face up to the demeaning fact that her mother, once so beautiful and adored, had to pay to have a man by her side, and supposedly, sickeningly, in her bed.

Flavia knew what she meant at once. She flushed deeply. 'It's none of your business, India. I really don't know why you're bothering yourself with my affairs. You should look to your own — there's Grace married and you not even engaged.'

India flinched as if she'd struck her. 'Grace tricked Jonathan into marriage,' she said icily. 'It won't last, you'll see.'

'Well, she's married, and he's such a nice man by all accounts, though it was sad that they lost the baby. Still, they're young and perhaps it's better to have a child a few years into a marriage. It'll give them more time for themselves at the beginning.'

'She lost the baby?' India said, hope suddenly rising in her.

Flavia looked uncomfortable. 'Oh dear, I forgot that Olivia told me not to tell anyone. Still, you're family and you'll keep it to yourself, won't you? She miscarried on their honeymoon night, had to spend a couple of days in hospital. Wretched for her.' She shrugged. 'Anyway it's better that you do know about it, so that when you see her you won't make any thoughtless remarks about pregnancy.'

India ate her food mechanically, not listening now to Flavia prattling on about Grace's miscarriage, miscarriages in general, and the most suitable time lapse, in her mind, between the wedding day and a conception. If the reason for their marriage had now gone, no doubt the end of their marriage would soon follow. It would not look good to separate straight away but probably by the end of the year the marriage would be quietly over and she would seize her chance to win Jonathan.

'Poor Grace,' she said thoughtfully, 'I must go and see her.'

'I have her address,' Flavia said, relieved that India was now showing more interest in Grace's affairs than Flavia's own. She delved into her handbag and after a moment came up with a small address book and handed it to India.

India, who only had Jonathan's office telephone number, copied the address down, then, handing the book back said, 'Thanks, I'll contact her, but to get back to you, Mummy. You simply cannot continue to see this man. He's bound to dump you when he's got what he wants from you and that will be really humiliating. Get rid of him now. What's happened to all those friends you used to go out with?'

Flavia gave her a tortured smile. 'I've lost touch — you know how people move on. But my dear, I really don't think it's any of your business who my friends are.'

India looked at her dispassionately. She was fed up with her parents' behaviour: her father setting up house with that dreadful trainer's wife, who made going down to Elmley such torture with her sucking-up to the staff and old friends of her mother, none of which fooled her for a moment; and now her mother carrying on with this creep who was obviously out to get all he could from her, no doubt impressed by her title, imagining her far richer and more influential than she was. She felt quite nauseated as she imagined him boasting about his conquest with his surely highly undesirable friends.

If only Caspar was in the country she was sure he would deal with it, though he'd been pretty hopeless over the trainer's wife. But seeing his mother with this frightful ponce would surely make him furious. There was nothing he hated more than beautiful male wimps.

'Caspar will be horrified,' India said coldly, 'and what do your friends think? I mean the ones of your own age? What do Aunt Olivia and Uncle Leo say about it?'

Flavia flushed, 'I haven't told Olivia and Leo yet. They've been so busy with Grace's wedding and then worried about her health . . .'

'If you're ashamed of your relationship with him then surely you can see that it's wrong,' India pressed on impatiently.

'I don't think it's wrong. He's not married, and nor am I any more, even though I'm not divorced.'

'I think it's an embarrassing relationship . . .'

'Only for you. Really, India, I'm surprised at you. You're of a different generation and your age group has fewer scruples and morals over this sort of thing, yet you criticize mine. At least I care for him and am faithful to him.' Flavia looked quite affronted.

India pushed her plate away from her and said wearily, 'Pity you weren't to my father

188

then. It's your generation that started this rot, leaving us yearning for the impossible, a love affair that never ends, a commitment that lasts for life. We find it difficult to settle with anyone, because at the slightest sign of a fault we leave, convinced we'll find someone better, remembering what a mess our parents made of their marriages.'

'India, I think you exaggerate. You've met some charming young men, that Freddie and Edward Porter, he's always been fond of you. He'll inherit that lovely house and huge farm, you know, just up the road from Elmley, that would suit you wonderfully.' Flavia made a great effort to sound soothing, as if India's bad temper was just due to over-tiredness or some disappointment in her life.

'Mummy, keep to the point. Please give up Jeremy, he's using you and you'll become, if you haven't already, a figure of fun. And' — she held up her hand as Flavia struggled to protest — 'wear different clothes. You're not eighteen, nor, I'm afraid, have you the stick-insect figure that you need for these skimpy things.' She gestured towards Flavia's tight-ribbed T-shirt worn under a slim-cut jacket with short sleeves and a very short skirt. 'You don't have to wear drab old lady's clothes, look at the way continental women dress. Somehow they always look elegant and attractive whatever their age. Shall we go upstairs when we've finished lunch and buy you some new things?'

Flavia looked as if she was going to burst into tears. She said, with extreme difficulty, 'I don't know why you are being so unkind, India. Jeremy likes me like this. He comes with me when I buy my clothes; he has very good taste.'

'That's debatable. Honestly, can't you see sense?' India banged her fist on the table, causing some of the other people lunching to stare at her. 'Please,' she said urgently, leaning forward so that her eyes were level with her mother's over-made-up face and brassy yellow hair, 'please stop this ridiculous affair before it's too late. I don't want you to be hurt, and believe me he will hurt you when he finds the next rich middle-aged lady with time and money to spare.'

'India . . .' Flavia's voice wobbled and her eyes shone with tears. 'You can't know what it's like to be lonely. I like men, flattery, I've always been used to it, as you are. My other . . .' She paused, gulping at her wine, 'men friends drifted away when your father chucked me out . . . but then I met Jeremy and he . . .' She stopped again, struggling with her composure, her face old now in its misery so that it touched India's heart.

190

'I understand, Mummy,' she said more gently, 'but don't you see how degrading this is? Give him up, then I'm sure you'll find someone nearer your age. You know that no self-respecting man will come near you while you've got him in tow.' She laid her hand on Flavia's arm. 'We'll give a party, ask all your old flames, everyone we know.'

Flavia smiled, looking for a moment more hopeful. India felt encouraged and was about to go into the details of a party when she sensed a slight hush in the surrounding chatter, an undefinable atmosphere of excitement.

'You said you'd be here, Flavia,' Jeremy sidled up to them, smiling. He bent down and kissed Flavia and might have kissed India too if she hadn't jumped up and away.

'How can you creep up on people like that, have you no manners?'

'Plenty, my dear, and how beautiful you are today, with that fire in your eyes.' His voice purred and she was aware that all the other women there were looking at him; all unconsciously preening themselves, sitting straighter, smiling, pretending not to look at him, but all the time taking in every tiny detail of his clothes, his hair and his beautiful face and body.

'I'm off. Don't forget what I said.' India threw the words at her mother, watching her frantically struggling with her previous near-tearful state to become the ever-young, amusing, happy girl again.

'Don't let me chase you away,' Jeremy drawled, absorbing all the admiring glances from the other women in the restaurant as a sponge sucks up water. 'I'll just sit over here' — he smiled towards a table of two attractive women who were eyeing him — 'and have a coffee while you finish your conversation.'

'Oh, no, darling, we've quite finished. India has to rush, she's so much to do.' Flavia beamed up at him. 'Sit here, let me get you something, have you eaten?'

India turned away without saying goodbye, her heart sick at her mother's humiliating betrayal.

★ ★ ★

India thought for a long time about how she could approach Grace and Jonathan.

The last time she had seen Grace was the night before her wedding and she still felt rather queasy when she remembered that scene. But she had been so angry, so angry and hurt that she, Grace of all people, had managed to *marry* Jonathan. She knew she should have thought it through and waited, because now things had worked out in her favour and surely soon, if not already, Jonathan would be bored of Grace and she could move in.

But that evening, arriving back from a lovely holiday, feeling rather deflated as one often did when one returned home, to be greeted by the news that Grace was to be married to Jonathan the following day had made her insane with jealousy, with panic at not being able to stop it, and had impelled her to act unwisely.

She realized she would probably have to apologize profusely for that outburst, lull Grace into accepting her as a friend so as to be on hand as it were, to scoop Jonathan up when he tired of Grace. But her apologies stuck like stones in her throat and for weeks, running into months, she put it off. At last, fearing Jonathan would forget her, might even now be flirting with another woman, she swallowed her pride and telephoned.

'Oh, India, hello,' Grace said rather guardedly.

'I feel I must apologize for my dreadful behaviour the night before your wedding,' India began, hating saying it. 'I was in a bad mood, I'd just got back and — '

'That's all right,' Grace said in a voice that

clearly indicated it wasn't.

India plunged on. 'It really was disgraceful of me and I can't say how sorry I am, or what came over me. I do hope you'll forgive me.'

'It's over now, India. I don't think about it,' Grace said, then added, 'we're married and very happy and that's very important to me.'

'Of course it is' — India fought to sound enthusiastic — 'so I wondered if you two would like to come round to dinner next Wednesday, I'd love to see you, catch up.'

'No . . . thank you, India, we've a busy week next week, then Jonathan is away on business,' Grace said firmly.

'I'd like to keep in touch,' India said, forcing herself not to sound bossy and order Grace to come.

'I must go now, I've something cooking,' Grace said, 'but thanks for ringing. 'Bye,' and she put down the receiver leaving India bereft and furious.

She poured herself a stiff drink and as she sipped it she ran over their conversation, such as it was. Perhaps their marriage had already come unstuck and Grace was determined to keep Jonathan from her. She'd have to try a different tack. She knew how Jonathan enjoyed shooting, she'd get her father to ask him to Elmley on the Glorious Twelfth, the first day of the new shooting season. He wouldn't refuse that invitation and she would be there watching them all weekend to see how the land lay.

The telephone rang; it was Freddie.

'As you won't marry me I've asked someone else to, and I want you to meet her. Can I bring her round and we'll all go out to dinner together?'

'Oh, Freddie . . . this is a surprise, who is it?' She felt weak with shock. She didn't want to marry Freddie herself, but he was such a good friend and so fond of her, so useful to go out with when there wasn't anyone else around. She didn't want him to marry anyone. 'I thought you didn't want to get married, or not yet anyway.'

'I know, but my sisters think as I have found Amanda I should marry her, get an heir.'

'But, Freddie, do you love her? I mean, *you've* got to live with her, not your sisters,' India said impatiently. Really, he was so wet; if she'd married him, he'd have done anything she wanted him to.

'She's a good sort,' he said, 'and I do love her,' he added as if it was expected of him. 'She loves the country life, dogs and shooting, she'll be perfect. So can I bring her round? I know you'll adore each other.'

'Perhaps another night, Freddie,' India said. She couldn't face anyone else's defection from her circle; perhaps she was losing her command over them all? She'd heard rumours that Ned Porter had a serious girlfriend; he certainly hadn't rung her lately. She rode over Freddie's protests with a story of already doing something that evening.

When he'd rung off she telephoned Max Dalbert, a rich, older man who'd shown an interest in her. She knew he would spoil her, give her a fabulous dinner and make her feel loved even though she found him rather boring.

As she bathed and changed to get ready to go out with Max she planned with military precision the shooting weekend at Elmley and how she would persuade Jonathan to give up dull, colourless little Grace and come to her. She had not given up.

Part Two

Part Two

13

1995

Grace stood on the pavement outside the smart private school in Eaton Square waiting for Sebastian to come out. Jack ran round and round in circles with Lucy, the friend he went to nursery school with.

'Can you both come to dinner next Thursday?' Sue, Lucy's mother, asked Grace. 'The Baxters are over from New York and I know Jonathan likes them.' She put out a restraining hand as Jack nearly knocked over Lucy with his exuberance.

'What fun, I'd love to if we can, but we've rather a busy week.' Grace took out her diary; every page was covered with her scrawling handwriting: *drinks Kate and Paul, gym boys, Sebastian judo, boys swimming, dinner Nicholas and Serena.*

'We have a drinks party with someone from Jonathan's office that evening, but if you don't mind us being late,' she began, inwardly feeling rather exhausted at the thought of yet another night out. She always left the house in such a frazzle, coping with

Sebastian's homework, feeding the boys or leaving something for the babysitter to give them to eat. That no babysitter could ever cook properly, let alone wash the dishes up afterwards, irritated her further.

She loved seeing her friends but life seemed so busy at the moment with her work, the children and a heavy social life, often connected with Jonathan's job. She felt, she joked sometimes, like a bemused tourist. If it's Tuesday it's Jack's day to lunch at nursery school and Sebastian's judo. Wednesday they both had swimming lessons. Every day spun past leaving both her and Jonathan exhausted, yet exhilarated by the speed of it.

'I don't mind at all, I'm never together much before nine anyway,' Sue said and Grace's heart sank as she remembered that Sue never seemed to start cooking until her guests had arrived — perhaps she didn't believe they'd actually come and didn't want to waste the food — and one was usually too drunk and too tired to enjoy the dinner by the time it did appear.

The school door opened and the nannies and mothers filed in. Some mothers were very elegant and had obviously spent most of the day getting ready for this moment. Others, like Sue, were in jeans. Grace was semi-smart in a suit, having just come from work via Jack's school.

Jack rushed ahead into the school despite Grace's pleas to stay quietly beside her in the queue. He would be coming here next term and she was always rather afraid that seeing his over-excited behaviour, the headmistress might change her mind about taking him. In horror she heard him calling out to his brother cheerfully, 'Sebastian, Sebastian, it's me you old poo poo.'

This greeting was followed by the more refined tones of Miss Becky, the young teacher in charge, who knew Jack well. 'Wait quietly, please, Jack. Sebastian must stay sitting still until Mummy comes.'

'I'll sit with him,' Grace heard Jack say and then as she filed slowly forward she heard a scuffle and a few yelps of pain as Jack accidentally trod on a few fingers as he tried to cram himself down into a tiny space beside Sebastian.

Miss Becky saw her and said quickly, 'Sebastian.' And Sebastian got up and so did Jack, squashing more fingers. 'Goodbye, Sebastian,' Miss Becky said, shaking his hand.

'G'bye, Miss Becky,' Sebastian answered.

'Goodbyeee, Miss Becky,' Jack said, thrusting out his left hand.

'Goodbye, Jack,' Miss Becky smiled at him.

Grace whisked them both out. Jack jumped like a frog all the way down the road to the car. Sebastian thrust his satchel at Grace and whirled after him, thrilled to be outside and free again, away from the confines of school.

Grace watched them with affection, socks down, hair wild, laces undone, but so full of vitality. She often marvelled at her happy life.

Losing the baby on her honeymoon night had been devastating. It was true they were barely used to the idea of having a child, or had not ever wanted one at that time, but as its life had drained from her so she felt sure would her marriage. When the sad business was over she said tearfully, but firmly, 'I'll quite understand if you'd like the marriage annulled, Jonathan. I mean, we don't have to get married any more.'

Jonathan had looked at her. He was pale, dishevelled with bewilderment and shock. 'Don't you want to be married to me?' he said at last.

'Of course I do, more than anything,' she'd burst out, too shattered to camouflage her true longings with pride, 'but if you want to finish it, I'll understand.' She'd thought of India then, India waiting for just such a moment to snatch him away from her.

He took her hand. He looked so young and yet so old too, like a child precipitated roughly into the reality of adult life. 'We promised we'd marry each other for better or worse, remember?'

'Of course but . . . ' She tried to find the right words to explain that though she would stand by him through anything, if he felt he couldn't stand by her now that the main reason for their hurried marriage had gone, she would let him go. Agony though it would be, she would rather let him go than live with his resentment, watching their love warping and dying.

'We've hardly given marriage a chance,' he said. Then he smiled, touching her cheek, 'Besides, I was looking forward to the honeymoon in that luxurious villa.'

She had sworn to herself then that she would do anything, suffer anything, to keep him, to make him happy. She had firmly tucked away the loss of the child, and done her utmost to be amusing and entertaining.

Grace had never forgotten the kiss India had given Jonathan on her wedding day. None of them had ever spoken of it. India had prowled around from time to time, occasionally offering invitations that Jonathan always turned down. He turned them down so quickly and so determinedly that in her more insecure moments Grace had wondered if he was afraid of being close to India, afraid he could not trust himself against her attraction.

The few times they saw her, India always looked wonderful. She would ask Grace pointedly how she was, as if reminding her of her threat on that dreadful night before her wedding, and that, despite her apology, she was still plotting how to snatch Jonathan. When she saw Jonathan she would give him most of her attention. Though Grace knew Jonathan loved her she felt uneasy the few times she'd seen him looking at India covetously from under his lashes, as if he was fascinated by her.

'She's so beautiful,' Grace said to him once, watching his reaction.

'She is,' he agreed and did not say any more.

Grace had been tired, having just nursed Sebastian through chicken pox. She knew she did not look her best and his confirmation of India's beauty, without adding a compliment for her, made her feel he could be wearying of her and might be tempted by India.

'She wouldn't look so good if she'd been up all night with an ill baby,' she'd said sourly, but Jonathan had only grunted and gone on reading, making her feel even more insecure. If she allowed herself to think rationally about her paranoia she thought it probably stemmed from their childhood, when India always got her own way and succeeded in everything she tried. Everyone wanted to be India's friend, later every man wanted to be her lover. Jonathan may have called her the praying mantis type but he was a passionate man and he might, given the encouragement, be tempted by her. There were weak moments in all marriages and she did worry that India might prey on him during one of them. It was always a great relief to her when India went off for a while with some other man.

The years had passed in a flash, bringing them Sebastian and Jack. Jonathan's job went well, most of the time. She used to show an interest in it, but when the boys were born she found she hadn't so much time or energy to discuss it. Nor, it seemed, did he. He threw himself happily and enthusiastically into his role of fatherhood.

They had never been quite without money, but three years ago they'd had to sell their large house in Kensington and move to a flat.

Busy with the children, Grace had not

perhaps paid enough attention to Jonathan's increasing agitation at that time. He'd been pale and restless and kept going out, telling her curtly that he had business to attend to. They went racing at Ascot for the week with friends and he hardly stayed by her side, but when she questioned him as to where he was going, he just muttered he had people to see. At the end of each race he seemed further sunk in gloom.

'Lost your shirt, Jonathan?' a friend quipped, and he jumped, flashing him a smile.

'Nothing I can't get back,' he'd answered, and she remembered while the others laughed and joked about it, his words had made her feel cold and sick inside, and try as she might, she could not laugh with them.

It had been difficult to question him too much in front of their friends, but when she got home she'd asked him if he had lost money backing the horses.

'A little, but don't worry about it, darling.' He'd thrown the words out casually but he could not hide the fear in his eyes.

'But I do.' The words had slipped out before she could stop them. His face had hardened, a look almost of dislike had flashed into his eyes. She felt herself dying inside.

'Don't you dare worry,' he'd demanded

and walked out, slamming the front door. He'd been away for hours, resurrecting her old fear that he had gone to see India. For though they didn't see much of India, she was the first person Grace thought of whenever she and Jonathan had a row. She felt India was always there, even when she was heavily involved with another man, waiting to snatch him from her.

When he'd returned, far into the night, he'd said nothing and she'd not dared question him, so afraid was she of what he might say, of what he might do to upset the loving nest she had built so carefully.

For a couple of weeks they'd skated warily around each other, then one night he had appeared trembling and ashen-faced, and she had thought he was mortally ill.

'There's been a crisis in the financial market — you must have read about it, darling, the recession, balance of payments. I'm afraid we've got to pull in our horns, sell the house, live somewhere cheaper, just for a while.'

His news had devastated her, yet everyone knew that times were hard, many of their friends had been made redundant or lost businesses. As he clung to her in despair, begging her forgiveness, she said: 'But you said it was the recession, that's hardly your fault.' As he went on telling her of the difficulties in the financial world, listing them as if he were taking an exam, she firmly pushed away any doubts. He must be speaking the truth about their collapse, he could hardly have lost the house and the generous amount they lived on by backing a few horses in Ascot week.

'We'll cope, as long as we're together,' she'd said bravely, his white haggard face and obvious distress tearing at her heart.

She was determined to make the best of it; after all they were all together, all alive and in good health. She cast off the nanny and the daily arranging a complicated, but cheaper, nanny-share with friends, and did up the small, rather cramped flat herself.

'You're wonderful, darling, so understanding,' he'd said, taking her in his arms. He had been so loving, so helpful with the boys and that one year before their fortunes had changed again had been one of the happiest in her life.

But things had looked up again and now they lived in a large house in Chelsea and had a cottage in the country. She didn't need to work, but she enjoyed her job in a small and exclusive interior decorators. Since working in an architect's office before her marriage, she had become interested in interior design and had done a few courses before being trained further by this firm. She also found she did not want a full-time, live-in nanny again, especially now both boys were at school. She much preferred the nanny-share, feeling that the presence of a nanny, however nice, intruded on their closeness as a family.

★ ★ ★

'Dad, Dad, will you take me karting on Saturday?' Sebastian said, the minute Jonathan arrived home exhausted from the office. He jumped round and round in the hall in a frenzy of excitement.

'Dad! Dad!' Jack threw himself at his father and clamped himself round his leg.

'Boys, give me a minute,' Jonathan said, pushing them away and taking off his coat.

'Can I look in your briefcase, Dad?' Sebastian said, seizing it from his hand. He loved the combination lock.

'No! Put it down at once.' Jonathan's voice was sharp.

Grace appeared, kissed him and shooed the boys away.

'Bad day?' she said sympathetically.

'Yes, hellish.' Then with an effort he said, 'It will be better tomorrow, just . . . some deals went wrong.' But he didn't look at her.

'Poor darling, I'll get you a drink,' she said, fussing round him. She hated to see that drawn, anxious look on his face. Whatever had gone wrong in the office didn't matter, here was his haven, his home, his family. Here he would find happiness and, if the boys would be quiet and stop playing at being Ninja Turtles, peace of mind.

In a few minutes he looked better. 'Thank you, darling,' he said, taking a another large gulp of whisky. 'It was a hell of a day, we lost quite a lot of money. We must economize a bit, I'm afraid.'

Grace felt faint. Not again, she thought. She looked round the large pale apricot-coloured drawing room with its fine antique furniture, the silk apricot and grey-blue curtains as full as ball dresses at the tall windows, the expensive limed-oak cupboards and bookcases, the Persian rug, all coming together to make a warm, elegant room. She'd spent so much time, not to mention money on it and it was her favourite room of all those she'd ever possessed. She could not bear now to leave this magnificent house, each room done up by her to perfection, and start again in a flat.

'How much?' she said, not daring to ask

him outright if they must move, sell this, sell the country cottage she also loved with a passion.

He seemed more revived now and smiled. 'Enough, but we'll fight back, we'll be fine. Just don't go mad and buy a fur coat or anything.'

She smiled, the tension lessening with his words. Everything would be all right after all, she was over-reacting. She squashed down the fear that she kept buried deep inside her, that something would happen to snatch away her happiness.

'Dad,' Sebastian ran into the room. 'Will you take me karting on Saturday? Mark's Daddy is taking him and so is Piers's and . . . '

Jonathan smiled at him, put his hand out and ruffled his hair affectionately. 'I can't this Saturday, Sebastian, old chap, I'm sorry. I'm doing something else.'

'What?' His face creased in disappointment. 'Can't you do it later?'

'I can't, I'm afraid. Is the karting place open on Sunday? I'll take you then.'

'Mark and Piers are going on Saturday. Saturday afternoon. What are you doing?' he demanded, his small face fierce. 'Can't you come back in time?'

'I won't be in London.'

'Where will you be?'

Jonathan smiled again, saying easily, 'I shall be at Newmarket, racing.'

Grace wondered why his words filled her with disquiet. He had raced so often these past years she'd ceased to remark on it. She hated to see Sebastian's disappointment, but he had to understand that Jonathan couldn't always be free for him.

'Can I come with you then?' Sebastian asked.

'What's Newmarket?' Jack said, determined not to be left out.

'You can't, I'm afraid, I've some business to do there. It will be very boring. Can't Mummy take you?' He grinned across at Grace. 'I'm sure she'd be a wow in a go-kart.'

'Only Daddies are going,' Sebastian said sadly.

'Well, I'm sorry. I can't manage it this time,' Jonathan said sharply, opening the *Evening Standard* firmly at the financial pages.

Grace tried with a heavy heart to think of another amusement for the boys. She knew Jonathan loved his racing, but she felt he could have, just this once, put it off. She thought she would put this to him later when they were alone, but he suddenly put down the paper and said, 'If the weather's nice on Sunday how about going to Thorpe Park?'

'Yes! Yes! Can we, oh, please, can we?' Both boys jumped up and down, their faces now glowing with excitement.

Grace felt warm again. She smiled broadly. Everything was going to be fine. The children were happy, the disappointment forgotten. In the general excitement and pleasure, the boys swarming over Jonathan, calling out what rides they were going on, could they bring a friend, could they stay the whole day until it closed, she forgot that a moment ago Jonathan had told her that money was tight and that they had to make economies.

* * *

Having just returned from taking the boys to school, Grace sank back with another coffee and a quick glance at the newspapers before starting on the housework. The doorbell rang and, thinking it may be the postman, she opened the door. It was India.

'Hoped to catch you,' she said brightly, depositing a quick kiss on her cheek, coming in before Grace could say anything.

'Oh . . . India.' Her heart sank at the sight of her.

'I hope I'm not too early, I just wanted to

talk to you. Oooh, is that fresh coffee I can smell? I'd love a cup.' She walked through to the dining room and sat down at the table amid the debris of breakfast. They'd eaten there today as she hadn't yet cleared up the kitchen from supper with the boys and their friends the night before. A couple of toy cars lay among the jam pots, a sticky spoon oozed honey on to the table, a half-eaten piece of toast lay on the floor.

Grace felt a stab of disquiet coupled with annoyance that India should arrive unannounced like this before she'd even had time to tidy things away. She decided not to apologize for the mess, but fetched another cup and poured her some coffee.

'So what's up?' she said briskly, vainly trying to quell her feelings of unease at the sight of India sitting there so smartly dressed, exuding superiority, in complete contrast to herself who, having rushed to feed the boys and Jonathan, find lost homework and projects, check they looked reasonably tidy before fighting through the traffic jams to pick up other boys and get them all to the school on time, was in jeans and a jersey, with no make-up and barely brushed hair.

India took a long drink of coffee. 'Mmm, I needed that, nothing like a good coffee to razz one up. This is excellent.'

'Italian,' Grace said, bracing herself for India's mission. She knew she had not just dropped in to be friendly.

'Very good.' India lit a cigarette, glanced quickly round the untidy room including Grace in her disapproval, then said, 'I was at Newmarket at the weekend. You know I don't often race now but Daddy had a horse running and we had a house party. I saw Jonathan.'

'Oh, he didn't say.' Grace felt cold inside. She'd often wondered if he'd run into India at race meetings or shooting parties in Scotland, but he'd never said he had, and she was afraid to ask, in case he felt she didn't trust him.

'I didn't speak to him and he may not have even seen me, there was an enormous crowd,' she said, smiling knowingly. 'But I saw what he was up to, and I really feel I ought to warn you before it gets out of hand.'

'What?' Grace asked fearfully, wondering if she was going to say she'd seen him in the arms of another woman.

'Gambling,' said India simply, taking another sip of coffee but scrutinizing Grace all the time over the top of her cup.

Grace forced herself to laugh and said unconvincingly, 'Oh, India, don't be silly, what's wrong with putting on the odd bet? We all do it from time to time, it makes the day more fun.'

'It didn't look fun to him, he looked very white and agitated. I saw him quite a few times putting on large amounts. But he didn't look happy, as if he'd won anything back.'

'Why didn't you confront him about it?' Grace said angrily. 'You know him well enough, surely you could have said something if you were so worried.'

'I didn't like to.' India was defiant. 'He looked so desperate that I knew he would only be furious with me if he knew I'd seen him at it.'

'You wouldn't want that, would you?' Grace snapped, upset by the news, fearful that India, bored of waiting for their marriage to fail, was determined to carry out her threat of taking him from her.

'No, I wouldn't.' India challenged her with her dark eyes. 'Anyway, it's your business to stop him before you lose everything. After all, you did once, didn't you, when you had to move into that dreary flat. Surely you don't want to give up all this.' Her hand swept round the untidy but expensively done-up room.

'We had to move into the flat because of

216

the recession. Lots of people were in financial difficulties then,' Grace retorted.

'Oh, Grace, don't be such a fool. The recession may have been part of it, but his gambling had as much to do with it. This isn't the first time I've seen him putting on large sums, believe me.'

'So why haven't you said anything before?'

'I didn't take much notice of it at first. As you say, lots of people do it and come to no harm, but on Saturday he looked different: more frantic, more obsessed, if you like. I think it's time you did something.' She blew out the smoke from her cigarette, still watching Grace carefully.

Grace felt sick. India was out to cause trouble, she knew she was. They had many friends who raced, who often went with Jonathan, but no one else had expressed this fear. Even if it was true, she did not want India to point it out, could not bear to think that India was watching them, waiting to bring them down.

'Funny how no one else has mentioned it,' she said, getting up and taking a handful of dirty plates into the kitchen.

'Perhaps they're as bad,' India called after her.

Alone in the kitchen Grace fought to calm her fears. Why shouldn't Jonathan put a bit on a horse every so often? He worked long hours for his money, he deserved a little pleasure with it. But she would speak to him, tell him what India had said. That may well antagonize him against India for her meddling, but the thought gave her no pleasure.

India came into the kitchen. 'Haven't you noticed anything about his behaviour, Grace? He must be in a different mood depending on whether he wins or loses.'

Grace looked round the cluttered kitchen, empty pizza boxes piled up on the side. Her cleaning woman didn't come today and she had all this to clear up, the beds to make, a load of washing to do, a trip to the supermarket and a list of telephone calls to make ordering materials for the company she worked for. All this before Jack was dropped home from nursery school.

'Look, India,' she said, briskly stacking the dishwasher, 'you don't know what it's like to be married with children and a job. Every moment of my day is crammed full. Jonathan and I, contrary perhaps to your hopes' — in her anger she could not resist this barb — 'are very happy together. It's all I can do to keep the show on the road. I don't want to waste time speculating on Jonathan's mood swings. He's a wonderful husband and father and works very hard to give us a good standard of living. I will not pry into how he spends some of his hard-earned money.' She crashed the pans together in the sink as if she would rather have hit India with them.

'I only thought it fair to warn you,' India said coldly.

'Thank you for your misplaced concern. Now, if you'll excuse me,' Grace said with as much strength as she could muster, 'I've got a hell of a lot to do before Jack comes home at lunchtime.'

'I'll leave you to it, then.' India looked with distaste round the disordered kitchen. 'But if I was you I'd take some time off your housework and take notice of his gambling. Perhaps if you went racing with him he wouldn't do it. I'll see myself out.'

Grace felt so shaken she had to sit down. India was exaggerating, she told herself. She was unable to accept that their marriage was a success and was determined to undermine it.

She spent a miserable day making excuses for Jonathan, trying to convince herself that India was out to cause trouble. But try as she might she could not get her cousin's words out of her mind.

That evening after dinner she told Jonathan

what India had said, trying to make light of it but determined to dispel her fears at once. His face was grave as she repeated India's words, then he suddenly laughed, took her hands in his and held them tightly.

'Oh, my darling, what a troublemaker she is. Of course I had a bet or two, and yes, I was unlucky that day. Two horses I was certain would win didn't come in, and you know how I hate losing.' He pulled her to him. 'But don't look so anxious, we're hardly on the breadline.'

'But at the weekend you said we had to make economies . . . ' she started, determined to see it through.

'We do, but nothing drastic, we'll soon be fine again, you'll see. Now stop worrying, my darling.' He kissed the frown lines on her forehead. 'I hate to see you so worried. I promise you everything's fine, you know I'd do nothing to harm you and the boys, you're all too important to me.' He looked deep into her eyes and cupped her chin in his hand. 'Surely you believe me and not your meddlesome cousin?'

She flung herself into his arms, holding him close, drawing in the scent of him, the feel of him. The sincerity in his voice calmed her.

'I love you,' she heard him say as he ran his hands down her body.

'I love you too . . . so much,' she answered, letting the leap of desire for him chase away her fears.

14

'Can we come and sleep in a box too, Marianne?' Sebastian asked his grandmother eagerly.

Marianne Wickham hesitated. It would certainly add a poignancy to their cause, two small boys sleeping rough in protest to the plight of the homeless.

Grace, divining her thoughts, hastily broke in. 'Oh no, darling, I think Marianne and her friends would find it difficult to — '

'Please, oh, please, we'll be so good and stay in our box, won't we, Jack?' Sebastian prodded Jack, who was lying on his stomach on the floor playing with his cars, rather heavily with his foot.

'Will there be a television there?' Jack asked.

'Darling, the homeless have nothing. They are cold and wet and hungry, they live on the streets because they have nowhere else to go,' Marianne began, sitting comfortably back on her large, comfy sofa to start on one of her speeches of the injustices of life.

'Can't they live here, then?' Jack asked, barely looking up from his game.

'Yes,' Sebastian said, 'you've plenty of room here and the girls could share their rooms with some of them. We could have our boxes here, right by the television!' He got quite excited as his ideas expanded.

'I don't think they'd be happy here,' Marianne began, looking rather awkward.

'Why not? It's warm and dry and you've oodles of food in the freezer,' Sebastian went on. 'B'sides, you could stay here in your box, not go out in the cold and get ill and be a nuisance to everyone, like Dad says you will.'

'Sebastian, that's enough,' Grace said sternly. She — indeed they all were getting rather tired of Jonathan's mother's do-gooding schemes. Since her last daughter had gone to university she had embraced what she called 'those less fortunate' with a vengeance. Although she was very fond of her grandsons she felt the title 'Granny' would give the wrong impression to her new collection of other socially minded friends. So she insisted on being called by her Christian name and wore her husband's old college scarf, jeans — designed by Versace — and a huge jersey or a long beautifully tailored shirt, and ran various campaigns from the drawing room in her large house in Ladbroke Grove.

'Well, I can't see why they can't come here,' Sebastian said loudly, annoyed that his plan had been put down.

To Grace's relief, Jonathan and his stepfather, Robert, came into the room. Sebastian ran at once to his father and began again on his plan. Robert's pale complexion went even paler. He raked his greying hair back nervously from his forehead, his dark eyes swivelling round the room as if he expected to see down-and-outs bedding down in every corner.

'Oh, Mother,' Jonathan said impatiently, 'not another hare-brained scheme.'

'No, darling, I've tried to explain to Sebastian that they wouldn't be happy here.'

'I'm sure *they'd* be very happy here, but I wouldn't,' Robert said irritably. 'Marianne, I've had enough of these extraordinary schemes of yours. Why can't you help the Red Cross or do Riding for the Disabled? There are so many other worthwhile causes that you could get involved with.'

'This is a worthwhile cause,' Marianne said icily. 'By sleeping out in boxes we will be drawing attention to the plight of the homeless. It is really quite disgraceful that in a so-called civilized country we have people sleeping rough on the streets.'

'I know it's a disgrace, but one of the worst things of being homeless must be the knowledge that they have nowhere else to go, or have any prospect of finding anywhere. You and your friends do have somewhere. Just bedding down for one night with your friends, knowing you'll be coming back to a warm comfortable house with a large breakfast, clean clothes and a hot bath makes your protest seem more like a romp. The real homeless will rightly feel patronized and put upon. I think you'd be far better employed handing out warm blankets and soup to them, or finding them permanent shelter,' Robert said firmly, thrusting his hands deep into his pockets and abruptly leaving the room.

'You don't understand . . . 'Marianne said, following him, going on about his prejudice.

Jonathan sighed loudly, 'Oh, God, my mother,' he said, then, giving Grace a sharp look, said, 'I hope you won't go peculiar when the boys go away to school.'

'You won't, will you, Mum?' Sebastian said anxiously.

'No.' She smiled, hugging him. 'I hope I won't.'

'Will you miss me?' he asked. He was starting prep school that term.

'Of course,' she said, feeling again the

pang of his going, 'but I'll be so busy writing letters to you and coming to see you in matches and concerts and exeats that I won't have time to go peculiar.'

On the way home in the car Grace asked Jonathan, 'Did your investment idea go down well with Robert?' Since she had confronted him with India's warning about his gambling he had been extra tender towards her. He had not been racing but had spent the weekends with them, hiring ponies at the local riding school, taking the boys out and teaching them to ride.

'Yes, he's quite interested. He's also got a few friends who might be interested too. He said he'd arrange a meeting for me with them. I must tell some of our friends as well. They'd get a good return for their money.'

'Explain again,' Grace said, who, though she wasn't madly interested in the financial world, was proud of Jonathan's achievements as an investment manager in the prestigious firm of Meadows and Laing.

'I'm starting up a new company investing in various commodities that have been missed by other markets, all run under the umbrella of Meadows and Laing. If I can get enough people interested, and I should because I've got some rock-solid ideas, they should get quite rich.' He turned and smiled at her, eager as a boy. 'We should make serious money then ourselves.'

She smiled. 'We're fine as we are, darling: two super houses, enough money for holidays abroad and the boys' schooling.'

'You're easily satisfied,' he said affectionately, 'but one should go on growing in life and the ideas I have are good ones. I'm pretty sure there's a big market out there waiting to be tapped.'

He was about to expand some more on his scheme when Jack called out, 'I'm going to be sick,' and promptly was, all over Sebastian.

Cursing Marianne under her breath for filling the boys with her rich Belgian truffles — she always did, however much Grace begged her not to — Grace hauled him out of the car and administered to him.

'Yuck, I stink,' Sebastian screamed. 'I stink, I stink.' He began to howl.

Jonathan sighed heavily, pulling off Sebastian's shirt. 'So does my car. There, we're nearly home, then you can have a bath.'

Jack stood white and shivering on the side of the road dressed only in his underpants while Grace wrapped up his dirty clothes and rammed them in the boot with Sebastian's shirt.

'Poor fellow,' Jonathan said, taking off his jersey and wrapping Jack in it, holding the small boy close to him and rubbing his back gently. 'You'll soon feel better. Do you feel well enough to get back in the car?'

'I'm cold too and I'm not having him next to me,' Sebastian said wanting Jonathan's attention as well.

'I'll give you my jacket when Mummy's cleaned the car.' He grinned at Grace who, grimacing, was mopping up the rest of the mess with some Kleenex.

'I'll take the car to be cleaned after we've washed you lot,' he said when they got home.

'You're such a nice person. So many fathers would run a mile at the sight of sick.'

'I'll run a mile if he does it again,' Sebastian muttered, prodding Jack surreptitiously in the leg and scowling disgustedly at him.

* * *

Curled up together on the sofa, watching the local news on the television later that evening, Jonathan and Grace saw Marianne and her friends parked cheerfully in their boxes among the homeless in the Strand.

'It's too shaming,' Jonathan said. 'Look at

their warm clothes and clean, healthy faces. They look as if they're having a midnight feast instead of a hard, cold night. What's the betting that once the television cameras go they'll escape into a pub.'

'Look.' Grace pointed to the screen. 'There's a down-and-out accosting your mother. She looks horrified.' Then the picture cut back to the studio.

'Trust Mother,' Jonathan said rather scornfully, 'it's so easy for her and her lefty friends to talk about injustice and do their little protests all cosily together, but to have to actually talk to or to touch one of her 'less fortunates' is quite beyond her. He looked quite angry too.'

The telephone woke them early the next morning.

'Jonathan!' Marianne shrieked down the phone. 'Guess who I met last night?'

'The Princess of Wales?' Jonathan said crossly. 'Really, Mother, don't you know it's six-forty-five on Saturday morning? I don't want to know who your social connections are at this hour.'

'No, your father!' Grace could hear her clearly from her side of the bed.

'My father?' Jonathan said stupidly. 'What was he doing there? Was he a cameraman, or part of your do-gooding group?'

229

'No, he was . . . he was homeless.'

'Oh, my God, he wasn't that man we saw talking to you on the television, was he?' Jonathan went white with shock. Grace laid her head against the receiver to hear what Marianne was saying. As she heard her hysterical description of how he was a drunkard and had lost everything, she suddenly remembered the tramp in the churchyard on the day of their wedding and her heart plummeted. She had imagined Jonathan's father as a suave, good-looking older version of Jonathan, with a string of attractive women, a sports car and an expensive house somewhere on the Continent, not a dirty, worn-out tramp.

'Where is he? How did he get like this?' Jonathan said in a daze.

'He's coming here, you must come too. Robert is furious,' Grace heard her say.

'I'll come.' After a few more panicked words from his mother, Jonathan hung up. He lay back in bed and stared at the ceiling. Grace could feel him trembling.

At last she said, 'I told you I saw a . . . scruffy type of man outside the church on our wedding day.'

'You said he looked familiar,' Jonathan said.

'He did, and now I know why. He looked like you, only . . . '

'So it was my father?' He sat up abruptly. 'I wish I'd seen him then, we may have been able to do something. I just can't believe it. How could he have sunk so low?' His face looked anguished.

'When did you last see him?'

'Oh, I don't know . . . when I was at school, I think. Yes, he came down to sports day with a beautiful girl in tow. Mother was not pleased, as you can imagine. He had a Rolls and had brought a huge hamper from Fortnums.' He smiled, remembering, then suddenly he looked sad again. 'It can't possibly be him, she must be mistaken.'

'If only we'd videoed the news, then we could have looked at him again. But it wasn't a very clear picture of the man anyway,' Grace said.

'I did hear from him again when I was at university,' Jonathan said slowly. 'He sent me a cheque for a hundred pounds, with just a note: 'from your errant father'. No address or anything, so I couldn't thank him, but it came in useful, I can tell you.' He sighed. 'I can't bear to think what happened to make him end up like this. I'd better get going.'

'Do you want me to come?'

'We can't bring the boys.' He blanched

again. 'They can't see their grandfather like that, if it is him.'

'What time do you have to be there?'

'I think it can wait an hour on so. Can we park them with someone?'

'They were going to lunch with Sue anyway, I'm sure she'll take them earlier,' Grace said, wishing for the hundredth time that her parents still lived in Kew. She occasionally felt, she knew unfairly, rather resentful of the fact that without discussing it with her they had decided to move to a tiny village in Portugal, explaining that the life and the climate suited them better.

They arrived at Marianne and Robert's house at eight-thirty. Jonathan gave the doorbell two short bursts, his signal for it being him, and Marianne opened the door. 'Thank goodness you've come,' she said, kissing them distractedly. 'I should never have told your father where I lived, but I was so stunned I gave him our address by mistake. He said he'd visit for old times' sake,' she rattled on, quite beside herself with anxiety.

Robert looked haggard. 'I knew this nonsense of hers would end in tears,' he said. 'Drawing attention to herself like that.'

'But none of us knew . . . my father was on the streets,' Jonathan said in fairness.

'No, that's true,' Robert said heavily, 'but now goodness knows what can of worms she's opened.'

'Is he here?' Grace asked.

'No. Maybe he won't come,' Robert said, without much conviction, 'but heaven knows what we do with him when he does come.'

Marianne shepherded them into the large, painted kitchen, still talking incessantly. Her usually pretty face was pallid and puffy. 'My God, how could he? Of course I always knew he'd end up in trouble, he cared for no one but himself. Pleasure, pleasure all the time. Women, wine, gambling. I thought he'd end up in prison, but not on the streets.'

'Tell me exactly what happened, Mother,' Jonathan said firmly. 'Is there some more coffee?'

Grace, seeing that the percolator was empty, and that no one else seemed capable of doing anything, said, 'I'll make some.'

'I was sitting in this box next to Marcus, you know, Albert's son, and Bunty and — '

'I don't care who you were with, Mother,' Jonathan said with irritation.

'I'm getting to it, you're so impatient. This . . . this person came up and said, 'Marianne, don't tell me you're homeless too? At least we can shack up together.

Your blanket looks far warmer than mine. From Harrods, no doubt."

Grace almost laughed. The whole thing was preposterous and she could imagine Marianne's outrage.

'So,' Jonathan said, 'did you recognize him?'

'I knew his voice, but . . . ' She shuddered. 'He used to be such an attractive man, so smart. To think . . . '

'Come on, what else did he say?'

'He said he'd had a run of bad luck . . . Well,' she said with a return of some spirit, 'I said he'd had a run of too much booze by the smell of him. He asked where I lived and if I had any money on me.'

'So you told him?' Jonathan persisted.

'I just said Ladbroke Grove, I don't think I said the number.' She looked bewildered again, as if she was suffering from a bad dream.

'And money?'

'I had just enough for a taxi home. Of course I didn't take my handbag, I'd have had it snatched off me in a second, but I gave him that and took the bus home instead. He went straight off then.'

There was a shrill ring on the doorbell. Everyone froze. Jonathan came to life first. He strode to the front door and opened it.

Everyone else clustered round the kitchen doorway.

A tall, shabby man came into the house. He stared at Jonathan. 'Saw you on your wedding day, my boy,' he said. 'How are you?'

'I don't know what to say . . . ' Jonathan struggled. Grace felt a pang of sympathy for him, knowing he, they all were completely out of their depth.

'Good morning, everyone. You must be Jonathan's wife.' He bowed towards Grace. 'And you' — he gave another mock bow towards Robert — 'my ex-wife's husband.' His bloodshot eyes took in the room. 'Well, at least he's done better for himself than I have.'

'Vincent . . . I . . . What has happened to you?' Marianne at last found her tongue.

'Is that coffee? Looks good and strong, may I have a cup?' he said.

'Of course.' Jonathan was about to take one of the bone-china cups from the cupboard when Marianne sprang forward and handed him one of the mugs she kept for builders or plumbers if they came to work in the house. Jonathan ignored this and poured the coffee into a cup. He asked his father if he'd like something to eat.

'Not just now, thank you,' Vincent said.

235

Grace watched him, horrified. He looked so old and ill; his clothes were ragged and dirty, he was far too thin, but his face was puffy, his eyes sunk in folds of flesh. He began to cough, a deep cruel hacking that seemed to rattle his bones.

'Do sit down,' she said, knowing it wasn't her house, but unable to bear his pitiful state. He made her feel revolted and afraid and yet, she thought, if they had to take him in, she would.

'Thank you, my dear.' For a second she saw the gleam of charm in his face, of an attraction that had now long gone. He sat slowly down in a large wicker chair with fat cushions. They all regarded him intently.

Jonathan broke the silence. 'What has happened to make you like this?'

Vincent shrugged, 'Life, my boy. I threw the wrong dice.'

'But you were rich, had a villa, a . . . '

Vincent drank his coffee as if he hadn't heard what Jonathan said.

'How could you lose it all?' Jonathan said, his voice sharp with terror at this spectacle of his father.

'Run of bad luck and I couldn't get it back. I thought I had friends . . . '

'Friends? You used everyone, you never stayed around long enough to have friends,'

Marianne said bitterly. 'You left me with a tiny baby, not knowing where the next penny was coming from!'

'All right, Mother,' Jonathan said and turned back to his father. 'How long have you been here, like this?'

Vincent shrugged. 'I don't know. I stayed in France. Things got better, then they got worse again and I came back here with a friend. I lost touch with her. Heard of your wedding though.' He smiled. 'I had no present, but I wanted to see who you had married.'

'Why didn't you ring us?' Jonathan said.

Grace, watching Vincent, wanted to say to Jonathan: 'Don't you see he didn't want you to know?'

'So why are you here now? They've been married almost ten years. Have you been living rough all that time?' Marianne asked.

'I've had good times and bad,' he said.

Then his racking cough took hold of him again. Marianne said crossly, 'You should be in hospital, chest like that.'

Robert had not uttered a word, but hunched himself against the wall taking in everything as if it were a play and he did not have a part in it. At the mention of hospital, he brightened. 'Yes,' he said, 'you should be in hospital.'

'Waste of time,' Vincent said. 'Have you a touch of brandy? Haven't tasted decent brandy for ages.'

'It's nine o'clock in the morning, you can't possibly drink brandy. You can have some more coffee.' Marianne walked over to him with the coffee percolator and poured some more into his cup.

'You always were a killjoy, Marianne,' Vincent said mildly.

'Have you nowhere to live at all?' Jonathan said. 'No job, nothing?'

'A friend took me in for a while, after your wedding, then I had a long run of good luck, but recently . . . ' He shrugged.

'So now you have nothing?' Jonathan asked again.

'That's about it. Nothing,' Vincent said wearily as if it had ceased to bother him.

Jonathan looked thoughtful and anxious. He cast a look at Grace. She knew what it said. I don't know this man. He abandoned my mother and me when we most needed him, he has given me a few extravagant gestures when it suited him, but nothing else, and now he has no one, probably through his own fault, a result of his lifestyle. What am I to do?

'Have you seen a doctor?' Grace asked him.

'What do doctors know?' Vincent said, seeming almost to fall asleep in the comfortable chair.

'Well, I'm going to take you to the doctor,' Marianne said briskly as if she could not bear him to stay another moment in her smart clean house. 'I'll take you over to St Mary's, they'll see you.'

Grace knew she would not take him to their private GP. It would not do among her smart friends; they might all shout about the treachery of the Government towards the weaker members of society but would not countenance one of their group being seen in close contact with someone as shabby as Vincent, let alone having been married to him.

'I'll take him to our doctor,' Jonathan said firmly. 'I'll give you some clean clothes, we're about the same size, and then we'll go.'

Grace gave him a warm smile, touched at his generosity towards this man who had caused him so much insecurity by abandoning him as a child. The situation was appalling, but they would cope with it.

'But, Jonathan, the hospital is used to . . .' Marianne gulped, waved her hand desperately in the air as if the word she was thinking of was too unpleasant to be uttered.

Jonathan shot her a despised look. 'I

will deal with it, Mother,' he said. 'So come on . . . ' He laughed awkwardly, not quite able to call him Dad. 'Vincent, shall we go?'

With a great effort Vincent stirred himself. 'What. Go? No thank you, my boy, I don't wish to go to the doctor. I'll be on my way now. Just wanted to see your set-up.' He ran his eyes wearily round the room. Robert looked decidedly uneasy as if Vincent was casing the place to return and burgle it later.

'But come back with us,' Jonathan said, 'have a bath, clean clothes, a meal.'

'No thank you.' He got up stiffly. 'No hope of a tenner from anyone is there?' He smiled feebly.

'Of course, here's twenty.' Jonathan took a twenty-pound note from his wallet and handed it over. Then after a second he took out a couple of ten-pound notes, all he had in his wallet, and handed them over too. 'But please come with us to the doctor.'

'No, I'll be off now. But I know where you are if I should need you.' He gave Marianne an ironic smile. 'Does it give you a thrill to sleep in a box on the Strand?'

Marianne had the grace to blush. 'I was just trying to draw attention to the plight of the homeless,' she muttered.

'I'd have thought we were pretty obvious, but I bet you never thought you'd actually know one of them socially, did you?'

'Please stop this. You must come home with us, get on your feet again,' Jonathan said firmly.

'Leave me be,' Vincent said. 'It's too late. I don't want to come with you, I have somewhere I can go. Thank you all the same.'

'I'll give you my number,' Jonathan said, writing it down and handing it to him. 'Promise you'll get in touch if you need anything. I'm sure we could set you up again.'

'Thank you.' Gravely Vincent took the piece of paper from him, folded it with the notes and put them away somewhere in his clothes. His eyes took in a bottle of whisky standing on the side and he said, 'Let me have that bottle, Marianne. It will keep out the cold.'

'You shouldn't drink, you . . . '

'Take it,' Robert snatched it up and handed it to him as if it would speed him on his way.

Vincent said nothing but took it, his hands shaking. He went at once to the front door, opened it and left without saying goodbye, leaving everyone staring after him, stunned.

A few minutes later when she went upstairs to the bathroom, Grace saw Vincent from the window. He was gulping greedily from the bottle right there in the street. The whisky was running down his chin as he desperately fought to fill himself with the alcohol. She was filled with pity and revulsion. She wouldn't tell Jonathan what she'd seen.

15

'I saw India today,' Jonathan said to Grace as they sat over dinner.

'Oh! How was she?' Grace felt the familiar stab of alarm in the pit of her stomach at the mention of her name. For the last few months, much to Grace's relief, India had been in New York with a rich financier, well out of harm's way. The knowledge that she was back in London filled her with unease. Had her affair finished? Would she be round here again accosting her with more malicious stories about Jonathan's gambling? Trying another tactic to take him away from her?

He laughed. 'She was terribly pleased to see me. I was quite surprised, you know how superior she used to be.'

'Where did you see her?' Grace fought to remain calm, searching his face for signs of attraction, of pleasure at seeing India again.

'In Bond Street. I told you I had a lunch up there today. It was after that. She called my name from the other side of the street and we had a chat. We haven't seen her for ages. We ought to have her to dinner, you know, she is your first cousin.'

Grace's lips felt too frozen to smile. Images of India, always smart, always beautiful, turning her full attention on to Jonathan, listening avidly to his words, swam into her mind. No man, unless he were made of stone, could fail to be attracted by her.

Sometimes Grace scolded herself for being too paranoid about India and her real hold over Jonathan. Were her fears not fuelled by the power India still had of making her feel inferior? Did she not still feel amazed, deep down, that Jonathan had chosen her and not India? Perhaps she clung on too hard to her love for Jonathan, wanting to be the centre of his life, as he was of hers. She had also learnt, especially since the birth of the children, that the joy of love was tempered with the fear of loss.

'So what is she doing? Has she come back for good? Finished with her American lover?' Grace asked in a rush, determined to know the worst at once.

'I don't know about the lover, but she told me she'd just been staying with Caspar and Sophie who are based in New York, as you know. He's enjoying his new career in the financial world. Sir William and his lady love are still at Elmley. I didn't actually ask about her mother, in case she's still with that odious young man she brought with her to

Caspar's wedding.'

'I suppose India's not thinking of getting married?' Grace asked hopefully.

'No, she doesn't think much of marriage, but she's not alone, she informed me.' He laughed. 'She's a beautiful woman, so elegant.'

Grace's stomach felt filled with stones. She felt irrationally that in praising India's beauty and elegance he was admitting that she had none.

He went on, 'But she's as hard as nails. There's a sort of ruthlessness about her as if she's determined to get what she wants.'

Grace looked at him sharply. She longed to say: Don't you see it's you she wants? Instead she asked, 'What do you mean?'

'She talked about one of her lovers, Max Dalbert. He's incredibly rich, you know, the jeweller. He wants to marry some young woman and have a son, but India's against it.'

'But if she doesn't believe in marriage and won't marry him herself — she's still got time to have children, after all — she can hardly blame him for wanting to marry someone else.'

'He's had two wives already, and has a daughter. He also feels this marriage would be a good one, businesswise. India wants things to stay as they are, with him staying free just for her.'

'How like India,' Grace said sourly. 'You seemed to have had quite a talk.'

'We had a coffee, talked about all sorts of things. I even told her about my new company. She seemed quite impressed, said she'd introduce me to Max and a few of his influential friends. Once I have a few well-known people interested it'll snowball, you see.'

Grace got up from the table and cleared away their plates. She wanted to be alone for a moment to control her fears. This was the first time Jonathan had talked so favourably about India. Was it just because he'd realised that she'd be helpful in finding rich people to invest in his scheme? Or was her obvious beauty and dogged determination to have him paying off? Now that India's lover seemed about to marry someone else, would his defection make India even more determined to have Jonathan?

She rinsed the plates and stacked them in the dishwasher, vainly trying to calm herself. She had never had any reason to believe that Jonathan no longer loved her or was bored of married life, but then she'd worked so hard to make their life together a success: watching out for any pitfalls ahead, smoothing them down and out of sight if they came, determined that everything would be wonderful. She knew that he still went racing and, partly to show herself she wasn't going to be fazed by India's tittle-tattle about his gambling and partly because their life seemed so happy and even at the moment, she did not enquire if he gambled or not.

Once you stop trusting the man you love, a woman friend had said to her recently, and feel you should be going through his pockets and listening in to his telephone calls, the relationship is over.

There was something else too in her mind that made her stop enquiring into his financial affairs. Only a few months ago she'd discovered that Uncle William had all but paid for her education at the small convent she'd been to. Her parents had never told her before. Her mother, apropos of something else, had mentioned it in a telephone call. When she'd questioned her, Olivia had airily dismissed it as something in the past and anyway, she'd said, surely Grace had known about it, it was never a secret. It had made Grace feel further beholden to her uncle. She didn't know if India knew about it, but she felt it gave her another reason to despise her; despise her father for not abandoning his painting and getting a more lucrative job, her mother for putting up with it and allowing them to take the money from her rich brother-in-law. Since then Grace had felt that maybe she was relying too much on Jonathan to keep them and she was now working hard as an interior decorator, determined to contribute more to their living expenses.

She began to wipe round the kitchen surfaces aimlessly, unable to quell the feelings of unease that had been stirred up in her at Jonathan's meeting with India. She wondered rather hysterically if there had been other meetings she didn't know about and which excused the slight changes in his character that she'd noticed recently.

It was, she told herself, hardly surprising that seeing his father again and in such a state would affect him. He'd become determined to find him, but even though he contacted the Salvation Army, walked the streets questioning other homeless people, visited all the refuges, he'd had no luck.

'He's sure to have found some gullible woman to take him in,' Marianne had said when Jonathan had asked her to enquire through her contacts with the various charities for the homeless. 'But he won't be found until he wants to be, believe me. I spent years searching for him when he left us, but every time I thought I'd caught up with him, he'd gone again.'

But apart from wanting to find Vincent, to help him, Jonathan had recently seemed to be driven by some fearful energy in his work. He toiled long hours to set up this new company, having dinner parties, meeting people, pushing his ideas at them as if time was somehow running out. It was a new side to him Grace hadn't seen before and it unnerved her, making her wonder now if it would make him more vulnerable to India's advances.

He came into the kitchen and picked up an apple from the fruit bowl and dug his teeth into it. 'I've got some work to do, darling, see you later.' He kissed her as she stood at the sink rinsing the dishcloth, putting his arms round her and holding her to him for a moment. She dropped the dishcloth and turned in his arms and held him tight, snuggling her face into his neck. They stood together for a moment, then he released her. 'I won't be long, darling, and we'll have an early night.'

'Do you really have to work so hard?' she said, still holding him.

'Yes, of course I do.' He smiled, pinching her nose playfully. 'This house, the cottage, the boys' education, all devour money.'

'I know they do, but if they devour too much we could move somewhere smaller. I don't want you to kill yourself working to give us so much. I'd rather see more of you in a smaller house, even sell the cottage, if you want to.'

He smiled affectionately. 'You really are the most unusual girl, you know, darling. You should see some of the poor bastards in my company, their wives demand so much from them, always wanting the house done up, or a new one, or an expensive holiday abroad. Their wretched husbands are like hamsters on a wheel, running round and round striving to keep up a standard of living that they are too exhausted to enjoy.'

'I don't want that to happen to us,' she said. 'We have plenty and with what I earn — I did very well doing up that house in Battersea, remember — you don't need to kill yourself for us.'

'I know, darling.' He took his arms from her and began to walk restlessly round the kitchen. His face had suddenly gone pinched and strained. 'This new company has got to succeed, it must, don't you see?' His fists were clenched now. 'I'm determined that it will work.'

'I'm sure it will, darling,' she said quickly, afraid now of this mood of his. She moved to take him in her arms again, to seduce him out of it. It made her feel so insecure and afraid, but he moved away.

'It must work, I couldn't bear us to be poor — '

'But we're not!' she broke in.

'No, and we never will be. Remember the time we had to sell the house and move into that tiny flat?'

'Yes. But that was only a hiccup, you got us out of it.' India's sneering words that it was his gambling that was responsible for it and she should admit it cut into her. To dispel them she went on. 'We are so lucky compared to lots of people, look at Michael Hilder being made redundant and . . . '

'Look at my father,' he said savagely, 'He had it all, money, women, a good life. Now look at him.' His voice was anguished, his body taut.

'I know, it's terrible,' she said gently, 'but he drinks. Surely that's what's destroyed him.' The picture of Vincent dragging greedily on the whisky bottle came back to her mind. 'There's no reason why we should be poor. Your job seems as secure as anyone's today, and I'm doing well, and if anything did happen we'd have to sell the houses. At least we have those.' Her soothing words were to comfort herself as much as him.

'I know,' he said unconvincingly, 'but I want to be sure of it. I want to have enough money so that we need never, ever worry.' He kissed her and abruptly left the room and she heard him go upstairs into his study and shut the door.

For the rest of the evening she felt jittery and unhappy. She remembered how long ago he had said he'd love to live somewhere like Elmley. She hoped he wasn't striving for that. The last thing she wanted was such a huge house that would surely swallow money by the bankful. She wished she could talk to him about it, but she knew that every time she asked him direct questions about such matters he would laugh, take her in his arms and tell her not to worry. Only recently, she'd noticed there hadn't been much laughter, but a hint of annoyance in his eyes at her probing, which made her afraid that such questions would make him irritated with her.

She went into Jack's room and sat by his bed listening to his breathing, sometimes touching him as if his warm, sleeping body would give her reassurance. She could not shake off the feeling that the stability of her family was being eroded, that the foundations which she'd thought were so strong were beginning to crack.

She told herself firmly that she was overwrought at Jonathan's mention of India, that she was merely imagining sinister shadows in the bright sunshine of her life. She forced herself to think of her blessings. Sebastian had taken to prep school with gusto, he had gone with two of his best friends and had made many more. Jack, with his easy temperament, was also flourishing at school, socially if not academically. Her job was going very well: she had two new clients who'd given her carte blanche for their whole houses. Most importantly she had Jonathan and their marriage was strong and happy. So why did she feel this unease? Was it just because India seemed to have come back in their lives again? India who always got what she wanted in the end?

★ ★ ★

'But I don't want to go down to Elmley,' Grace said to Jonathan, when he told her with excitement that India had invited them all down for a weekend. She was suspicious of his obvious delight at the invitation. 'Besides, you never wanted to go when we were asked before.'

'Well, we probably had something better to do. Anyway, Caspar and Sophie will be there,

253

and I haven't seen them for ages, and we can bring the boys. They'll love it, especially the horses,' he added, his face glowing.

She couldn't be selfish and refuse the invitation when she knew they would get such pleasure from it. Running free in the grounds, climbing the vast old trees, visiting the stables as she had as a child. Why should she let India spoil such a wonderful place for them? She scolded herself fiercely, mocking herself for wanting to say, stupidly, I'm afraid India will take you from me, break up our happy family. Besides, it would hurt him to think that she trusted him so little.

It was the end of July and the weather was perfect for a summer weekend in the country. There was a scent of flowers and new-mown grass; the sun touched the old house, making it glow like a jewel among the ancient trees. The soft blue of the sky made a perfect backdrop to the idyll of an English summer.

'Isn't this magic,' Jonathan said, slowing down the car as they came up the drive, to take in the house standing proud among the trees. 'I swear there is no more beautiful country in the world than Britain on a summer's day.'

'It is lovely,' Grace agreed, feeling, despite her dread of seeing India, the slight frisson of excitement that Elmley always invoked in her. In any season it had its beauty, even in the grey rawness of winter.

'Where are the horses?' Sebastian said, wriggling in the back seat, impatient to be out of the car and running over the grass.

'We'll see them soon,' Jonathan said as they arrived outside the massive front door. Jack and Sebastian opened the car door and almost fell out in their eagerness to be free.

Frobisher, looking rather old and faded now, opened the door to them. 'Everyone's by the pool,' he announced.

After they'd been shown to their rooms they took out their swimming things and went through the house, across the garden to the pool. Sir William thought swimming pools ugly things and had built it behind a wall smothered in tumbling roses. Their scent was quite intoxicating in the still, warm air.

Grace braced herself to meet India, feeling just as she had as a child when India used to put her down. They went through the wrought-iron gate into the pool enclosure.

'My dear, welcome.' Uncle William, in an enormous pair of faded, baggy bathing shorts, lumbered over to greet her. 'And these are your boys?' He surveyed them with interest. Grace prodded them to remind them of their manners.

'Hello, Great-uncle William,' they intoned, staring at him with interest.

'Right, first one in gets a quid,' he laughed, awkward under their gaze. With a quick glance at their mother to check this was all right, the boys rushed to get changed. Jack was in first, having no qualms about undressing right there in front of everyone.

Anthea was drinking a Pimms, having just finished a game of tennis with Caspar, and Sophie was there with their two little girls, but there was no sign of India.

Caspar and Jonathan quickly paired up, laughing and ragging each other as if they were still at school. Grace sat down beside Sophie, who looked pale and ill.

'How pretty your girls are, Sophie.' Grace said, smiling at them. One was about three and sat solidly at Anthea's feet wearing a sunhat and playing with some little animal figures; the other, hardly more than a baby, slept under a canopy on a sunbed.

'Thank you.' Sophie smiled as if she was used to her daughters being complimented. 'Your boys are just like Jonathan, very good-looking. They are older than I thought.'

They talked of the children for a while, then Sophie confided that she was pregnant again and so hated it, feeling ill all the way through. 'Let's hope it's a boy this time,' she sighed, 'you are lucky having two of them. Caspar will be furious if we don't have a son to inherit Elmley.'

Grace glanced over to Caspar and Jonathan. He was a very handsome man, but he'd never attracted her, even in her teenage years, because he looked too much like India. She knew too that he had the same determination as India, and she could imagine him bullying Sophie into having lots of babies until they got the son he craved.

'There's not much you can do about it,' Grace said lamely. 'There have been all sorts of theories since time began on how to get the sex you want, but I don't think there is any proven way, do you?'

Sophie sat up slowly on the sunbed. 'I don't know. I tried washing myself out with bicarb this time. Caspar has a theory that I am too acid and kill off his male sperms, only allowing the female ones to get through. I just hope it works. I hate pregnancy. Apart from feeling sick all the way through, the births are always long and difficult. I just hope this is the last one I have to put up with.'

Grace smiled sympathetically, not knowing what to say. The Gratton children, she thought with foreboding, usually got what they wanted, regardless of anyone else.

India appeared at lunchtime with Max Dalbert. 'How good to see you, Grace,' she said without enthusiasm, kissing her briefly. Grace watched her kiss Jonathan, searching for the smallest sign of flirtation, but she did so quickly and without fuss, introducing Max to them.

Max was about ten years older than India. He was a tall, broad-shouldered man with the colouring of someone who'd lived a lot of the time in the sun. He had a well-cared-for look about him, sleek and polished. His hair was dark, just going grey, and he had a full mouth and deep-set eyes that seemed to home in and study people intently as if he could see into their souls. He took Grace's hand and raised it to his lips.

'Enchanted,' he said. She detected a slight mid-Mediterranean accent, and to her annoyance she felt a sliver of warmth as his eyes appraised her. Foreign men, she warned herself firmly, pride themselves on their hold over women.

'And how are you, my poor Sophie?' he said, kissing her hand. 'You must walk, you know, all this lying about is making you sick. My sister, who has six children, walks a lot while she is expecting. She says it disperses the toxins in the blood.'

'It's too hot,' Sophie moaned, but Grace thought she seemed to perk up at Max's attention.

'Come walk with me, we will go in the shade of the trees,' he said, pulling gently at her hand.

Grumbling, but only mildly, Sophie obeyed him and, tucking her hand into his arm, he took her away.

Grace watched India's reaction to this, but she seemed not to notice. She said to Caspar, 'I wish you'd sell that hunter of yours before you go back to New York. He's too bad-tempered for anyone but you to ride.'

'I won't just yet,' Caspar said. 'Now, have you heard Jonathan's investment plan? It sounds good.'

'Tell me some more about it,' India said, turning to Jonathan with a smile. 'Max will be interested too.'

'Investment, what investment?' Sir William, who'd been dozing in his chair, perked up. 'Got something hot, Jonathan? I'm always asking Caspar for some tips, but he doesn't seem to put me on to anything.'

'You're fine as you are, Father,' Caspar said. 'You don't want to take risks at your age.'

'I don't know.' He winked at Anthea who smiled back at him. They still love each other, Grace thought with pleasure, seeing this. The people who said she'd thrown herself at him for his title and money were wrong. She saw that India had seen the look too, and it had annoyed her. Her expression tightened for a second, but then she smiled, put her hand casually on Jonathan's arm and said, 'So, will you make me a fortune?'

'I hope so,' he laughed, and launched into a description of his ideas. India listened spellbound, her soft red lips slightly parted in wonder as if he were spouting endearments instead of flat, financial details. Grace busied herself with the boys, praising their diving and swimming efforts loudly, determined to remind Jonathan where his loyalties lay.

Grace would have enjoyed the weekend more if she hadn't had to be so vigilant over India's interest in Jonathan. India never flirted openly. She'd once told Grace that only desperate women needed to sink so low. But then she'd never needed to, for it was the men who swarmed round her. However, to Grace's relief Jonathan seemed more intoxicated by his investment plans than by India's charms.

Grace spent a lot of time occupied with the children. Sophie had given her nanny the weekend off and Grace found herself helping her with Natasha and Alice too, India taking no notice of her nieces at all, except sometimes to swat at them distractedly as if they were annoying wasps. Caspar seemed to ignore them altogether, as if they were a species quite unknown to him.

Normally Grace wouldn't have minded; she felt sorry for Sophie's ill health and enjoyed being with her own boys. This time, however, she couldn't help feeling that India belittled her by it, seeing her as no better than a childminder, and certainly a dull companion for Jonathan. She was also disconcerted by Max, who watched everyone intently, reminding her of a lizard on a rock, eyes always alert. She felt that he guessed at her fears and got some sort of pleasure from her discomfort.

'I don't like him,' she said to Jonathan when they'd gone to bed.

'Why? He's nice enough,' Jonathan said, 'he seems quite interested in my new company. We're to have a meeting in London soon. He knows some quite influential people he could put my way.'

'What about his relationship with India? At times he seems to be quite fond of her, yet at others he's almost detached, and she seems often to ignore him altogether.'

She thought back to dinner where Max had fussed over all the women, including Anthea, while India seemed to take no notice. She talked animatedly to everyone else — they had further guests who came in for dinner — but ignored Anthea pointedly at all times. Grace knew she could never forgive her stepmother for living at Elmley, bringing a different atmosphere here and, as she saw it, siphoning her father's love and attention away from her.

'You have to be a strong character to cope with India,' Jonathan said, putting on his silk pyjamas and getting into bed beside her. 'And I think it's a good thing he's so much older than her. He's known her some time, I understand, before her fling with that American in New York. But I can't help feeling he's a sort of stopgap and she's using him, and if anyone else better comes along she'll ditch him.' He picked up a few of the books arranged on the bedside table and idly looked through their titles.

'Why do you think that?' Grace asked, terror striking at her. Had India been flirting with Jonathan when she wasn't there?

'Well, she had her American, and various other men have been linked with her, and when she's had enough of them she comes back to Max, and he seems to put up

262

with her behaviour. Odd, other people's love lives.' He tossed aside the books and took her in his arms. 'Let's forget about them, darling. Remember that time at New Year? Thank goodness we can make love here in bed instead of in those dusty old attics. Remember those stuffed birds and things?' He laughed. 'So unnerving, like voyeurs watching our every move.'

'Yes, we've come a long way since then.' She forced herself to laugh with him, clinging tight to him as if he was going to be snatched away from her.

The next afternoon Grace found herself alone with Max. Caspar and Jonathan had taken the children to the stables. Uncle William and Anthea had gone out to lunch with friends. She'd got caught up with Sophie, who gave her a blow-by-blow account of her last labour, leaving Grace feeling thoroughly relieved that she was not going to have any more children herself. Max then appeared and Sophie announced that she was going to lie down on her bed. She and Max were left together in the garden reading the Sunday papers. She had not seen India since after lunch.

Grace felt on edge. She wondered if India had somehow extricated Jonathan from the rest of the stables party and was alone with him somewhere. She was about to get up and go and join them all when Max put down his paper and said: 'Your husband is a charming man. You are a charming couple' — he smiled — 'and your sons are very good-looking boys.'

'Thank you.' She felt herself blushing.

'What do you think of his new company, his investment scheme?' he asked her unexpectedly, watching her intently.

'Oh, I . . . ' She felt very stupid suddenly. Jonathan had explained it to her quite a few times, and she had listened, making a few comments. But he seemed to change his ideas quite often and he became impatient when she pointed this out, saying it was too complicated for anyone not in the market to understand properly. She felt now that she had no real knowledge of the intricate ins and outs of it.

'I'm sure it's very sound,' she said with more confidence than she felt. 'After all Meadows and Laing are so respected and since they seem to value him so much, he's obviously very talented in that field,' she finished proudly, knowing Jonathan wanted people like Max to join his new company.

'But you don't really know anything about it?' Max said.

'Y . . . yes . . . I, well, I leave most of that

to him. I mean I'm an interior decorator and good at that, and — '

'I'm sure you are,' he broke in.

'And Jonathan wouldn't dream of telling me how to do my job, unless I asked him of course, but even then, he might not know the best fabric, the best colour scheme or whatever.' She laughed rather frantically under his gaze. 'I feel like that with his job, a bit out of my depth. He's the expert in that field.'

'Has he started any other new companies?'

'Not exactly, not like this one. This is his own idea, just his.' Then seeing Max's thoughtful expression she pushed on, 'But he's brilliant at his job, knows exactly what he's doing, it's bound to be a success. He's working so hard to set it up.'

'Really.' He gave her another intent look, then suddenly smiled, a warm and almost tender smile that made her feel quite flustered. 'My dear, you are a wonderful wife. What a lucky man he is, and two strapping sons. How I envy him.'

'*I* am lucky,' she said, feeling awkward at his words.

'Then you both are. I wish I had a son, and so I understand does Caspar. Well, of course he has a title and all this for a son to inherit.' He swept his hand round the garden

'Ah,' he sighed, 'there are some things money and position cannot buy.'

Grace did not know what to say, not really knowing what Max's position was with India, remembering Jonathan had told her he wanted to marry some other woman and have a son. As if he guessed this he said, 'I shall not marry India. I cannot imagine her as a wife, can you? Some women make better mistresses, others better wives.' His eyes were warm on her. 'You, for instance, are a perfect wife, India a perfect mistress.'

'Do you think so?' She found herself feeling rather put out. A mistress sounded far more exciting, even though she didn't want to be one.

'I do. I think arranged marriages are the best idea, a sort of business arrangement that can be mutually satisfactory and civilized.'

'Best for whom?' Grace burst out, annoyed now with his arrogance.

He laughed, a deep rich sound. 'Now you are cross with me. For both people, of course. I know the day when women needed a man to support them is supposed to have gone. You women are so clever at making your own money these days, but don't fool me that most don't still crave the protection — socially, I mean — a man gives them. Women don't look good alone.

266

If you don't believe me go and look in any large international hotel and see the sad collection of business women dining alone in their smart executive suits.'

'You exaggerate,' Grace said. 'I like having a husband, I agree, well, one I love. Marriage must be hell if you marry a brute.'

'Or a bitch. Believe me, I know,' Max said with feeling. 'That is why an arranged marriage can be so much better. You both like and respect each other, have a role to play and take it on gladly, and don't fight and squabble for a different pecking order.'

'I suppose for some people. I prefer to choose who I want to live with, and to love them.' Grace felt uncomfortable talking with him. It seemed to her that he was out to ridicule her simple, happy life, make her feel somehow inferior and rather naïve that she had settled for it.

As if he guessed this he laughed. 'You are very lucky then. I married two women I loved and they both did their best to destroy me.'

'So why marry again, if you're happy as you are?'

'I want a son. I have worked hard to build up my business. I shall not bore you with the old story of a poor Jewish boy who started with nothing' — he smiled sardonically — 'but now I have an empire of sorts and I want a son to take it on.'

'But you have a daughter, don't you?'

'Yes, but she is stupid like her mother. Very beautiful and a sweet person, but' — he shrugged — 'no good for business. Besides, I have old-fashioned ideas. I want a son.'

'I see.' Grace closed her eyes from the glare of the sun. She felt suddenly rather exhausted. No one is content, she thought. Caspar has all this, a lovely wife and two dear little girls but he wants a son too. Jonathan wants more money, though we are comfortable enough as we are. Why do people go on striving for more without enjoying what they already have?

'You disapprove, Grace, don't you?' Max said gently.

'I don't understand why people are never content. You, Caspar, us, we have so much and yet . . .'

'You stagnate if you stay cosily in one rut. Besides it is human nature to strive for more.'

'Until it destroys you,' Grace said without knowing why. Suddenly she felt cold as if a wind had cut through the warm sun.

'It destroys the weak,' Max said easily. 'Ah, here is India. No one can accuse her of being weak. She knows just what she wants and will get it too, no matter what, will you not my darling?' He made space for her beside him on the bench.

'Of course, as you will.' She laughed as she sat down beside him and leant up against him. 'And you, Grace,' she said in the old superior voice Grace dreaded, 'you know what you want too, don't you?'

'Yes, and I'm lucky enough to have it,' Grace said defiantly, feeling distinctly uneasy as if they were both ganging up against her, exposing her weakness through their strength.

16

She could now really begin to enjoy her own dinner party, Grace thought with relief. The first two courses had been eaten with relish and now they sat comfortably round the table enjoying the pudding and the cheese and she could stop wondering if the vegetables were over cooking or the sauce congealing. It was all but finished and it had been a success.

'So you will come with us to Méribel at half-term?' Miles Godwin said, smiling at Grace. 'It'll be fun for the boys all being together.'

'It would be lovely,' she said glancing down the table at Jonathan for confirmation of the idea.

'And do try and come to Cornwall in the summer,' Sue said, 'Mummy will be away and she's lent us the house for a month. It's so nice to get out of London in August.'

Grace agreed and sat back in her chair and looked at them all, feeling happy and secure. They were lucky to have such good friends, people whose children fitted in with theirs giving them lifelong friends too. Most of her childhood friends had moved away

270

from London, but she'd barely time to miss them with all the new ones she'd made since her marriage to Jonathan. Having children helped as they had met many nice parents through the schools and they had a very full and enjoyable social life.

'I must say I'm delighted with your investment scheme, Jonathan, I made quite a tidy sum last month,' Richard Kenyon said. He was flushed and Grace suspected a little drunk.

'Good,' Jonathan said briefly, busying himself pouring more wine.

'I hope to do better this month than last,' Miles said. 'How's it looking?' Grace thought he sounded a little belligerent, and wondered whether to suggest the women left the room and went and gossiped in the drawing room leaving the men to discuss the investment. Jonathan had explained to her that some people had done better than others, but by the end of a year or so, everyone would have about the same return for their money. It was unfortunate that Richard seemed to be pleased with his return, and Miles did not, and she did hope the evening would not disintegrate into bad feeling because of it.

Jonathan smiled easily. 'It'll all work out, Miles, believe me,' he said. 'Let's lunch next week and I'll go over it again with you.'

271

'The paperwork was quite clear, but I won't say no to lunch,' Miles said. 'I just assumed if we all invested the same sum in the same projects, we'd get back the same return.'

'It's probably all above you, old chap, don't worry about it. Jonathan will look after you. You always were a thicko over difficult words,' Richard guffawed. Then he said to the rest of the table: 'He once wrote a whole essay on Macduff instead of Macbeth, got them muddled up and got no marks for it. Imagine that.'

'He just gets muddled because he's dyslexic, not because he's stupid,' Pandora, Miles's wife, said sharply. 'He'd hardly be running his own business if he were stupid, would he?'

'Keep cool, love, I was only teasing,' Richard said. 'I just think Jonathan's scheme is brilliant, you have to be a bit patient, that's all. That's right, isn't it, Jonathan?'

'Yes.' Jonathan smiled at Miles. 'Things will get better, I promise you.'

'What is all this? I seem to have missed out, stuck away in Frankfurt,' Gerald Sheldon said. 'I haven't been told of this goldmine. Is it too late to cash in on it?'

'I'd be pleased to tell you about it,' Jonathan said. 'Let's meet next week.'

'Coffee, tisane?' Grace said cheerfully, catching Jonathan's eye to remind him to go into the kitchen and make them. She felt she'd had enough of this discussion and with Richard a little worse for wear, it might easily get nasty. Pandora was very protective of her husband and his dyslexia, more so as her son suffered from it.

Jonathan got up and began to take coffee orders: 'Two proper, one decaff, mint tea, yes, I think we have camomile.' He ticked them off on his fingers then when Richard said, 'Any hope of an Irish coffee?' lost count and had to start again.

'I wish Richard hadn't brought up how well he was doing with your company,' Grace said when they at last went to bed. 'I hate discussing money at dinner parties, someone always feels hard done by.'

'I agree, darling, but you know Richard when he gets a bit on board,' Jonathan said. He kissed her, then turned over on his side to sleep.

'But things are going well with it, aren't they? I mean, why has Richard done so much better than Miles if they put in the same amount at the same time? They invested in the same things, didn't they?' She could feel Jonathan tense beside her.

'It's late, darling,' he said, 'I'll explain

another time, but everything's fine. Good-night.'

''Night,' she said, but she lay awake for another hour, for some reason quite unable to sleep.

* * *

'That fireplace is quite dreadful, wrong period entirely,' Marsha Reid said to Grace, 'and what colour shall we have in here? It's quite a bright room.' She strutted about, a small, plump, overdressed and over-made-up woman. Grace hated her.

'I thought a soft yellow with touches of blue, and some white,' Grace said, taking out her books of fabrics and wallpapers. She was tired of Marsha who changed her mind almost every day and obviously had nothing else to do but redecorate her house. She moved fairly often, getting easily bored.

'I wonder if her husband is one of the poor bastards in your firm, working their guts out so their wives can relieve their boredom by spending their money,' she'd said exhaustedly to Jonathan after a particularly bad day with her.

'I . . . I wouldn't know.' Her words seemed to startle him from his thoughts. He had been so introspective recently, almost secretive, shutting himself away for long hours in his study, snapping at the boys if they made a noise. She was beginning to worry about it, worry that he was getting bored with her, worry that India might be worming her way into his affections through her frequent telephone calls to fix up yet another meeting with a rich friend who professed interest in his investment scheme.

'And I think glass shelves in that recess, what do you think? No, perhaps not. Why don't we make a cupboard, put on some pretty old doors. Do you know where we can find some?' Marsha went on, breaking into her thoughts.

Grace struggled to smile and remain polite; after all, this was her client, paying her a lot of money to do up her house. 'It would be better to have doors made from old, seasoned wood, if that's what you want. Now, let me leave you with these pattern books. We'd better get the stuff ordered, it can take some weeks,' she said briskly, wanting to go and collect Jack from school, but not saying so as even though she'd given Marsha most of her day, her client would become sulky if Grace suggested that she had another life to lead.

'I thought we'd discuss the bathrooms,' Marsha said moving towards the door to go upstairs.

'We've agreed they've got to be completely gutted and I thought you wanted to go round your friend's bath shop,' Grace said, remembering Marsha's enthusing about this shop and its elegant baths.

'I did.' Marsha looked like a spoilt child, her bright red mouth drooping in her little-girl face. 'But I wanted to discuss a few things first.'

Somehow Grace managed to extricate herself from this pink and perfumed middle-aged child and she ran into the school to find Jack alone in the classroom with his teacher.

'Mum, where were you?' he said, jumping up, relief and annoyance bunched on his face. Miss Becky looked rather annoyed too.

'I'm sorry, darling, I had a rather difficult client,' she looked to Miss Becky for sympathy, but Miss Becky just held out her hand to Jack.

'Goodbye, Jack.'

Jack stuck his grubby hand in hers, and as soon as he'd left the school began petulantly: 'I thought you'd forgotten all about me, and I could have gone home with David, *he's* going to McDonald's for tea with his nanny.'

'I'd never, ever forget you, darling,' Grace

said, feeling sick with guilt and fury at Marsha. 'You do know that, don't you?' She suddenly felt desperate that he would ever think that again.

'Can we go to tea at McDonald's?'

Grace, who knew David's nanny preferred to take him out as often as she could to save her having to cook at home, said, 'No, darling, not today. You could choose a cake at the French baker's though, would you like that?' A peace offering, she thought, for her being late.

'I'd rather have McDonald's, why can't I?' He looked sulky. 'I wish I had a nanny, then I could go there every day.'

Grace ignored this and said as brightly as she could to divert him, 'Tell me about games, did you play football today?'

Later that night when she'd read to him and tucked him up in bed, she sat idly reading the paper waiting for Jonathan to come home. Dinner, a lamb casserole, was keeping warm in the oven. It was twenty to ten and she was fighting to ignore the feelings of panic that were churning around inside her. He was often late when there was a crisis, or he had to contact people on the American stock market, but he always rang to tell her. A few days ago he had mentioned vaguely that he may have to go away suddenly on business. This was nothing new, but she began to wonder now if he'd gone without telling her.

These last weeks he'd sometimes been quite agitated, which concerned her, too. It was so unlike him. When she had questioned him about it, he had told her not to worry, not to imagine things, so she had reluctantly left it alone, knowing how he hated interference. If he wanted to tell her anything, he would do so in his own time. She wondered now if he was going through some sort of a breakdown from overwork, or if there was some other reason and he'd forgotten to tell her that he'd gone.

She'd left the house before him this morning, and with a sinking feeling of terror she wondered if he'd just packed and gone, or left a note somewhere that she hadn't seen, or told someone to tell her he'd gone and they had forgotten. She could solve it at once by going upstairs to see if he'd packed, but she refused to give in to what she told herself was an irrational fear.

For a few seconds she allowed panic to take over. She imagined him dead in some traffic accident, or collapsed with a heart attack, then she forced herself to stop this hysteria, brought on no doubt by exhaustion and guilt at being so late for Jack that he had worried that she had forgotten him, and her present anxiety, until now successfully hidden inside her, about Jonathan's health.

She would try and ring him in twenty minutes, though if there was no answer she would feel even worse if he didn't get home in exactly the half-hour it usually took him to travel from the office.

She opened the paper again and began to read an article about an actress who'd discovered that her husband was having an affair. She mentioned him 'working late', having to go away on strange, sudden trips, then finding receipts for expensive underclothes and scents that she certainly had never received. This woman's distress now transferred itself to her. Was Jonathan having an affair? Was that the explanation for his apparent lack of interest in her and the boys recently, for locking himself away for hours in his study, or being away from home so much?

Sitting here alone with just the sound of the traffic in the street outside, she became convinced that it was, and that although she knew that many women found him attractive, she could not help thinking that India had got him at last. India, who cheerfully rang to set up these meetings which were perhaps a front for romantic trysts. Her mind was tortured with images of India sneering at her shortcomings, easily seducing Jonathan with her beauty and her determination. Of course she'd questioned Jonathan about these meetings but he'd been offhand about them, often in fact said he hadn't time to go to them, yet now, feeling so alone in this large house with only a sleeping child as company and the dark night outside, her fears of India winning him took shape and grew into reality.

She sat there in her beautiful drawing room gripping her hands in her lap. The clock ticked on and her emotions whirled out of control. She couldn't live without him, she couldn't. Whatever he was doing she would put up with it, even share him with India if she had to; after all she was used to sharing love, hadn't she done it with her parents all her life? She would put up with anything as long as he would stay with her.

Then she heard the front door open and Jonathan come in. She rushed out into the hall and threw herself into his arms, just stopping herself saying: Don't leave me, I love you. India will never love you as I do.

He clung to her; she could feel his body shaking. 'Oh, Grace.' His voice sounded exhausted. 'Oh, Grace.'

She thought: He *is* having a breakdown,

what do I do? They stood there locked in each other's arms for a long moment while she thought about ringing the doctor, or putting him to bed to rest. Then he suddenly released her and said urgently, 'We've got to pack, leave at once.'

'What?' She looked at him incredulously. His face was white as milk, stiff with tension. 'Go where?'

Still holding her arm he walked with her into the drawing room. 'You've got to trust me, darling, just do as I say. Pack what you need for a few days — easy clothes, nothing smart. Get your passport, and any money you have. Now, quick . . . please, darling, we haven't a minute to lose.'

'But there's Jack, what about him?'

'Oh, Jack, of course.' He ran his hand distractedly through his hair. 'I'll ring Mother, just pack . . . for both of us. Please.' His eyes, large and dark with pain beseeched her.

She didn't move but said, bewildered, 'Is it this business trip you said you might have to go on?'

'Y . . . yes, that's right. It's very urgent, and I'd like you to come with me. We must hurry to catch the ferry.'

'Ferry? Don't you mean plane?'

'No. Look please hurry, darling, I don't

want to miss it. I'll tell you all about it when we're on the way.' He went to the telephone to ring Marianne.

Grace obeyed him like a robot and went upstairs to their bedroom. She was dressed in smart wool trousers, a shirt and matching jersey, clothes that would do for the journey. She packed a couple of skirts, more shirts and jerseys and a pair of designer jeans, with underclothes and night things. She packed a suit, shirts and some casual clothes for Jonathan. She did this all mechanically, her mind now intoning: He wants me to go with him, he's not having an affair. India hasn't got him after all. The sheer relief of this, after having convinced herself otherwise, made her temporarily forget her concerns about his health, forget to question this hurried departure.

He came upstairs pulling off his clothes. 'Mother is coming at once, she'll cope with everything.'

'But what is happening? Where are we going? And why so fast? Why didn't you ring me earlier to warn me? I could have been better organized then.' Her words tumbled out.

'Don't ask me now, please, darling. We won't be away long.' He looked so haggard she was afraid that if she questioned him he would collapse. 'The boys will be safe with Mother,' he said as if he was reciting a mantra. 'They will be safe.' He went into the bathroom.

She heard the doorbell and went downstairs to let in Marianne.

'I don't know what's happened,' she greeted her mother-in-law, 'this sudden business trip that I have to go on too. I don't know what would have happened if you hadn't been able to come.'

Marianne kissed her. 'I'm glad to be of some use. Robert is away and I feel quite bored and useless. Of course it sounds mad, but you know businessmen. They think they're so important and have to dash round the world at a moment's notice when a telephone call would probably do just as well.' She put down the small overnight bag she carried and took off her coat.

'Jonathan did say a few days ago that he might have to go away suddenly, but I never thought it would be this suddenly and that I'd have to go too. Oh God! My work! I'll have to telephone the dreaded Marsha and tell her I have to be away a few days.' She followed Marianne into the drawing room.

Marianne gave her a cryptic look. 'You both work so hard and, with the children, you never seem to have enough time for

283

yourselves. Take my advice, dear, for what it's worth, and use this time to enrich your relationship.' She sat down on the sofa, opened her enormous handbag and took out a paper and pencil. 'Now, tell me what time Jack goes to school, what he wears, his favourite food at the moment, everything.'

Jonathan came into the room, dressed in jeans, a shirt and jersey and a blue blazer. He kissed Marianne. 'Thank you for coming, Mother.' His voice was calm now, there seemed to be no sign of his previous agitation. Marianne gave him a long, penetrating look. Grace thought: She knows that something is up. Her advice of using this time to enrich their relationship rang in her ears. Had Jonathan confided in her about something that was bothering him in their marriage? Was there something, her working harder, earning good money, or giving too much time to the boys, that had upset him?

'Off you both go, and enjoy yourselves, remember you must make time for each other,' Marianne said. 'It's a good idea of yours, Jonathan, to take Grace with you. Jack and I will have a lovely time, so mind you do too.'

'We will. Now, are we off?' Jonathan said mechanically, moving to take the suitcases.

'I must say goodbye to Jack,' Grace said, moving towards the staircase, determined to question Jonathan the minute they left the house and were alone.

'Don't wake him up, dear, I'll explain everything to him in the morning. You'll ring him tomorrow no doubt,' Marianne said, but Grace had run upstairs and into his room.

In the soft light from the landing she gazed down on him. His body was flung down as if he'd been playing and had suddenly fallen asleep. Half of him was uncovered, the duvet almost on the floor. Gently she covered him up, then bent and kissed him. ''Bye, my love,' she whispered, hoping he'd hear her, 'I'll be back in a day or so.'

'Hurry, darling.' Jonathan was on the landing.

'I really find this so odd,' she said, feeling mean at leaving Jack so suddenly, without an explanation. 'Why can't we go tomorrow? What's happened? And if it's so urgent why aren't we flying?'

He took her arm and led her down the stairs. 'It's better to drive this time. Just trust me, darling. It's very important to me. Please just come.' Again he looked so strained that she followed him without another word, determined that once they

285

were away together she would get to the bottom of his distress, his strange behaviour over these last weeks, and however hard it was to bear, cope with it.

She said goodbye to Marianne, who hugged her, told her not to worry about the children and to be away 'as long as it takes, relationships need nurturing'. She went out into the street with Jonathan, the exhaustion and emotions of the day making her feel dazed. She thought with sick dread: Has Jonathan told her our marriage is in trouble, some trouble that I am not aware of? She wondered if India was responsible for his panic. Had she seduced him and he, feeling guilty for his action, was now taking her on this trip to reinforce their commitment? Or worse, the thoughts stabbing her like arrows, was he going to tell her that their marriage was over?

When they reached their car Jonathan walked straight past it. 'No, we're going in this one,' he said, unlocking a dark Ford Escort and loading in their suitcases. 'It's easier. I've rented it on the business.'

'Curiouser and curiouser,' she said, attempting to make light of it though her stomach lurched with further dread.

'Then Mother can use ours,' he said quickly, as if the idea had suddenly come to him. He drove away quickly, looking round frantically as if he expected someone to stop them.

'But she has her own car. Jonathan, you must tell me where we are going, and why you want me to come too,' Grace said firmly, bracing herself for a confession. 'You know I love being with you, and would normally snatch at any excuse to go abroad with you on our own, but so suddenly, at dead of night like this, you must admit it is peculiar.'

He turned to her, his face ghastly in the streetlights. 'We're going over to France,' he said, 'and I wanted to be with you. I want to concentrate on the driving now, but once we are there I'll tell you everything.'

17

'So where is the bastard? I have rung his office and they say he's not there. Give me his home number, I will screw him for every penny he has lost me!' Max Dalbert snarled at India. He was flushed, his solid frame quivering with fury.

India looked at him dispassionately. God, how he bored her, with his obsession with money, his tedious convictions that people had done him down. It was time she dumped him. He'd been useful just taking up with her again when she'd returned from New York, not asking any questions about her affair there — not that she thought it any of his business, he had never been faithful to her. She'd known about his discreet liaisons for ages, but as long as he was there when she needed him she hadn't said anything.

'Oh, do calm down, Max, I don't know what you're talking about,' she said now in a bored tone, carefully painting the last of her fingernails and surveying them critically.

He marched over to where she sat at her dressing table. 'That bastard Jonathan Sheridan has scarpered with my money.

288

Every bit I invested with him has gone.'

India felt as if he'd slapped her. With extreme effort she controlled herself. 'How do you know?'

'I suspected something was up weeks ago. I was expecting a cheque, promised a cheque, and it never came. He gave me endless excuses in that charming way he has,' he spat contemptuously, 'saying next month. Well, when I asked for it, in fact demanded my original stake back, he got quite panicky. He promised he would see to it straight away and now he has gone. His firm were very cagey at first when I rang them, but when I got angry, threatened them with legal action, they admitted he was not there, they did not know where he was, and they had never heard of the company he set up.'

India felt cold, but the sight of Max squawking away like a turkey irritated her. She said offhandedly, 'He goes away on business quite often, doesn't he? Whenever we've asked them to dinner he's been away. You've got masses more money, just be patient. He's sure to deal with it when he gets back.' She carefully tested that her nail varnish was dry and got up, pushed past him and began to put on her blouse and skirt.

'There is more to it than that. Bruce Peyton and Mark Shaffer have also asked for their money back. They are both shrewd businessmen, they smelt a rat too, and they have been fobbed off with some lame excuses.'

'If they were so shrewd why did they invest with Jonathan in the first place when they distrusted him?' India said, smoothing down her skirt and checking her reflection in the mirror. 'Now I must go, I'm chairing a meeting for the Save the Children ball at Grosvenor House, I can't be late.' She took her jacket out of the cupboard and put it on. 'See you later?' She gave him a dazzling smile, though inside her feelings were raging: boredom and irritation with Max and fear that Jonathan was in trouble.

'Give me his home number before you go,' Max demanded, 'I must get hold of him at once. His wife will know where he is. And the number of anyone else you know who invested in his damned scheme. I will contact them too.'

India took a deep breath, 'I'll find their number for you this evening,' she said evenly. 'I must rush now.' She blew him a kiss and, taking no notice of his protests, ran downstairs. In the pretence of collecting up her papers, keys and things she managed to slip the leather address book she kept by the telephone into the back of the bookcase before he saw what she was doing. With another kiss and a wave she was gone.

Leaning back in the taxi on the way to Grosvenor House, she wondered how she could find out if Max's allegations against Jonathan held any truth.

Although she had shown great interest in his investment scheme she had not joined it. She had toyed with the idea as an ideal way to be in contact with him, ringing him up, arranging meetings to discuss it, but on reflection and after overhearing Caspar swearing about 'some bloody client who seems to want to sit in my office and watch his money grow before his eyes', thought that that might be the quickest way to bore him. So, instead, she had introduced her rich friends to him and lapped up his gratitude, such as it was. It had at least given her access to him without Grace. Grace was so weak, she thought, remembering that time she'd gone round to warn her about his gambling. She'd obviously taken no notice as she'd seen him again at the racecourse, placing bets. Grace let him do whatever he wanted, made no demands on him, laid herself out like a mat on the floor for him to walk over. No wonder he stayed with her, not many women would be so considerate — or so foolish. But then, she reflected, hadn't Grace's mother done the same, lived in poverty while Uncle Leo idled his way through life with his painting?

But it was certainly not her own way, India thought, to become the *femme fatale*, setting up some seductive nest and luring him in. Even if she managed to get him into bed she was certain that afterwards he would go back to Grace and his children. Grace, of course, would forgive him anything, but India wanted him to love her, to leave Grace and live with her for the rest of his life. She wondered why she wanted him so much, apart from the fact that he was undeniably attractive, elusive, charming. As she idly watched the buildings through the taxi window, an uncomfortable thought edged into her mind.

She had always been jealous of Grace. Grace, whose parents loved her and had time for her. Grace, who did not need the sumptuous backdrop of Elmley as a security prop to her life. Was she determined to get Jonathan just out of revenge, or was it her pride that once resolved on something would not give in? Hastily she pushed these thoughts from her mind. She loved him plain and simple. She had been waiting patiently for some crack, some disaster to appear in their marriage which would deliver him to her. Now it looked as if at last her patience had been rewarded.

When she got to Grosvenor House she rang his home number. There was no reply, which was hardly surprising as Grace was surely at work. Unable to curb her impatience until the evening when she would be home, she rang Jonathan's mother. She had over the years got hold of all his telephone numbers. Marianne answered.

'Hello, Mrs Wickham, it's India Gratton here, how are you?'

'Very well, thank you, my dear. How are you?'

'Fine. I'm trying to contact Grace and Jonathan. I'm organizing a weekend house party, and they don't seem to be home. Are they on holiday?' she asked her brightly.

Marianne stalled. After their mad rush to go on their business trip, Jonathan had rung her and told her to take Jack to her house and if anyone, anyone at all, wanted to know where he was to say she didn't really know. He would keep in touch with her and Jack, but she was to say they were away on business and would be back soon. He had been very insistent upon this and Marianne had not liked to question him further.

'They're not here,' she said airily, 'they're away on business.'

'When will they be back? You see, I want to organize this party and if they can't came . . . '

'When is your party?' Marianne said with false cheerfulness.

India had not thought, so she laughed and said, 'I have two dates in mind. When do you expect them back?'

There was a loud screech down the line followed by spluttering noises and gunfire.

'Whatever's that?' India said.

'Oh,' Marianne laughed rather hysterically, 'that's Jack being a bomber, don't worry about it.' She sounded harassed. 'I'm learning not to jump every time I'm held at gunpoint or bomber.'

'So you're looking after Jack?'

'Yes, dear, just for a few days.' The noise got louder, ending in a bloodcurdling scream. 'At least I hope it's only a few days,' Marianne finished weakly.

'So you don't know the exact day, or, better still where they are staying so I could ring them there.'

'No, not exactly. Look, I'll take your number and get Grace to ring you the moment she gets back. OK? Your parents well?'

India tried a few more tactics, but got nowhere. Something was up, she was sure, and she was determined to get to the bottom of it.

Later that evening, before going home to a surely by now apoplectic Max, she called in on Caspar at his office. He had now moved back to London with his firm.

'Have you heard anything about Jonathan Sheridan's investment scheme?' she asked, throwing herself down on one of the leather armchairs in his office.

He looked at her intently. 'What sort of thing exactly, India? You haven't invested any money with him, have you?'

'No. Did you?'

'Yes, as a matter of fact, I did. What do you want to know about it and why?' He leant back in his chair, his handsome face now beginning to thicken with good living, his dark eyes watching her.

India was sure that he'd guessed the truth about her feelings for Jonathan, he knew so much about her, but as he had lived abroad for so long he might have forgotten them, or assumed she had abandoned them with Jonathan's marriage. She said, 'Max is in a dreadful tizz, says Jonathan has run off — scarpered, he put it — with his money. I wondered if there was any truth in it?'

Caspar sighed and jiggled on his chair. 'He's such an old friend I'm sure things will work out. Sometimes these schemes hit bad patches and the best thing to do is to sit tight, or double up the stakes at the lower prices until they rise again.'

'So something has gone wrong?'

'I don't know,' he said carefully, studying the wall behind her. He paused. 'Of course, you won't discuss this with anyone else, India, but at this moment it looks very bad. There may be a perfectly acceptable explanation for it, but until we can talk it over with him, we don't know what to make of it.' His face became drawn, a deep furrow showing between his eyes. 'I don't like to think he's done anything dishonest, but the fact is, large sums of his clients' money have gone missing. Most of them are wiped out completely.'

'I don't believe it!' India exclaimed vehemently. 'There's obviously some cock-up with the computer or something. I mean, investments do go wrong, go up and down like yo-yos, they'll probably pick up again next week.'

'Of course, but I don't think that's what's happened in this case. Details are very sketchy at the moment. No one but Jonathan seems to know much about it and as you can imagine Meadows and Laing are keeping as quiet as they can until they know the truth.

I know someone who works there and I've tried to get something out of him, but all he'll say is that as far as he can see the company Jonathan set up for our investments doesn't exist.'

'Doesn't exist? But it does! I've seen receipts, letters on their headed paper about it. Max got quite a bit of money from it in the past. They must be mistaken,' India said with feeling.

'I hope they are, but it seems that Jonathan has disappeared and until he is found and questioned, we can't do anything.'

'He's gone with Grace, they've left the children here,' India said, then remembering Grace's obvious devotion to her sons added, 'but she won't stay away from the children long, she adores them.' She also adores Jonathan, she thought sadly to herself, and for a second she felt a pang of sympathy for Grace, torn between her children and her husband.

'Do you know where they've gone?' Caspar asked hopefully.

'No, but I rang his mother. I'm sure she knows more than she let on to me.'

'She must know . . . I mean they'd leave a contact number in case the children were ill or something, wouldn't they?' he said eagerly. 'Perhaps we ought to go round.' He looked thoughtful for a moment. 'But then again he may not have told her anything.'

'Max is livid, and his friends are too.'

'A lot of people will be baying for his blood if he's lost their money,' Caspar said grimly. 'Look, let's go round to Marianne, see how the land lies. I'll just ring Sophie, tell her I'll be late.' He reached for the phone.

★ ★ ★

Robert opened the door to them. He looked surprised to see them. 'India and Caspar, hello. Were you passing? Come in,' he said, concealing with difficulty his annoyance at being disturbed.

'Thank you,' India said, ignoring his look and giving him a huge smile, following him through the hall into the drawing room.

Robert called ahead, 'Darling, it's Caspar and India Gratton.'

A small body hurtled out of a door at the end of the passage, arms outstretched, tore past them and up the stairs emitting a loud and ear-piercing noise.

'Jack!' thundered Robert, 'stop that infernal din. Surely it's time you went to bed.'

'Nope,' Jack said. 'I go at seven now, Marianne agreed I could.' He came back down the stairs again looking hard at Caspar and India. 'Hello,' he said.

'Hello . . . Jack, isn't it?' Caspar said.

'Yup. You're friends of Mum and Dad. Have they been staying with you?'

'Not recently,' India said. 'Do you know when they'll be back?'

'Soon,' Jack said. 'In time for half-term. Mum promised.'

'Oh, India, Caspar, how nice.' Marianne appeared looking rather flustered. 'Come and have a drink. We're having one.' She said to Jack, 'Get into your pyjamas, darling, I think we'll go without a bath tonight.'

'I especially wanted a bath tonight to try out my experiment,' Jack said. 'I'll have it on my own.' He turned to stump up the stairs again.

Marianne went rather pale, 'No, Jack, wait for me,' she said desperately. 'We don't want another flood. Just wait, I'll be with you in a minute.'

'All right,' Jack said good-naturedly and walked downstairs again to join them. 'I'll give them ice in their drinks,' he said. 'I could pick up the ice with my grabber and drop it in the glasses, then you won't get cold fingers.' He beamed proudly.

'I think we'll be fine, thank you, Jack,' Marianne said weakly, staggering towards the drinks cupboard.

They were settled with their drinks making small talk when the telephone rang. Jack, who was hovering about with his grabber hoping that someone might like to try it for ice, snatched it up.

'Hi, Mum,' he said, 'I knew it was you. When are you coming home?'

Caspar and India exchanged glances. Marianne, gulping back a stiff gin showed no emotion at the call, only Robert seemed to become more alert.

'But when will you be back then?' Jack said. 'I am being good, ask Marianne, so you can bring me a present. Two presents. I want some new games for my Gameboy.'

India got up and went to stand beside Jack. Just before he said goodbye she took the receiver from him, and put it to her ear.

'So, darling, I miss you and I'll . . . ' she heard Grace say.

'Grace, it's me. India . . . I'm just round here for a drink. How are you?'

She heard a gasp from the other end and then the line went dead.

'I've something else to say,' Jack said, putting out his hand for the receiver.

'She's gone,' India said, looking at Caspar. 'She hung up.'

'But I wanted to say something else to her,' Jack wailed. 'Mum, Mum,' he called down the phone. 'Come back, I have to tell you something.'

'Can't you ring her back?' India said, hoping to use the child's distress to persuade Marianne to contact them.

Marianne got up and gently took the receiver from Jack's hand and hugged him. 'The call gets cut off sometimes if it's very far away,' she said. 'I'm sure Mummy will ring you again.'

'I forgot to tell her something,' he sniffed. 'I wish they'd come back.'

'So do I,' Marianne said with feeling. 'Now let's go and have that bath so you can do your experiment,' she added bravely, leading him away.

'Can't you ring them back?' Caspar asked Robert.

'No,' Robert said. 'I'm afraid we can't, it's difficult for them to leave a number. They just ring us from time to time.'

Caspar studied him for a minute, then said, 'I invested some money in a scheme of Jonathan's and suddenly things don't look good. I need to contact him urgently about it.'

'I know,' Robert sighed heavily. 'I don't mind saying this to you, as you're in the same boat, but I'm getting very worried indeed. I haven't said anything to Marianne — didn't want to upset her if there was nothing in it, you understand. She dotes on that boy. They had a tough time when that first husband of hers left her. But . . . ' He paused, staring into the fireplace. 'I've been away in Sydney on business. I only came back two days ago to find Jack here and Grace and Jonathan gone off suddenly on a supposed business trip. At first I took no notice, Marianne loves to have the boys, she misses our daughters, you see, but then I heard some rumblings of our investment being worthless. I'd accepted Jonathan's story of there being a slight dip in the market, but then when a couple of other investors rang me with their concerns, and Marianne told me we couldn't contact Jonathan, I began to feel uneasy.'

'I did too,' Caspar said and told Robert his story, and about Meadows and Laing saying they didn't know about the company Jonathan had set up. 'I'm going to fax them some of the papers that Jonathan sent me, all on Meadows and Laing's headed stationery, then they might be able to find out more about it.'

'I don't like it,' Robert said frowning. 'Grace and Jonathan are devoted to the boys, and although they know that Marianne, and I too, of course, will take good care of them, it's not like them, especially Grace, not to leave a contact number. In fact the few times she's left them with us before she's been almost paranoid about her movements so we can reach her at any time.'

India sat there listening to them talking. She felt numb inside. Jonathan couldn't be dishonest, surely he couldn't? She remembered a friend of hers who'd come unstuck in the commodity market and when an investor asked for his money back, he'd had to borrow it from another client's account. Then he couldn't pay that back when it was asked for and after shifting money from one account to another in a frantic attempt to get things straight, he had ended up losing everyone everything. Had something like that happened to Jonathan and he was fighting to sort it all out?

She put her point to Robert.

Casper broke in, 'India, an inexperienced person might do that, but Jonathan's been in the game for years. I don't want to think he's been dishonest — after all, he's been a friend since childhood. But I'm afraid at the moment it looks very black indeed, and him disappearing like this can only add to people's worst suspicions.'

'I'm sure there's a perfectly logical explanation . . .' India began. But then an image came to her of him standing in the queue at Newmarket to place a bet, his eyes fixed ahead oblivious of other people as if he was willing himself to chose the right horses. She had warned Grace, but she had done nothing. He must have some reason to be so hooked on gambling. Surely something to do with his marriage, she thought suddenly. Perhaps Grace demanded more from him than his salary allowed — their house must have cost a packet. That was it, India decided with a flash of inspiration. Grace, having been brought up in virtual poverty, wanted a good life for her children and was somehow pushing him to provide it, or was just standing by letting him get on with a sometimes lucrative occupation which she had obviously benefited from. She must have pushed him too far and if he'd lost this money gambling it was undoubtedly her fault.

'Let's hope so,' Caspar said dryly and went on discussing it with Robert, both talking in sombre tones as if they were sentencing him to death.

India, listening to them, could not help but feel uneasy about Caspar's explanations. He was not someone who jumped to hysterical conclusions, but she was feeling a bit hysterical herself, she thought. It had all come as rather a shock, though. Then she scolded herself for believing the worst about Jonathan. He would never gamble with someone else's money and was too strong to allow Grace to influence him. She was sure now that whatever had happened was beyond Jonathan's control. Something must have gone wrong in his company and they were using him as the scapegoat.

She knew how Grace would be torn between staying with her husband or coming home to her children. Maybe she would even begin to hate Jonathan for putting her in a situation that forced her to make such a choice. Maybe this was the crisis she'd been waiting for all these years? Grace was not strong like she was. Grace would buckle under the strain and Jonathan, especially if he was ostracized by everyone over this, would be alone. But she, India, would be there waiting for him.

The thought made her glow inside, her eyes shine and her mouth curve in a smile. Caspar, noticing, said sharply, 'What's up with you, India? You look like a particularly sleek cat who has devoured a whole pot of cream.'

'Nothing,' she said vaguely, but seeing he was still staring at her said, 'poor Grace, she won't be able to stand all this, will she? She'll be quite out of her depth.'

'Possibly, but that's no reason to look pleased. If he has been up to something it will be hell for her.'

'I know and I will stand by her and support her,' India said sweetly, daring Caspar with her eyes to challenge her.

Robert sighed. 'Yes, poor Grace. It will be tough on her, but' — he smiled at India — 'how comforting to know that she can rely on you.'

18

The room smelt of cheap carpets, stale smoke and suffocating dreariness. Grace lay on her back on the rough sheets on the small bed and listened to Jonathan's breathing.

She could not believe that this was happening to them. It was as if she were looking down on the scene, quite apart from it. Her eyes felt dry and scratchy with weeping, her body chilly and on edge. Today they would move on again to yet another soulless hotel in yet another nondescript French town.

So often in the past they had stayed in France in cheerful, bustling hotels, rich with the aroma of good food, or in the faded elegance of small *châteaux* renowned for their cuisine and filled with congenial, cultured people. But that seemed another life, she and Jonathan different people, wandering in the scented hills of the South, or in the elegant streets of Paris. Now they were in hiding, slinking from dismal hotel to dismal hotel, choosing the dullest of towns to keep out of the way of the authorities.

Jonathan stirred. He woke and took her

in his arms, holding her close to him. 'Are you all right, darling, did you sleep?' he said, looking at her anxiously.

'A bit.' She hid her face in his shoulder. She did not know how to behave towards him, torn between wanting to support him, yet devastated at his actions, ashamed at what he had done. When he had told her, at the back of her mind she realized that she had been waiting for something like this to happen. Ever since India had warned her about his gambling — although she'd been determined not to believe her, could not bear it to be India, since childhood the superior one, who'd told her about it — she had known that the hairline crack in his behaviour was slowly developing into a crevice.

Jonathan had not talked much on their dash to the ferry. She had noticed his agitation, especially when they had handed in their passports to the man at the check-in. But the official had smiled and waved them through. The ferry was not crowded, being the middle of the night, but Jonathan had searched until he found an isolated corner and settled with her there.

When he felt the ferry was free of its berth and out in the open sea, he said abruptly. 'This may the last time we will be together.'

'Why?' She jerked up, wildly clutching on to him, as if he was suddenly going to be spirited away from her.

'I've done something terrible. I'll be punished for it. I don't mind that, but I mind not being with you. I mind what I've done to you, you and the boys.' His voice cracked and she saw him fight back the tears. She held him tightly to her, half in her own fear, half in trying to comfort him.

'I don't care what you've done, I'll always love you, always be with you.' The words spilled from her, but even then the first thought that hit her, no doubt brought on by the newspaper article of the wronged wife she'd read earlier in the evening, was the thought that there was another woman; and the only other woman she could think of was India. She felt very empty, but she recognized these feelings, resigned herself to them as something inevitable, something she had lived with since India's threat the night before her marriage, the fear of losing him to her.

She turned to him to exclaim: Don't you love me and the children any more? Has someone else taken you away from us? when he said, firmly as if it was an unpleasant duty but one that had to be performed at once, 'You know this investment scheme, this company I set up? Well, it's gone wrong. I've lost all the money and more besides. There is nothing left for anyone — '

'But,' she broke in, relief momentarily flooding her that he hadn't confessed a love for India, relief that it was only business, something she could cope with, 'deals often go wrong, shares go down, they must have realized that. No financial dealings are without risk.'

'It's not like that, Grace,' he said slowly. He looked out of the porthole at the dark sea as if he could not look her in the face. 'I gambled it away. On the horses. Oh, at first it worked, I put it on accumulators, made a killing and paid it back to them. They were pleased, amazed at the return.'

'Did they know you were gambling with their money?' Her eyes stared wildly at him, horror creeping like icy fingers through her.

'No.' Now he stared at his hands. 'I used the headed paper from Meadows and Laing with . . . bogus investments, figures, you know. They all swallowed it because I often enclosed a cheque, quite large ones sometimes. But then it started to go wrong. I suppose I got over confident, it was so easy to do.' He turned to her now, his face flushed with a strange excitement. 'It was so exhilarating to see those horses thundering past with the one I'd bet on in the lead, or snatching the race at the last minute. You don't know what power it gives you, what excitement to bet on a whole clutch of horses and have them all come in. You think you're God.'

'Oh, Jonathan,' she said, faint with dread, staring at this man who suddenly seemed a stranger to her.

'I felt so good giving them all that money and then' — his face sagged, his body slumped — 'it all went wrong. I couldn't get a horse right. I put on more and more money, thinking this time it will win, this time I'll make it back again. But now it's all gone and I've lost everything, for myself, for us, as well as for all those investors.'

'So what will happen?' Grace said, feeling as if she were having a nightmare but knowing with sickening horror that it was one she would not wake up from.

'I'll go to prison, I expect.'

'No,' she cried, clutching at him, 'no, you can't.' The full agony of his crime hit her and she began shivering uncontrollably. She did not want to believe what he was telling her, and yet incidents from the past thudded back to haunt her and India queened over them all, sitting there in their dining room telling her she must stop his gambling. She

311

had been so happy with him and the children she hadn't wanted to know. If it had been anyone but India, she thought, I might have paid more attention, but she has always acted as though she knew more about life than me, which I hated, and I was so sure she was doing it to undermine my marriage that I refused to take it seriously.

'Hush darling, calm yourself,' he said in a resigned voice. 'I've had a few days to think about this, and I know what will happen. I'll be arrested, put on trial. I just had to get away, be alone with you to tell you everything. I want you to know everything, before it's splashed all over the papers, before I'm caught.'

She could not speak to him, her thoughts were in such turmoil, nor could she stop shivering. When they arrived in France he led her like a sleepwalker back to the car. She thought that at any moment the French police would arrest him. But they were waved on without their British passports even being looked at and as they drove on into the night, she relaxed a little.

They had been in France two days now. He had explained to her that they'd had to go abroad, because one always bumped into someone one knew in England, and by keeping away from the obvious places in France they would be safer. Both were being very careful with each other, but apart from knowing they would move on today, she did not know what they would do. Neither of them seemed to want to discuss it, as if by ignoring the problem it would die a natural death and slip away.

Once she had said, slowly, as if to herself, 'Your father was a gambler too, wasn't he?'

'Yes, and look where it got him. Oh, I know I'm mad, darling, but ever since seeing him like that, filthy and homeless, I felt I could not bear that to happen to me. I was determined to make money, masses of it, to keep us safe. Don't you see?' He'd begged her to understand, and she had, but she was devastated at the way he'd gone about it. She wished he had told her about his fears. But then, she thought with frightening clarity, would she have listened or would she just have soothed him, tried to brush it all away, hide it before it could tarnish their happy home? She too had not had the strength to face up to him becoming like his father.

As she watched him over those days, she wondered if he knew that he was a gambler. Some of the things he said made her think he thought it was just a run of bad luck, and that if he got hold of some more money it would be all right again. But though she despised herself for still being weak, she did not say this to him, afraid of making things worse, of leaving nothing to salvage from the life they used to have.

She missed the boys terribly. She was also afraid that Jonathan's crime would be snatched at gleefully by the press, that Sebastian would see it in the papers at school and she would not be there to shield him, to explain it to him. But how, she thought, anguished, do you explain to children that their beloved father is a thief? That he must go to prison for his crime? Would the older boys read about it and use it to bully her son?

If they saw any English papers in the shops she looked at then surreptitiously. She was terrified that she would see Jonathan's picture on the front page and that the newsagent would recognize them and call the police. Yet again she could not tell him this. In a strange way she wanted to protect him from her fears as if he couldn't think of them himself. She bought a paper once when he wasn't looking, searching through it secretly to see if he was in there, but there was nothing.

'When will everyone know?' she said now, shifting in his arms. 'What will we tell the boys, your mother?'

He was silent. 'I don't know, but we

must tell them. It will break soon. People — Max, you know, India's paramour, was already demanding his money back. So are two of his friends. Others will follow.'

'India was at your mother's last night,' she said in a small voice. She hadn't wanted to tell him, hearing India's voice at the end of the phone had given her such a fright.

'Was she? How do you know?' He shot up in bed, panic in his face.

'I was talking to Jack, as you know. She took the receiver, said she was having a drink with Marianne. I just put the phone down. I didn't know what to say.'

'Why didn't you tell me?'

'I was so shocked . . . I . . . ' Then she said defiantly, 'She wants to ruin our marriage. I just don't want her to have any more ammunition to do it with.'

'Ruin our marriage?' He looked puzzled, but the thought that now people would know where they were prevented him questioning her further. He jumped out of bed. 'We must move on,' he said. 'I wish you'd told me about this last night. They may have traced the call, they may be downstairs waiting for us.' He pulled on his clothes. 'Hurry up,' he said brusquely, 'just hurry up.'

As she obeyed him she felt fear grab her again. Were they going to spend the rest of their lives running? And what of the boys? An intense desire to be with them took such a strong hold of her she almost cried out. She could not live without her boys, could not disappear like this without telling them. She wondered what Marianne had said to Sebastian yesterday. He'd been playing in a match and Marianne'd promised to go down to watch him, to explain that Mummy would be back soon. But would she? She glanced at Jonathan who was counting out some cash from his wallet for the bill.

'We'll pay cash,' he said, 'I've brought out quite a bit. Credit cards can be traced, and besides they can see our signature on them.'

'We can't leave the boys for long,' she said desperately.

'Hurry up, we'll talk about that later,' he said, picking up their suitcases.

They paid the bill to the sour-faced woman downstairs. The smell of coffee and croissants made Grace feel sick, whereas before they would have made her hungry.

Looking round as if expecting a whole posse of police waiting to arrest him, Jonathan slipped quickly outside and to the car. He had rented it, he told her, from a not-very-well-known firm, hoping that it would take a few days for the authorities to trace it. Now he said, 'We might change the car, leave this somewhere, in case they've caught up with it.'

'Are you sure? I mean, you said we were going home soon,' she said.

'Not yet.' He opened the map and studied it a moment. 'We'll go on down to the South,' he said. 'Marseilles. We can take a boat from there if necessary.' Before she could protest he thrust the map at her and said, 'We'll take that small road, see, and on down there until we come to Avignon. OK?'

She nodded, another fear hitting her now. He had told her he would give himself up after a day or two alone with her, and go back to face the music, but now he seemed to have forgotten all about that. He seemed almost to revel in being a fugitive, pitting his wits against the authorities, outwitting them. There was a note of ridiculousness in his furtive behaviour, almost like a little boy playing a part.

She said, 'We are going home, aren't we?'

'Mmm . . . Look, there's a garage, let's stop for petrol.'

He filled the car and came back from the garage shop with a coffee for her and a packet of madeleines. 'These will keep you going, I don't want to stop until we get to Marseilles.'

'Jonathan,' she said as they edged back on to the road, determined now to settle this, 'you told me you were going to go home and give yourself up.'

'Yes, that was yesterday, but now' — he looked excited — 'well, no one seems to have come after us. I'll buy a newspaper to see if anything's in there, but we'll go on for a few more days.'

'But the boys!' she said. 'I feel dreadful leaving them like this. And if anything does come out, I want to be with them to explain.'

He was silent for a moment, then he said, 'I'll ring Mother, explain everything to her. She'll know what to do, don't worry, she loves them. She'll look after them.'

'I know she will, but I feel it should be . . . ' instead of saying 'me', she said '. . . 'us' with them. They must be so afraid, so bewildered without us.' Frantically, she watched his face tighten, his hands clench on the wheel.

'Mother will protect them,' he said firmly. 'There is no need for us to rush back to it all just yet. Look, there's a payphone, we'll ring her now. I just hope the police aren't at her house. I'll have to risk it. Mother's pretty

318

switched on, she'll warn me if someone's there.'

Grace felt awful as she watched him go into the phonebox, as if she was forcing him to do something that he was convinced would hurt him. Yet, she thought, he has changed. A few months ago he too would have worried about leaving the boys to face any trauma alone. When Sebastian had started prep school, he had written almost every day, determined that Sebastian should know he was still as much part of the family and in their thoughts as ever.

She watched him come back to the car, slower, whiter somehow. He sat motionless in his seat for a moment, staring in front of him, before turning on the engine again and going back on to the road.

Grace waited. Her whole body seemed to be strung so tight she felt it would snap. At last, unable to bear it any longer, she burst out: 'Did you get her?'

'Yes. Caspar came round with India. He's invested some money too, you know, as has Robert. They told Mother. She's . . .' His voice tailed away; he sighed heavily. 'She's distraught, didn't believe it. I had to tell her that it was true.'

His expression was so anguished it tore at her heart. She put her hand on his thigh.

319

'And the boys? What about the boys?'

'She'll shield them as best she can. It's not in the papers yet, but I suppose it will be. She's going to bring Sebastian home later today. She thinks it's better to have them both with her, in case there's any flak.' He looked at her, ashamed. 'You know, bullying.'

'Do the . . . police know where we are?'

'I don't think so. They've managed to contain it so far, but it'll break soon. Some of the investors are very angry indeed. It's only a matter of time until they come for us. Mother has managed to persuade Caspar that we are in America.' He almost laughed.

'America?'

'Well, you know how she is. However shocked and horrified she is, she'll fight for me, stand by me, as you are. I'm so lucky having two such wonderful women in my life.' He touched her hand. She didn't know why she didn't feel any pleasure at his remark. He went on: 'She doesn't know where we are, I never told her. She might even believe that we are in America.'

Grace sank back in her seat. She didn't know what to do. It seemed almost as if Marianne was collaborating with him. She realized she'd assumed that his mother would persuade Jonathan to come back at once and give himself up, but she hadn't and here they were still running, and she wanted it to end. She loved Jonathan, would stand by him whatever happened, but she wanted to go home now, home to her children.

The hotel they found in Marseilles was cheerful compared with the others they had stayed in. There was a rich warm smell of cooking that almost made Grace feel hungry.

They stayed in their room until dark then Jonathan said he was going out.

'I want to come with you. I can't bear to stay here alone,' she said. 'I also want to ring the boys, see if Sebastian is home.'

'OK, we'll find a phone on our way.' They left the hotel and he took her arm, held her close to him as they walked.

They wandered through the small streets until they reached the Vieux Port. There was a sharp smell of the sea. Jonathan let go of her arm and walked up and down the quay stopping every so often to stare at the boats that rocked gently in the harbour. Then he said, so quietly that she had to strain to hear him: 'Morocco. We'll go to Morocco. We'll be safe there. I'm sure I can find a boat going that way, and with a bit of money we should be able to get aboard.'

'We can't.' She stood stock still beside

him. 'We can't go on running. We must go back, face whatever is in store for us.'

His face was white and tense in the lamplight. She felt sick, terrified of the future, of losing him, but standing here at the busy waterside, the possibility of escape before them, she knew she could run no further. She could not leave her children.

'I love you,' she said, 'I will stand by you whatever happens, but I can't leave the children. You must see that?' She was crying now, tears slipping unnoticed down her face, knowing with a heavy heart that if he chose to go from her to Morocco she would let him go alone, would risk losing him for her children's sake. They were too young, still too vulnerable to be without her.

She realized that while they were away from home he and she were in a sort of limbo. The stark reality of his crime could be avoided, minimized. This she wanted to say to him, wanted him to know that she understood this feeling, but she could not find the words so she stood there, silent and helpless, clinging to his hand.

He stood for a long moment by the sea, looking out into the blackness beyond, the sky dotted with stars. She felt as if he were leaving her, slipping away as a dying person slips from one world to the next, and she

322

knew she could do nothing.

He turned at last and smiled, a sad, weary smile that tore at her heart. 'Do you know what's out there?' he said, and when, bewildered, she shook her head, he went on, 'Château d'If, the fortress that used to be a prison. Remember the Man in the Iron Mask, and the Count of Monte Cristo?'

Her eyes widened in horror and she shivered as if she could hear the clang of the gates behind him and the sharp, lonely cry of the forgotten prisoners.

19

They drove back to England like two strangers. It felt to Grace as if the real Jonathan, the man she had known and loved for so long, the father of her beloved sons, had left her, and in his place was a lookalike, a replica of his body that was empty of his character. But somewhere like a faint glimmer of light in the darkness of her pain was the reassurance that India would no longer want him after what he'd done. Whatever other horrors she'd have to face at least she could be free of the fear that India would take him from her.

It was uncomfortable, though, knowing how India would sneer at her, how she would taunt her with being so weak as to let him fall so far, echoing her own guilt that maybe her indifference to what was going on under her nose had caused him to commit this crime.

When they spoke it was only of practical matters. They needed more petrol; should they stop here for the night, or a meal? Only in the anonymity of the dark did they cling together, making love with a kind of desperate passion. Wordless, neither daring to unleash the incriminations, the anguished fear of what would happen to them.

He told her briefly that he had contacted a lawyer, but apart from making some non-committal remark at his news, she remained impassive. She felt as if she were holding the shattered pieces of their life together in her hands and that if she moved or spoke of her terror the whole lot would fall out of her her control for ever.

As they reached Calais, Grace braced herself for the police to take him from her. There was a terrible pain inside her, knowing of the inevitability of this parting, a yawning emptiness. How would she cope without the warmth and stability of his love, deal with the disruption to their family life, the bewilderment of the children. She forced herself not to think about it, just to get through each hour, each day, leaving the future to itself. But now this moment must be got through. She wondered bleakly if she would have to drive home alone, or if they would be accompanied by a police convoy. She could not look at him, or offer one gesture of comfort, knowing he felt the same dread and if either acknowledged it they would give the other away.

But yet again the person at the ticket

check-in waved them through. She felt Jonathan relax a little and she thought: Perhaps they can't be bothered with him here, it's on the other side that British police will be waiting, waiting to haul us off.

On the ferry he said, his eyes fixed on the grey turbulent sea, 'I've always felt that my father let me down when he abandoned me as a baby, and when I saw him homeless, I felt so angry with him for allowing himself to sink so low, for betraying me again by his hopelessness. But now it's my turn to let down my sons.'

Grace understood what he meant, but didn't know what to say.

'I must ask you one more thing, Grace, please tell them I didn't mean to do it. Things just got out of control. I know I shouldn't have started it in the first place. I know I was wrong to gamble with other people's money, but I never meant this to happen. I never even suspected it would happen. I thought I was in control all the time.'

Still she said nothing, but put her hand on his arm, her thoughts raging. She fought to hold on to the good times they had had, the joy of being with him, the delight of having the children. He had been so easy to love, with his good looks, his sensuality, his kindness — yes, he had been so considerate, so kind. She thought back to the time she was ill on their first romantic holiday together, him standing by her during her first pregnancy and later miscarriage and the years after with the boys. They had had a good marriage, surely they had. Indeed, compared to some of their friends who had confided their marital difficulties to her, it had been more than good, with genuine love on both sides. All this churned away inside her as she searched in vain for the deep love she'd once felt for him to surface again.

'The idea seemed so good, *was* so good,' he continued. 'I never thought of losing, of the consequences. It was the thrill of it that encompasses all reason. You lose one day, but you win it back the next time, or the time after. It was the outsiders that brought in the real money, you see.' He turned to her, a slight gleam of excitement in his dull eyes. 'If an outsider came in at say thirty to one, you were made, don't you see?'

Grace looked into his face, and realized it was the face of a man she did not really know. A man who had kept a major part of his life, perhaps the most vital part of him, away from her.

'Oh, Jonathan . . . ' Her voice was barely

more than a whisper. 'Don't you see this . . . this idea of yours has ruined our lives, ruined the lives of your investors.' She saw the pain cross his face but before he could say anything she hurried on: 'I felt cross with your father too, I couldn't understand how a man . . . a man of his background and education could sink so low. When I saw him gulping the whisky from the bottle in the street, not even able to wait until he was somewhere less public, I was revolted, furious that he had allowed himself to get like that. But now I see how easy it is.'

'We won't be like that,' Jonathan said furiously.

'We might,' she said, angry too now, all the pent-up fears surging up in her and spewing out. 'You say you've lost everything, so where will we live? I only have a little money, my parents have none. If you go to prison where will we live? On the streets with your father?' She was shaking, terrified of this spectre that had haunted her since he had told her the truth. She knew his investors would demand as much back as they could get, which meant that there would be nothing left for her and the children. The thought devasted her.

'It won't be like that. I've told you I can salvage something,' he said grimly. 'Anyway, there's the married women's housing act, or something like that, to protect you. You'll have a roof over your head.'

'Are you sure? And the children's education? At least we have that insurance scheme for them, even though they'll probably have to leave where they are now to escape the bullying. They can go somewhere else, get a good education.'

A deadly silence made her stop. He would not look at her. She felt as if she had been kicked hard in the very pit of her stomach.

'Oh, no, don't tell me you took that too?' Her voice was almost a howl of agony. 'You couldn't have taken from your children, you couldn't.' But even as she made her plea she knew that he had and that nothing and no one was safe from his addiction.

He looked ashamed, knotting his fingers tightly in his lap, then he said defiantly, 'Don't worry so, something will work out.'

'Oh, Jonathan,' — she leapt up, making the other passengers look at them even more curiously — 'why can't you learn that nothing will turn up! We're not in fairyland. You have lost everything you, I, and all your investors worked for. And you think, I suppose, that an outsider will win the race and bring it all back to us.' She sank back on her seat weeping bitterly.

She could feel his shocked horror at her words, knew that at last she had made him see how hopeless their situation was, how deadly his gambling was. Knew that until that moment he had nurtured a secret thought that once back at the racecourse, his luck would change. She wanted to help him in his agony but she could not, the anguish of her own despair overwhelmed her.

She stayed slumped there beside him, her face in her hands, until they arrived at Dover, too weary, too shocked at him and their plight to move. He took her arm and led her back to the car. As they went she felt as if they were on their way to be executed, for whatever punishment was in store for him she would doubly share it in her imagination.

He helped her gently into the car as if she was an invalid and did up her seatbelt for her. The huge mouth of the ferry opened, letting in the dusk outside. The car in front of them drove off and Jonathan moved slowly after it. She wanted to shout to him to stop, as if once out of the safety of this noisy, petrol-smelling hold they would be lost, but her voice would not come and he drove down the ramp on to the tarmac, following the tail-lights of the car ahead.

It will happen now, she thought as they slowed down by immigration. The man will come out of his box, or the police will appear and take Jonathan away. She longed to open the door and escape from what was to happen, but she could not move.

Jonathan slowed down and held up their passports and the man behind the glass nodded and flicked his hand. For a split second Jonathan paused as if surprised. The man looked up at them again with impatience and waved them through. This time Jonathan drove away on up the road above the port and the old houses tucked into the cliffs, the sea pounding below, the gulls whirling and calling in the darkening sky.

They stayed in silence until they reached London, then he said, 'Shall we go home first, ring the boys at Mother's, pick them up in the morning?'

Grace longed to hold her children to her again, but also she dreaded it. Dreaded telling them their father had done wrong and that their lives were now changed for ever. She did not know, apart from her dreadful imaginings, what the changes would be, but she knew she could not face the honesty in their eyes tonight.

Once home Grace switched mechanically into her housewife role. She made a list of the essentials they needed to see them through this evening and for breakfast: milk, butter, bread, eggs. She knew as she wrote each item down carefully that she was only putting off ringing the children. Putting off the animosity, the sad disappointment that would come from Robert and Marianne, putting off having to face up to the consequences of Jonathan's actions that would hurt the most.

It was Jonathan who rang them. She did not hear what he said to his mother, she came into the room as he was talking to Sebastian. His voice was clipped and firm. 'Hello, Sebastian, we're back. We'll come and get you both tomorrow.' There was a pause, then she heard him say: 'We'll talk about that tomorrow, old chap. Now, have a word with Mum.'

She knew as she took the receiver from him that he couldn't bear any more. She forced herself to sound cheerful. 'Hello, darling.'

'Hi, Mum. Mum, I've got to go back to school by Wednesday 'cause I'm in a match and if I don't get back they'll put Barnsley in and he's hopeless.'

'We'll talk about it tomorrow.'

'Why not today? Why not come round here now, we're not in bed. Marianne makes us go to bed far too early anyway and she thinks the television makes us noisy, which is silly, isn't it, Mum? I mean we're sitting down when we watch it.'

'Darling, we'll talk about all this tomorrow. Daddy's . . . tired now, and he's got some work to do.'

There was the sound of a scuffle and a few shrieks and 'get orf', and Jack came on the line.

'Mum, it's me, Jack,' he said as if she wouldn't recognize his voice. 'Did you bring me a Gameboy game? Is it nice? Did you bring me two? I've been good. Miss Becky gave me a gold star for my writing.'

'Show off,' Sebastian said in the background.

Grace felt even sicker. She hadn't remembered to buy a present for them. 'They didn't have any,' she said lamely.

'Oh, Mum, you must have looked in the wrong place,' she heard him wail. In the old days she'd have popped out to a shop here and bought him one, pretending that she'd got it while she was away. But there was no money now for presents. There could be no more spoiling them. Life was going to be tough and there was no way she was going to be able to protect them.

She slipped out to the all-night shop and as she left the shop carrying her purchases she saw Sarah Lewis, whose son was a friend of Sebastian. Sarah was a cheerful woman who liked to chat and Grace felt she couldn't really cope with that at this moment, but there was no way to avoid her. Clutching her shopping and trying to look as if she was in a rush, Grace called out, 'Hello, Sarah,' forcing a friendly smile as she attempted to hurry past.

Sarah stopped, looked at her then, with a face full of hatred, spat, 'How can you show your face after what you've done?'

'What . . . what do you mean?'

'Losing us all our money like that. You must have known about it, yet you said nothing, went on enjoying spending it, I suppose. You make me sick. I hope they lock you up and throw away the key.' She turned abruptly and whirled off into the darkness.

Grace stood stunned as if she'd been hit. She hadn't even known that Sarah and Paul had invested money with Jonathan. She stumbled, almost fell, on her frantic way back to the safety of her house. How many people had he involved in his scheme? How many people would hate them now?

She was very quiet while she cooked their scrambled eggs for supper. They ate mechanically, not getting any enjoyment from it. She felt ashamed of the scene with Sarah and did not want to tell Jonathan about it. How could he have done these things without her knowing?

How could she have lived with him so closely and yet not known this side of his life? Yet she had known about it, even before India had so thoughtfully warned her, but she had chosen to dismiss it as a wild exaggeration, a bit of mischief on India's part. But she had never suspected it would get so out of hand, that he would be driven to steal to feed his addiction. Now she felt the full force of her own shame as if in her indifference to his gambling she was as guilty as he was.

After supper Jonathan went into his study and she did not see him again until he got into bed beside her.

'I've had a long talk with my solicitor and I'll make sure you and the boys have somewhere to live,' he said, his face and voice strained with exhaustion. He stroked her cheek with his fingers. 'I'll never forgive myself for what I've done to you and the boys. It's that I care about more than anything. I can understand you hating me, but I want you to know I never meant to do it. I only wanted what was best for you.'

'I know,' she said. They clung together, weeping together, lost in wretchedness.

***

There was a terrible thumping and pounding, the house seemed to be shaking as if in an earthquake. Grace woke with a shock, wondering what she had been dreaming of. But the noise continued. Jonathan was awake now and as they lay there they realized with horror that someone was battering on their front door.

He turned to her, his face that of a terrified child. Then he kissed her, his expression changing to one of resignation. He got up and put on his dressing gown.

She followed him, thinking of Sarah Lewis, terrified it was an angry pack of investors coming to lynch them.

'Don't open the door, call the police,' she begged, suddenly starkly awake, pulling her wits about her. She went into the drawing room to the telephone.

But she heard him put the chain on the door and open it.

'Jonathan Sheridan? Police. Can we come in, please?'

Each word was like a bullet. She heard the door open and some people come in. Jonathan led them into the drawing room. She sat there transfixed, seeing these hard-faced men surrounding Jonathan, hearing the

336

police officer cautioning him, asking him to get dressed and come down to the station with them.

She heard Jonathan's voice, calm and firm. 'I'll come with you, but I want you to understand that my wife has had no part in this whatsoever. She is completely innocent.'

She did not hear what the officer said. Then a policewoman thrust a cup of hot tea at her and she thought: It has happened, but I can't go to pieces, I have the children. Thank God they were not here to see their father taken off like a murderer.

This thought made her angry and she said, 'Why do you have to batter down our door like this so early in the morning? Couldn't you come quietly at a decent time of the day?'

The officer looked at her. 'We have our job to do, madam,' he said.

She drank a few sips of tea automatically, hardly feeling the scalding liquid running down her throat, but the tea gave her life. Putting down her cup she sprang up to go upstairs to Jonathan.

'Just stay there, please, Mrs Sheridan,' the woman officer said quietly.

'I want to see my husband.'

'You can in a minute.'

337

Grace was about to protest, to insist on going to him, when Jonathan appeared. He had on a grey suit, a blue shirt and a dark red and blue patterned tie. He looked clean and spruce but very pale.

'I've rung my solicitor; I'll be back as soon as I can. Go to my mother and the boys at once. She's expecting you, I . . . I've rung her too.' He spoke to her calmly as if it were an ordinary request and that he was just going to a meeting and everything was as it should be.

They did not touch each other, standing at opposite ends of the room, as if the easy camaraderie between them had never been, but the look in his eyes smote her heart. She stood there, stupid, unable to help him, but knowing that if she obeyed her instincts, and ran to hold him, screaming for him to stay, she would destroy what dignity he had left. She heard him walk through the hall and into the street, and the door shut firmly behind him.

20

Marianne Wickham looked ten years older than she was. Grace, even in her distress, almost reeled back in shock as her mother-in-law opened the front door. Her face and her body seemed to have sagged and collapsed. Her hair, once so jauntily styled, was limp and lifeless. She was dressed in an old pair of shapeless slacks and a beige cardigan. She looked as if she had given up on life and relegated herself to the dowdy obscurity of old age.

The two women clung together a moment, both too frightened by the events to say anything. But both of them, Grace thought later, must have been thinking: How can the man we love have betrayed us so?

'Mum, Mum!' Jack ran to hug her, jumping about like a puppy. Sebastian followed him more slowly, regarding her solemnly. He did not move to kiss her.

'Hello, darling,' she said, forcing herself to smile, wondering for a moment if he wanted to kiss her but was inhibited by boarding school, or whether he knew a little of what had happened and was blaming them both.

'Hello.' Still he did not move. She went over to him and kissed him, putting her arms round his sturdy body, holding him to her.

Jack was jumping about saying, 'Where's Dad? When's Dad coming?'

Grace heard a sob from Marianne and saw her run from the room, her hand over her mouth. She felt very alone and bereft. She longed for Marianne's comfort; she loved Jonathan too. She looked anxiously at her sons. Sebastian, so like Jonathan, was watching her with the wisdom and the wariness of an old man. Jack was like her father, slim, small-boned, and brown-eyed. He seemed to know nothing of Jonathan's disgrace. Perhaps he was too young, or too immersed in his games to have picked up any vibes.

She sat down on the sofa and pulled the children with her. Jack wriggled and jumped away to go and find some toy to show her. Sebastian allowed her to pull him down beside her, but he made no attempt to cuddle up to her or to speak.

When Jack came back, she swallowed and said as clearly as she could, 'I have something very difficult to tell you. You have to be very grown up and try and understand what I have to say.'

'Is someone dead?' Jack said offhandedly,

fiddling with his Transformer. 'Philip's granny died. Miss Becky told us and said we must be extra nice to him.'

'No.' Grace thought it might be easier to tell if . . . but no, Jonathan was alive, she couldn't wish him dead.

'It's Dad, isn't it? He's going to prison,' Sebastian said abruptly, his little mouth tight, his face chalk-white.

'Why's he going to prison?' Jack said, running his Transformer down his leg and over his thick shoe. 'Only bad people go to prison.'

If there were tears left in Grace she would have shed them now. How could she tell them the truth about their beloved father? But how did Sebastian know about it? She supposed he must have overheard Robert and Marianne talking about it. She had not been here to comfort him. She thought of him, alone in bed, a small child hugging to himself the appalling knowledge that his father had done something bad enough to go to prison for.

Her eyes caught a photograph of Jonathan standing on the table. His hair was blowing in the wind, he was smiling out at them, his eyes crinkled with laughter lines, and she hated him. Hated him for the pain he had caused his children.

'Daddy used other people's money in the wrong way,' she began. 'He gambled — do you know what that means?' She looked at them both, hardly able to meet Sebastian's solemn, grey-blue eyes. He shook his head.

'It's a bit like a bet, you know, how you say to Jack I bet you some jelly beans or some of my Premier League stickers that you can't climb that tree.'

'I bet I can,' Jack said, crawling on to her lap and putting his thumb in his mouth, something he hadn't done for ages.

'But instead you bet a sum of money that a horse will win a race or sometimes a certain number will come up in a game. If you win you win some money, sometimes lots, but if you lose . . . ' She tailed off, then rallied. 'Daddy won a lot, then he lost it, but it wasn't his money to play with.'

'Did he steal it?' Sebastian asked in a very small voice.

Grace hesitated, wishing she could fudge the answer, say he didn't really, he'd borrowed it, but by mistake he'd lost it. He had done wrong, but he hadn't meant to. But somehow, faced with Sebastian's unwavering gaze, she could not.

'He shouldn't have taken it,' she said, 'he thought he would make them more money, but he lost it all. He did wrong, he knows he did, and he's very upset about it and knows he will be punished.'

'Did he hold up a bank?' Jack said.

'No, it wasn't like that.'

'Thomas Fairbain says he's a thief and he'll go to prison, and no one wants to be my friend 'cause my father's a thief,' Sebastian burst out, tears running down his face.

His hands were clenched by his sides, and Grace took him tightly in her arms, holding him to her. She wished with all her heart that she could take the pain from her children and bear it for them. It must have leaked out at school before Marianne had managed to take him away and he must have been harbouring this anguish for days on his own.

'Did they talk about it at school?' she said gently.

'I saw Thomas at the weekend, it was an exeat. I saw him in the street. He says the whole school knows and they won't let me back and I wanted to be in the match against Ludgrove . . . ' Grace couldn't think of a reply, of any way to help, for surely the hardest thing of all was coping with other people's anger and hatred over an offence that was not of their doing.

The day dragged on and on. Marianne did her best to be strong, she cooked them all sausages and mash and let the boys melt

343

Mars bars to pour over their ice cream. Grace helped her mechanically, washing up things, even though there was a dishwasher, drying them, wiping round the kitchen like a zombie. Robert was away on business and would be back in a couple of days.

'He didn't want to leave me on my own, but I insisted I'd be all right. I think we needed to be away from each other for a while,' Marianne said to Grace when they'd finally eaten lunch and cleared it away. 'I feel as guilty as if I'd done it myself,' she continued as they slumped dejectedly together in the drawing room while the boys watched television out of earshot at the other end of the room. 'Robert was so good to him, to me. When Vincent left me like that, suddenly without warning, I had five pounds in my purse and twenty pounds in a post-office account. He hadn't paid the mortgage on the flat and it was repossessed. I had to go round to my friends begging. He'd gambled it away, you see.' She sighed, her mouth working. 'I never thought Jonathan would be the same, he didn't seem like that at all. He loves you, adores the boys, seemed happy to have his own family, not like his father who hated commitment. I just don't understand it.' She ran her fingers up and down the arms of the chair, picking and

344

rubbing at the fabric as if she wanted to wear it away.

'When did you meet Robert?' Grace asked, really just to divert her.

'I went to stay with a friend from school, and Robert lived next door. He'd just broken up with a long-term girlfriend. I think I rather threw myself at him' — she smiled wanly — 'but I loved him. I *do* love him, as well as being grateful to him for rescuing me and Jonathan, and giving Jonathan a good life. That's why I feel so hurt that Jonathan has done this to him and the girls. They can't believe it either.' Her voice wobbled.

'Where are they?'

'They want to stay on in their rooms at Bristol. I don't think they can bring themselves to see him. You know how they adored him, their wonderful older brother, even though there was such a large age gap . . . ' Her voice tailed off. After a while she said, 'Caspar and India came round, without ringing first, which was strange. They told Robert about it, but I couldn't believe it. You know how arrogant and spoilt they are? I thought they had some axe to grind against Jonathan, or were making it up.'

'I can't believe it either, and what's worse I might have stopped it, if only I'd asked him about his racing, insisted on going with him. India . . . ' She paused, not really wanting to go into India's motives. ' . . . warned me, she said she'd seen him putting on huge sums of money but I thought it was just her exaggerating.'

'India has too much time on her hands, if you ask me. It's all very well her noticing these things, but when one is so busy bringing up children, working, coping with a husband like you are, I know it's all you can do to keep to the job on hand. One hasn't time or energy to go digging about looking for trouble,' Marianne said as if she knew how it was.

'I know but, Marianne, I loved him so much, felt lucky to have him.' Grace leant forward in her chair and said earnestly, 'You know how he married me when I got pregnant? When I lost the baby I was so . . . grateful, I suppose, that he wanted to stay married to me, I swore to myself I'd do anything to make him happy. I didn't question it when small sums of money went missing.' She smiled sourly. 'After all in marriage you're meant to share and he was always so generous I thought it unfair to make a fuss if he borrowed a little money from my bag from time to time. Besides, he told me once he hated people prying on his life, so I swore to myself I wouldn't.' She raked her hands through her hair. 'I know this all sounds as if I'm pathetic, but once you stop trusting someone everything is over, isn't it?'

'Of course. But, my dear, we all feel at fault, and besides it is so easy to be wise after the event. So easy for other people to accuse us of being naïve, but so often one's instincts and emotions at the time are tied up elsewhere. In bringing up children, for instance.' It was a road she knew, well, after all. 'But in the end it is up to him. He knew it was wrong; he should never have let himself get in so deep. I'd have thought seeing his father like he is would be enough to keep him away from gambling.'

'That made him worse. Seeing him like that made him reckless, determined not to let us sink so low. But now . . . Oh, Marianne, he will go to prison, won't he?' She said the words fast as if they stung her. 'What shall I do?'

Marianne shuddered. 'I don't know. If only I could help you, but he lost so much of Robert's money that things are going to be very difficult for us. We may even have to sell this house. What about your parents, can they help you?'

'I must tell them about it,' she said, 'but

they have nothing. They live in a tiny place in Portugal with hardly enough room for us. Anyway I can't live there, the boys need to go to school.' She began to shiver again remembering that Jonathan had cashed in their education policies. 'I'll need to get more work. Talking of work, I'd better ring one of my clients. I promised to finish her house by the end of the month. I must keep to that, I'll need every client I can get now.'

She took out her diary and looked up the number of June Bradley, a woman who had enthused over her ideas and begged her to decorate her house in Chelsea, no expense spared.

'Oh, Mrs Sheridan.' June's voice was cold. 'I won't be requiring your services any more. Goodbye.'

Grace put down the receiver as if it were a poisonous snake. Marianne saw her shocked expression and said gently, 'I'm afraid a lot of people are going to hate you. They're going to vent their anger on you as well as Jonathan.'

'I know.' She walked heavily back to the sofa, telling Marianne about Sarah and then about what a boy at school had said to Sebastian.

'They'll have to leave their schools,' Marianne said. 'I don't suppose you can afford to keep sending them there anyway, but I think it's too much to expect them to put up with other people's vitriol. Lucy's mother rang and said that in the circumstances she didn't want Jack to go to Lucy's birthday party. I didn't tell him, so he doesn't know he's missed it. He hasn't been at school for the last two days. I kept him here with Sebastian.'

'I suppose one can understand their anger, but it's a bit unfair to take it out on the children,' Grace said wearily, knowing she couldn't bear to tell Marianne about Jonathan taking the children's education insurance.

'I know, but this is only the beginning. I think you should take the children away. Perhaps they could stay with your parents for a while?'

'Perhaps they could, during the trial. Oh, God, will it be in the newspapers? I'll have to get them away from London. It'll be such a squash in my parents' tiny house, we always stay in a hotel when we visit them, but I'm sure Mummy and Daddy will have them.' At least she thought, she had parents who'd stand by them.

★ ★ ★

All day they waited in extreme agitation for news from Jonathan, but none came. They fought to hide their feelings from the boys. Grace felt heavy with misery and completely helpless. She didn't know where to contact him. She rang Paul Cartwright, his lawyer, but he was out. All she could do was leave a message begging him to ring her, then wait.

With half of herself Grace longed to see Jonathan, have him here safe, away from the indignities he must be suffering at the police station; the other half of her could not bear to see him again after the pain he had caused his children.

It was ten o'clock when he finally rang. 'I've got to stay here tonight, I . . . I can't find anyone to put up ten thousand pounds surety for me.' She could barely hear his voice, it was so sunk in despair. Before she could find words to comfort him he rang off leaving her crying after him, swearing she would find the money.

'What's happened?' Marianne said fearfully.

'He can't find anyone to stand bail,' Grace said in a small voice; then she remembered her jewels, beautiful pieces that Jonathan had bought her over the years. They were in the safe at home. Each piece meant something special to her, their first anniversary, the birth of each child, but this was no time to be sentimental, it was the only way she could raise the money to get him out.

'It's too late to fetch them tonight. Besides,' Marianne shivered, her voice breaking, 'I'm afraid he'll have to get used to prison. Go tomorrow.'

But Grace could not wait. She went straight back home to get her jewellery. She knew she would not sleep thinking of Jonathan locked away, alone. She needed to have it safe in her hand tonight so she could take it to his lawyer first thing in the morning.

She opened the safe and took out the large blue leather box that held her treasures. It was surprisingly light and she barely had to open it to know that it was empty.

She stared in horror at the empty velvet cushions inside. How could he take these things he had given her with such love? Take them without asking her? He had sold the only way she had to pay his bail.

She knelt there on the floor beside the open safe for a long time, cursing the poison that had invaded him, the poison that would ruin them all. She saw the yawning blackness before her and felt helpless in the face of it. Then anger kicked in. How dare he do this to them? Serve him right if he had to stay

351

in custody until the trial.

But when she got back and told Marianne and saw her bitter tears she felt again the agony of hopelessness. She felt too the fear of having to go on, living with his shame, having to make a life for her children, alone.

★ ★ ★

So tired and defeated was Grace by his latest act of betrayal that she drifted through the next day doing nothing about Jonathan, knowing he had taken away her only means of helping him, or starting a fresh life for her and the boys. Then, to her amazement, at half-past nine that night, Jonathan came back. He looked a hundred years old. He sank into a chair, closing his eyes. Both women hovered round him offering him sustenance, momentarily forgetting their anger with him. But he shook his head and waved them away.

The two women sat apart from him in the drawing room. There was only one lamp on and they sat as if in vigil. Marianne kept falling asleep and at last Grace persuaded her to go to bed. She sat on alone watching Jonathan who lay flung back in the chair, one arm thrown across his face, his eyes closed. Yet she knew he was not asleep.

At last he stirred. 'I've had a terrible time,' he said, as if each word hurt. 'I thought I'd never get out; I couldn't get bail. I thought I had a few friends, but in the end I have none.'

Grace did not trust herself to speak.

'I have nothing left, but we can say most of the furniture and pictures are yours. Someone I know . . . who's not involved with all this mess, may strike a deal with me. If I give him the good bits of furniture, he'll give me, or rather you, a cottage he owns, but wants to sell. Then at least you'll have somewhere to live.' He didn't look at her as he spoke.

She heard his words but she didn't take them in. She knew she wanted to go away, away from all the people they had once thought of as friends, the people he had wronged. Away from him. But even as she acknowledged this, looking at his broken form, his haggard face, she knew that somewhere beneath her feelings of pain, anger and betrayal, part of her still loved him.

'How did you get bail?' she asked.

'Oh, India put it up for me,' he said with a slight smile.

'India!' Her mouth felt dry. 'But surely India wouldn't want to have anything to do with this.' Hadn't she convinced herself that India would drop all ideas of wanting him now he'd committed this crime? She felt sick with envy, with fear that still India had a hold over him. 'How did she know you needed the money, did you tell her?' she demanded, stung to the bone.

'She found out about it through someone who'd refused me. She rang my solicitor this afternoon and said she'd put the money up for me. It's awfully good of her.'

'Awfully good!' Grace spat. 'I was prepared to sell my jewellery to raise the money for you, but you've sold it, sold it without telling me!'

'Darling . . . I . . . '

'Don't make any more excuses, I'm sick of them. India has got you exactly where she wants you,' she flung at him, 'grovelling at her feet.' She whirled from the room, so hurt, so furious with both of them. India with her money and her connections, had always been superior to Grace, except this once — she too could have saved Jonathan with her jewellery. But Jonathan had sold it, giving India the chance she needed to get him.

21

'So you put up Jonathan's bail, India. Whatever's in it for you?' Freddie said, lying back languidly on the sofa in her mews house. 'I mean, he's as guilty as hell, isn't he? He's bound to go to prison.'

'I put up the bail because what he did was a mistake. He didn't exactly set out to steal from his investors. Anyway, like most of these City scams, if it had worked no one would have said anything,' India said. She didn't want to talk about her action. She'd done it on impulse and now, well, no, she wasn't regretting it at all.

'But he was a bloody fool, gambling it all on horses like that. The court isn't going to like it. Public-school boy who should have known better. At least he didn't go to Eton.'

'They say the prisons are stiff with old Etonians,' India said coolly. She closed her eyes. It was a terrible business. If only Caspar hadn't invested money with Jonathan. It was a relief it hadn't been more than he could afford to lose, but he'd been furious when he'd heard she'd put up the surety, accused her of betraying the family. Max had said the same thing, though her affair with him was finished now she'd got bored of him — though she'd used the fact that he'd gone and married that girl to produce his son and heir, without telling her, as a valid enough reason to dispense with him.

'Why did you do it, anyway? You haven't said,' Freddie asked again. 'I'd accuse you of being after a bit of rough, but he's hardly rough, is he? Is it him being a criminal that appeals to you, or is your new good work adopting a felon?' he teased her.

'Don't be silly, Freddie,' she said irritably. She didn't want to tell him or anyone why she had done it. It was sheer luck that she'd heard of it. She'd gone to have a drink in Green's Oyster Bar with a friend and Bertie Milne had been in there, saying at the top of his voice, 'Bit of cheek, what, Jonathan Sheridan asking me to stand bail for him?'

It had been easy to get the story and the number of Jonathan's solicitor from Bertie, who was only too glad of a bit of interest in what he considered a grave insult to himself.

'How he dare ask me, I wasn't even at school with the bastard,' he muttered into his drink.

She had rung Jonathan's solicitor and

sorted it out at once. Jonathan had been very grateful and to her surprise she hadn't liked that. She had thought . . . what had she thought? That he would toss her that devastating smile, drive off with her, make love to her with abandon, as if he'd loved and wanted her all along, and was treating this business with the law as just a tiresome aberration in an otherwise enjoyable life? But when she'd met him at the police station he'd just looked ashamed and sheepish and her heart had sunk.

He'd asked her to drive him to his mother's when she'd offered to give him a lift, but he had barely spoken to her on the journey, and had not asked her in when they'd arrived.

'I don't know how to thank you,' he'd said, not looking at her. Then he got out of the car and went into the house without looking back.

But she couldn't go back on it now, she told herself defiantly, stung also by Caspar's and some of their friends' reaction to her conduct. Jonathan must be shattered, two days and a night spent in police custody would test the strongest of men. She must be patient a little longer, wait until he was rested. He would soon be himself again.

'There must be a reason for you to help him. Are you having an affair with him? Or

357

did you do it to be a rebel?' Freddie said. 'It's quite a lot of money. Would you have done it for me?'

'I might have. I just hate the hypocrisy. So many people in the City fly too close to the wind and no one says anything while it's working,' India said lamely.

'The crime is to be found out,' Freddie said, looking at her intently. 'Now answer my other question. Are you having an affair with him?'

'Don't be silly, Freddie,' she said sourly. 'Now tell me, how is Amanda, any babies yet?' She didn't want him to guess how much she wanted Jonathan, or worse, see that she was disappointed in the result of her action.

'No babies, only the imminent arrival of spaniel puppies,' Freddie said, looking awkward. He sighed. 'The fact is, India, I . . . well,' he laughed, embarrassed, 'I don't really fancy her that way. She's a great girl, we have a lot of fun together, but . . . well, you know.'

'Oh, Freddie,' she sighed, knowing he had never been exactly keen on sex. He wasn't gay either, he just didn't seem to care for it. She wondered if he and Amanda had silly nicknames for each other, put valentine messages in The Times, 'Piggy Wiggy loves

Froggie Woggie', all baby talk but no real action. The British, she thought, love childish jokes about sex, chocolate willies and boob pasta. Perhaps they would rather laugh about it than do it. Freddie would anyway. 'You must make an effort,' she said. 'You only need a couple of children.'

'You sound like my sisters,' he said. 'Do your bit for Queen and Country, an heir and a spare. But look at Caspar with three girls. Is he having another shot at a son?'

'I don't know, I suppose so,' India said, wincing as she remembered again Caspar's anger at her standing bail for Jonathan.

'He's a rotter of the worst kind, taking money from his friends,' he'd thundered. 'How could you, India? You've put the whole family into a very embarrassing position. I don't know what Father will say. I can only hope up there in Scotland he might not hear too much about it. But wait until the papers get hold of it, they'll have a field day at our expense.'

'Doesn't Amanda mind?' India said to get her mind off the memories. 'Doesn't she want babies?'

'We will get one,' Freddie said as if babies could be produced as easily as another spaniel. 'I've been in London rather a lot lately, I'll go back to Scotland soon.'

'It would help if you were with her,' India said, but not too strongly. She enjoyed having him back as an escort, he was good fun and there were no strings attached, but now all her energies were going to be focused on Jonathan.

Although she'd rather die than admit it, India was disillusioned with her life: the round of parties, the fawning men, the charity committees. Even though her father and Anthea had moved out of Elmley, leaving it to Caspar and Sophie, and gone to Scotland, she no longer enjoyed going there so much now that it was full of whining children. Standing beside Jonathan would be a new challenge. She would succeed where poor Grace would fail, be the strong supportive friend. She smiled to herself, feeling a frisson of excitement as she pictured herself in her new role. She'd always got what she wanted in life and this would be no exception.

'How long will your criminal get, do you think?' Freddie too was tired of discussing his ability to father a child.

'What . . . Oh, I don't know.'

'At least five years I should imagine, unless he gets Community Service. That seems to be the thing these days, doesn't it? I suppose he'll paint pensioners' flats or something.

Will he be good at that, do you think? I know I'd be hopeless.'

'I really don't know, Freddie.' She wished he'd leave it alone.

'He's married to your cousin, isn't he? What will she do if he's put inside?'

'I don't know. Her parents live in Portugal; she may go there.' India did not like to think of Jonathan going to prison and rather hoped that Freddie was right about Community Service. She knew nothing of the legal system. She supposed that with good behaviour and various other vague reasons like he didn't set out to be a thief, or the judge might have been at school with him so give him a lenient sentence, Jonathan might be out in a matter of weeks, if he went at all. She rather fancied herself as a prison visitor, imagining naïvely he would be with a whole group of public-school boys all in for similar offences. She thought of sustaining him with long letters and managed successfully, in her mind, to write off Grace as not being able to cope and anyway living away from England with her children. Then having so much time to think while he was incarcerated would surely make Jonathan realize that he wanted to be with her, instead of Grace. All these thoughts she carefully nurtured.

'Let's go and eat, I'm starving,' Freddie

said, getting up. 'I think you're bored, India, you ought to have married me, you know, you'd have had lots to do then.'

'You've got Amanda, Freddie, remember?'

'I could have two wives. But talking of wives, how is your mother and that creepy boyfriend?' He laughed, then seeing her pained expression said hurriedly, 'Poor India, you've had the most dreadful time with your parents' love lives.'

'I think he's going off her. I hate him, he makes me feel . . . sort of grubby.' She shivered with revulsion. 'I wish it would finish, but now I see it will be a disaster for Mummy if it does. She's always had men falling at her feet, but now what with her age and her stupidity at going off with someone like that, the few nice men of her age that she could have made a life with have gone elsewhere.' As she told Freddie about this she felt a small chill inside herself. It upset her seeing how a beautiful, charming woman like her mother could so easily be left alone. It made her afraid she too could suffer the same fate. The spectacle of her mother fighting to keep her dreadful creep at any cost because of her fear of not having a man by her side, made her more determined than ever to secure Jonathan.

Jonathan rang her three days later to thank her again for putting up the surety money. 'I'm sorry, I was so whacked that day I could hardly speak. I had a hell of a day, going to court, searching for bail money, not to mention a sleepless night.'

'I understand,' she said, her heart lifting. 'How's it all going?'

'It's pretty much hell,' he said, then paused.

'Do you want to talk about it?'

'N . . . no, thanks, India. I must sort out things here, see that Grace and the boys have somewhere to live. You will . . . well, she is your cousin so I'm sure you will see her sometimes when if the worst happens and I get put inside. We haven't any friends left. It's all my fault, I know . . . but . . . '

India swallowed. She didn't want to be nice to Grace. She had thought for a moment that he was ringing her to arrange to see her, to confide in her because he couldn't get through to Grace or his mother.

'I'll understand if you don't want anything to do with either of us,' he said and before she could protest he went on, 'none, and I really mean it, of this business is in any way Grace's fault. I didn't tell her what I

363

was doing and thank God she's never been one to pry, so I don't want her and the boys to take the flak for what I did. Do you understand?'

'Yes, of course. But . . . ' Her mind swung into action. ' . . . you know what people are like when they lose money, they're so furious they want to hit out at anyone who's involved, however remotely, and as your wife of course people will think she knew all about it. Wouldn't it be far better for her, better for the boys, if they went away while all this was going on? Surely she could stay with her parents in Portugal until it's all over?'

She saw a picture of herself at his trial, standing tall and beautiful, dressed soberly yet elegantly, the mysterious friend standing by while his wife was out of the country with the children.

'I'll discuss it with Grace,' he said, 'it might be the best idea. She's been wonderful but, well, it's getting to her a bit now. The press, everything.'

'It must be so difficult for her, and having the children to cope with too,' she said in her most sincere voice. 'You know, Jonathan, sometimes it helps talking things over with someone else, someone not so close to you. Please come round whenever you feel the need to talk, or just get away from it all.'

'India, I don't know what to say.' He laughed sourly. 'I don't know why you're being so kind, after all I've lost your brother money and your . . . er . . . Max, not to mention what I've done to your cousin.'

'Max and I are finished,' she said firmly.

'Oh, I hope not because of me, oh, God . . .'

'No, I got bored of him, it was nothing whatever to do with you. But I mean what I say, Jonathan. Come round whenever, day or night, when you need to. You know my address?'

'Thank you . . . I'd like that. It's . . . ' He paused again, then said in a rush, 'It's dreadful here, all of us trying very hard not to hurt each other any more. I could shoot myself for what I've done to them, but that would only solve it for me, and leave them worse off.'

'Jonathan.' Her voice was strong, 'I know you're a man of courage and honour but that you made some misguided mistakes. I'm sure it will be sorted out and that when everyone's calmed down, things won't look so bad.'

'Thank you, India,' he said and then just as she was about to ask him round that very day she heard him say, 'Grace, it's India. I know she'll be a good friend to you. Do you want to talk to her?'

'No, thank you,' India heard Grace say in the background and then something else that she couldn't catch.

'Poor Grace,' India said to Jonathan in her most understanding voice, 'she sounds absolutely exhausted. You must insist that she goes away to her parents for a while. You can always stay here if you like, I have a spare room.'

22

Grace sat on the huge rock staring out to sea. She felt the warmth of the sun on her back and for a moment it soothed her. Below her the boys played on the beach, their tight, white bodies relaxing a little at last so she felt that for long periods now they went without thinking of the terrible disgrace and unhappiness their father had inflicted on them.

Jack, at six, seemed not to have been too badly affected by it. He was a happy, carefree child still locked into his baby world of make-believe. He knew his father had done wrong, had witnessed the tears, the clenched-teeth recriminations of his grandparents and his mother, but those had, as far as Grace knew, washed over him. It was easier to protect him from the hatred of his friends' parents. It was Sebastian she was afraid for.

He was almost nine and he saw and felt far more than Jack did. He idolized Jonathan and she knew he felt desperately betrayed by him. Yet he was too young to know exactly what he'd done, too young to see that though he had done wrong, Jonathan had not set out to steal from his clients, his family and his friends. Some people might say putting money on the stock market was gambling and should not be surprised if they lost it, Jonathan had chosen to put the money on the horses — admittedly without telling his clients first — but if it had not gone wrong and had made his clients money instead, it would have been a different story.

She had tried to explain to the children that although their father had done very wrong he was not a bad person, he still loved them. They must still love him, but even as she said this, holding Sebastian's tense body to her and trying to smooth away the tightness in his face, she felt her own love for Jonathan falter. The man she had thought she'd known and loved for all these years, had gone. It was this she found so hard to take, the fact that he had lived another life without her, running parallel beside the life she knew.

India, who as yet had not accosted her in person, telephoned her from time to time, 'to give her support', as she put it, had said, 'You always were naïve, Grace, you let your love blind you to the truth. You know that sort of love is rather unrealistic, but of course your mother loves your father like that so it's hardly surprising you'd go the same way.'

Grace, hating the familiar sneer in her voice, shouted, 'Leave me alone, India, leave us all alone,' and slammed down the phone. But her words had stuck like burrs, painful in their truth. She dreaded seeing her, the old feelings of inferiority adding to her turmoil, but making her determined to fight on, to keep Jonathan with her.

She could, she told herself, have withstood any amount of pain from Jonathan for herself, but not for her children. They should not have to suffer so much because of him: lose their way of life, their friends, who themselves were too young to understand why they could not play with them any more, who had to witness the angry hatred of their parents over the misdeeds of their friends' father.

She felt a movement beside her and Leo, her father, sat down and put his arm round her. 'I wish I could help, darling.'

'You are,' she said, 'by having us here, giving the children a haven.'

'I wish I could do more: financially, I mean.' He smiled sourly. 'I suppose I've been selfish in my life, painting instead of getting something more lucrative, more secure. We are so happy out here, we need so little and luckily your mother — unlike her sister — doesn't demand an expensive way of life, but it's at times like now that

I wish I had money to help you.'

'Money's not everything,' she said, praying suddenly that he wasn't going to suggest that Uncle William might help as he had with her school fees. 'I know you've both always been there for me, and that's more important. I can't tell you what it means to be here with you, away from it all.'

'Money would help you with the more practical things.' He sighed. 'You know, darling, you can all stay here for as long as you like. But the boys need to go to school and there is nothing much near here. I really do wish I could pay for them.'

'Daddy, don't.' She laid her head against his. Much though she loved him she couldn't bring herself to tell him that Jonathan had lost the children's money. It was the thing that she found the most hurtful in the whole of this ghastly matter, that he had used his children's future to feed his gambling.

'I just want to get through the trial then I'll decide what to do. Jonathan has made some deal with a friend, exchanging some of our wonderful furniture for this holiday cottage in Aldeburgh. I've never been there, but there are bound to be schools nearby. I just can't think that far ahead.' She didn't say that she had another worry, a worse worry than Jonathan's disgrace; that he no longer loved her and wanted to be free of her.

After a few difficult weeks, they had gone down to their country home in Wiltshire to get away from London, but it had not been any easier there. Although it was easier to hide in the cottage, surrounded as it was by its large garden, the atmosphere in the village had been as hard to bear as life in town. Many of their friends there had lost money with Jonathan and there had also been some hate mail, which wounded her terribly.

She had opened one letter just addressed to The Sheridans and there in thick, black ink were the words: *I hope you all rot in hell for what you have done, ruining all our lives.* It was not signed.

Fortunately the children weren't there at that moment, but Jonathan, seeing her stricken face, had taken it from her, torn it up and thrown it away, and told her not to think of it again. 'It's obviously from a madman, who's probably got nothing to do with the affair but has read about it in the newspapers and decided to take it upon himself to torment us,' he said, stamping out of the room and leaving her to bear the shock of it alone.

When Jonathan was with them they tried to live as normal a life as possible, though the atmosphere was strained and they had no friends to relieve it. But he was often up in London, seeing his solicitor, making his monthly visit to the court, and when he came back into the house, she could feel the tension tighten in the air, and see the boys, especially Sebastian, close in again upon themselves. It did not help that most of the money they lived on came from one of her savings.

Many times Grace caught Jonathan watching her. She knew she looked dreadful; white-faced, hollow-eyed from tiredness. She tried to make an effort, but all the time she felt he was silently criticizing her, angry at the way she was reacting, at her looking as she did, tortured by the pain he had inflicted on the children, unable to sleep with the worry of what their future held.

One day he'd said, 'I think it would be a good idea if you took the children to your parents. The trial will be a dreadful time, I don't think they should be here for that. I'll find some money for the tickets and to help pay their board with your parents.'

She didn't ask where the money would come from. Knowing he had hidden some pictures and silver, she was fearful all the time that he'd put more on the horses to try and win everything back.

'They have offered to have them and

you're right, I'd like them to be out of it,'
she'd agreed. 'But I'll be here for you.'

He'd looked at her, then burst out in
anguish: 'I don't want you here. Stay in
Portugal with them, stay until it is all
over.'

'What? Why can't I stay with you? I want
to be with you.' The words were wrung out
of her.

He had seized her arms and shaken her.
'Don't you see? I can't bear to see the
hurt I have caused you. I can't bear to
see your strained face and the children's
tension. I understand now why my father
wouldn't come with us, he couldn't bear to
see the pain and the pity . . . yes, the pity
in my eyes.'

'Oh, Jonathan.' She felt the tears rise up
in her and struggled to stop them, knowing
they would add to his hatred — his hatred
of himself.

He dropped her arms and took a few
steps away from her. 'I'm sorry,' he said
levelly, 'I know I'm to blame for everything,
for destroying your lives. It's pointless to
say I never knew my actions would have
such a devastating effect, but don't you
understand, Grace, seeing you, seeing the
boys, seeing my mother so affected, seeing
the huge effort you're making to stand by

me, makes me feel worse. I want to go away, even to prison, where I won't be tortured by it, by your reproachful face any more. *Do you understand?*' His voice was desperate, his eyes burning in his drawn face.

'Yes,' she said in a small voice. Catching sight of herself in the mirror that hung above the mantelpiece she hated the cringing, pale creature she'd become. She thought of India and how she would despise her for her weakness. Every day among the battles she emotionally girded herself to face was the fear of India coming or telephoning and the knowledge that her beauty and her strength would be a far more attractive champion for Jonathan.

One night, almost defeated by it all, she said to him, 'Would you rather be with India?'

'India? No, why should I?' he'd said, frowning at her, and had then asked again how she thought the children were coping and if it wouldn't be better for them to go to her parents in Portugal.

She'd felt torn between supporting Jonathan and staying here to guard him against India, and doing what was best for the children, but their lives were still so new, so easily bruised. She knew it would be so much better for them to be with her parents, away from all this. She knew she must take them, settle them in, even if it did leave the coast clear for India.

'I'll take them to my parents and then I'll come back for the trial,' she said firmly. 'Somehow we must remain a family.'

'So how long will you stay with us?' her father said gently.

She turned to him and smiled. 'I wish I could stay for ever, escape what lies ahead, make a new life with you and Mummy and the boys, but I know I must go back, stand by Jonathan.'

'What will you do when it's over? I'm afraid if he's found guilty he's bound to go to prison.'

'I know. I . . . I'm afraid he'll be so different when he comes out. Already I feel he's a different man. I'm frightened that I'll no longer love him.' She did not add that she was also afraid he no longer loved her and that India would get him if she had not done so already.

He held her close. 'No one can answer that, my darling. Time and his experience — and by God, I pity him despite what he's done — if he is locked away, will decide. Just take each day, don't burden yourself with any more.'

They heard the children running up behind

them, her mother following close behind. She was smiling and Grace knew she was happy to have her grandsons with her.

'Come and see my castle,' Jack said, flinging himself down on the ground beside her. 'It's so big, Grandpa, you won't believe it.'

'I'm sure I won't. What about you, Sebastian, did you build one too?'

Grace's heart warmed. Without her saying anything her parents had understood the situation with the children. Her father had made a special effort with Sebastian and he seemed to be responding, loosening up a little, taking an interest in Leo's painting, asking to do some too.

'No,' Sebastian said, 'I made a sort of sculpture instead.'

'Good, I can hardly wait to see these amazing things. Let's go and look at them.'

The boys ran on ahead and Grace walked slowly between her parents. The terrible agitation of the last months seemed to have calmed in her. One of her worst worries had eased: the boys seemed so happy here, and her parents, although horrified by the reason for it, were delighted to have them. They would be safe here, they might not be in school, but they were loved and secure, far away from the hatred and the misery caused by their father's crime.

'I think I'll have to go back on Wednesday,' she said with a sigh, linking arms with her parents. 'I can't tell you what a weight it is off my mind knowing the boys are here with you.'

'We'll keep them safe until you come back,' her father said.

'I wish . . . I wish I could bring Jonathan with me,' she said, suddenly realizing what it would be like to come back to this bright and beautiful country alone leaving him behind in prison. But she knew deep inside herself that she wanted to return to the old times, bring back the Jonathan she had loved so much, not this stranger who had been poisoned by his addiction.

'Hush,' Leo said. Her mother tightened her grip on her arm. 'Remember that old cliché,' Leo went on. 'Just one day at a time. Put away your imagination, just take life as it comes.'

377

23

India lay back in her bed and watched Jonathan dress. It had happened; she had seduced him — or perhaps he had seduced her — but it had not been at all how she had imagined it would be. She was left feeling sadder and emptier than ever, for she felt that he would never really love her.

He had come round to her mews house quite a few times, just to sit staring into space, or to talk. He told her how he couldn't bear to see Grace and his children and witness the pain his actions had inflicted on them staring him in the face day after day.

She had thought that she'd got him then. She recognized that it was his own guilt that had turned him from Grace, but still it had made him free of her, and he had come to her, just as she'd always hoped he would.

'I do so understand,' she said gently, moving closer to him on the sofa where they sat side by side. 'You need to be with someone who is not affected by the situation, who can stand back and see it from your point of view.'

'But you are affected, after all Caspar and

Max lost their money because of me.'

'I know, but it won't cripple either of them, and I know it was a mistake. It'll all come out in the trial and then everyone will see you didn't mean to do it. After all,' she laughed, 'if you'd continued to make them money, they would have praised you.' She let her eyes linger on his face, his mouth, yearning to kiss it, be kissed back with passion, but he didn't seem to notice her. His eyes, once so bright, so seductive in their careless glances, were now dull and blank.

'A drunk may not mean to run over a child and kill it, but if he does he's guilty,' he said. 'Oh, India, don't you see? I'm like my father, I can't help it. The thrill of gambling is something I can't explain. It's not so much winning money, having it without doing a day's work — though that's attractive too — it's the flow of adrenaline. To keep that going I'll do anything.' His voice was rough, his eyes frantic and for a moment she felt out of her depth.

'You can't imagine what it's like to see your horse win, especially if it's an outsider,' he said. 'I loved your father's stables, it was there that I first got that buzz seeing the horses riding out, the smell of them, the speed of them. It all gives me such a kick.' He'd grabbed her hands excitedly. 'I had a good win the other day, I had some money from a picture I'd sold, I put it on an accumulator and I won.'

She looked into his face with curiosity and not a little fear. He was as excited as if he were just about to make love, as if he found her the most arousing woman in the world. But she knew it was not her that enflamed him now, it was the gambling.

Neither Grace nor I, she thought miserably, as she listened to him, and saw the light coming back into his eyes, can have him. He is lost to this other mistress who is far more attractive and compelling than either of us.

Then suddenly he did kiss her and the passion for gambling seemed to transfer itself to his lovemaking, and although her body enjoyed it, her mind was thinking, It's not me he loves, nor even Grace, but this deadly compulsion.

'Jonathan,' she said watching him now, admiring his still attractive, lithe body, 'you should get help for your gambling, you know. Does Grace know how bad it is?'

'Help?' He gave her a quizzical smile, pausing in doing up the buttons on his shirt. 'Why should I need help? I can stop it any time I want to. It's just a bit of fun, and can be very lucrative too.'

'How can you say that when you've just lost so many people their money and you've been arrested for it?' she said, afraid for him now, sad that her victory in getting him into bed had been such a hollow one.

'I didn't set out to rob them. I'm not guilty really, you see, just unfortunate. I could get it back, if I had the time,' he said. 'I would have stayed abroad and done so, then I wouldn't be in this mess now, but Grace was missing the children, and my mother wanted me to come back.' He looked bitter for a moment, then he smiled, a little too brightly. 'I've got to go now, it's my day for calling in at the police station to show that I haven't done a runner.'

'You'd better not as I've put up the bail for you,' she said with feeling.

'I can never thank you enough for that,' he said gently and came over and kissed her again. 'I always thought you were so superior — indeed you were when we were younger, but deep down you are a really kind, tender person.'

She felt the warmth of his remark flood her and she drew him to her and kissed him again on his lips.

'I must go,' he laughed, kissing her breasts, her mouth, then all down her body until, throwing off his clothes, he made love to her again and this time she felt that he did love her, or anyway want her enough to come back to her.

He left her at last, promising to return later, but though she waited in all day he did not come and it was not until she turned on the television news later that evening and saw the results of the day's race meetings that she suspected he had gone to one of them and had forgotten her.

She should have dismissed him from her mind then, she knew, remembering her earlier conviction that gambling was his only love, but she couldn't forget how he'd said how kind and tender she was, and how soft and loving his face had been as he did so.

His words flowed through her like balm, making her feel more loved than she had ever before. She would save him from this fatal flaw, she promised herself. Surely she could. She knew of alcoholics who had been cured. She would help him, stand by him through the trial. Once it was known he was addicted to gambling surely they would give him a lenient sentence, if any at all? Grace would not be able to cope, after all had she not refused to acknowledge the fact that he gambled all these years? Also she had the children to worry about, she'd said it was being so occupied with them that stopped her finding out. She'd certainly be too busy with them to help him now. Filled with this enthusiasm she rang his house. Grace answered.

'Oh, India,' she said, 'what do you want?'

India smiled to herself, feeling the passion of Jonathan's love-making as if they had only just stopped. 'Is Jonathan there?'

'No, he's not. What do you want him for?'

If only you knew, simple, poor little Grace, India thought, seeing him again in her arms. 'Just tell him I rang. Are you going back to . . . wherever with your parents?'

'After the trial. I am staying here for that,' Grace said firmly, putting down the receiver.

'So we will both be there,' India said to the empty room. She went into her bedroom to choose clothes to wear each day at the trial. She was determined to look her best: beautiful yet mysterious. She imagined that the press coverage might be a little like it had been for the Maxwells' trial. After all, quite a few well-known people were affected. She imagined how the newspapers would speculate over her role in the affair. The telephone rang; it was Caspar.

'I understand you've been seeing Jonathan.'

'So? It's a free country. How do you know anyway?'

'So it's true?'

'Why shouldn't it be? Look, Caspar, who has been spying on me?' India said impatiently, wondering if it was the police, or even if Grace, unable to ask herself, had gone running to Caspar.

'That boyfriend of Mother's. He said he was just passing your house and saw him come out.'

'The swine, what was he doing just passing my house, and anyway how does he know it was Jonathan?' India spat.

'His picture was in the paper, remember, and I don't know or care what Jeremy was doing outside your house. What are you playing at, India? First you set up bail for him, now he's seen leaving your house. It doesn't look good. What are you up to?'

'It's none of your business, Caspar,' she began, furious with Jeremy for spying on her, for running with tales to Caspar. 'Jeremy is a troublemaker, yet Mummy still insists on holding on to him even though it's quite obvious he's sick of her. I wish she had some pride — '

'I think it is my business,' Caspar broke in. 'Jonathan has after all lost me and many of my friends a considerable amount of money, and is standing trial for it. If you had any family feeling at all you'd be ostracizing him, not giving him hospitality. Or have I got it wrong? Is he pestering you?'

'No, of course he's not. It's just . . . well, you wouldn't understand, Caspar. Jonathan didn't mean to do wrong, he wanted to make you money, not lose it. He's mortified, he — '

'India, don't tell me you're in love with him, or any such nonsense!' Caspar sounded horrified. 'He's married to Grace, poor girl. Don't tell me that you're after him?'

'What if he loves me?' she said defiantly.

'I'd run a mile,' Caspar said. 'Look, we'd better meet, this is worse than I thought. I admit I thought that creep Jeremy was trying to cause trouble, but you've got to see sense. The man's a criminal, and your cousin's husband. You cannot, must not, have anything to do with him.'

'He's innocent until proved guilty and I'll live my own life, thank you, Caspar, and you live yours.' India said furiously, slamming down the receiver. Fury whirled through her. How dare that creep Jeremy spy on her? She detested him.

She snatched up her bag and her coat and went round at once to her mother's.

'That bloody boyfriend of yours,' she began as Flavia, her hair now an alarming auburn, opened the door. She was dressed

385

in a little-girl cream dress that looked very like a petticoat. The sight of her done up like this infuriated India even more.

'India! Wh . . . what do you . . . want?' Flavia bleated fearfully, her over made-up eyes bulging like a fish's.

India marched into the house and flung herself down on the sofa in the drawing room. Flavia followed her anxiously muttering to her to stop, to keep her voice down.

'He's been spying on me, then ringing Caspar with stories about who I see,' she said. 'Really, Mummy, we've all had enough of him. Can't you get rid of him?'

'Hello, India, my you are het up today,' Jeremy glided into the room, his streaked hair perfectly groomed, an amused smile on his lips.

She turned on him. 'All because of you, you creep. How dare you spy on me? It's none of your business who I have in my house. If I catch you at it again, I'll tell the police you're stalking me.'

'Really.' He smiled again, sitting down slowly and gracefully on a large armchair opposite her.

'Oh, India, darling, I'm sure he didn't mean . . . ' Flavia began vainly, wanting to smooth everything over.

'I'm sure he did,' India spat. 'Why do you

always hang round older women, playing on their vulnerability? Can't you make it with your own age group?'

'I can make it very well with my own age group, as you put it,' he said suavely, smiling sensually at her.

'Oh, India, do please go,' Flavia said desperately as if feeling the electric sexual vibes coming from Jeremy.

India felt them too and was disgusted with herself for feeling a small stirring of desire. Repellent though he was he obviously had a great animal attraction, and would feed on the basic instincts of a woman, enslaving her with his sexual prowess. She saw now how helpless her mother was under his magnetism, and how easy it would be to succumb to it herself. In her anger at her discovery, she hit out again. 'I shall go,' she said, 'but, Mummy, use your sense and what dignity you have left and throw him out. He'll destroy you.'

'Don't be silly, dear,' Flavia said shakily, trying to smile at Jeremy.

'Look forward to seeing you again, India,' Jeremy said smoothly.

'Just keep out of my life.' She stormed from the room and out into the street.

As she pounded along the pavement towards Harrods she tried to calm the raging turmoil inside herself. She wanted Jonathan; despite everything, she still wanted Jonathan. Now that Grace was back and Caspar so angry about her seeing him, it seemed to increase her determination to have him. What could she do? If only he would come to her again she would tell him that she had always loved him, that together they would win the fight against his conviction, that she would see him through.

But the memory of the burning fervour in his eyes when he'd talked of gambling haunted her, merging with her mother's frantic fear of losing Jeremy. That was her mother's addiction. There were some obsessions, she thought grimly, that were stronger than love, stronger than life itself. Yet she was determined to outdo them all and make Jonathan love her.

24

There was a month to go before the trial. Grace, who had just got back from a few days with her parents and the boys in Portugal, still felt as if her life with Jonathan was unreal, like a film running quite out of her control.

Sometimes she went over to Marianne's, but always when Robert was not there. He'd never said anything but she couldn't help feeling that he held her in some way responsible for not knowing what Jonathan was up to. But being with Marianne depressed her further.

Sometimes Marianne didn't even bother to get out of bed, just lay surrounded by the pills the doctor had given her: pills to wake her up, pills to put her to sleep. She was quite unable to cope. Other days she was better, then she would endlessly try and reason why Jonathan had turned out to be like his father when she and Robert had given him such a good upbringing. Her two daughters seemed to have opted out completely, preferring their own life far away at university or staying with their friends, leaving their parents to fend for themselves.

To help pass the creeping time Grace had got herself a few temporary jobs. Once she'd started, anonymous in some busy office, she felt better, part of the human race again. She could do a day's work and get paid for it then disappear back to her disembodied life beside Jonathan.

She noticed he had become not quite happier but more purposeful. This surprised her, for each day as the trial got nearer she felt worse, more afraid of the ordeal ahead and their eventual separation. For though her feelings for him now were mixed, she did not want to lose him, holding on tight to the fact that one day everything would be all right between them again. Each day he left the house and sometimes she didn't see him until late in the evening, but he always came back to her. She wondered what he did with his day, but when she asked him he smiled and said, 'There's so much to do, you wouldn't believe.'

'Like what?'

'Oh, this and that. Don't worry, darling, there's just a lot to tie up . . . you know.' He'd looked at her meaningfully as she had nodded, imagining he was getting ready for his time in prison. She didn't question him much these days, the wound of his betrayal was painful enough without her digging further into it.

One of her chief fears was that their creditors would obtain a court order on their property. Jonathan had no other assets and she had terrible visions of bailiffs coming at dawn. When she asked Jonathan about this he said, 'I've looked into that. The creditors have got to get a case against me first. That's why I'm trying to sell a few things before they can get them.'

She had tried to get more information from him, certain they would not be able to keep the money from the sales of the houses. But he just smiled, told her to stop worrying, everything would be fine. His attitude added a further anxiety to her already overwhelming load: had this crisis turned his mind so that he had convinced himself nothing was wrong and they would be safe?

Both properties were now on the market. Grace found this further torture, especially selling their London house. She'd done it up with such care, such love, seeing it as the epitome of all her dreams, a beautiful, happy home to bring up her family in. Now it would soon be gone. She hated showing people round it, feeling as if they were voyeurs picking through her life, tearing away her warm memories. She could not bear to think of other people living here, or other people's children growing up inside this haven, her haven. She tried to distance herself from it, finding it painful to clean it, to care for it as if by doing so she was pouring more love into it, so that when it was sold these feelings would be thrown back at her to wound her further.

There were huge gaps where the wonderful antique furniture that they had bought so carefully together had once stood, gone now in exchange for somebody's holiday cottage. One morning when she wasn't working, Jonathan said to her, 'I want to take you down to the cottage at Aldeburgh so we can see it. It'll be your home, unless you go to your parents while I'm . . . I'm away.'

'All right,' she said listlessly. She did not like to think of him in prison; it tortured her nights, making her wake in fear. She had heard such terrible things about prison. He was sure to be bullied for what he was, and she was so afraid he would be damaged mentally for ever after it. Once he had joked that it couldn't be much worse than public school, but she was sure that it could. She wondered if he would make friends, have someone else like himself to help him through.

It was almost Christmas. After much

thought they had decided that the boys should come over for Christmas, stay with Robert and Marianne — this idea had given Marianne a new lease of life — so as not to see the lack of furniture and pictures in their own home. It might be the last Christmas they would spend together.

As they drove down towards the Suffolk coast Grace thought of that day long ago when Jonathan had driven her down to Elmley. She wondered if she would ever see it again. She did not know if Uncle William and Anthea in their new home in Scotland knew of Jonathan's disgrace. She felt ashamed of them knowing, ashamed too that Jonathan had lost Caspar's money. India, however, had dismissed her fears, saying, 'Caspar has plenty of money and he'll come round when he realizes that Jonathan was caught up in something out of his control.'

'What do you mean, India?' Grace had said, having to her annoyance found India waiting on her doorstep when she had crept back from a quick sortie to the shops.

'His gambling, he can't help it, it's an illness. I've been looking it up, he needs help and he must get it. Then everything will be fine again.' Her face was smug and she'd sat there on the sofa as if she would organize everything knowing that it was quite beyond Grace.

'I wish you'd leave us alone,' Grace said, getting up. 'Please go now. I've things to do.' She hated seeing India so sure of herself while Grace could hardly get through each day. 'I can't think why you're still hanging round Jonathan after what he's done to your family.'

'You're still hanging round and he's done worse to you.' India watched her intently.

'That's different. I'm his wife, the mother of his children,' Grace said defiantly.

'So you do it for duty, not for love?' India said quietly, her dark eyes peeling away more layers of Grace's defences.

'Just go, India, do,' Grace said. 'Have you nothing else to do in your life but loiter around my husband?' She loathed her now, her beauty, her wealth, her self-confidence, all surely much more attractive to Jonathan than her own pale face and tired eyes.

'OK,' India said, getting up with dignity and leaving the room. But she stopped and turned round in the doorway. 'If I were you, though, Grace, I'd stop acting the victim, go to your children and leave him to sort this out on his own!'

She swept out triumphantly, banging the front door behind her, leaving Grace seething.

But her words shook her up enough to take more care over her appearance and take more interest in him.

They arrived at the Suffolk coast at last and Jonathan, following a map given to him by his friend, soon found a row of cottages facing the sea. It was very cold as they left the car and Grace could almost taste the salt that came in on the wind from the raging North Sea. She felt nothing. This place was alien to her, cold, grey and friendless. She tried to make herself realize that this was where she would live with the boys. She followed Jonathan towards a small white-painted cottage with a royal blue door and window frames. There was a tiny garden in front with rather windswept plants in pots by the gate.

Inside it smelt unlived in and musty. There were dead flies at the windows and no furniture; the carpets were stained. Its bleak, lost feeling made her feel even more unwelcome. She could not bear to stay inside, so she made an excuse to Jonathan, who was busying himself taking measurements, and went out again to the front, telling herself firmly that she must make the best of it. She would make it comfortable and cheerful with what was left of their own furniture. She could cut down their curtains from the

London house, perhaps even use some of the carpets.

'I think you'll be happy here,' Jonathan said brusquely when she went back inside to ask him to come away. 'There are three bedrooms and two bathrooms. Shall we walk about the town a bit, get to know the place, ask about schools?' He did not look at her and she knew he still felt ashamed that she had to give up her homes for this. It was a pretty cottage but it was tiny compared to what she had been used to.

As she stood there in the dusty, empty room, she thought: He will hate me more if I complain. Anyway I have nowhere else to go. Surely once our houses are sold, the money will be taken by the courts. She forced a smile and said, 'The boys will love being so near the sea.'

'I'll think of you here,' Jonathan said suddenly, his hands clenched by his side. 'I wanted to come and see it so I can imagine you here.'

'Oh, Jonathan.' she bit back her tears. 'One day we will all be together again. I know we will.'

He took her hands. 'You always believed in me, Grace, never tried to own me or pry into my life. Whatever happens, will you try to still believe in me a little, know that I love you and always will?'

She looked into his face and wished she could read what lay behind his eyes. She wondered why she had the feeling that he was hiding them away down here. If they sold this cottage they could surely buy a tiny flat somewhere in an unsmart part of London. Yet she felt that he did love her and she knew he loved the boys, but his shame at bringing them to this blighted his love.

'Why must we live here so far from anyone we know?' she said, determined not to be pushed into a corner and discarded.

He looked embarrassed, then said in a rush, 'It will be better for you to be out of the way of people's vindictiveness. When I'm away, they might go for you if they can't get me.'

His words made her feel sick, but she said, 'I'd rather risk it than start afresh somewhere I've never been to.'

'No, darling, I want you here, safe. You'll like it, there's sailing, a music festival . . . lots of interesting people,' but as she watched him trying to convince himself as well as her that they would be happy here, she realized that he couldn't bear their past friends and acquaintances to see how far they had sunk.

25

A week before the trial Grace was going through her letters and accounts. She did not have a lot of money but she had saved some from her richer interior decorating days and was now earning a little with her office jobs. She was paying for their food and a few of their other living expenses and the money was going fast. Every penny had to count now. Jonathan both resented and appreciated this. Sometimes he appeared with a little money saying he'd sold something, which helped with the immediate outgoings.

She had a hundred pounds in her wallet which she'd cashed that morning. She no longer used her credit cards and forced herself to take out a sum and keep to it for as long as she could. Not liking to carry so much money around in her bag in case it was stolen, she went to hide some in her writing desk. The money wasn't in her wallet.

At first she couldn't believe it and searched the other compartments in the wallet, then she searched her bag and then her coat pocket, but it wasn't there. She felt cold. She could not afford to lose it. She forced herself

398

to remain calm and thought back through her day. She had not worked that day, but had gone out about ten, done some chores, got the money, come back here, cleaned up, had a snack lunch with Jonathan, then he had gone out and she had read the paper before settling down to her letters and accounts.

She felt a slow, burning, sickening anger. Surely Jonathan wouldn't have taken it all? In the past when twenty or so pounds had gone missing from her bag, she had never said anything. It hadn't really mattered when money was plentiful; besides it could be said to be his money anyway as he gave her so much for housekeeping. But now when she needed every penny and he knew that she did, it was unforgivable, especially taking such a large sum. She didn't want it to be him. Perhaps she hadn't even taken it out of the cash machine, but left it there sticking out for the next person to take. But she knew she hadn't. She could almost see herself taking it out of the slot and putting it safe in her wallet, snapping it shut and putting it in her bag.

She knew she was kidding herself. He had stolen her jewellery, sold his children's education policies, cheated his friends and clients, even his own stepfather, why could she not accept that he had taken her money?

He'd been gone over two hours. She sat waiting for him as the room got darker and darker. She could not move to put on the light or draw the curtains. She just sat there, poleaxed by his latest treachery, praying vainly that it wasn't true, that she was becoming forgetful and had put it somewhere else. Praying that he'd kept to his promise and would never take anything that wasn't his again.

She thought of Christmas and how they had tried so hard to be happy. How even Sebastian had seemed to forget his anger and hurt with his father and for a few days they had been a real family again. She thought of Jonathan holding her in his arms in the cottage in Aldeburgh and how the tension had lessened between them and she had felt that everything would be all right again one day. It was the one hope that kept her going, that they had built up such love, such a stable relationship over the years, that like an old clinker-built boat battered by many storms it would still float in the end. But now she saw that her hopes were false and there was no future for them.

She heard the front door open and Jonathan came in.

'Sitting in the dark?' he said cheerfully, snapping on the light. 'Were you asleep?'

he continued, going to the window and drawing the curtains then switching on the table lamp.

'No, I was waiting for you.' She looked at him, thinking with a pang how attractive he looked in his dark, well-cut coat and how she had loved him so.

'How nice of you, darling.'

'I've lost a hundred pounds from my wallet,' she said harshly.

His smile wavered, then it increased. 'I have it right here, my love. I only borrowed it. Look.' He took his wallet from his inside pocket and opened it. She saw it was bulging with money.

'How have you got so much money?' she whispered, shocked by the sight of it.

'Don't worry, it's all above board and legal.' He counted out a hundred pounds and added another twenty, 'for lending it to me', before tossing it into her lap.

'You've been gambling again. You promised you'd stop,' she accused him. 'Oh, God, you must stop. You must get help. I'll come with you, Jonathan, but you must get help. There's Gamblers Anonymous, isn't there?'

She was halfway out of her chair to look it up in the telephone book, when he laughed and said, 'Oh, darling, what a fuss. What help could I possibly need? I'm good at gambling, look at all this money. If I went on I could win everyone back their cash and the case would be dropped. Think of the saving to the taxpayer on the legal fees.'

Grace suddenly felt too weary and desperate to argue with him. When he'd lost the huge sums of his clients' money he admitted he'd done wrong, sworn to change his ways, but now that he was winning he could see no harm in it. She didn't know how to cope with it.

She got up from her chair, taking the money, and went to her room and hid it in a book in her bookcase. She did it guiltily, as if it were she who had stolen it.

★ ★ ★

The next day India rang. Jonathan had gone out early and Grace answered the telephone.

'Oh, Grace,' she said too brightly, sounding disappointed that it was she who had answered the telephone and not Jonathan. 'How are you?'

'Fine,' Grace lied wearily, but determined not to let India know how devastated she felt.

'You don't sound it, can I do anything?' Her voice was almost kind. It crept into

Grace's misery, nudging aside her fake wall of well-being. She ached to confide in someone. Her parents were too far away, Marianne was too upset and all her friends were against them. But she couldn't confide in India, or show weakness in front of her.

'We're fine,' she repeated stoically. 'What do you want?'

'I wondered if you'd both like to come and have lunch? It's such a gloomy day.'

'Jonathan's not here.'

'Oh . . . well, you then. Actually it would be better if it was just you. I want to talk to you about Mummy. It might be a bit embarrassing in front of Jonathan.'

'Well, India . . . ' She felt she couldn't take on any more problems. One of the gossip columnists had got wind of Flavia and her young man and made some rather disparaging remarks in his column.

'Please come. We'll have something here. I know you don't like to go out at the moment in case you meet someone who's lost money through Jonathan. I do understand.' India put on her most persuasive voice.

'All right then,' Grace agreed reluctantly, knowing from past experience that India would go on at her until she got her own way. She supposed that at least talking about Flavia would be a different subject to Jonathan and the coming trial. She also, though she hated to admit it, felt so lonely that even being with India was better than being on her own.

'So you see,' India said a while later as they sat over the debris of a delicious lunch bought at a French delicatessen, 'it really is too shaming. One's own mother behaving like a teenager. This man is . . . *vile*. The sort of man you pay to go to bed with. I mean, how can Mummy demean herself so? I'd rather go without.'

'It must be the loneliness,' Grace said feebly, feeling that now she could understand the desperation loneliness could bring. But she found it hard to imagine Aunt Flavia, of all people, actually paying someone to sleep with her. India must be exaggerating; after all, she'd always hated her parents to love other people. Look at her behaviour over her father and Anthea.

'She needn't be lonely if she dressed properly, had her hair a normal colour, and ditched that creep. She had lots of friends, even though the men were rather old. Past it, I would imagine, but then so should she be at that age. She should be playing Bridge and things, like my friends' mothers.' India stubbed out her cigarette in anger. 'Perhaps you would go and see her for me, Grace, and tell her to act her age. She won't listen to me.'

'Me, India? I couldn't possibly.' Grace felt rather sorry for Flavia having such an unsympathetic daughter. Her parents were certainly not past it, but then they were still so much in love, she thought enviously, yearning for the love she and Jonathan once shared.

India seeing her expression and perhaps guessing her thoughts went on firmly: 'Well, then your mother must come over and tell her. I know, couldn't they have her to stay with them in Portugal, right away from the ghastly Jeremy? Then tell her?' India leaned forward eagerly in her chair as if she'd struck on the perfect solution.

'No, India,' Grace said firmly. 'They have their hands full with the boys at the moment. I'll tell Mummy about it if you like, maybe she'll write to her.'

'That's not the same.' India looked cross.

'Maybe . . . ' Grace stalled not wanting to mention the trial, her life afterwards.

'It's not as if he cares for her,' India went on vehemently. 'He's just taking her money and she's sitting there letting him. It makes me livid seeing him use her like that. I'm livid with her for letting him. I hate feeble women, don't you? Women who let men get

405

away with anything?'

'Yes,' Grace said, feeling sick. She studied India out of the corner of her eye, sure she was talking about her letting Jonathan get so out of hand with his gambling. India lit another cigarette and went on.

'Some of these women seem to be so ridiculously grateful for a bit of male attention. I suppose it's sex. They're a bit past their sell-by date to get it on the open market as it were. The men of their own age group tend to go after girls younger than their own daughters, so I suppose it's hardly surprising that creeps like Jeremy have a field day. It makes me sick!'

'What does Caspar say about it?' Grace tried to get off India's views on feeble women. 'Surely it's up to him to say something?'

India sighed heavily. 'You know what he's like. He's horrified, especially after the bit in the paper, but he doesn't dare to say anything to her. After all,' she said sarcastically, 'there might be an emotional scene. His mother crying and screaming. He couldn't handle that.'

'I suppose not.' Grace felt immeasurably tired. India's energy alone, her strident voice and frantic hand gestures were enough to exhaust her. She also had the feeling that she was including Jonathan, and her in this tirade, insinuating that she should give Jonathan up after the way he had behaved towards her, though she was sure India would be the first to pounce on him if she did. This feeling renewed her loyalty to him. A few hours ago when she'd found he'd taken her money she'd been on the verge of leaving him, now she felt she would stay, hold fast to her hope that everything would one day come right again.

'I think the creep is going to dump her any minute. I just wish she'd dump him first. It's so pathetic just to hang on to him like that. Has she no pride?' India's face was screwed up in anger and disgust. 'It beats me how some women will put up with anything however degrading just to keep their man. Don't they have the guts to live on their own?' She glared at Grace.

Grace was certain now that some of India's anger was directed at her. She was about to say that since Flavia had lost Elmley and her place in society, she seemed also to have lost a string of so-called friends and that loneliness might well be at the bottom of her behaviour, when the doorbell rang, interrupting her train of thought.

'Oh! . . . I wonder who that is?' India said irritably and got up to open the front door.

'Oh, Jonathan,' she said loudly enough for

Grace to hear. 'What a surprise, have you come to collect Grace? We were just having a gossip over lunch.'

'Oh, good.' Grace could hear that he'd put on a voice of false jollity. He came into the room behind India.

'Hello, darling,' he said, smiling at her. 'I thought I'd find you here.'

'Did you? I didn't say I was coming. I didn't even know I was until a couple of hours ago.' Grace said sternly, some of India's disgust at weak women taking a hold on her.

She looked at him; he was smiling directly at her. India began to stack their dirty plates and put away the food, her back to them. But Grace felt suddenly as if she had interrupted something between them. Before she could suggest they left at once to visit his mother, just to get him away, India said nonchalantly, 'Stay for a cup of coffee, Jonathan? I'm just making some. And there's some delicious Charbonnel et Walker chocolates I was given the other day. They're quite the best, aren't they?'

She picked up a large, round box done up with a pink ribbon and put it on the table in front of Grace.

'Open it, do, Grace. I've been longing to, but I decided to save it until someone else

408

was here or I'd eat the lot.'

Jonathan sat down on the padded bench beside Grace in the tiny kitchen. He put his arm round her and kissed her, rather, Grace felt as an apology than as a gesture of love. She did not respond but began to undo the ribbon on the chocolate box as if the task needed enormous concentration. She felt rather than saw India's jealousy of what she no doubt thought was a show of affection.

Don't think, she warned herself, holding the turmoil of mixed emotions tight inside. She took off the lid of the box releasing the rich aroma of the dark chocolates inside. Don't ask him why he is here. Her nerves were so stretched that she knew now she would not believe any explanation he gave to her.

The only good thing about prison, if he does go, she thought sadly, is that I will know where he is and the lying will stop. She drank her coffee but could not eat a chocolate and sat there between them feeling like an outsider, although they both made a great effort to include her in the conversation.

How long can I go on fighting? She thought wearily. What am I fighting for? A man I once knew who has gone away?

26

It was a great relief to Grace that the divorce proceedings of the Prince and Princess of Wales took over the newspapers. There had been a few paragraphs and one small picture of Jonathan when he was first arrested, but now, with pages taken up with analysis of the breakdown of the royal marriage and what the outcome would be, there was no room for or interest in Jonathan's case; even though quite a few members of the aristocracy had lost their money through him.

On that first morning of the trial Grace dressed in a pale amber suit which brought out the lights in her hair. She walked beside Jonathan to the courtroom, holding his hand, her head held high, though inside she felt like running away, leaving them all and escaping to her children. But she felt that it was expected of her to stand by him, and she had not forgotten how once she had loved him so.

India was already there. She looked wonderful in a dark red suit, her hair newly done.

'Good morning, Grace,' she said, but she did not kiss her.

'Why are you here?' Grace said coldly as she sat down.

'Jonathan needs all the support he can get, don't you think?' she said, her dark eyes boring in on Grace. 'He may well get off, you know. Where do you think he will go to then?'

'Home with us, of course,' Grace said with more conviction than she felt.

Since the day Jonathan had stolen the hundred pounds from her, she realized with alarm that her love for him was slowly shrinking like a drying plum. The succulence of trust, of hope was little by little seeping away. She could not bear to lose the warmth and passion they had once revelled in, the happy family life they had once led. She over-compensated when he was there with love and support, convinced that once the trial was over, whatever the outcome, all would be well between them again. This sham, though she hated to admit it, grated on them both. He took to going out often which in a way she found a relief. But once when he had come back late at night, although she was half asleep when he crawled into bed beside her, she was sure she had smelt a scent on him, a scent that was not hers, but

411

she pretended to herself she was imagining things and did not question him, unable to bear another uncomfortable truth.

India smiled her superior, pitying smile that Grace remembered from childhood, making her feel ill and insecure, but before she could say anything, the clerk of the court appeared and the trial began.

Throughout it all Jonathan was amazingly calm. This surprised Grace, knowing how afraid he had been when he had first confessed his crime to her. Perhaps, she thought, he was now resigned to it, or felt somehow better that he was seen to be atoning for the wrong he had done. To her astonishment he pleaded not guilty, telling her later that he had not, after all meant to rob them. He answered each question clearly and fully as if he wanted to be helpful.

At the end of each day he came home with her, but she noticed with a pang of envy that he always greeted India warmly. India would slip her arm round him, or squeeze his hand. Her body language convinced Grace that he had made love to her. But Grace said nothing, determined to bide her time and wait until the end of the trial. If he was, as everyone including his solicitor said, probably going to prison for two years at least, it was pointless making a scene about

412

it now. We will have all that time he is in prison to sort it out, she thought. Surely India won't be bothered to wait that long?

So each day Grace sat with India. The two women who loved him: one fair, the other dark. Grace felt as if she were acting a part, standing by a man she no longer knew. He is the father of my children and I love him, and I must keep our family together, she kept saying over and over to herself, but sometimes the last image she had was of his own father. He too had once been attractive, respectable, well off, but that had not saved him from his addictions.

Once when they left the courts she saw an old man dressed in the dingy clothes of a vagrant approach them, and for a second she thought it was his father. She clutched on to Jonathan in terror, but then she saw with relief that it was not Vincent. Jonathan understood her fear at once. She saw his face blanch and he hurried her away. From that moment it was as if a fever had possessed him. He stayed up late most nights, refusing to tell her what he was doing. She could hear him packing away his things, sorting his papers as if when he went to prison he would leave nothing of himself behind.

The trial neared the end. Grace sat impassively through the evidence of all their friends, of Caspar and of Max and Robert, each word they uttered piercing her to the core. She pretended not to see the looks of hatred and contempt that some of her one-time friends threw her way as if she too was as guilty as Jonathan.

Paul Cartwright, Jonathan's lawyer, told him the trial would probably end the next day or the day after.

India came up to them after the day's hearing. 'Jonathan,' she said, her eyes full of meaning, 'why don't you come round this evening, after all, tomorrow . . . ' She left the words unsaid, but everyone knew that tonight could be Jonathan's last night of freedom.

He smiled at her and touched her face. Grace turned away. She wondered if he loved her, would go to her after all, or if he was just showing his gratitude for her standing by him. After all, they had lost all their other friends.

'Not tonight, India,' he said.

Grace felt relief running through her, she turned back and heard India say with a brave smile, 'I'll write, visit you, be there if you need anything. Though . . . I still think they might let you go free.'

'Thank you,' he said and before he could walk away she took him in her arms and kissed him passionately on the lips.

'India, behave yourself,' Caspar cried out at her. He took her arm and pulled her away. 'What an exhibition you're making of yourself,' he said angrily, but she didn't seem to be listening, she was looking back at Jonathan.

Jonathan was not looking at her. He smiled at Grace and said, 'Ever dramatic, your cousin.'

'Have you given her cause to hope you'd go with her?' Grace said as they walked quickly to a taxi.

He said nothing until he had got in and sat down beside her. 'I want to be with you, with you and the boys,' he said. 'Whatever happens, always remember that.'

She wished that she could feel pleased that it was her that he wanted, but she did not. He had lied so easily, perhaps hardly knowing that he did so, about his life of gambling, might he not just as easily lie about wanting to stay with her?

She felt so ill, knowing that tonight could well be the last night they would be together. When he came out of prison, how different would he be? And yet, she thought looking out at the passing street, do I love him, do I trust him any more? Would prison cure his gambling? Give me back the man I once so loved?

He dropped her home, then said he wanted to see his mother.

'But you've just seen her outside the court!' She was fearful now that he was going to India.

'I want to see her again. I'll be back here in under an hour. I promise you that, darling. Trust me.' He looked so earnest that she swallowed her protests. She would believe him this last time.

'OK, in an hour then.'

'Let's go out to dinner, you get dressed up and book a table. Where shall we go?'

She was about to say she didn't feel like going out, but she swallowed her words. If this really was to be their last night together, it would be better to give him one to remember, a last good dinner before he went inside.

He was back within the hour, subdued, yet strangely calm. He took her out to Chez Nico's and despite her saying they had no money, urged her to choose the best on the menu. He ordered lots of wine, making sure her glass was always full and as their evening progressed she almost forgot that tomorrow he might be taken away from her.

When they got home he said, 'You must sleep well tonight, my darling, not worry about anything.'

416

She gave a bitter laugh. 'Sleep well, when it might be the last night we spend together?'

He looked ashamed and said, 'I don't want you, or the boys to worry about me, do you understand? I shall be fine, remember that.' He took her in his arms and kissed her.

'I can't bear to think of you suffering in prison. They say it's so horrible, tiny smelly cells, rough people, who'll hate you because you're from a different background . . . I can't bear it, whatever you've done you shouldn't have to go to prison.' She was shaking now, unable to keep back her terror at what lay ahead for him.

He held her close. 'Don't you worry, my darling,' he said, 'just think of how I love you, how one day we'll all be together again.' Gently he undressed her and made love to her, and she clung to him wishing they could suddenly die together, stop now before he would be torn away from her.

'We've had some happy times, haven't we?' he said as she lay spent in his arms, fighting off the effects of the wine. 'Think of those when I've gone and how I love you, will always love you, no matter what.'

She fought to stay awake and yet she longed for the oblivion of sleep; his voice, soft with endearments in her ear, and the wine soothed her until she did fall asleep.

She woke in the morning feeling terrible. Her head was aching and she felt as if it was filled with cotton wool. She was alone in bed. She struggled up and went into the bathroom. After splashing cold water on her face she felt slightly better and she went slowly downstairs to have some coffee calling for Jonathan as she went. There was no answer.

In the middle of the table, propped up against a honey pot, was an envelope with her name on it in his writing.

Her heart stopped. He had left her after all to go with India. She felt the pain deep inside her as if her very soul had been torn apart. She remembered India kissing him, remembered too the way he'd turned up at her house that day. He had gone to her for his last day. Then she remembered how he'd said he'd always love her and the boys. How could he lie so convincingly?

For a long time she stared at the letter. Then she picked it up, held it in her hand staring at the letters of her name. She decided to throw it away unopened, unable any more to cope with his excuses. But then, she thought, she'd better know the worst of it.

My darling,

Get on with your life and don't think of me. I can't go to prison, be locked away from the world. I've gone away, and I pray no one will find me and bring me back.

I know I have ruined our life together and that of the boys, my mother and Robert, not to mention my friends. That is a punishment I will carry with me for ever.

I love you always,
J.

She sat there at the table and read it and reread it and beneath her pain she felt a small glimmer of relief. If only he could get away . . . but where would he go? She decided that he must have been planning this all along. That from that moment they stood together at the quayside in Marseilles he had decided he would not go to prison. He had taken her home, owned up to it all, stood trial, and now just before the end he had said his goodbyes and vanished.

But had he gone alone? The terror struck again, winding itself tight inside her. Had he gone with India?

Quickly she dressed. She would confront India, see for herself whether he was hiding at the mews house, or whether India had gone with him. She would not telephone her, she didn't want to give her any warning.

There was half an hour before she should leave for the court; she dressed quickly and drove to India's house.

As she drove into the mews she saw, to her immense relief, India coming out of her house alone. Grace stopped the car and called sharply, 'India?'

India came over and peered into the car. 'Grace? Is Jonathan with you?'

'Is he with you?' She felt very calm as she got out of the car and stood confronting her. India looked wonderful, a sort of tragic, strong beauty.

'What did you say?' India said imperiously, putting her doorkeys into her handbag as if that was more important than answering Grace's questions.

'I said, is Jonathan with you? Did he spend the night with you, are you meeting him somewhere later?' Her voice was harsh.

'No, he didn't, more's the pity, and how can I meet him later? He might be in prison.' India looked at her with contempt as she had when they were children, when Grace couldn't act properly in Charades or serve the ball over the net.

Grace felt a smile of relief break over her

face. 'He's gone,' she said. 'I've a letter here from him telling me he's gone. I thought he might go with you, but I think he's left us both.'

'What!' India was furious. 'What do you mean gone? I stood bail for him, remember! He can't go.'

'Oh, God, so you did. Well, he has. Like his father, he's slipped away.'

'Did you know he was going to do this?' India said accusingly. 'There'll be such a stink over this, you'll see. They might even arrest you for conspiring to help him escape.'

Grace felt a sudden chill at her words, but she said bravely, 'I knew nothing, I'll swear to that. But I admit I'm pleased, I know he did wrong but I couldn't bear to think of him locked up.'

'Come into the house,' India said after a moment. 'I must think what to do.'

'We must do nothing,' Grace said when they were inside. 'I'm sorry about you losing the bail money, but I have to say I'm glad he's free.'

'He won't be for long. I thought the police took his passport.'

'I was thinking about that on the way here, but then I remembered that in fact he had two. A couple of years ago he had his briefcase stolen. He thought his passport

421

was in it and got another one, then the old one turned up at home, one of the boys had been playing with it.'

'They'll soon trace it,' India said.

'When we went to France, that time it had just happened, hardly anyone looked at our passports. I was terrified, especially coming home, that they would arrest him, but we were waved on without them even being opened. If he got into France last night, and if he caught the ferry in the middle of the night, like we did before, the same thing might have happened. And they wouldn't take much notice of an Englishman, unless they'd already been informed of his escape. He could have been on a plane to almost anywhere from France before anyone knew to look for him.' Grace paused, looking at the clock. 'It's nearly ten o'clock. He could have left me about half eleven, that's over ten hours and presumably still no one knows he's gone.'

'They will any minute, we're due in court now,' India said. She had slumped down on a chair and was looking pale and agitated. She looked intently at Grace. 'Everyone will be at court now, I can't ring Caspar, anyone. Do you think we're the only people who know he has gone?'

'Yes.'

'What about his mother?'

'I don't think he'd tell her, it would be too risky in the state she's in. Anyway, Robert would make him stay.'

'So that's that, then,' India said bitterly. 'In the end neither of us got him. But you at least have his children.'

'Did you love him, India, or just want him because he was mine?' Grace said, suddenly no longer feeling afraid of India, or inferior to her.

India lifted her beautiful eyes, her face sad. 'I loved him,' she said, 'I loved him more than any man I'd ever met and I wanted him. I was furious with you for having him.' She gave her an acid smile. 'Maybe he would have come to me in the end if it hadn't been for that fatal flaw in him, his gambling.'

'He loved me, he loved his sons,' Grace said.

'He could have loved me too,' India said, thinking of their lovemaking, 'but in the end he loved gambling more. That won and both of us have lost him.'

They sat there in the small drawing room together, waiting to see what would happen next. Would the police batter down their door? Would Paul Cartwright, or Caspar, or even Max come rushing round to find out where Jonathan was? But as every minute ticked past they felt calmer, almost happy, knowing it was giving Jonathan more time to get away.

It was India who broke the silence first.

'I suppose I ought to tell you now that we were lovers.'

Grace felt as if she'd been slapped. She stared at her stupidly for a moment. 'When?' she said, wondering wildly if Jonathan had been sleeping with her all through their married life.

'Recently. Surely you guessed, Grace? Or is it really true that wives are always the last to know?'

'I wondered, but . . . Oh, India, I so hoped it wasn't true. How could you? Why do you always have to take everything?' Grace howled in anguish, clenching her hands as if any moment she would jump up and scratch India's eyes out.

India looked rather uncomfortable, but said defiantly, 'It takes two, you know. The truth is, Grace, he found your miserable expression, your sort of martyred look, I suppose, impossible to live with.'

Grace took a few deep breaths. She knew it was true, there'd been so many signs left littered about that she'd pretended not to see, just as there had been with his gambling. She thought of all the love she'd poured over him, how she had been determined to keep her family safe and happy and how she could not bear to admit that he'd betrayed her. She longed suddenly, with a pain that almost made her cry out, for her children, the only good, honest part of their relationship. She got up.

'I'm going straight to Portugal to be with the children. I can't bear any more of this, India, they'll be my only reason for carrying on.'

'I doubt they'll let you leave the country. They'll think you've gone with him,' India said brusquely. Then in a softer tone she said, 'I'm sorry, Grace, but you have got more from him than I have. All those years of married life; the children.'

'But he wasn't yours, India, he was mine, *my* husband, the father of *my* children, and he loved me, I swear he loved me,' Grace cried. 'You just wanted him because he was mine, you could have had anyone.'

'He doesn't belong to anyone, no one does, Grace. The only thing he'll be faithful to is his gambling. But I did love him, do still love him. I don't mind telling you, if he'd asked me to go with him I would have.'

Grace couldn't look at her anymore. She got up and left the house, just wanting to get away from India, from Jonathan who had so utterly betrayed her. She drove out to Richmond Park and walked a while under the ancient trees trying with each step to rid herself of her misery. She was determined to get to the children, even if she too had to slip away in the night. She would go and be with them; nothing else, she thought, matters any more.

But why, she wondered, as she pounded over the grass, had she fought so hard for Jonathan? Was it because she could not bear to face up to the fact that his gambling had strangled their love? Or that she could not bear India to win as she always had when they were children? But why should she not fight for him, the father of her children — had she not promised at the altar to love him for better or worse? She demanded these questions of herself as she walked. But he had gone, gone without either her or India, leaving his children just as his father had left him. She saw with sickening clarity that the reasons she had clung on to him were illusions, mere dreams that had now evaporated in the stark light of the day.

27

When Grace got back from her walk she found a couple of policemen at her door. She was not surprised to see them and felt curiously light-headed and detached from the situation. They were courteous but stern.

'I really do not know where he has gone,' she said, handing them Jonathan's letter.

When at last they left her, after making her feel as if she was the criminal, she had a long, hot bath as if to wash away the feeling of guilt.

She visited Marianne frequently over the next few days.

Her mother-in-law took Jonathan's escape very badly. It was worse for her, Grace thought, because Robert was so furious, and Marianne had convinced herself that as she was Jonathan's mother, his behaviour, and now his disappearance before he could be seen to pay for his crime, was entirely her fault.

'I can't face Robert,' she wailed at Grace who'd gone there after her walk in Richmond Park knowing Marianne would need her. 'After all he's done for us, taking Jonathan in as his own child, paying for his education and now look at what he's done.' She was past crying, she slumped in a chair, looking like a rag doll that had lost its stuffing.

'And where's he gone? How will I know if he's dead or not? How can I carry on not knowing where he is, how he is?' She lifted her faded eyes piteously to Grace, as if she had the answer. The suffering in them smote Grace to the core. At first part of her had been glad that Jonathan had escaped the confines of prison, but now she saw that it was worse for Marianne not knowing where he was and in a way despising him for not facing up to his punishment like a man.

Grace realized, seeing this defeated woman, that if Marianne had had Jonathan to visit in prison her do-gooding feelings would have overtaken her despair. She would have made it a cause, befriended other prisoners and their families, harangued the Home Secretary over prison reforms, possibly even made it quite chic to have a son in prison. But now she had nothing to hold on to, nothing to plan and live for. Her daughters had escaped to their own lives and their own friends, but what was worse was that she felt she had let Robert down and was now not good enough for him.

'He might get in touch when everything's

died down a bit,' Grace said to her unconvincingly, wondering why she and Marianne were wasting their energy feeling guilty about Jonathan's actions. He was, after all, an adult of sound mind and body, capable of choosing right from wrong. 'We must hope for that,' she said to comfort her, knowing that she didn't want him to get in touch with them, couldn't bear the pain of seeing him again.

'I'm going to go to Portugal and get the boys, now that I've answered the police's questions,' she said. 'I thought I'd leave the day after tomorrow. We have them to live for, Marianne.' She tried to rouse her mother-in-law from her apathy, but she only shook her head.

'Poor little things, you must watch they don't go the same way. I tried, my God, I tried with Jonathan, but his father's genes must have been too strong. Do watch your boys.'

Grace couldn't bear much more of this, she felt it was only making them sink deeper into the mire of misery. When Robert came back from the office that evening she said, 'I must go home now, pack up a bit. The house has to be vacant in a month and I'll have to think about moving to that cottage. I want to fetch the boys too.'

Robert looked wearily at her. He too had become more faded, his skin, his hair, even his clothes seemed to have lost their colour. 'You've had a terrible time, Grace. What will you do?'

'I'll spend a few days with my parents, then come back and move down to the cottage, put the boys in the local school and try and find a job.'

'It's a hell of a mess,' Robert sighed. 'I don't know what to do about Marianne, he's broken her completely, and the girls have gone. I just don't know what to do.'

'The girls must come back and stay with her a while. I'm sure they would if you asked them,' Grace said without much optimism. She felt they were selfish to opt out because they couldn't face their mother in this pitiful state. She felt guilty too that she couldn't take much more of Marianne's misery herself. It pulled her down when she should be fighting to make a new life for herself and the children.

'I'll ask them. If only Jonathan hadn't done a runner, but it looks as if he's just like his father.' He frowned. 'Bloody fool with a wife like you, but then I said that twenty-odd years ago to Marianne about Vincent. The truth is if they're rotten at the core there's nothing you can do.'

Even after everything Grace didn't like to think that Jonathan was rotten at the core, but she said nothing. She got her few things together and went back to her house, refusing Robert's and Marianne's suggestion that she stay until the morning.

She stopped at a supermarket, bought some groceries and got home about seven-thirty. The house smelt musty; it was empty and silent, and though once she had loved it so, it now felt as if it no longer welcomed her. She busied herself with washing and putting the food away, knowing that she was trying to cram things into every moment until bedtime so that she wouldn't have to think. If only she had someone she could talk to, but India was the only person left, and she was not her friend. She had never felt so lonely.

The doorbell rang, making her jump. She decided not to open the door. Even though she was desperately lonely she didn't want to see anyone — it might be the police again, and she'd had enough of them. The bell rang again more insistently and, putting the chain on, she opened up cautiously.

Max Dalbert stood on the step, scowling. 'Hello, Grace,' he said curtly, 'I have come to find out where Jonathan is. Let me in and tell me.'

'I . . . ' She felt she would faint. She tried

431

to shut the door but he put his foot in it.

'Just open it, please,' he said. 'I'm sure you don't want to conduct this conversation on the doorstep where any roving reporter might overhear it.'

The authority in his voice and his mention of a reporter made her open the door. He came in and without being asked went into the drawing room. She followed him, feeling mesmerized, like a mouse caught by a stoat.

He turned to confront her. 'I want to know exactly where he is. What he did was a serious crime, you know, not some public-school boy prank. He lost me — and others — a great deal of money. I am well aware that he probably cannot pay it back, but I want to find him and see what I can get out of him. So will you tell me where he is, please?'

Max stood there in the middle of the room, his dark eyes pinning her to the floor like a helpless butterfly. Hysteria began to rise in her. She didn't know what to do; she couldn't take any more. She heard someone screaming, she felt her legs buckle and the woolly, dusty taste of the carpet in her mouth as she fell face downwards on the floor. She thought she would die with the utter torment of it all. She was choking now, her face wet, her nose too stuffed to breathe, she was drowning, she longed to die.

She felt herself being lifted up, then a stinging slap to her cheek, then another and she was put on the sofa and Max was calling her name, telling her to remain calm. She felt as if she'd come to the end of her tether, the excuses she'd made for Jonathan were stripped away and all she felt now was the vast agony of his betrayal.

She felt Max's arms round her, heard his soft words of comfort. She clung to him sobbing, craving the comfort of a fellow human being, yearning for some release.

After a while she felt calmer. She lifted her wet, blotched face from his shoulder and saw to her horror his silk tie all stained from her tears.

'I'm so sorry, I've ruined your tie,' she said weakly.

He took a handkerchief from his pocket and gently wiped her face, and held it to her nose to blow.

'I must look awful,' she said, wondering how to get out of this embarrassing situation.

'You do,' he said gravely. 'You must have had a terrible time over this.'

The kindness of his voice made the tears well up in her eyes again and drip down her face.

He got up and went over to the drinks tray. 'Have you any brandy? I think you need some. I could do with some too.' He found a nearly empty bottle and poured two glasses, threw his down his throat then came and held a glass to her lips. Obediently she drank it. It burned all the way down her throat.

'I . . . I must go and wash my face,' she said, and fled upstairs to the bathroom. The sight of her face in the mirror horrified her. She was red and blotchy, her eyes fat little slits, her nose swollen. She washed her face, holding a flannel soaked in cold water over it for some minutes. She didn't look much better, but she felt a little stronger and she went back downstairs feeling small and ashamed at her outburst.

'I really am sorry,' she greeted him. 'I don't know what came over me. Only I don't know where Jonathan is. He left a note and just went. I showed it to the police.'

'Where are your children?' He was watching her all the time.

'They are with my parents in Portugal, they live there, my parents, I mean. I'm going to fetch them on Thursday.'

'Then what will you do?' Again he watched her as if he was interrogating her, looking out for the slightest mistake that would lead him to Jonathan. She found him worse than the police.

'A friend of Jonathan's took all our valuable furniture' — she gestured round the nearly empty room — 'in exchange for a cottage in Aldeburgh. I shall go there and live with the children.'

'And will Jonathan join you, or will you join him?'

'Max, I honestly don't know where he is. He hasn't even told his mother where he's gone. He might get in touch with us again, he adored the boys.' She paused, biting her lips to stop the tears starting again.

There was a silence for a moment and Max broke it by saying, 'This is a very pretty room, with good furniture it must have been spectacular. I especially like the way these shelves are done in the alcoves. Who designed it?'

'Oh, I did,' she said, surprised at his change of tack.

'You, on your own?'

'Yes. I once worked in an architect's office and got ideas there. I used to, when things were, well, you know, before, do interior decorating, but since everything, I've lost all my clients.'

'I see. Have you any friends left, Grace?' His eyes were back on her face.

'No.' She felt as if she was naked under his scrutiny.

'Poor little Grace. You know your fault was that you loved him too much?'

'What do you mean? No one can love someone too much.' She said sharply.

'They can and they do. My mother did the same with my father. He had lots of affairs, could not leave a pretty woman alone, but instead of making a fuss about it she turned a blind eye, made excuses for him. You did the same with Jonathan's gambling. At first I suppose it was nothing, and you said nothing, so he got worse.'

His words made Grace feel uncomfortable and angry. She did blame herself, but so did Marianne. It was so foolish of women always to blame themselves for everyone's faults. She bet men rarely did, even when it was their fault. 'I couldn't pry into everything he did, nag him all the time,' she said crossly.

'No, but you must have known things were getting out of hand. You should have insisted that he got help, stopped it at once or you would leave him.'

'I couldn't do that, there were the children! Besides, I loved him; he loved me; we were a family. It wasn't a question of just leaving him, I couldn't have broken up the family, our whole way of life.'

'It is broken now, smashed beyond repair, with all the disgrace that goes with crime,' he said seriously. 'You and India are so different, she would not stand for anything she did not like. She was too bossy, I agree, but . . . '

'If you must know she did put up with it too! She slept with him and stood bail for him, she put up with it,' Grace almost screamed at Max. She felt the fury rise in her. How dare he come here and criticize her? More fool him for investing his money so rashly.

Max raised an eyebrow, a slight smile playing on his lips. 'So she got him in the end. Trust India. She always wanted him, said she loved him, but I always thought it was because he loved you.'

She felt a little sliver of warmth. 'He did love me, didn't he?' she said anxiously.

'Yes, he loved you as much as he could love anyone. He loved you for not interfering, for letting him get on with his addiction. My guess is, though, that in the end that would have made him hate you.'

'That's not true, we were so happy.'

He said nothing for a moment and she went on trying to convince him of their happiness but he didn't seem to be listening. Then he said, 'I knew India put up the

437

bail — now of course she has lost it, but I did not know she got him into her bed. So has she gone with him?'

'No, not that I know of. I was with her all yesterday morning, she seemed as surprised as I did that he'd left.'

She wondered why she was standing up for India. Why not let him believe India knew where Jonathan was? He could go round and plague her then.

'Now, will you please go? I've things to do,' she said, hating him now, hating the things he said. She just wanted to be alone with her misery and her shame.

He didn't move from the sofa. 'I know you are angry with me and I do not blame you, but surely you see that by loving him so much, making excuses for him, not facing up to what he was really doing, in a way you were telling him it was all right to go on gambling. All right not to accept that he had a real problem and should try and tackle it.'

'You don't know anything about marriage,' she flared up. Perhaps his words had some truth in them, but she didn't want him of all people to tell her.

'I have had three, my dear, I should know a little about it by now.'

'But I was so busy with the children, my

job . . . Jonathan himself.'

He shrugged and held up his hand. 'OK, OK, now tell me what you are going to do now. Can you stay here?' He looked round the room.

'No, the house is all but sold. I've a month to move out. I'm going to live in Aldeburgh.'

He smiled. 'Do you want to live there?'

'I have no choice,' she said angrily. 'Now please go, Max. Go and torment India instead.'

He laughed. 'No, thank you.' He looked at her intently again. She felt angry at his scrutiny, but before she could say anything he went on, 'I am about to open a new shop in Knightsbridge. I wonder if you would design it, possibly if you're up to it, run it for me. There's a small flat above it, you and the children can live there. I would pay you a decent salary, of course.'

'What? You must be mad, why would you want to employ me?' He was laughing at her. First he'd interrogated her, then he'd done the psychiatrist bit, now he was mocking her.

'My shops have not been doing well lately. You have great taste' — he looked admiringly round the room again — 'great choice of colours. It may be style, but you have something that the other designers I have used don't have. Maybe it is being brought up in Elmley Park. I am serious, Grace,' he went on before she could protest again. 'I am not being kind or feeling sorry for you because you married a loser. You have what I want, what I think will put my shops back in the centre of the marketplace again. Sort of stylish class, but amenable to everyone. I want the sort of interior which will make everyone, rich or poor, feel a little luxurious, a little special. Feel if they come in and bought a piece of my jewellery, whether it be worth thousands of pounds or less than a week's wage, that they have bought something good, something that will make them feel a little richer because of it.'

'I can't do that,' she said, wondering what else he would demand from her. She knew he was newly married, but only because he wanted a son.

He fitted the tips of his fingers together, gravely concentrating on them as if it were a complicated manoeuvre. 'The choice is yours, Grace. Either you take the job, and do it well, start to build your life again by your own efforts for yourself and your children, or you go and huddle in your cottage on the dole, or find work — in some little office or seaside souvenir shop I suppose.'

Grace was furious with him, and mortified at how she'd cried in his arms. She wanted to shout back at him that he could take his job and go, but she knew in her heart that he spoke the truth and she found it very painful. How was it that he seemed to see into her very soul? She couldn't work for such a man.

'There will be no sexual strings,' he said, 'unless you want them. But it is complicated enough India seducing your husband without you ending up with me, her ex-lover.'

'I wasn't thinking of that,' she lied, 'but why don't you offer her the job? She's got tremendous style.'

'Not the kind I want, nor has she the right temperament. She has never needed to work and she would only play at it until it bored her.' He got up from the sofa and walked over to the door. 'Shall I expect you Monday then? That gives you five days to sort yourself out. I will get details of the position, flat etcetera sent round to you. You can move in over the weekend. It is clean but dull, you can have it done up if you like.'

'I have to collect my children,' she said, thinking she could never be ready to start work on Monday.

'They are only in Portugal, my dear,' he said, 'not Australia. See you in the shop on Monday morning at eight-thirty on the dot.

I will see myself out. Goodbye.'

'Goodbye and . . . thank you,' she added mechanically, not feeling grateful at all. She felt as if she had been hounded into something against her will. Then on reflection she knew it was a great chance, one she should grab with both hands.

Sitting there in the dusk thinking back over the last couple of hours, she knew in part that Max was right about her loving Jonathan too much. Ever since losing the baby that had precipitated them into marriage she had vowed she'd put up with anything to keep him. In a way her life with him had been a sham, as if she'd put on an act of what she wanted it to be instead of what it really was: life with a gambler who was destroying their and many other people's lives.

The terrible hysteria Max had somehow unleashed in her had left in its place a steely strength. She felt that she never wanted to be under any man's power again, whether by loving them too much or by being used by them for whatever talents they thought she possessed. She needed to find a good job, and she was damned if she was going to hide away in the country. Yes, she would work for Max, but she would pay back every penny that Jonathan had lost for him, then she would not be beholden to him.

Part Three

28

Despite the flurry of snowflakes the Christmas party in Max's shop spilt out on to the pavement. There seemed to be a never-ending stream of cars and taxis dropping off people at the gleaming shop to buy their presents.

Max and his wife Carla, looking a little pale after the birth of their son, stood just inside the shop to welcome the guests. Grace stood a little apart, keeping her eye on the waiters, making sure that the champagne and the luxurious food was being constantly circulated.

Behind the glass counters stood the assistants, each dressed in a cream silk shirt and dark skirt ready to help any customer with their purchases. They were being kept busy. The whole ambience of the shop, with its soft, yet warm yellow decor, its dazzling white woodwork just touched with a thin gold line and glass shelves and showcases clear as water, evoked a feeling of largesse among the clients, champagne added to their mood and perhaps they showed off among themselves a little too, but they seemed to be spending and that was all Grace minded about.

She was glad that she had kept some of the expensive clothes she'd bought when they were rich, for she would never be able to afford new designer ones now. She knew that she looked good, indeed Max had insisted that she have her hair done frequently and dress smartly at all times. This advice she might have resented, but somehow it wasn't so bad coming from him rather than India. She was glad now that Max had insisted on so much from her, it made her forget her unhappiness, or at least gave her less time and energy for it. It also gave her back her self-confidence.

But she kept herself aloof from the men she met here and there, smiling, being charming, but determined to discourage anything more intimate.

Max had been no trouble that way. In fact it seemed that he preferred to keep to the boss/employee footing, which was a great relief to her. She knew he had mistresses, had seen them come into the shop to meet him for lunch, or arrive early in the evening to look idly among the jewels, the beautiful glass paperweights, the rich leather desk sets, perhaps even choosing things they'd ask him for later, until he was ready to whisk them away. She said nothing, but she refused point blank to cover up for him when Carla rang.

'I am here as a designer and a manager,' she said firmly, 'not as your secretary or your minder. It's up to you to reassure your wife.'

'You have become quite hard, Grace,' he grumbled. 'I am not asking you to tell any fantastic lie, just say I am in a meeting, which is true. It is just I conduct some meetings in bed.' He'd smiled then, a smug, boastful smile that insinuated that she was jealous, which she certainly was not. This infuriated her.

'I'm just not interested,' she'd said, walking out of the room, annoyed with the selfishness of him, of all the men who seemed to think they could live their lives to their own rules and even be admired for doing so, and when criticized, blamed their mothers or their wives for indulging it.

She looked now at Carla; her smile of welcome was fixed on her face, she was gracious and polite. She knew it wasn't a marriage of love, Carla had extravagant tastes and Max indulged them in exchange for a son and her presence, when needed, as his wife. She was an empty woman and Grace hadn't much time for her, all beauty and femininity with no brains. It did not surprise her that she bored Max rigid, but she rather despised him for marrying her.

India and Caspar came over to her. Flavia was with them. Her boyfriend had finally left her and she looked faded and dispirited. Before she could greet her Grace saw her stop and admire a showcase of jewelled boxes with India.

Although India wouldn't have wanted the job she seemed rather piqued that Max had given it to Grace and when she had first heard of it she kept appearing 'just to give Grace ideas', as she put it. Max had been strict with her. 'You can come back and spend all your money when we are ready, my dear India. I do not want Grace distracted, we are working to a tight schedule.'

India had not been pleased.

'Quite a place,' Caspar said coming over to her. 'Not bad champagne either. How are you, Grace?'

She hadn't seen him for almost a year since he too had come round and tried to find out about Jonathan.

'I'm fine, and you and Sophie? Congratulations on your son.'

'Thank you. How are your boys? At public school yet?'

'Good Heavens, no,' she laughed. 'They go to the local schools, I can't afford school fees.'

Caspar looked amazed. 'But didn't you have a school insurance scheme?'

She blushed, still feeling hurt at the loss of it. 'It went,' she said simply.

'I suppose that bastard took it. I'm so sorry, Grace, you must have had a hell of a time.' He looked down into his glass, biting his lip. 'I'm sorry,' he said again, 'I was so angry at the time I didn't think of your suffering. Look, come down to Elmley one weekend, bring the boys. We'd love to have you.'

'Thank you, I'd like that.' Grace smiled at him. She felt that he did genuinely mean it and had probably not thought about how Jonathan's gambling had affected her and the children. India would not have told him.

There was a slight lull for a second in the shop and Grace heard India say to Max, 'A big discount for me, please, darling. After all, I did introduce you to Grace.'

'And you introduced me to her husband, so no discounts for you at all, my dear,' Max answered her firmly before greeting Flavia.

The gibe, though true, dug into Grace painfully.

Caspar seeing her discomfiture, said, 'I see you've done well, Grace. I must say this shop is so much better designed than his other ones — they were all, well, a bit middle-European, weren't they? I understand you're doing them all up in the same sort of way.'

'Yes. Bond Street is finished, as you know. He wanted me to work there but I like being here near the boys' school. I can pop out and meet them if I have to and they are just upstairs when they get back from school.'

'How are they coping?'

'All right now, but it was very difficult at first.' The pain she'd suffered when she told them Jonathan had disappeared still affected her. She had, after discussing it with her parents, decided that it would be best to tell them the whole truth so they would be armed against the taunts and stories from outsiders.

'You mean he ran away?' Jack said. 'And he's hiding somewhere?'

'Yes.'

'I must look for him, tell him not to worry,' Jack said and had spent hours 'looking' for Jonathan. Often he'd thought he'd seen him and said in anguish, 'It looked just like Daddy from the back but when I saw his face it was someone else.'

It broke Grace's heart and even though she and her parents had explained that he was more likely to be far away in another country, and they would not find him, Jack continued to look for him for a long time.

Sebastian closed his mind to him. He was becoming very good at and interested in art and would lose himself for hours in his painting and his sculptures. Grace didn't know whether to be relieved or concerned about this. But the suffering of her children finally killed off any feelings of love she had left for Jonathan.

Grace couldn't talk to Caspar for long as she was meant to be looking after the clients. They loved to be spoilt and have their purchases, even if it was only a tiny package, carried for them. She didn't mind this with some of them, but there were others that she hated and despised. They may be millionaires but their manners would have disgraced a pig. They demanded this and that in loud grating voices like spoilt children and she could never get over their ugliness. Money had not given them beauty or style.

One man, who was popping out of his red silk shirt with gold buttons and still wearing his floor-length fur coat inside the shop, pushed through the crowd, stepping on quite a few of them as he made his way to the counter. His companion, a cheap-looking girl in a gold leather mini-skirt and an over-tight fake-leopard top, squeaked her delight at everything. He jabbed his fat white fingers, like sausages encased in flashing rings, at the things his companion pointed out in the showcase and inspected them as if they were dirt instead of exquisite jewellery made from the finest gold and precious stones.

Grace tried not to catch the eye of Felicia who was serving him but she knew that both of them were nearly being sick with revulsion at him. As he tossed aside the pieces of jewellery his hand shot out now and again to snatch a tiny sandwich or other delicacy from a passing tray, which he would cram into his mouth, chomping loudly. Grace wondered if he might chomp a piece of jewellery by mistake and hoped it would break his teeth. She could bear no more. Max and Carla had finished greeting people and were now circulating. She grabbed Max's arm and pulled him over to his hideous client.

'Here is Mr Dalbert to assist you,' she purred at the monster, unable to resist a sarcastic smile at Max who, understanding exactly, gave her a curt nod and took over. She knew he would later be annoyed with her — it was clients like these that kept her in work — but she didn't care. The more she saw of this kind of rich person the more she found herself yearning for a life like her parents, simple yet filled with friends and small pleasures, many of which, like genuine affection, good conversation, wonderful views and sunsets, were free.

India and Flavia came over to her. She kissed her aunt, thinking how like Marianne she was, completely destroyed by a man. What was worse about Marianne was that now Robert was bored with her. No doubt he had fallen in love with the brave, strong young mother struggling to bring up her son alone and who had spent most of their married life battling for some good cause or other, but now that she was lost, destroyed by her son's betrayal, Robert couldn't cope with her weakness.

'Lovely shop,' Flavia said vaguely, taking another glass of champagne.

'Ghastly people,' India said looking over at an over-made-up woman laden down with more jewellery on her than a Christmas tree.

Grace giggled. 'Shh, some are dreadful, I agree.'

'I don't know how you can work here,' India said with a hint of jealousy in her voice. India, she knew, was at a loose end. She often rang Grace to discuss the slow decline of Flavia, who was also bored out of her mind and giving her children a difficult time. India often went down to Elmley, where she criticized poor Sophie in her running of the place.

Grace knew too that India chose to see a lot of her to ask about Jonathan. Not that Grace would ever talk about him apart from telling India how unhappy Marianne was and about the children. India was not interested in that, she wanted to know if he had been in touch.

'No, never. He probably doesn't know where I am, and I don't want to talk about it, India. I want to put it behind me,' she'd said firmly more than once.

Seeing Flavia and India now, India looking wonderful in black and gold, but so restless, quite dismissive of any admiring glance thrown at her, and thinking of Marianne, Grace felt a shiver run through her. She could so easily have turned out the same, given so much of herself to a man, whether he be her son, lover or husband, or as in India's case, an illusion of someone she wanted to own, that when he had gone she could no longer function. Jonathan could have destroyed her too, but Max had saved her.

She looked over at him, still struggling with the hideous man draped in fur and his awful girlfriend, and suddenly feeling an enormous surge of gratitude for him, went over to rescue him.

29

India pounded across a field at Elmley, Caspar's dogs at her heels. She felt so restless and dissatisfied with life. She'd come here for a change of scene, hoping to find some inner peace, but she had not. If anything it had made her feel worse.

It was not as if she spent her life lying about doing nothing. She ran, successfully, many charity committees organizing social events to raise money. She was taking a computer course and brushing up her Italian. She had a full social life and at the moment she had two boyfriends whom she idly played off one against the other, not really knowing which one she cared for most, if indeed she really cared much for either of them. But they were useful, a sort of accessory for the evenings, someone to amuse her and drive her here and there.

Freddie, who had at last managed to get his wife pregnant, said on one of their many evenings together, 'You need to get married, India, and start breeding. I told you to marry me. You wouldn't have felt so bored then.'

But she thought now that she didn't

want marriage and children. One hour here with her three nieces and baby nephew was enough to convince her of that. And now that Grace had come with her two boys it was chaos. Sophie seemed to let her children have the run of the place; there were toys everywhere, even in the wonderful long gallery which the girls appeared to use instead of the garden on wet days. She sympathized with her mother's horror at the sloppy way Sophie was running Elmley. Caspar didn't seem to notice. He still had a job in London, but much of his energies were spent here running the estate, the farms, the shooting. He didn't seem to mind that the beautiful house was beginning to resemble a nursery school.

Then there was her mother, another drain on her life. Flavia was driving her mad with her misery over Jeremy dumping her for, India supposed, yet another gullible middle-aged woman. She was hoping to persuade Caspar to keep her here a week or so. It really was his turn to put up with her.

She reached the wood and a pheasant ran out in front of her. One of the dogs gave chase, snapping at its tail feathers as it flew away. She heard a shout and saw Grace's boys come running down the field; they disappeared into the trees before they reached her and she could hear them calling to each other and the snap of twigs as they crashed through the undergrowth. Their noise sent up a few more birds and the young dog went wild.

India called it sharply to her and tied her belt round its neck.

'I don't think you'll be much of a gun dog,' she said to it, feeling annoyed now — not with the dog, but with Grace. She knew she was still jealous of Grace. After all these years she still felt Grace had come off better than she had. Grace, who should have collapsed weeping into a hideous wreck after Jonathan's disgrace had, admittedly with the help of Max, picked herself up and blossomed. She bet she didn't feel bored with life or wonder what the point of it was. She'd been in good form last night when they'd had friends over to dinner. Ned and Charlie Porter had been pleased to see her; Charlie was married now, but Ned was not. He was still in love with her, India supposed, though she'd ignored him most of the evening and he'd had to make do with Grace. But her mother, never leaving the subject alone, had suggested that she marry him.

'He's a very sound young man, India,' she'd said, as if describing a stallion. 'He's inherited that lovely house and farm. You could do worse you know.'

India stamped hard on the rough ground, scuffing up the turf with her feet. Trust her mother to imagine that marriage would be her daughter's salvation, especially when she'd made such a mess of her own. She hated to admit it but she knew in her heart what was really the matter with her. She wanted Jonathan, despite what he'd done, even the way he'd run away, which — unlike Caspar who thought it a cowardly thing to do — she rather admired, although it had cost her a great deal of money. She thought of him rather like the Scarlet Pimpernel, giving his captors the slip at the eleventh hour. His elusiveness added to his glamour. She wanted to be with him. There was something about him that still intrigued her; his way of distancing himself, his way of not quite giving everything in his lovemaking, of keeping something back, yet making her feel that if she found the key to him he would be entirely captured. She wanted to find that key; she wanted him to give himself completely to her.

She had asked Grace many times if he had contacted her and Grace, growing more irritable with each demand, had assured her he had not, and even if he had she did not want to see him again.

'I can't bear to, don't you understand that, India? I loved him so much, but that Jonathan has gone. Now I feel completely betrayed by him, not least because he slept with you,' she'd retorted last night when India had asked her again. 'The boys are settled at school now, have made friends and are coming to terms, slowly, in their own way, with Jonathan's disappearance. I don't want their lives disrupted any more. He chose to leave us and that as far as I'm concerned is the end of it. So please, India, don't keep on about it.' She'd got up and left the room making India furious, but determined not to follow her.

As she stomped her way back to breakfast, India wondered if perhaps Grace did know where he was and was keeping it a secret from her.

The dining room was chaos, three small girls clambering about demanding things. Caspar had breakfasted early and Sophie and the 'girl' who passed as a nanny were vainly trying to make them eat. Only Grace seemed unruffled, she sat there drinking her coffee and reading the *Daily Mail*.

'Can't think how you can concentrate in this racket,' India said, sitting down beside her.

Grace smiled. 'I'm used to it. The boys

460

aren't exactly quiet; I've sent them outside to run off some of their energy.'

'I never want to get used to it,' India said. 'It's like a bear garden. Remember when we were children? We stayed upstairs in the nursery until we were about twenty-five.'

'Not quite twenty-five, India,' Grace laughed, 'more like fourteen.'

'Why are you so cheerful today?' India demanded, wondering again if she knew where Jonathan was.

Grace smiled. 'I don't know. It's just so nice being back here and I feel . . . well, you don't how dreadful I've felt for so long, India, and at last that seems to be lifting and I can enjoy life again. It was such fun seeing the Porters last night, just like when we were young. You know, there were times when I never thought I would enjoy life again.'

There was a scream as one of the girls spilt her milk and another refused to eat up her toast, screwing up her face and chanting, 'Shan't, shan't.'

India said sharply, 'Be quiet at once and, Charlotte, eat up your toast before one of the ghosts living in those suits of armour comes and eats it for you. He might drop his spear on you by mistake.'

'Is there a ghost?' Charlotte's eyes widened in fear, her lower lip trembling.

461

'Oh, India, don't be so silly,' Sophie said anxiously. 'Of course there's not a ghost, darling, Aunt India's only teasing.'

'Don't bet on it,' India said fiercely, glowering at her three nieces who stared back in terrified awe. Charlotte crept on to her mother's knee and there was complete silence from them for at least ten minutes.

Grace went back to her newspaper but when the girls had left the room with their nanny, giving anxious sideways looks at the suits of armour as they passed, Sophie cried out, 'Really, India, how could you say such things to them? You can deeply disturb them, you know, you should never frighten children so.'

'Rubbish,' India said, 'a bit of fear never did any of us any harm. We were often terrified, weren't we, Grace, when the wind howled at night right down the long gallery, and there were creepy shadows everywhere. Do you remember the attics, Grace? Those horrid stuffed birds and animals with their staring eyes, trapped in those glass cages, I hated them.'

Suddenly Grace looked as if she was going to cry. She got up and ran from the room.

India shrugged. 'You see, it still frightens her. Funny really, as it was me who was really terrified of them. She loved them.

Wanted them in our playroom.'

'I think you are very unkind, India,' Sophie said. 'You must realize that small children do believe the things we tell them. Maybe you've triggered off some forgotten fear of Grace's childhood here, and upset her again.'

'I doubt it,' India said airily, then suddenly a thought struck her. That New Year all those years ago when she'd crept off with Jonathan, had they gone up to the attics together? They hadn't been in their bedrooms when she'd looked and all the other bedrooms were occupied, and they'd hardly have stayed downstairs to be discovered by one of the staff.

She finished her coffee and went to find Grace and question her. Grace was in the sitting room with the large fireplace where she and Jonathan had hidden all those years ago playing Sardines. Grace's face was streaked with tears. When she saw India she got up and made to leave.

'Don't go,' India said, feeling suddenly rather mean and sorry for her.

'Your remarks brought it all back,' Grace said, defiantly wiping her tears away with a handkerchief. 'I just wanted to be here for a minute, to feel if he was here. Silly, I know, but I loved him so much. Max says I loved him *too* much, and let him get away with his gambling.' She looked at the deep fireplace. 'It was here that it all started really. I was so young and innocent, I never suspected there would be anything wrong with him, did you?'

'No, and I didn't for a long time. Well, until it all happened really,' India said, flopping down on one of the faded old chairs. 'You don't believe I loved him, do you, Grace? You think I just wanted him because you had him.'

Grace looked at her. 'I don't know what I think any more. In retrospect I suppose I should have seen there might be a problem, his gambling was always there. He told me here, in that fireplace, how he loved racing and putting a bet on the horses.' She laughed sadly. 'If only I'd known.'

'Would it have changed your feelings for him?' India asked, wondering if despite her denials, Grace did still love him.

'No, not at the time. But he changed, gambling changed him, made him so ruthless. You know he stole all the jewellery he gave me? I went to get it to put up the bail when he was arrested and it had gone. It was lucky for him you put it up,' she said, seeing how shocked India looked. 'He took the children's education trust money too, and he repeatedly took money from my bag.'

India didn't like the sound of this. It suddenly sounded rather sordid, not glamorous and daring at all. 'Are you sure?' she said weakly.

'Yes, I'm sure,' Grace said. 'And you should see his mother. She struggled so hard to bring him up, was so happy with his stepfather, Robert, but now she's a neurotic mess'. She looked strained. 'Robert is still with her, but he keeps going away on business, and I don't think he always goes alone.'

'But Jonathan probably didn't know all this would happen,' India said, not wanting her picture of him to tarnish. After all, she'd held on to it for so long.

'I'm sure he didn't. If you could stand on the edge of your life before you'd lived it and see what havoc certain mistakes of yours would cause, you might live it another way. On the other hand, perhaps you wouldn't, perhaps you can't help it, or are sure you can control your life. Or maybe you're not strong enough, or are too selfish, arrogant or whatever.' Her voice trembled. 'I'll never love anyone as I loved him, but I never want to see him again after what he's done to us all.'

India looked at her and knew that she was serious. She knew without Grace spelling it out that she was saying India could have him, if he ever turned up again. 'What about his children?' she asked tentatively, having visions of them wanting to be with him too. 'Haven't they a right to see their father again, if he does turn up?'

'When they are grown up, yes. If I know where he is by then, I'll tell them, let them make up their own minds. I've never, India, even in my worse moments, said anything horrible about him to them. I've explained as best as I can how his gambling has led to all of this but I don't know if gambling, or alcoholism for that matter, is inherited. His father did it, you know.' She told India all about Vincent being down and out and Marianne finding him when she did her homeless protest in the Strand.

'I don't believe it,' India said, feeling rather sick. 'But Jonathan would never let himself get like that. I mean, he doesn't drink, does he? It's alcohol that rots your brain, makes you unable to hold down a job. Gambling doesn't affect you that way.' She was desperate not to imagine Jonathan dirty and unkempt.

'Nor, apparently, would you have thought his father would end up on the streets,' Grace said. 'He may have taken to drink when his gambling failed. But *is* gambling a disease, something you can't help, or could any of us get like that if we let ourselves, do you think?'

'I've heard there's an addictive personality, but I can't help feeling you should fight against it — well, against it getting out of hand, if you can, I suppose,' India said. 'But perhaps like other diseases you can't help it.' She could not believe that Jonathan would sink so low, he was far too elegant and fastidious for that. She remembered how clean he always was and his freshly laundered clothes: he would never allow himself to end up like that.

Then, remembering him making love to her, she looked guiltily at Grace. For the first time she realized how much he had made Grace suffer and she felt sorry for her. But then as Grace had never had her own money she had needed to rely on a man for that, until recently of course. India was lucky enough to be rich, and however much she cared for someone she would never let them have access to her money, or become dependent on them. In any relationship, she would call the tune. Grace, having the children to consider, probably couldn't threaten to leave him unless he stopped his gambling. India saw that now. If you had little children to bring up, she thought, you were, despite the welfare state, very vulnerable as a woman; without them you had more control over a man.

'*Do* you know where he is, Grace?' she asked nonchalantly.

'No. I don't even know if he is alive, but I suppose if he wasn't his body would have turned up by now. I sometimes wonder if he did a John Stonehouse. You know, left a pile of clothes on a beach somewhere hoping we'll think he's dead, but I haven't heard anything. Nor do I want to. I told you, India, I never want to hear from him again. It's hell for his mother, she longs to know if he's all right, and I suppose later the boys will wonder where he is, but . . . I'm afraid to know. I don't want him back, yet if he contacted me, swore he loved me and everything was all right again, I just hope I wouldn't be weak enough to go to him.' She gave India an apologetic smile.

'Would you tell me if he contacted you?' India said, feeling closer to Grace than she ever had before.

Grace looked at her a moment. 'Yes I would,' she said, 'maybe he wouldn't have behaved like this with you. Max was right in a way. Ever since I lost that first baby — you know, the reason we had to get married — I promised myself I'd put up with anything if

468

he stayed with me. You know how much my parents love each other, I wanted that, I suppose. I did love him too much.

'Oh, Max and his crackpot theories!' India laughed. 'I wouldn't lose much sleep over those. But you've done well for him, his shops are all the rage.'

'I know. I can move on now.'

'Move on, where to?' India was surprised; surely Grace wasn't going abandon her golden egg?

Grace shrugged. 'I was determined not to just let him pick me up and give me a job because he was sorry for me. I've just about doubled the money Jonathan lost him and I'm going to leave. Though don't say anything yet, I haven't quite finalized my plans.'

'What plans?' In spite of their conversation, India still couldn't help but think she was going to Jonathan.

'I don't really like doing up shops, it's too impersonal. I'd really much rather do houses — houses like this if I could. You know, get the right materials, colours and everything to suit the period of the house. I've found a firm who'll take me on and train me. I need more training. The money will be less but if I sell that cottage in Aldeburgh instead of renting it out I'll have enough to put down on a little house somewhere and pay the mortgage.'

'But the boys' school, you'll never manage to live in Knightsbridge,' India said. As far as she was concerned you could only live within walking distance of Harrods.

'They'll let them stay for the moment. Anyway, *if* everything goes to plan I hope to be able to send them to public school,' Grace said.

India could not help but feel admiration for her, though she felt too the old pang of envy. Envious that she was getting on with her life, having a purpose to it. India didn't feel she had anything. Oh, people would contradict her, remind her how much she had raised for her various charities, and it would be true, she wasn't just a spoilt rich bitch, but she needed something else.

'Do you have a boyfriend?' she asked Grace, wondering if that was the reason for her strength.

'Goodness, no!' Grace laughed, then said more seriously, 'I don't want Jonathan back, but I don't feel I can love anyone else.'

India looked at her gravely, 'I don't feel I can love anyone else either, I never have, you know. Are we both doomed never to have a decent love life because of him? Do we love him, or are we just frantically attracted to him?'

Grace did not answer for a moment, then she said, 'I was attracted to him, yes, but I did love him too. In a strange way I feel quite content with what I had, before it went wrong. I don't feel I could better it. After all, they say some people only love once.'

And there was another reason for India's old envy of Grace. Whatever Jonathan had done, and even if they never heard from him again, Grace had had the best of him. She felt immeasurably sad. 'If he should contact you, please tell me,' she said, 'I would like to see him again, even if it's just to lay old ghosts.'

Grace smiled. 'He doesn't know where I am so he'll have to contact his mother, and I think they'll move on soon, the house is too big and too expensive for them, *if* Robert stays with her. So unless you move, I expect it will be you he'll contact.' She reached out and squeezed India's hand. 'We've been together on and off all our lives, both of us so different, and yet we loved the same man and he ruined us both. He's still tied to us both, will always, whatever happens, be linked to us. I don't believe he'll be able to resist getting in touch with one of us again, but I hope it won't be me.'

'I suppose you're right,' India said, suddenly feeling hope stirring in her. Surely he wouldn't stay away from them all for ever. He'd get bored and lonely and contact them, wouldn't he?

30

'So, here is just about double the amount Jonathan lost you.' Grace pushed a sheet of figures across Max's desk. 'I can't thank you enough for giving me the chance to pick up my life again and now, at your convenience, I'd like to move on.'

'What? Grace, what are you saying?' Max glanced quickly at the sheet of paper in front of him and then jerked his head up sharply to look intently at her. 'Moving on? What do you mean?' He frowned deeply and before she could answer said savagely, 'Do not tell me you're going to that no-good husband of yours. Do not tell me you're still nannying him.' He flicked at the sheet of figures.

'No, Max, of course I'm not,' Grace retorted. 'I've no idea where he is, or even if he's still alive. I just didn't want to be under an obligation to you. You had faith in me to design your shops, and thankfully it paid off, but now I want to move on, do up houses instead. I just prefer doing them to shops . . . ' Seeing him take a breath to protest she ran on quickly, 'And anyway we've done your chain, the last one was finished last week and I don't want to do anyone else's.'

'I did not take you on so you could pay me back,' he said, but his eyes gleamed as he looked at the healthy columns of figures on the paper in front of him. 'I took you on because you had the kind of taste and style I wanted for my shops. I was right, business has never been better.' He sat back in his leather chair and regarded her seriously. 'We have worked well together, Grace, and you know I wanted you to stay on to help buy for the shops; you have superb taste. You have a good salary, a nice flat — why are you really moving on?' He'd put on a pained voice, as if she had committed a terrible crime against him.

Grace's spirits were sinking. She'd known he'd make it difficult for her to leave. He liked to feel that he owned his employees. He was kind to them; fair over time off, bonuses, and praise when it was deserved; yet he hated it if they wanted to leave. She'd seen it with Felicia when she'd left to look after her new baby. He'd even offered to pay for a nanny, refusing to accept the fact that she wanted to bring up the child herself. But if he didn't like someone they were out at once with no second chance.

'I told you, Max, I prefer to do up houses

and I've been offered a job, with training attached, at Bickham and Walshe.'

'Have you been touting about for work?' he demanded, looking sternly at her as if he was going to dock her wages for looking for another job in his time

'No, of course I haven't, when have I had time? I became friendly with Sarah Bickham when I went to her to ask about the best floor covering for the shops, remember? She suggested it.'

Max frowned, chewed his finger, not taking his eyes off her. He said suddenly, 'So where is Jonathan?'

'Jonathan? I told you I don't know. Max, what is this? I know you hate any of us to leave, but this has nothing whatever to do with Jonathan. If you like' — humouring him — 'I'll always be there to help you if you should need me. I'm hardly leaving the country, their shop is only up the road, as you know.'

He ignored her. 'I am pretty sure India knows where he is, so I assumed you might too.'

Her heart gave a jolt. 'India knows where he is? Are you sure, Max?' A moment ago she'd felt in command of the situation, almost elated that he thought her such a success he didn't want her to go. Now she felt leaden, sick with the feeling of doom.

'I lunched with her last week, for old times' sake. She was very animated, excited to see me, but not because she felt anything for me, but because she was so happy. Quite unlike her, as you will agree. She has been complaining that she is bored with her life for ages.'

'Yes, she has. Maybe she's got a new boyfriend,' Grace said, determined that Jonathan had not come back into their lives.

'I asked her. She laughed, looked at me coyly and said wouldn't I like to know. At once I thought of Jonathan, and when I asked her, all she would do was smile mysteriously and say she was bound to secrecy. I asked her if you knew and she said not, but now when you tell me you're moving on . . . ' His dark eyes drilled into her, his mouth tight with displeasure.

Grace closed her eyes. She was finding it difficult to breathe. For months now she'd managed to live her life without Jonathan, put him aside in another compartment of her life and get on with the present. The boys were doing well at school and she, to her surprise, for she thought that no one would like her once they knew about Jonathan's fraud, had made new friends among the parents there. Ned Porter had taken her out a couple of times, which had been fun and comfortable, and Caspar had asked them to Elmley. Life was beginning to be good, but now it looked in danger of being swept away again.

'I want to know, Grace,' Max said.

She opened her eyes. 'I don't know anything, Max, believe me.' Her voice broke, but she recovered herself quickly. 'I don't want him to come back. I loved him, but that is in the past. I can't go back after all he's done. I can't put the boys through it all again. Their sadness at losing him is easing now. It's them that I live for now. He didn't mean to destroy us, but it was touch and go, wasn't it?'

Max nodded and began to fiddle with a gold pen. 'I understand his mother is in a very bad way.'

'Yes. I could so easily have been like that, and the boys too, but thanks to you . . . '

'You had the guts to get up again,' he said gruffly. 'I would not have taken you on if you had been a basket case. I support enough charities each year, I do not want one in my office. But these sort of people . . . ' he paused as if he was remembering an experience of his own. 'It is an addiction, you know. He might swear he is cured, has turned over a new leaf, but just by being back in the same environment, with you and the boys, might lull him into thinking the occasional flutter on the horses will do him no harm.'

Grace felt the old wound of guilt painfully reopen in her.

Seeing her expression Max said at once, 'Grace, my dear, it was not your fault. It was the wrong combination of characters. It was just bad luck your sweetness and indulgence brought out the worst in him; neither of you could possibly have known that at the beginning.' He came round his huge mahogany desk and put his arm round her. 'You are a wonderful woman, Grace, warm and giving. That is rare these days, everyone is too obsessed with themselves, snatching at what they want with no regard for others. He took away his arm and went over to the window to stare out at the busy street below. 'I do not mind telling you, if I had had a woman like you as my wife, my life would have been far happier. I probably would not have run after all these other women.'

'Nonsense, you adore women,' she said quickly to hide the quick wave of embarrassment that swept over her at his words.

'I do, but I often think I am always looking for the perfect one.'

'She doesn't exist,' Grace said, 'nor the perfect man for that matter. But, Max, if it's not prying too much, have you ever tried to be faithful to any woman?'

He turned and smiled at her, a sad smile. 'With my first wife yes. I really loved her.' The sadness took over his face, making him suddenly look old and gaunt. 'She could not stay faithful to me, like a greedy child in a sweet shop of men. I never let myself love anyone else so deeply again. It makes you too vulnerable.'

'I know,' Grace said, thinking of Jonathan, wondering if he really had been in contact with India, or if she was just teasing Max, wanting his attention, even if she didn't care for him. She sighed; she would find it very difficult to get on with her life if she knew where he was. He would take on flesh again, no longer be a ghost safely buried in the past. But it had to be faced. Deep down, though she'd half dreaded to hear from him again, she'd half longed to too. She had to know the truth.

'Will you excuse me if I go and find India? I want to find out the truth about Jonathan,' she said, getting up.

'As long as you let me know where he is?'

'But I've paid you back his debt — twice

the debt.' She gestured towards the paper that lay beside the pictures of his baby son.

He smiled. 'Thank you, but I did not ask or expect you to do it. I do not respect men who get their women to pay their debts.'

'He didn't know I was going to do it, and I haven't done it for anyone else,' she said, cold again inside. She thought: Now it all begins again, just talking about Jonathan brings up hostilities, ruins my relationships with other people.

He came back again and stood in front of her. 'Whatever you do Grace, do not go back to him. He dumped you and your children right in it and you have won through. Do not weaken and go back, for your children's sake if not your own.'

'I won't.' She looked into his dark eyes and felt his power. She knew that he did care for her and that if she chose she could have him, have his love, his protection, but she knew too there would be a price and she wanted to be free. She smiled, leant forward and kissed him on his cheek, laying her face against his for a moment. 'I'll always be very fond of you, Max,' she said, backing away before her gesture could be misinterpreted, 'and I'll keep in touch. If you need any more help with designing, I'll be there. I'll move in a month, if that's all right with you. Out of the flat, too, I'm looking for a little house in Wandsworth or Putney.' Her voice was businesslike, her expression cheerful yet aloof.

'Why must you move house? The flat is not needed by anyone else. If it makes you feel better, you can pay a small rent for it.' His eyes held regret. She knew he wasn't going to plead with her.

'The boys need a garden, even a tiny one, and much though I love living in Knightsbridge I think they'd like to be somewhere a little greener. Hyde Park's lovely, but they can't get there on their own yet, and I've seen a couple of houses I like not too far from the park.'

'As you wish.' He turned back to his desk as if to force himself back into his role as her boss. 'A month's notice will be fine, give it to me in writing please, and remember' — he fixed her with his eyes again — 'let me know if you find out where Jonathan is.'

★ ★ ★

Grace called India but on finding her number engaged went straight round to her house and rang the bell. Mrs Glen, India's daily, opened the door and Grace went into the drawing room to see India on the telephone.

481

She looked up guiltily, muttered something into the receiver then put it down. The smile she gave Grace was bright enough to light up a dark room.

'Grace, what a surprise,' she said extravagantly. She jumped up and came over and kissed her. 'Don't tell me Max has sacked you, surely you should be working.'

'I've just told him I'm moving on,' she said.

'How did he take it?' India walked restlessly round the room. Grace felt she wasn't really interested in her.

'Max thinks that you know where Jonathan is. Do you?'

India looked awkward then she said defiantly, 'What if I do?'

'You must tell me if he gets in touch. I must tell his mother, she's frantic with worry. Do you know where he is?'

India wandered over to the table, slowly took a cigarette from a silver box and lit it. She turned round, leant against the table and faced Grace, exhaling a long stream of smoke into the air. 'Yes, I do,' she said. 'He rang me last week.'

Grace sat down suddenly. She remembered Max's words and forced herself to remain calm. 'Tell me everything, India. Everything.' She looked at her sharply.

India took another long draw on her cigarette. 'He's in Marrakesh, bored out of his mind. He . . . ' She paused but Grace's stern look made her go on. 'He asked me to go out and see him. He can't come here, of course.'

Grace felt as if she'd faint. After all these months of uncertainty and worry, of wondering if he was alive or dead, he had turned up again.

'You were right he didn't know where you were and he hasn't yet contacted his mother,' India said not looking at her.

'Would you have told me if I hadn't asked you?'

'Yes, I would, but not until after I'd seen him.'

'So you're going? Was that him on the phone when I came in?'

'Yes to both things. I am going, Grace, you know I love him and I've nothing here.'

Grace waited to feel a stab of hurt, of envy that India had got him in the end, but she felt nothing, just a weary, sad emptiness. 'Is he well?' She felt she was asking about a vague acquaintance, not the man she had loved so completely.

'Yes, very well, just bored. He asked after you and the boys, but, well . . . ' India looked as if she was fighting with herself, then she said generously, 'He did ask if you had anyone special.'

'What did you say?'

'I said no, but I also said you didn't want him back, that you'd said that the Jonathan you had loved had gone.' Her face was set hard, her eyes defiant.

Grace was about to protest, but she knew in her heart that India spoke the truth, she had said that and she meant it, however hard it might be. She knew that she must not be tempted to go back to him, that what Max had said about the combination of their characters was probably true; back with her he would no doubt start gambling again. She must accept that she had lost the man she once loved a long time ago. 'Please, India, ring his mother, or better still go round and tell her he's safe and well,' she said and, making sure India had Marianne's number, she went out into the street and walked slowly back to the shop.

She didn't know what to do or what to think. She went aimlessly up to her flat and sat down on the sofa by the window. It was quiet; the boys were at school. She stared out at the bustling street below. Jonathan was back, back in her mind now as warm and living as when she'd last seen him. When she didn't know where he was it had been easier to put him from her thoughts. Now she could feel his presence in the room even though he had never been there. She could hear his voice tender with words of love, of excuses. She tossed her head to get them from her ears. She could almost smell the scent of him. If he had been standing there before her she would not have been surprised. An overwhelming feeling of longing for him came over her.

She jumped up, moved round restlessly picking up things, straightening a cushion, the curtain, as if looking for him. She picked up a photograph of the two boys when they were not much more than babies; Sebastian grinning at the camera; Jack's chubby baby face staring intently ahead. Now you would hardly recognize them; they were grown, tough lads, Sebastian almost an adolescent. She mourned her babies, remembering suddenly the softness of them, their gurgling laughter, their sheer joy each time they saw her. Those babies had gone, slipped into the recess of time, and so had Jonathan. She could not go back in time; like her boys' babyhood the past could only be reached in dreams.

She kissed the photograph, put it back on the table and went downstairs to her office.

Sally, who coped with everything, said, 'You had a phone call.'

Her heart stopped, now she knew where Jonathan was would her life ever be safe again? She watched Sally delve about on her desk. 'Here it is.' She pounced on a piece of paper and handed it over. 'Ned Porter, says he's in London, can you ring him?'

'Oh, yes, thanks.' She tried to hide her agitation, thinking it had been Jonathan who'd called her. Now each time the telephone rang or the postman came would she not think that it was him?

Sally smiled at her. 'Someone important?'

'No, just an old friend. I've known him since we were children.'

Max came in and stopped Sally asking any more questions. He gave Grace a piercing look and said evenly, 'Have you time for a quick word?'

'India is going to him.' She told Max all she knew in a flat voice as if she were discussing a recent diagnosis of a serious illness.

'How do you feel about it?' His voice was concerned.

'India told him I didn't love him any more.' Again she stated the fact without emotion. It was agony but there was nothing she could do.

Max smiled. 'Trust India. Is that true? Your feelings for him, I mean?'

'Yes,' she said firmly. 'It is true. I still hanker after the old Jonathan, but I've just been looking at a picture of my boys as babies.' She smiled at the picture of his son, tiny and crinkled, not yet grown into his skin. 'Of course I love them madly now, but it was a very special time when they were tiny. You can't go back in life, you can't ever go back.'

'No.' He too smiled at the picture of his child, taken some months ago. 'I'm always here for you, Grace, come and talk if ever you need to, but ditch the past, keep going forward, that's the only way to survive.'

'Thank you, Max. I'll try, I really will.'

31

'So that's the story,' Grace said to Ned as they sat over the debris of dinner in her flat. They moved away from the table to the sofa and chairs, she put the coffee pot and a bottle of Kummel, his favourite liqueur, between them.

'Oh, Grace, you poor girl. I didn't know the half of it,' he said with concern. 'Caspar told me about losing the money through Jonathan but I thought it was more a straight case of fraud. This is far worse. Gambling can be such an addiction, and taking everything of yours and the children's' — he shook his head in disbelief — 'how dreadful to be in so deep that you cease to see reason and steal from those closest to you.' He looked up at her. 'Are you divorced?'

'No. I didn't do anything about it. I didn't really want to rake up any more for the boys' sake as much as mine,' she said, 'and I didn't know where he was . . . and . . . ' She gave him an ashamed look. 'The more people that looked for him the more likely it was that they'd find him. Whatever he's done I don't want him to go to prison.'

'Do you still love him?' His voice was serious. He took another sip of his Kummel, pretending to concentrate on that.

'Not what he is now,' she said quickly. 'There were too many betrayals and the worst one was . . . ' Apart from Max and India, who had bulldozed much of it out of her, and of course her parents, she hadn't told anyone about the hurt Jonathan had caused her. Yet she felt the concern in Ned, felt so comfortable with him. He cared enough to listen without judging. She went on, 'He slept with India. Oh, *she* must have seduced him, but all the same.' She still hadn't quite lost her apologetic tone when she talked of his treacheries.

'India always gets what she wants, as you know,' Ned said quietly, 'but once she's got it she gets bored of it. Remember how I used to love her?' He gave a self-deprecating laugh. 'Those teenage years when one's emotions were so raw and so near the surface. I really loved her, even though I was crucified by her almost every day. If I'd only been more sophisticated, tougher, I'd have acted as if I could take her or leave her, like Jonathan did. Then I'd have got her.'

'Do you want her?'

He laughed. 'Goodness, no, not any more. I know it was said I took to the bottle because I couldn't have her, but the truth is I went through a rather wild stage, girls, drink, you know, retarded development I suppose.'

'Lots of people do that. Better to get it over when you're young.'

'I suppose so. Anyway I didn't sit around and pine for her, I had other girlfriends. I wasn't going to remain a hermit because she didn't want me. But as the years went by I saw how destructive she is, how she's incapable of really loving anyone but herself.'

'She says she loves Jonathan.'

He shrugged. 'I can't imagine India ever really loving anyone. She always wanted to be the one in command, taking, never giving. I think she craved love from her parents, but never got enough, so expected it from everyone else instead. She got it too, with the one exception of Jonathan, who loved you instead.' He looked at her warily. 'I don't think she's ever forgiven you.'

'There's certainly some truth in that,' she sighed. 'Love covers a multitude of emotions far more complex than the poets would have us believe. Fear of loneliness, wanting to belong. Maybe she loves him in her own way. Maybe she likes that edge of danger about him. He was, after all, the only man who wasn't head over heels in love with her.' She hoped she wasn't hurting his feelings.

His smile was wide. 'That's true, but I hear from Caspar . . . ' He paused, then went on gently, watching her all the time in case he was upsetting her. ' . . . that she's gone to Marrakesh to live with him. Her mother's gone with her and so I believe has *his* mother.' Seeing that she was smiling, he said, 'Hardly the passionate love nest she'd hoped for, and how do you think they're living? Off India's money?'

'I don't really know, there was some talk of him doing something in tourism. Maybe he's gambling on camel racing,' she joked.

'But I'm glad Marianne has gone to him. She completely collapsed after he'd gone, you know. Funny, I always thought she was such a strong woman, with all her causes and good works. Though of course it was during one of those that everything began to come unstuck.' She told him about Vincent.

'You've had a terrible time, Grace,' he said with admiration, 'but you and the boys have come out of it magnificently. Still enjoying your new job?'

'Very much, though I've been spoilt just walking up the road to work. Max was sweet letting me stay here while the builders were

491

in the house. I move next week. It's going to be quite a business.' She leant back on the sofa and surveyed the room. It had been rather gloomy when she'd first moved in, now it was bright and comfortable, she'd miss it and she'd miss Max. She wasn't attracted to him but something about him, above his insistence that she looked smart, had made her hold her head a little higher, made her take more care with herself, given her back her self-respect. She'd always be grateful to him for that.

'Have you seen Jonathan since he reappeared? Spoken to him on the telephone?' Ned asked her quietly.

'No, India put paid to that, she told him I no longer loved him. I know it's for the best. His mother can keep him informed about the boys, and I can keep them away from Morocco until they are old enough to make up their own minds about seeing him.' She said it as cheerfully as she could, though in truth she resented India taking charge like that.

'Casper is furious about India going to him, in fact I'd say most of her social set is. After all, he lost everyone a considerable amount of money,' Ned said tonelessly as if he really wanted to say something else, but this had come out instead.

'I know,' Grace sighed. 'She's got what she wanted all right, but she's stuck with it. If she dumps him and comes home she'll find most of her friends won't speak to her. Caspar's even banned her from Elmley. By choosing to be with Jonathan she's made herself an outsider here.'

'She may think that rather glamorous,' Ned smiled, 'going against the grain of society.'

Just then Jack lumbered into the room rumpled with sleep. He grinned at Ned.

'Can't you sleep, darling?' Grace put her arms out to him; he snuggled down beside her, but kept his gaze firmly on Ned.

'Can I come to your farm and see the lambs?' Jack said to him. 'You said I could. Are they born yet?'

'Oh, Jack,' Grace laughed, 'what made you think of that at this time of night? It's almost midnight, you should be sound asleep.'

'Of course you can come. They're all born now, you can come any time you want,' Ned said.

'Tomorrow?'

'Not tomorrow, you've got school,' Grace said, 'and we can't just invite ourselves, darling. Ned is very busy.'

'I'm never too busy to see you,' he said, looking directly at Grace, his eyes very tender. 'Come for the weekend, and see the lambs.'

'Good, we will . . . thanks,' Jack said and got up and trundled back to bed.

When he'd gone Grace smiled apologetically. 'Sorry you were bamboozled into that, Ned. I don't know why he suddenly thought of the lambs. We can't possibly come though, I've far too much to do here before we move.'

Ned leant forward in his chair, holding his glass in his cupped hands, studying it thoughtfully. 'You've got great children. I'd love them to come down. It would do you good, too, to get away. Won't the removal men pack all this for you?' Again she felt he was saying something different to what he really wanted to say.

'I suppose so, but . . . '

He looked up at her, put his glass down carefully on the table and said, 'I know I'm probably going to ruin everything between us if I say this, but I feel that at our age . . . What I mean is we're no longer gauche teenagers and we can't go on pussyfooting around our feelings. I know you've had a hell of a time and probably will always love Jonathan. But don't let the memory, perhaps rather rose-tinted by time, of a past love cut you off from the possibility of a new relationship. I love you, Grace. I've always been fond of you, but during these past months since we met up again, saw more of each other, I soon realized that my feelings were becoming deeper, that I love you.'

'Oh, Ned.' She didn't know what to say, she was fond of him too, but she wished he hadn't spoken to her of love, she didn't want love any more.

'Don't say anything now,' he said putting his hand up as if to stop her words. 'We get on so well together, and the boys seem to like me too. I like them enormously and we can't disappoint Jack over the lambs, can we?'

'You don't have to let him see them at once,' she said, still wondering what had triggered off Jack's request. He hadn't mentioned anything to do with the farm when he'd seen Ned earlier. Then she thought back to a couple of weeks ago when Jack had said to her, 'Lots of boys in my class have two daddies. We want another one too, don't we, Sebastian?'

'Only a nice one.' Sebastian had barely looked up from his drawing.

'Well, darling, perhaps one day,' Grace had said lamely, not quite knowing how to handle this.

'I want someone with a farm,' Jack had said, 'someone who buys us sweets and listens to what I say.'

She had managed to change the subject and they had not brought it up again until Jack had appeared just now to ask to see the lambs. She smiled, wondering if in his way he was trying to matchmake. The little devil, she'd speak to him in the morning. He couldn't go round asking every man she met for an invitation.

Seeing her smile, Ned said, 'We'll take it easily, I promise I won't pressurize you.'

She looked at him sitting there, an attractive man, someone she'd known for ever. He was so dependable, so kind and, she was sure, so honest: all the qualities, except for perhaps dependable, which in those days had added to his charm, that she'd thought Jonathan had. They did get on, were comfortable together, which would be a relief after the endless strain of living with Jonathan, and yet something was missing, the capacity for excitement that Jonathan possessed in abundance. You can't have everything, she told herself now, recognizing suddenly that she was attracted to Ned, would like him to make love to her. The excitement that Jonathan provoked had been their undoing.

'I don't know what to say,' she said, still holding back. 'I feel I want to be free, but I can't do without good friends.'

'That's a start,' he said and got up to go. He held her for a moment in his arms, and she liked the feeling of being close to him, but fearful that Jack might come in again with some other ruse did not relax herself against him. 'I'll see you all this weekend, then.' He released her reluctantly.

'Perhaps just the Sunday?' she said lightly.

'Saturday night.' He smiled into her eyes, stroking her cheek.

'All right, I'll ring you with the time. Goodnight, Ned.'

When he'd gone she sat for a long time. She missed having a man about; she would like to be loved again. The boys and her job were not enough, even though she'd tried to convince herself that they were. But she hadn't wanted another man before: the memory of the good times with Jonathan had been enough. But only in fantasies were relationships perfect. Life had a funny way of playing jokes. India had got the man she'd always wanted. She thought of them lying in the sun round some pool in a villa somewhere in Marrakesh, Jonathan and the two mothers and India. She wondered if Flavia was chasing the dark, lithe Moroccan boys.

Grace felt a sudden lightness in her; she wished Ned was still here so she could describe the picture to him. Poor Jonathan, she thought, how will he cope with nothing to do?

India was right when she said they would always be linked, not just by family ties but by Jonathan. She had had good times with him and now it was India's turn to make what life she could with him. Grace smiled and found all the past rancour she'd felt for India had left her. She wished her happiness. Perhaps, she thought, with a burst of hope, she and the boys might find the same with Ned.

THE END

McLEAN AT THE GOLDEN OWL
George Goodchild

Inspector McLean has resigned from Scotland Yard's CID and has opened an office in Wimpole Street. With the help of his able assistant, Tiny, he solves many crimes, including those of kidnapping, murder and poisoning.

KATE WEATHERBY
Anne Goring

Derbyshire, 1849: The Hunter family are the arrogant, powerful masters of Clough Grange. Their feuds are sparked by a generation of guilt, despair and ill-fortune. But their passions are awakened by the arrival of nineteen-year-old Kate Weatherby.

A VENETIAN RECKONING
Donna Leon

When the body of a prominent international lawyer is found in the carriage of an intercity train, Commissario Guido Brunetti begins to dig deeper into the secret lives of the once great and good.

A TASTE FOR DEATH
Peter O'Donnell

Modesty Blaise and Willie Garvin take on impossible odds in the shape of Simon Delicata, the man with a taste for death, and Swordmaster, Wenczel, in a terrifying duel. Finally, in the Sahara desert, the intrepid pair must summon every killing skill to survive.

SEVEN DAYS FROM MIDNIGHT
Rona Randall

In the Comet Theatre, London, seven people have good reason for wanting beautiful Maxine Culver out of the way. Each one has reason to fear her blackmail. But whose shadow is it that lurks in the wings, waiting to silence her once and for all?

QUEEN OF THE ELEPHANTS
Mark Shand

Mark Shand knows about the ways of elephants, but he is no match for the tiny Parbati Barua, the daughter of India's greatest expert on the Asian elephant, the late Prince of Gauripur, who taught her everything. Shand sought out Parbati to take part in a film about the plight of the wild herds today in north-east India.

THE DARKENING LEAF
Caroline Stickland

On storm-tossed Chesil Bank in 1847, the young lovers, Philobeth and Frederick, prevent wreckers mutilating the apparent corpse of a young woman. Discovering she is still alive, Frederick takes her to his grandmother's home. But the rescue is to have violent and far-reaching effects . . .

A WOMAN'S TOUCH
Emma Stirling

When Fenn went to stay on her uncle's farm in Africa, the lovely Helena Starr seemed to resent her — especially when Dr Jason Kemp agreed to Fenn helping in his bush hospital. Though it seemed Jason saw Fenn as little more than a child, her feelings for him were those of a woman.

A DEAD GIVEAWAY
Various Authors

This book offers the perfect opportunity to sample the skills of five of the finest writers of crime fiction — Clare Curzon, Gillian Linscott, Peter Lovesey, Dorothy Simpson and Margaret Yorke.